Like Kent State in the late 1960's, Hayes University was in a sleepy Ohio college town. Julia Brandon, an innocent sorority girl, was in for an awakening, both emotionally and physically. Trouble begins when she tries to bail her radical roommate out of jail and escalates as she becomes increasingly involved with the protest movement, which erupts in violence, death, and destruction. She falls irrevocably in love with handsome, carefree, soon-to-be drafted Win, who steals her heart, entombing her emotionally.

Fifteen years later, trapped in an arid life, Julia catches a glimpse of a man whom she believes to be Win while on a cruise. She embarks upon a journey which leads her to the brink of devastation. Can she accept the truth about what happened so long ago without destroying herself and those she loves?

THE PIPE

DREAMERS

THE
PIPE
DREAMERS

SANDRA GURVIS

OLMSTEAD
P R E S S

Published in 2001 by Olmstead Press: Chicago, Illinois

Cover art: Victoria Waltz.
Photos: Victoria Waltz, Georgi Likovski/Agence France,
Ohio University Archives.

Cover design: Hope Forstenzer

Text designed and typeset by
Syllables, Hartwick, New York, USA

Printed and bound in Toronto, Ontario, Canada by
Webcom Inc.

ISBN: 1-58754-008-8

Publisher's Cataloging In Publication Data
(Prepared by Donohue Group, Inc.)

Gurvis, Sandra.
    The pipe dreamers / by Sandra Gurvis.
    p. ; 22 cm.
    ISBN: 1-587-54008-8
            1. Vietnamese Conflict, 1961-1975—Protest movements—Fiction. 2.
        Peace movements—United States—Fiction. 3. Love stories. I. Title.
PS3557.U43 P57
813/.54

Editorial Sales Rights and Permission Inquiries should be addressed to: Olmstead Press, 22 Broad Street, Suite 34, Milford, CT 06460. Email: Editor@lpcgroup.com

Manufactured in Canada
1 3 5 7 9 10 8 6 4 2

Substantial discounts on bulk quantities of Olmstead Press books are available to corporations, professional associations and other organizations. If you are in the USA or Canada, contact LPC Group, Attn: Special Sales Department, 1-800-626-4330, fax 1-800-334-3892, or email: sales@lpcgroup.com

To Ron
with love

All civilization has from time to time become a thin crust over the volcano of revolution.

—Havelock Ellis

It was but yesterday we met in a dream.
You have sung to me in my aloneness, and I of your longings
    have built a tower in the sky.
But now our sleep has fled and our dream is over and it is no
    longer dawn.
The noontide is upon us and our half waking has turned to a
    fuller day and we must part.

—Kahlil Gibran
"The Prophet"

ACKNOWLEDGMENTS

This novel has been the result of many years of hard work and would not have been possible without the help and encouragement of many people, including the following: Rena Vesler, who read the first draft and offered supportive and insightful suggestions; Charles Steinman, who rescued the manuscript from Atari oblivion; Kali Tal, who published a portion and started me on the rocky but rewarding road of book publication; my daughter Amy, who encouraged me to try yet again; and my son Alex simply because. Also many thanks to Barb Kuroff, Ellen Greene, Tom Hodges, Sherry Paprocki, David Wilk, Maureen Owen and others too numerous to mention here. And last but not certainly least, Ron, who was there for me from the very beginning.

I also owe a debt of gratitude to my friends from those years who provided the spark which fired my imagination. Some of you may no longer be among the living or may be out of the loop of communication, but you will live in my heart and mind, forever young.

Whenever possible, I have tried to be accurate. Because this is fiction, I have played with certain historical facts and places to fit various situations. Thus, responsibility for any errors is mine.

PROLOGUE

March 1985
Ocho Rios, Jamaica

Julia would never know what made her turn around. Perhaps it was the familiar reddish glint of the Irish setter racing along the brilliant white beach, followed by its master. Perhaps it was her desire to escape what she was doing, making the supposedly easy climb up Dunn's River Falls, an intimidating drop of several hundred feet of slippery limestone terraces. Or perhaps it was fate, an unexpected tipping of life's scales.

Whatever the reason, she nearly fell when she saw the man. His hair was the same color as the dog's. A shining, almost incandescent russet, it hung to the middle of his broad shoulders. His back was to her, but his body — slim, tapered hips balanced on sinewy legs — and his precise, graceful motions were unforgettable. He wore a torn T-shirt that revealed muscular arms and cutoffs which left little doubt as to the firmness of his well-proportioned buttocks.

It can't be, Julia thought, stopping in mid-step, much to the dismay of the people in line behind her. As instructed by the Jamaican guide, they'd formed a human chain, holding hands to support each other. The pudgy fellow behind Julia gave her an encouraging shove, but she stood frozen to the spot, a broken link.

Only Win sprinted like that, a physical fitness buff before it became a requirement of a generation that had once denigrated clean living. "I don't believe it," she said, not aware she was speaking. "What could Win be doing here?" She'd last seen him fifteen years earlier at Hayes University, in a small college town in Ohio. Soldiers were fighting in Vietnam, the campuses were engaged in a different kind of battle. She and Win had been in bed, naked.

"Move along please, lady," the guide urged in his soft Jamaican cadence. Accustomed to doing what was asked of her, Julia took a step forward.

Not that she'd always been so accommodating. During the days of Win and her best friend, Valerie, she'd believed she'd seized control of her life. But since then, she'd learned to pick up cues from her environment, to follow the most propitious route. As when her husband, a United States Congressman, became tied up in a subcommittee and was unable to accompany her on this cruise. "Go anyway, Julia," he'd urged. "Time away from the pressures of work and the boys" — Adam and Abe, their 7-year-old twin sons — "will only do you good."

And so she had, inviting her friend Rachel, a freelance artist like herself, along as a companion. And it had been fun to a point, and relaxing. With a few vicarious thrills thrown in, such as watching newly divorced Rachel flit from shipboard romance to shipboard romance in the brief span of a week. Not for Julia, the roller coaster of involvement, innocent or otherwise. That sort of thing was in the past.

But now this particular remembrance seemingly materialized before her, rudely throwing her back in time. And all the anger, anguish, and passion she'd suppressed for nearly a decade and a half suddenly roared to the surface of her consciousness. She simultaneously wanted to strangle Win and to go to bed with him. Valerie had been right — love and hate could be two sides of the same emotion. Fifteen years later, Julia finally grasped the essence of that statement.

The same force that had initially drawn her to Win now propelled her down Dunn's River Falls. Unassisted she began the perilous slide towards the beach. Like the murmur of the water that grew increasingly strong towards the peak of the falls, an-

noyed comments arose in proportionate crescendo from the
climbers behind her. In a country where everyone said, "no problem" Julia was definitely creating one.

The guide reached for her arm, but she pulled away, elud-
ing his grasp. In her scramble towards solid ground, she nearly fell
several times on the wet limestone rocks.

She stumbled onto the beach. For a moment, the sun
blinded her. The falls had been a cool, leafy refuge from the daz-
zling Caribbean heat. She couldn't see the man or the dog, only
the glistening sand and the blazing midday sky. But then her eyes
adjusted and there they were — cooling off at the Jamaican version of a snack bar, a wooden hodgepodge of buildings and picnic tables. The man, still with his back to her, stooped down,
giving the dog something to drink.

What if he wasn't Win? Somewhere, they said, everyone has
a double. The face could be that of a stranger, indifferent and
amused by her flustered case of mistaken identity. Julia's eyes
dimmed with more than adjustment to the light. Perhaps it
would be for the best...Did she really have the courage to confront Win? To grapple the demon of unrequited love that had
grown from the seeds of his casual attentions? A feeling of unreality, the likes of which she hadn't experienced since Hayes, engulfed her.

The guard came abreast of her. "Lady! Why you run away?"
He seized her elbow.

The man looked up, and Julia came face to startled face
with what had nearly destroyed her an era ago.

PART ONE

THE DREAM

May 1969 – May 1970
Hayes University, Hampton, Ohio

CHAPTER ONE

On the evening of the May Music Fest, Julia Brandon sat with her sorority, wondering why she was there. The air was unbearably close, despite the cloudless, pink-streaked dusk. And Julia sweated, even though she wore a lightweight dress. Yet with her dark hair, seaforest eyes, and satiny skin, she looked cool and composed. But it was a deception, like most of her life at Hayes.

The Music Fest, which fell on the last weekend before finals, usually served as a barometer by which Julia measured her year. When she was a freshman, she'd regarded this tradition, in fact, the entire Alumni Reunion Weekend, with enthusiasm and awe. She'd been a pledge and the older girls seemed so polished and self-assured, handling the alumnae Beta Gamma Phis with charm and facility.

When Julia was a sophomore, she was thrilled to be part of the festivities. She helped organize the tea for alumnae and their husbands, and led the sorority in its theme song during the Music Fest. She'd felt so proud standing with the BGPs, one of the top sororities on campus.

Now, in her junior year, Julia was less enthusiastic. She noticed chinks in the girls' behavior; barbs masked with delicate laughs, whispered comments not meant for all ears.

And she had a growing certainty her presence in the sorority had been a case of mistaken identity. During rush week last fall an outstanding freshman candidate, a National Merit Scholar and former prom queen, had been dropped from consideration when the sisters learned her last name was "Goldberg." Would they have accepted Julia, had they known about the "stein" Julia's grandfather had excised before debarking on Ellis Island?

Which was why Julia's roommate, Valerie Stazyck, was as refreshing as a spring charging through a desert. Valerie had been assigned to the room at the beginning of spring quarter. Nancy, her predecessor and Julia's former "big sis," had dropped out due to "family problems," BGP lingo for "knocked up." Poor Nancy had been grist for the sorority gossip mill, although Julia refused to discuss the matter with anyone.

"Look, you're a sorority chick and I'm a hippie," Valerie had announced, plunking her carpet bag down on the empty bed. "And the goddamn Administration thinks it can suppress me by putting me in a dormful of Greekoids. As long as you do your thing and I do mine, they can continue with their delusions." Then Valerie proceeded to plaster her side of the room with black-light Peter Max posters and pictures of President Nixon grinning under the captions "Would you buy a used car from this man?" and "Dick Nixon before he dicks you."

Rather than being appalled or even slightly offended by Valerie's brash dress and language, Julia was fascinated. Valerie radiated spontaneity and humor, two things Julia's life lacked.

Soon the girls became friends, although they never ate at the same times or went anywhere together. An unspoken agreement to maintain their separate lives made their relationship almost clandestine.

Valerie was careful not to push her radical ideas on Julia, although she used any conversational opening to espouse her beliefs on ending the war in Vietnam, free love, and the legalization of marijuana and LSD. Then one day at the Student Center she stopped Julia in the cafeteria line and introduced her to Adrian. Julia had never met a man interested in a woman's mind before, although his satirical humor was often biting. And his discourses on Lenin vs. Marxist philosophies and surrealistic vs. street theatre confused her. The sorority she at least understood.

So when Valerie and Adrian invited her to participate in an anti-Vietnam demonstration to be held during this May Music Fest, Julia gently refused. She told them of her obligation to sit with her sorority. Besides, she asked herself, what did she have to gain by refusing to stand for the national anthem? A chance to antagonize the Administration? To be ostracized by her sisters? The last thing Julia wanted was to make a spectacle of herself.

Adrian volleyed a witticism about Julia's lack of commitment and Valerie shrugged, her impish mouth a straight line, her stonewashed blue eyes downcast.

Now, turning her attention to the crowd, Julia told herself she was foolish to feel guilty. She'd only known Valerie and Adrian two months; relationships and loyalties in the sorority had taken years to establish. BGP wasn't perfect, but it was familiar. Be honest with yourself, Julia, she thought. Where would you be on this big, lonely campus of 12,000 plus bodies without your Greek security blanket of ready-made friends and dates?

Not that the dates were much. Mostly Betas and Sig Eps who tried to slip sweaty hands under her skirt and sweater as soon as they were alone. But at least they reassured her that she was attractive, although she often wondered why they never bothered to get to know her first. There was a mating ritual, and Julia could nearly always anticipate the boy's next move.

Lately it depressed her so much she'd confined her longings to a handsome profile glimpsed on the Slantwalk or a nice build in the back row of class, where Julia rarely sat. In addition to being pretty and poised, BGPs were expected to maintain good grades so they stayed in the front of the room next to each other, of course.

From her vantage point at the topmost bleacher, Julia viewed a scene straight out of Norman Rockwell. Administrators, leading citizens from the adjoining village of Hampton, and assorted honorees sat in front of the steps leading to the portico of the Performing Arts Center. Behind the VIPs stood the singing groups and soloists resplendent in long, flowered dresses or suits or matching robes. On the side lawn to the right was the band, clad in military-looking uniforms of red and yellow, the school colors. On the left sat the orchestra in somber grey.

The audience, too, reflected Rockwellian decorum. Alumni lounged in folding chairs or blankets on the grass. Some strolled through the adjoining, full-bloomed Formal Gardens. Their children stayed close, undoubtedly discouraged from racing about by the heat. The rest, undergraduates, grad students, and an occasional professor, sat directly on the lawn below Julia. Only sororities and fraternities had the privilege of bleachers and a total view of the goings-on.

Julia's "little sis" Betsy leaned over and said, "It's beastly, isn't it?" Betsy waved her program back and forth, a makeshift fan. "I thought it'd cool down when the sun began to set."

Julia examined a strand of what once was her perfectly straight, shoulder-length flip and sighed. "I'd say the humidity's about 95 percent."

She started to ask Betsy if she could borrow her hair-straightening iron when they got back to the dorm. But Lydia, president-elect of the sorority, shushed the group, telling them the program was about to begin.

Julia searched for Adrian and Valerie during President Carrell's opening speech about the greatness of the University and its tradition of excellence. She didn't spot them until just before the band struck up "The Star Spangled Banner."

They sat a few feet away from the bleachers while the audience rose en masse. Julia had a good view and could see the five of them: Adrian, Valerie, an overweight couple with an American flag draped around their shoulders, and an aesthetic-looking blonde holding a sign bearing a blue-and-white peace symbol. Adrian and Valerie waved placards labeled "Stop the War" and "War is Not Healthy for Children and Other Living Things."

With a mixture of relief and disappointment, Julia realized the demonstration was doomed. Not only did their distance from the portico render them practically invisible to the crowd, but they'd been swallowed up by the standing, singing audience. With their small number and poor location, no one would notice the demonstrators unless they really looked.

Julia began to check out a groovy-looking guy a few rows below her when a blur of blue caught her eye. She leaned forward, astonished, as three Hampton sheriffs approached the protesters. Her first thought was, what are the police doing here? Valerie and the others aren't breaking the law.

Yet two officers seized Adrian and the couple by the scruff of their necks, dragging them towards an unmarked, idling van. The protesters offered no resistance. The blonde girl followed peacefully.

But Valerie's reaction was different. Struggling violently, she kicked and shouted at the third sheriff, a heavyset, bulky man. In his attempt to restrain her, he hit her in the face. A ribbon of steel flashed across his fingers.

Iron knuckles, Julia realized in horror. She'd seen prison movies where guards used them to torture inmates. Little did she know they'd be employed on her own roommate.

Valerie's outcry alerted the audience that something was amiss. Heads began to turn and bodies shifted, making it difficult for Julia to see. But she couldn't miss the blood streaming from her roommate's cheek, nose, and mouth. Bright red rivulets ran down her neck, staining her loose cotton top. And it wasn't cushioned by celluloid like film clips of the Chicago riots or the makeup used in movies. It was real.

The policeman shoved Valerie in the back with the others, jumping in the driver's seat and slamming the door. The van jounced down the gravel side road, just as the band finished the last strains of "The Star Spangled Banner."

Julia was stunned. The altercation had been so sudden, so cruel. And Valerie and the others hadn't done anything wrong! Pointing in the direction of the retreating van, Julia shouted, "I can't believe it! Did you see what just happened?"

Several of the sisters stared at Julia. Betsy said, "No, I didn't, but you'd better sit down. Everyone is looking at you."

"I don't care," Julia was filled with helpless rage. "Those," she wanted to say "bastards" but didn't dare, "those *cops* just brutalized my friends for exercising their freedom of speech. This is America, not a dictatorship. They had no right to do that!"

Betsy laid firm hands on Julia's shoulders, forcing her to sit like the others. "Calm down, Julia. If you're referring to that crazy roommate of yours, she probably asked for it. You should have requested a transfer — there are plenty of empty rooms on my floor."

If Betsy hadn't been her closest friend in the sorority, Julia would have pulled a Valerie and told her where to get off. How dare Betsy talk that away about someone she didn't even know! Julia fumed while the Hayes Choraliers stepped onto the portico and began a tune about being on top of the world.

Julia squirmed, conscious of the sweat between her breasts and under her arms. Between the heat and the curious eyes of her sisters, she felt physically and mentally stifled. Valerie could be bleeding to death, and here she sat with these pampered princesses as if nothing had happened. And what of Adrian and the other protesters? What kind of treatment would they be receiving, alone, in the hands of the police?

There was a $100 bill stashed in her suitcase back at the dorm. In case of an emergency, her Mom had said. It might be enough money for bail. And she couldn't think of a more justified use. So without a word of explanation, she clambered down the rickety metal bleachers.

"Julia, where are you going?" the soon-to-be president, Lydia, demanded in her haughty voice.

But Julia didn't answer. And as soon as she was out of sight of her gaping sisters, she started to run. She'd explain her abrupt departure later. Right now she had to help Valerie and Adrian.

CHAPTER TWO

Flushed with exertion and triumph at her own resourcefulness, Julia rushed into the reception area at the Hampton police station a few minutes later. Thrusting her money at a skinny, young cop sitting with his feet on a desk, she announced, "My friend Valerie is hurt. Here's $100 bail money for her and the others."

The policeman swung slowly around on his chair. He leaned forward to examine Julia. His gaze traveled up and down her body, stopping at her skirt which rose six inches above her knees. "You mean the hippies?" he drawled, not removing his eyes from Julia's well-shaped legs. "Now what's a nice girl like you doing with the likes of them?"

A blush crept upward from the flat collar of her dress, deepening the pink already on her cheeks. "I have cash," she snapped, resenting his insinuating look. "You take cash, don't you?"

"Sure we do." As he smirked at her, she noticed his face was narrow, like a fox's, with small, mean eyes. "But we haven't set bail yet. Could be anywhere from $50 to $1000 per head."

"But that's not fair! These people haven't broken the law!"

"Ah, but they have, magnolia blossom. Refusing to stand for our national anthem is an offense. And Judge Wilkins went fishing this weekend, so it's up to me'n Sheriff Mitchell to make the determination."

Belligerence was getting her nowhere, so she'd try to appeal to his sense of humanity. He was supposed to watch out for the public good, after all. "Please give them a break," she pleaded. "Valerie may be seriously injured. She needs a doctor!"

Glancing around, the cop licked his dry, cracked lips and quietly suggested, "Then come in back with me, magnolia blossom. Give me some of that free love, and maybe we can negotiate."

How dare he speak to her that way! As if she were a slut and not a member of the most respected sorority on campus! Who did he think he was? Tears of rage welled into her eyes. "You owe me an apology," she cried. "Now take my money and release my friends!" She nearly shoved the $100 bill in his face.

"Trying to bribe an officer of the law, eh?" he snarled, plucking the money from her. "Here's my evidence. You're under arrest for solicitation." He seized her arm.

The harder Julia struggled to break free, the firmer his grasp became. "You can't do this!" She barely noticed the tears spilling down her cheeks.

She could smell the chewing tobacco on his breath. "Go ahead and fight me, flower child. I can add the charge of resisting arrest to your record. That'll explain the bruises on your pretty body after I pay a visit to your cell later."

Now Julia was really scared. Until tonight she'd never even talked to a policeman, and now she was about to be raped by one. And she barely let the boys she dated touch her.

A door slammed open; they both jumped. Julia buried her face in her free elbow so no one could see her mortification.

"Excuse me, officer," a clear male voice spoke. "But my friend and I couldn't help listening in on your conversation as we approached the station. I'm sure you're aware that sexual harassment of either male or female suspects is a violation of Section 201.4 of the Hampton Village Police Code and could result in immediate dismissal. Incidentally, just how was this young lady breaking the law?"

Releasing his grip, the cop backed away. Julia peeked through her fingers and glimpsed a sturdy young man of medium height a few years older than she. He had a pleasant, open face and could have been mistaken for a professor, save for his faded, frayed bell bottoms and frizzy tan hair tied back in a ponytail.

Tilting his head so his eyes met hers, he smiled at her as though her situation was another minor inconvenience of everyday life. Julia wanted to run and hide behind him, but restrained herself. She straightened up, trying to maintain her few remaining shreds of tattered dignity.

He said to the cop, "I'm Louis Wexler, president of the Student Mobilization Committee to End the War in Vietnam. It's my understanding you have some of our people in custody: specifically, Adrian Shaffley, Valerie Stazyck, Shawn Collier, Stu Moseko, and Laura Sturdivant. I'm here to discuss the nature and constitutionality of their internment."

Julia remembered Valerie and Adrian talking about Louie Wexler. He was supposed to be brilliant, with plans of becoming a lawyer. He'd been a medic in Vietnam and as a result of that experience, was totally committed to stopping the war. Julia had never met a Vietnam veteran before. Military service was not a part of her or her friends' lives.

The policeman was obviously intimidated by Louie, for he kept edging towards the back of the room while Louie spoke. "Yeah, right," he mumbled. "We got 'em in the holding cell. I'll get Sheriff Mitchell. I'm just the deputy." Then he disappeared.

Louie turned to Julia, his pleasant mask replaced by a look of anger. "You should press charges. Sexual harassment is heavy stuff, and it would serve that bastard right."

"I don't want any more trouble," Now that she was safe, Julia began to shake violently. She tried to conceal her emotions by fumbling in her purse for a tissue and wiping off her remaining mascara and eye shadow. "But thank you so much for rescuing me."

"What were you trying to do, anyway?"

"I'm here to bail out Valerie and Adrian, too." For the first time, she glanced at Louie's companion, a tall, muscular fellow. He leaned against the door, his face mostly hidden by a purple felt hat.

Louie raised his eyebrows. Was he studying her sorority pin or her breasts? "That probably won't be necessary." He sounded amused.

Valerie, Adrian, and the others were ushered in. They seemed fine, albeit somewhat disconcerted. Julia saw with relief that Valerie only had a cut on her cheek, which she nursed with an ice pack.

But Julia recognized the burly policeman who accompanied them. "This man assaulted Valerie for no reason!" she cried, pointing to a piece of gauze wrapped around his right hand. "He even hurt himself hitting her!"

The man, obviously Sheriff Mitchell, cast a disgusted glance in Julia's direction. "You kids have all the answers, don't you? You think you know everything." Quickly unwinding the dressing, he revealed bloody deep indentations on his hand, the obvious marks of human teeth. Everyone gasped, and Julia felt her stomach rise to her throat. Even Louie turned away.

"Your friend bit me," Mitchell continued, covering up his wound. "Because she was resisting arrest, I tried to handcuff her. I struck her in self-defense." So the flash of steel had been handcuffs, not an iron knuckle. And Valerie hadn't been the totally helpless victim after all. With dismay, Julia realized she'd jeopardized both her personal safety and position in the sorority for a situation she hadn't fully understood.

"You mean I went to all this trouble..." she began, and was stopped by the gentle pressure of Louie's fingers on the small of her back.

"Officer Mitchell, may I speak honestly?" He didn't wait for an answer to his rhetorical question. "We appear to have a Mexican standoff of sorts. You've arrested three out of five of my people on unconstitutional grounds. Only Stu Moseko and Laura Sturdivant were wearing the American flag in what you might consider an inappropriate manner. Although you can press charges against Valerie Stazyck for resisting arrest, the reason behind her internment might not hold up in court." Valerie hung her head as if ashamed, and Julia recalled her praising Mahatma Gandhi and his methods of nonviolent protest.

"But Randall Winfield and I caught your deputy," Louie's well-modulated voice turned to steel, "making sexually threatening actions towards...."

He looked at Julia and she softly supplied, "Julia Brandon."

"...which is a hell of a lot more serious than a bunch of college kids demonstrating against Vietnam during a University-sponsored function."

Sheriff Mitchell sighed, settling his heavy bulk at the desk so recently vacated by his wayward deputy. "Look, son. I don't really want to tangle with you or your organization. But the University's worried about the trouble on campuses these days and gave us specific instructions to halt any unauthorized protests." He rubbed his tired-looking face. "Believe it or not, I'm not totally unsympathetic to your cause. The way you go about things, maybe, but I'm not sure I'd want to fight in that jungle war myself. Why don't you try working within the system?"

"That's impossible and you know it," Valerie retorted, pressing the ice pack against her injured cheek. "Look, I'm sorry I freaked out and bit you, but getting the word out to the kids is the only way we're going to accomplish anything. The Administration refuses to recognize Student Mobilization and won't grant us the right to assemble."

"We could argue politics for hours," said Louie. "But the facts are we have an even trade. Drop the charges against these five people and we'll overlook the incident of sexual harassment." Julia shot Louie an alarmed glance — she hardly wanted to testify in court — but Louie reached over and gave her hand a squeeze.

"You've got to understand about Deputy Adams," Sheriff Mitchell said. "He lost his brother in 'Nam six months ago. So contact with your friend Julia here, or anyone against the war, is like waving a Viet Cong flag in his face. We even leave him at the station whenever we go on campus patrol." He shook his head, a middle-aged man overwhelmed by society gone awry. "When Ike was President, everything made sense. Now all of you get out of here."

Louie and the girl named Shawn went with Louie's friend Randall to get their car which was parked in an alley across the street. The rest restrained their whoops of joy until they were fifty yards away from the police station.

Stu hugged Laura and cried, "Far out! I was afraid we'd have to get married in the fuckin' jail cell!"

Adrian bent over from his height of six-one and kissed Julia on the cheek. "Oh, wow, I can't believe you actually came to bail us out. Won't your sisters have a shit fit?"

Valerie turned to Julia, her eyes deep pools of apology. "I'm so sorry I created this hassle for you, Julia. I had no idea you'd go to such lengths for me. Even though you're a sorority chick, you're a real human being."

"Thanks a lot!" In spite of everything, Julia had to chuckle.

"Did that young pig hurt you? With your looks, sweet innocent Julia, you need to take karate." Holding onto her injured face, Valerie did a fractured kung fu imitation, her golden hair flying. "Hi ya! Kickee in the balls!"

Julia released her tension over the incident with hysterical laughter at Valerie's theatrics. But she stopped when she remembered the $100 bill. "That deputy took my money and never gave it back!"

"You didn't ask for return of the bail?" Valerie demanded.

"So much was happening I forgot," Once again Julia was near tears. "What will I tell my parents?" She hadn't thought of how Dr. and Mrs. Harry Brandon would react during her impulsive flight to help Valerie and Adrian.

"Say someone ripped you off." Adrian suggested. "Besides, who cares what the old fogies think anyway?"

"Shit, that pisses me off," Valerie scowled. "I'm going back there and insist that Deputy Asshole return your bread." She began to walk back to the station.

Julia grabbed her arm. "Don't, Valerie. It's my money and we've had enough for one day. I'll explain I lost it. In a sense, it's the truth." Although her father would be annoyed, she would never frighten her mother by telling the whole story.

A blue '59 Chevy rumbled alongside them, and the driver — the one called Randall Winfield — leaned on the horn. "Any of you goddamn hippies want a ride?" he drawled. Julia, Valerie, and Adrian declined while Stu and Laura climbed in back next to Louie.

Winfield glanced at Julia. "Well, don't say I didn't offer to get you out of this heat," Pulling off his hat, he shook out his hair, revealing his face for the first time.

Julia had to force herself not to gasp. He was the most beautiful man she'd ever seen. His magnificent red-brown mane tumbled to his shoulders in a shining mass. He turned towards Julia, his chiseled features alight in a radiant smile usually found only in a very young child. His eyes, which matched his hair, sparkled with laughter, but hinted at greater depths.

"Isn't this yours, magnolia blossom?" He handed Julia her $100 bill. "I encountered the good deputy as he tried to sneak out the door while Louie was negotiating everyone's release. I reminded him we'd overheard your entire conversation and that jogged his memory. He returns this to you with his sincere apologies and hopes there will be no hard feelings."

"That's not the only thing of his that's hard!" Adrian roared at his own joke.

"Thank you," Julia could barely manage the words.

"Win is quiet but effective," Sitting next to him in the front seat, Shawn leaned over his lap with a proprietary air. "You guys are coming to Stu and Laura's wedding tomorrow, aren't you?"

"Oh, wow, I wouldn't miss that," Adrian said. "Sex and drugs and rock-n-roll."

"Sure," Shawn snorted, an unexpectedly genteel sound. "Right in front of the entire theatre department on the steps of the Performing Arts Center." She turned to Valerie. "Three o'clock. Wear your most far-out duds."

Of course they don't want me there, Julia thought with a stab of disappointment. I don't even know them, and besides, I'm an outsider. "You're coming, too, Julia." Surprised, Julia looked up to meet Win's unflinching gaze. It was less of a question, more of a summons. If she'd been a Popsicle, she'd have melted on the spot.

"She'll be there," Valerie promised. "If it wasn't for Julia, we'd still be busted. Once you save someone's ass you're their responsibility for life. Isn't that a proverb or something?"

"It's either Chinese or in the Talmud," Louie observed.

"Not to take anything away from your friend, but I think we all kind of rescued each other," Shawn commented. "But the more the merrier."

The Chevy puttered off. Adrian and Valerie offered to walk Julia back to her dorm. They'd invited her to get high at Adrian's to celebrate the end of their ordeal but as usual she declined.

A breeze cooled her sweaty clothes as she strolled through the brightly lit campus. Instead of worrying about the sorority or the near-tragedy with Deputy Adams, she found herself wondering why they called Randall Winfield "Win."

CHAPTER THREE

Because Julia slept so late the following morning, she skipped Saturday brunch in the downstairs cafeteria and ate crackers and oranges at her desk instead. By early afternoon, Valerie still hadn't returned to their spacious room in Henderson Hall but the rare time alone gave Julia an opportunity to think. What if Valerie and Adrian were right? What if it was the responsibility of young America to end the war in Vietnam? "By any means possible," Valerie had said.

That's what this whole rebellion thing's about, Julia decided. The long hair, the wild clothes, the drugs and sex were a statement of sorts, a way of letting adults know Vietnam was morally wrong. And our generation has to fight it while older people get rich making napalm, or shipping parts, or manufacturing the plastic bags bodies are sent home in, she realized with a shudder. She remembered the 6:00 news at dinnertime at home, and the announcer's dry reports of "body counts." She'd never thought of those statistics as flesh-and-blood boys her age or a few years younger. Separated from her world by social class, skin color, or education, they had neither the money nor the awareness to avoid the war. Or perhaps they wholeheartedly believed in America, and felt an unquestioning commitment to fight.

When Julia was a student at Bexley High in Columbus, Vietnam had just begun to escalate. The affluent, mostly white school had neither radicals nor even the slightest whiff of marijuana. Boys automatically avoided the draft via college, marriage, or cleverly devised medical deferments. Like the civil rights movement and the general sexual and social upheavals of the '60s, Vietnam was an abstract involving other people. Such issues were cocktail fodder for parents; the kids were mostly absorbed in dates or getting into good universities.

Julia followed the same accepting path at Hayes. She threw herself into becoming a BGP, getting high grades, finding the "right boy." She was studying to be an art teacher because she loved to draw and felt teaching was the only way she could find a job. Yet the thought of standing in front of primary graders day after day alternately terrified her and filled her with emptiness.

Julia had given up on marriage. With only a year of school left, all the decent boys her age were either pinned, engaged, or involved in a steady relationship. And Julia suspected she was frigid, for even though she wanted love, a man's touch failed to move her. Her fantasies and realities seemed light years apart. For as much as she could imagine herself coupling passionately with a boy, once her crush evolved into a pair of lips meeting hers, or a hand touching her breasts, all feeling stopped.

She'd been living in a cocoon during a decade where the foundations of civilization and even the reality of God had been challenged and pulled apart. It wasn't until she believed someone she cared about was in danger that she allowed the outside world to affect her. Valerie had tried to break through her protective sphere, but she'd been too preoccupied to respond. Perhaps selfish is a better word, she amended.

It was 2:00, nearly time to get ready for Stu and Laura's wedding. Where was Valerie, anyway? Although her roommate often risked suspension by staying out overnight, she always returned for meals. Yet Valerie remained skinny while Julia struggled to keep down her weight.

Julia decided to dress, even though she would never go to the wedding without Valerie. She went over the closet made even roomier by Valerie's lack of wardrobe, and selected her prettiest outfit, a pink chiffon mini-confection with ruffles around both the open collar and the billowed sleeves and three layers of frills at the bottom. It would be perfect with matching hose, flats, and a pearl choker.

Thirty minutes later, after carefully putting on her clothes and makeup, Julia examined herself carefully in front of the full-length mirror that covered the closet door. Did the dress make her rear end look big? Flatten her already somewhat small breasts? At least her legs were good, a blessing in this era of short skirts. She imagined Win's admiring glances as she made her entrance at the wedding. He would take one look at her, then ask her out on a date.

A disheveled Valerie burst in, vaporizing Julia's daydreams. "Goddammit, I'm late!" she exclaimed. "Adrian and I stayed up all night rapping. We just woke up a half-hour ago." She glanced at Julia, then did a double-take. "What the hell are you all decked out for? Aren't you coming to the wedding?"

"Of course I am," Julia replied uncertainly, not understanding why she felt so embarrassed. "I'm ready whenever you are."

"Oh, Julia," Valerie lowered her head, unsuccessfully hiding an amused grin. "You're dressed for a straight ceremony, with bridesmaids and preachers and rice and all that shit. This is, like, an alternative wedding where people make up their own vows and everyone wears whatever they want. Adrian was thinking about coming in the nude, but I saved the theatre department from being grossed out and talked him into a tie-dyed toga."

Opening the closet, Valerie pulled out a full-length Indian print dress with a plunging neckline and matching headband and a skimpy halter top that looked like an oversized handkerchief and low-slung bell bottoms. Valerie thrust the dress at Julia. "I think you'd look funky in this." She began to peel off her blood-stained clothes from the night before.

Julia couldn't imagine herself in anything that freaky-looking. What would people say when they saw her? "I can't," she mumbled.

"Why not? The dress will flatter your figure. And don't worry about the hem; just watch where you walk." Tying up her top, Valerie yanked the bell bottoms over her narrow hips.

As Julia averted her eyes at Valerie's nudity, she marvelled at how quickly Valerie put herself together. Between deciding on outfits, picking shoes and accessories, applying makeup and straightening her perpetual curls, Julia could take an hour or more. Valerie's secret was simple: she regarded clothing as a utility, rather than a way of attracting and keeping a man.

But Julia neither wanted to hurt Valerie's feelings nor adopt her dress code. So she said lamely, "I'm such a klutz, I know I'll trip. And besides, the neck's too low."

Valerie ran a fast brush through her straight, shoulder-length hair. "Hey, what you have on isn't exactly prudish. Make it quick, though. Adrian's waiting in the lobby."

Julia still didn't move and Valerie looked up. "Oh, I get it. You don't want to compromise your image by dressing like a hippie." She lifted her shoulders in an abrupt gesture. "Have it your way, then."

Someone rapped softly on the door and Valerie grimaced. "Speak of the devil. I can tell by the knock it's one of your sisters. They're so fucking po-lite. Enter!" she barked.

Sure enough, it was president-elect Lydia, who smiled sweetly at Valerie. "Hello Valerie. How are you today?"

Valerie ignored Lydia's cheery greeting. "I'm going to the bathroom to wash up, Julia. Adrian and I'll meet you downstairs."

"That's a good idea. Cleanliness is next to godliness," Lydia commented, wrinkling her nose at Valerie's back. "I'm glad to see you're ready, Julia. And don't you look nice!"

Julia stared at Lydia in confusion. How did Lydia know about the wedding?

"What's wrong, Julia?" Lydia queried, a slight edge to her sugary voice. "Have you been smoking some of your roommate's marijuana?" She emitted an exaggerated giggle. "Just kidding! I've come to fetch you for the Alumnae Tea."

She'd completely forgotten about the annual gathering of past and present BGPs. Her visions of seeing Win at the wedding vanished in the face of a stultifying afternoon listening to alumnae preface each sentence with, "When I was in BGP...."

"Weren't you planning on coming?" Lydia demanded, the sorority watch dog hot on the scent of a potential aberration. "Why did Valerie say she'd see you in the lobby?"

Julia hated confrontations, and she'd had her share in the past day and a half. Yet she had to see Win again. There must be some way to placate Lydia and still attend the wedding. "You're right, Lydia, I did make plans with Valerie," she said in her most contrite voice. "The tea slipped my mind and I'm really sorry. Can I make it up by sketching out those murals for fall rush?" Lydia had asked Julia to paint wall-sized posters of the sorority's various activities when they returned to Hayes in September. Julia had declined because she was student teaching and didn't know what her schedule would be. "The other girls can just fill in the colors," Julia suggested.

"Of course you can do the murals, but your obligation is with us. Always. " Lydia's tone remained even but her pasty skin grew blotchy, reminding Julia that Lydia was one of the least attractive girls in BGP. Perhaps that's why she could be such a meddler, Julia thought resentfully. Although she should be happy and secure as president and pinned to a groovy-looking Sigma Chi. "I expect you in the suite in fifteen minutes." Lydia turned on her heel to leave.

"Now wait a minute, Lydia." Last night's frustration with BGP returned in a rush. "You're not being fair to either Valerie or me." Julia started to follow Lydia out the door.

"And you're doing justice to the sorority?" Lydia whirled back around. "I wasn't going to say anything, but you certainly didn't make us look good when you ran off after those hippies."

"How can you judge others when you've never really talked with them?" Julia could hear her voice escalating. "Certain things are wrong with this country, and Valerie and Adrian sincerely want to help."

"That roommate of yours has been a bad influence, Julia. You'd better straighten out or you'll lose the friends who really count."

"Valerie has nothing to do with this! I just see her and the others trying to put an end to the slaughter of innocent people, both American soldiers and Vietnamese alike." Julia stopped, surprised at the depth of her feelings. She noticed several girls had gathered in the hallway to listen.

"Don't you spout that Communist rhetoric at me, Julia Brandon!"

"Adrian and Valerie love this country as much as we do!" Their audience was growing. What the hell, she fumed, maybe they'll learn something. "Unlike most of us, they refuse to ignore the lies of politicians, big businesses, and the military."

"How dare you compare me with those filthy freaks!" Lydia shrilled. "It's obvious you no longer care about Beta Gamma Phi. I'm going to the Panhellenic Council and recommend that you be investigated for subversive activities."

Julia almost laughed. Since when was a wedding subversive? But she knew more was at stake than a mere conflict of plans. Although she was tempted to apologize to Lydia, her newfound convictions held her back.

So she kept silent. Lydia started to walk away again, nose in the air, refusing to look at the other girls. But Valerie, coming out of the bathroom, blocked Lydia's path. Julia had never seen her roommate so furious, not even when she was struggling with the policeman.

"Well, we finally see your true colors," Valerie sneered at Lydia. "You know you're wrong, don't you?"

Lydia's complexion went from splotchy to purple. "Get out of my way you...you terrorist!"

"Gee, I went from Valerie to a terrorist in less than five minutes," Valerie tilted her chin and cocked her fists. "Make me, cunt."

A collective gasp rose from the group. Julia was amazed the girls even knew what the word meant. She wouldn't have, except Valerie explained it to her one night when they were discussing various sexual positions. "How dare you call me that!" Lydia squeaked. She looked ready to explode. Julia wished she could somehow turn the clock back and prevent this whole fiasco. If only she and Valerie had left a few minutes earlier!

Valerie edged closer to Lydia. "Apologize to Julia or I'll do more than talk, fuckface." Another gasp. A theatre major, Valerie knew how to hold an audience. Except this wasn't one of Adrian's experimental plays.

Lydia turned ashen, then began to back away. "You wouldn't touch me," she whispered.

"Oh, yes I would, " Valerie's eyes glinted as she closed in on Lydia. The others stepped back, leaving the two warring girls exposed in the middle of the corridor.

"You're out of your mind!" Lydia looked around desperately, a cornered animal searching for an escape route.

Julia wanted to beg Valerie to stop, to tell her it wasn't worth it, but an almost perverse fascination with the unfolding drama held her back.

Valerie laughed. "You'll get no assist from these tender chicks. Unlike them, I grew up on the streets and learned how to fight dirty at a young age." She was practically on top of Lydia.

"Somebody call campus security!" Lydia sobbed, cowering against the wall. No one moved. Like bystanders at an unexpected crime of violence, they were paralyzed into inactivity.

"But I wouldn't waste my time on a chickenshit like you," Valerie dropped her aggressive stance, and Julia caught her breath. She felt a surge of annoyance now that Valerie had put a rein on her temper. Julia and Lydia's argument was no business of hers.

Lydia, sensing that physical danger was past, began to pull herself together. "I don't know why this concerns you, Valerie," she said, echoing Julia's thoughts. "This involves BGP and has nothing to do with you."

"Oh but it does, Lydia," Valerie mimicked her condescending tone. "You're trying to hamper Julia's personal freedom by threatening her. It's her free time and she can do as she damn pleases."

"A sorority expects certain standards of behavior from its members. Julia is no exception."

"Cut the bullshit." Valerie retorted. "She hasn't done a damn thing wrong except express ideas you don't agree with." Valerie looked around and several girls, most of whom belonged to other sororities, nodded.

Lydia noticed also and equivocated, "Well, perhaps I was a bit hasty about calling in Panhellenic." She flashed a pallid smile at Julia, but her expression remained tense and angry. "Vietnam brings out the worst in everyone. We'll discuss this later, Julia." Without waiting for any other comments, she ran down the steps.

CHAPTER FOUR

"You should've seen me, Adrian," Valerie gloated. "My greatest performance ever. I think I even had Julia convinced." They were finally on their way to Stu and Laura's wedding.

Adrian giggled. "Oh, wow. How did you get those sorority chicks to believe you belonged to a street gang?"

"I sort of implied it," Valerie radiated glee. "I grew up in a rough neighborhood but didn't mention I went to strict Catholic schools or the fact my stepdad wouldn't let me out on weekends 'til I was seventeen. What they don't know won't hurt them." Valerie's real father had died of cancer when she was twelve. She claimed to be an atheist ever since, embracing the "God is dead" philosophy.

"Well, you practically ruined me," Julia attempted to keep the tears from her voice. "I'll never be comfortable in BGP again."

"Hey, cut that out, Julia," Valerie stopped underneath the arch linking the two wings of Cassidy Hall, the English and Journalism building. "I'm sure people will see Lydia for the bitch she is."

"She isn't the nicest person in BGP, but she adheres to a code of honor. And she tries to be objective. That's why we elected her president."

"I'd hardly say she was fair in threatening to call you in front of your Greekoid counsel."

"She is opinionated. And once you get on her bad side...." Julia shook her head, overcome with emotion. As far as she was concerned, her life at Hayes was over.

"If you cry, you'll destroy your makeup," Adrian admonished, smacking his lips. "And you look so delectable. Rather like a strawberry sundae topped with hot fudge and whipped cream all around."

Valerie put her hands on her narrow hips and glared at him. "You couldn't resist, could you?" she demanded. "I told you to save the stuff until after the ceremony. Now you're stoned out of your gourd and have the munchies to boot. How many did you take?"

Adrian pulled a foil-wrapped paper plate from beneath the layers of his tie-dyed toga. "Only a few." He lifted the foil, revealing a congealed brown mess that reminded Julia of something found in her two-year-old cousin's diaper. She recoiled in disgust.

"Alice B. Toklas hashish brownies," Valerie explained. "Stu and Laura's wedding present. Or former wedding present, since this asshole ate nearly half. Adrian and I baked them last night."

She selected something that, upon closer examination, did resemble edible food — sort of. "Want one, Julia? It'll blow your mind along with curing your blues."

"No thanks."

"Aw, c'mon Julia," Adrian pleaded. "Just one. At least try getting high. It's like sex, though. You don't get off until the second time." He reached for another brownie.

In spite of her worries, Julia cast an amused glance at her roommate. Wouldn't Adrian be shocked if he learned Julia had smoked once in the room with Valerie! He was right though, except for a slight headache, she hadn't felt a thing.

"You've had enough, Adrian," Valerie snatched the plate away from him and covered it up, but not before taking a second brownie for herself. "Let Julia make up her own mind about things."

"I had the situation with Lydia pretty much under control before you interfered," Julia said to Valerie as they approached the

Performing Arts Center. "She probably wouldn't have gone to the Panhellenic Council once she cooled off, and the whole argument would've been forgotten by fall. Now the damage is permanent."

"I wouldn't be too sure about that. Like you said, Lydia's ultraconservative and you pissed her off pretty good." Valerie observed. "I just added a finishing touch. But maybe I should've kept out of it. Still, what a wonderful opportunity for street theatre...."

"Dorm theatre." Adrian amended. "God, I wish I'd been there!"

Perhaps it hadn't totally been Valerie's doing. Hadn't she, Julia, baited Lydia by implying she was unfair and loudly voicing her changing political beliefs?

"Look, Julia, I don't want to tell you how to run your life," Valerie said. "But it's becoming really obvious that you have to make a choice between us and the sorority."

"A get off the pot or go predicament," Adrian amended. "Or, in our case, turn on to pot. Get it?" He tittered. No one enjoyed his own humor more than Adrian.

"But it shouldn't be like that!" Julia cried. "In a way, I like those girls as much as you and Adrian." She remembered late nights in the BGP suite munching popcorn and gossiping with her little and big sisses, Betsy and Nancy. And she'd had fun during rush week and at fraternity parties and beer blasts, especially during her freshman and sophomore years.

"But it's two different worlds. And because of where people's heads are at, you can't be part of both," Valerie sighed. "I'm sorry I fucked over your relationships. It might've been easier for you if we'd never met."

"Don't say that!" They paused in front of the long driveway leading to the Performing Arts Center. "I'm glad we're friends. You two care about what's going on inside me, something no one's ever done before. And you've also made me aware of things that are wrong with the world. The problem's with me. I just don't fit in anywhere."

"You need to take some time and get your shit together," Valerie advised. "What do you, Julia Brandon, really want?"

"Enough group therapy for today, girls," Adrian interjected. "If we don't haul ass we'll miss the wedding."

Julia barely recognized the Performing Arts Center from the evening before. Gone were the bleachers, the musicians, and the neatly dressed alumni. The theatre department had reclaimed its territory, with an abundance of colorfully-patterned dashiki tops, afros, pink and yellow-tinted metal rimmed glasses, capes and ponchos, antique and long dresses of all fabrics, and even a few costumes. And of course the staple, faded blue jeans strategically patched with lurid red lips, peace signs, or other symbols of the movement.

Perhaps it was because the bright day was cooler, but it seemed to Julia that the Performing Arts Center had changed also. Surrounded by rustling pines, the ancient red brick structure gave off an air of dank mystery, of hidden creakings and silent watchfulness. Like all Hayes students, she'd heard stories about the historic old building. Originally constructed during the Civil War and named after the prestigious Taft family of Cincinnati, it was initially part of Mt. Airy College for Men, as Hayes was called before 1890.

Taft Hall underwent a number of incarnations. Because it was so far away from the rest of the campus, the college, in the dire financial straits typical of state-funded institutions during the 1870s, rented it out to the nearby hamlet of Hampton. Hoping to attract tourists and add to its population, the village fathers advertised the idyllic setting as a health resort. When that venture failed, it was used as a sanitarium for wealthy, mentally disturbed women.

The university reclaimed Taft Hall in the latter part of the 19th century. A presidential name and government support brought students and prosperity. The college was by now coeducational, although Taft Hall spent the following half-decade as a men's dorm. The next conversion, to Navy officer training headquarters, resulted from World War II.

By the 1950s, Taft Hall was once again a residence for male students. The building's popularity soared, due to its nearness to the Formal Gardens and subsequent "blanket dates," along with a liberal reputation regarding curfews and dress codes. But one bitter January night in 1955, a junior named Pete Edison vanished, leaving all his personal belongings untouched. There was no body, no clues, no witnesses. A few months later, residents began to hear moaning in the halls. A mysterious figure appeared on the portico. The students organized search parties, and only succeeded in scaring each other.

Perhaps the "ghost" was someone's idea of a joke; nevertheless, a year later the building was declared unfit as a dorm. The official explanation was that Taft had never been completely rennovated and had unsafe electrical wiring and inadequate bathrooms.

In 1960, however, the rapidly expanding music and drama departments needed larger facilities. So the first and second floors of the renamed Performing Arts Center were remodeled to include a full-sized stage, a theatre in the round, and several studios and practice rooms. Administrators, faculty, and students were currently embroiled in a controversy over whether to completely revamp the old building or raze it and build a new Performing Arts Center closer to the middle of campus.

Despite the changes, the phantom of old Taft Hall stayed on, at least according to students. Valerie told Julia she heard the ghost clattering around on the boarded-up third floor and rattling windowpanes. Even a ZBT Julia once dated made a middle-of-the-night visit on a dare and returned with stories of shadows peering through windows and tapping sounds underneath the portico.

Presently, though, Julia was only concerned with the living. After looking around, she realized her pink ruffles and lacquered flip were horribly out of place. People cast curious glances in her direction, even though she tried to make herself inconspicuous by shrinking behind Adrian's lanky form. She felt like an interloper, a neon sign screaming "straight," and desperately wished she'd borrowed Valerie's dress. How foolish she'd been to think Win would find her attractive, much less ask her out!

She failed to notice the wedding procession had begun until Valerie gave a low whistle. Win and Shawn strolled past the spot where she, Adrian, and Valerie stood. Julia's knees weakened at the sight of Win. He was so *big*. Not just tall -- he couldn't be much over six feet -- but muscular with broad shoulders, slim hips, and strong-looking legs. He must exercise, Julia decided.

That in itself was unusual. Other than team sports, physical fitness was considered a boring waste of time by most of her peers.

But what drew every eye to Win was his confidence. He moved with the animal grace of someone with complete control of his body. And only a man sure of his sexuality could carry off that brown velvet vest and pants and beige silk swashbuckler-type shirt with elegance and grace.

The sun shone through the pines, highlighting the red in Win's mane, casting shadows on his deep-hewn features. Julia felt drawn to him by a force that had nothing to do with her intellect, a primitive urge so powerful it almost frightened her. Slowly, something slumbering inside her began to come awake.

She forced herself to focus her attention on Shawn, who was just as fabulous, with platinum hair that hung a foot below her tiny waist. She looked like a Dresden flapper in a paneled, peach sleeveless dress with a wide, hip-hugging bow and feathered headband. She and Win seemed a perfect match. But it was a theatrical pairing, like the maid of honor and the best man in the weddings they so decried.

An admiring murmur followed their path to the portico. "They are outtasight!" Valerie whispered.

"The costume shop can work miracles," Adrian commented, bitchily, Julia thought. She wondered if he was envious.

Win and Shawn outshone even Stu and Laura, who lumbered behind them in floor-length matching white cotton tunics. Stu and Laura seemed slightly dazed, undoubtedly from a prenuptual joint. Or maybe they were just nervous.

Julia paid little attention to the brief ceremony on the portico, which consisted of made-up vows recited by Stu and Laura. Her thoughts buzzed around Win. He had to be more than another campus infatuation from afar. Simply looking at him made her ache, flooding her with feelings she'd never before experienced. She wanted to be next to him, to touch him in places she didn't even know about.

"Oh shit!" Valerie exclaimed, grabbing Adrian, who appeared to be falling asleep on his feet. "He's starting to crash. Maybe we ought to sit down."

Julia didn't want grass stains on her dress and was about to refuse, when the wedding came to an abrupt halt. Adrian shook himself awake, and Valerie, seeing he was all right, went over to congratulate Stu and Laura.

There were more tearful hugs than smiles surrounding the bridal couple. "Why is everyone so sad?" Julia asked Adrian. "This is a wedding!"

"Personally, I find even the mere idea of marriage disgusting, but Stu and Laura are splitting for London in a couple of weeks," Adrian told her. "Everyone will miss them -- Stu got a scholarship to the Royal Academy of Performing Arts and Laura wants to support him. Marrying Stu is the only way her asshole parents'll let her go."

"It must be difficult moving so far away." An only child whose family lived in Columbus, Julia was close to her parents, grandparents, aunts, and uncles. Most of her mother's relatives had died in the Holocaust, so Julia's every accomplishment and failure was a cause for great triumph and concern.

"Shit, they're lucky," Adrian retorted. "Getting out of Amerika with a "k" and all the repressive bullshit that goes along with it. In fact, we all plan to escape to London after we graduate."

It sounded like a pipe dream to Julia and she said, "Adrian, you make things worse than they really are. This is a good country. We're just going through some troubled times."

"I'll drink to that, except I don't drink," Louie Wexler came up to them. Taking Julia's hand, he gave it a brief squeeze, then asked, "How are you today, Julia? Have you recovered?" His touch was firm, reassuring.

"More or less." Amazing how quickly she shoved the unpleasant incident with Deputy Adams into a distant corner of her mind. "Lovely afternoon for a wedding, isn't it?"

"Julia, if you don't quit acting like you're at a goddamn rush party, I'll put you on top of the cake over there," Adrian threatened with a good-natured smirk. "No one'll notice the difference."

"Except for people's clothes, I find this whole experience rather conventional," Julia challenged him. "The procession, the vows, the cake and punch...."

"Wait 'til you see the real reception," Adrian retorted. "Actually, you'd better not. It might freak you out." Adrian was always implying Julia was missing out on things. But what was she supposed to do to get herself included?

"Well, I'm here to invite Julia to join the Student Mobilization Committee," Louie said. "Are you interested?"

"I don't know. I have a lot of thinking to do this summer."

"Well, don't strain your brain too much," She sensed Win's presence behind her before he spoke. "Vacations are supposed to be fun." He flashed his radiant smile. "You look lovely, Julia." God, the hair on his chest was magnificent. Julia wanted to run her fingers down his open neckline. And then what? She could feel herself turning as pink as her dress.

"I do?" she stammered.

"That's what the bride's supposed to say," Win teased.

Adrian began to complain. "Oh, wow, Win, I'm starting to crash. And this is such a drag. When do we split for the reception? Will it be everything Stu promised?"

Win looked at Julia, then at Adrian. "You'll have to ask Stu," he replied, suddenly distant. For some strange reason he seemed almost embarassed.

"I want to congratulate Stu, too," Louie said. "If I don't see you around, Julia, have a nice summer. And give the SMC some consideration." He and Adrian disappeared into the rapidly dwindling crowd.

For a moment, Julia and Win stared at each other. "Do you..." Win began.

"Why do..."Julia spoke at the same time and they laughed.

"Ladies first," Win told her.

Not wanting to seem too personal, Julia changed her mind about what she was going to ask Win. "Thanks for inviting me, but I guess everyone's leaving." She frowned, remembering the confrontation with Lydia. "I have to get back to the dorm. I'm having some problems with my sorority."

"I've almost forgotten that kind of life still exists on this campus," Win observed. "We've all come so far these past two years." What did he mean by that?

Before she had a chance to frame the question, he said, "You'd better straighten it out, then. I'll walk you back part way."

"What were you going to say?" Julia asked as they headed in the general direction of campus.

"Nothing important." Obviously Win decided to censor his words also. Later when she mentally reviewed their conversation she would realize he probably intended on inviting her to the reception but changed his mind. That stupid pink dress! She was definitely going to invest in some blue jeans for fall. "Adrian's a pretty-spaced out dude when he's ripped," Win said.

What did Adrian have to do with anything? Julia decided to play along, pretend she was part of the group. "It's strange, but I can never tell when Valerie's stoned," she replied with what she hoped was nonchalance. "But then it didn't affect me much when I tried it."

Win examined her, a perturbed, almost guilty, look clouding his face. "Certain people handle this whole scene better than others." Had she said or done something to make him feel bad? They reached the end of the driveway. "Well, I guess we part here, Julia. Finals are coming up, so maybe I'll see you in the fall." He stood with his hands clasped behind his back, a polite schoolboy waiting to be dismissed.

"Thank you..." she hesitated. What should she call him? Randy? Randall? She didn't know him well enough to say Win. It seemed like such an intimacy.

"Win," he supplied, as if reading her mind. "That's what my friends call me."

"Why?" Julia posed the question she'd originally intended to ask.

"Which reason do you want? The one I give everyone or my true feelings?"

"Both," she whispered, thrilled that he chose to confide in her.

"Well, people at Hayes think I'm a freak on Winnie-the-Pooh and it's a far out play on my last name," he explained almost shyly. "They even got together and bought me a giant Pooh bear for my twenty-first birthday. But the truth is, I despise the name Randall, and Randy sounds like a lecherous goat."

"Funny how little things bother you. I get upset when people call me Julie or even Brandon."

"I'll remember that," He turned and waved to a cluster of people who were waiting for him. "I've got to split. See you later, Julia." He strode off.

Julia watched him go. He was the most incredible man she'd ever met. And like Valerie and her friends, he expressed his feelings and vulnerabilities. I like these people and their ideas, she realized. They're genuine and caring. The sorority seemed superficial in comparison, and Julia knew she'd made her choice.

CHAPTER FIVE

That summer, Adrian called Valerie and asked if she was interested in taking over the lease on his tiny, free-standing house for the school year. Valerie couldn't believe her good fortune: she'd actually have a place by herself! She'd been so excited she offered to drive to Cincinnati or Hamilton or wherever Adrian was currently crashing and give him the deposit check. Of course he refused, saying he'd stop by and pick it up as soon as she got back to school.

The red clapboard doll house, set several hundred feet behind Hampton's old-time grocery store, was a privacy lover's dream. And for all her contacts and involvements, Valerie relished solitude. During her first two years at Hayes, she'd been shuffled from dorm to dorm, unable to get along with roommates because they either tried to reform her or found her too eccentric. Valerie was beginning to wonder if she could ever be compatible with anyone in close quarters when she met Julia, who accepted her for what she was.

Still, Valerie refused to endure the bitchiness endemic in dorm life any longer than she had to. Until this, her junior year, she'd been forced to live on campus by a University policy that prohibited females under twenty-one from taking residence elsewhere. And being off campus was cheaper, although over the

summer Valerie still had to work double shifts as a waitress and
sell marijuana on the side. Her family could barely afford tuition
and did so grudgingly (after all, she was a female, what did she
need an education for?), so Valerie tried to make as much money
on her own as possible.

Originally she'd planned on staying with Shawn, Win,
Louie, and three others in a house on Maple Street. But when
Adrian told her the rent was about the same on his place, she
phoned Shawn in Toledo, with the intention of suggesting Julia
as a replacement. Before Valerie could give voice to the idea,
Shawn mentioned she had someone in mind. Vicki Viorst was
transferring from the University of Louisville to be near Bill
Gordon, another one of the roommates. So it worked out beautifully.

Valerie moved in a week early. She needed time to settle in
and get her head back together after a summer with her uptight
family. And now, the night before classes were to start, she'd finally finished decorating the one-room efficiency. And she hadn't
done a bad job, considering her financial straits. She'd draped
Indian print bedspreads across walls that also held posters of the
three J's: Janis Joplin, Jimi Hendrix, and Jim Morrison. The
kitchen was separated from the living-cum-bedroom by brightly
colored, plastic beads. The end table sported a cheap fringed
lamp Valerie had bought at a secondhand furniture store. A bong
dominated the long coffee table which sat in front of the worn,
flower print sofa bed.

Valerie especially loved the miniature back yard with its ancient sycamore tree. She could plant a garden in the spring and
stretch out in the sunshine when it was nice. She'd come a long
way from the cramped two-bedroom apartment that once over-
flowed with Valerie, her three sisters, and her mother and stepfather. She'd been the first one to go to college, and now she'd
made another breakthrough: a place of her own.

But where was Adrian? He'd left the key under the mat as
prearranged, but she hadn't heard a word from him. Since he was
always secretive about where he spent his vacations, she had no
way of contacting him. She figured they'd connect at their usual
uptown hangouts, Hampton Square across from the main drag

of shops or Lenny's, the hippie bar. But they somehow must have missed each other.

Or maybe he's found a lover, Valerie thought with a twinge of envy. Although she told herself heavy relationships were a hassle, she sometimes felt empty inside when she saw couples entwined in the standard passionate embrace in front of buildings and under trees. Valerie liked to compare sex to a handshake: quick, impersonal, and as unsweaty as possible.

Valerie hadn't seen Julia yet either, but her friend had only arrived that day. They planned to meet in a few minutes in front of the Campus Ministry building where the first Student Mobilization Committee meeting of the year was being held.

If she left now she'd barely make it to the meeting, but Valerie couldn't resist getting high. Especially since there was no paranoia involved; she simply rolled the joint from her stash in its plastic baggie and lit up. Of course, some of the excitement of smoking grass was tied up in the drama of avoiding discovery — shoving rugs underneath doors and lighting incense sticks to contain the odor; cramming paraphernalia under a pile of dirty laundry at an unexpected knock. But Valerie doubted if she'd miss the anxiety too much.

After feeling the requisite rush of relaxation, she stubbed out the roach, adding it to the quickly accumulating pile in the ash tray. It was good stuff, and would make mind-blowing grist for the bong.

Valerie knew she was late for the meeting, but when she arrived at the Campus Ministry building she thought she'd come to the wrong place: scores of students swarmed up the steps into the small white stucco structure. But as she got closer, she saw many sported long hair, beads and peace symbols of all types and sizes and fringed vests and bell bottoms extended even further by ripping open the seams and sewing in brightly colored pieces of cloth. Radical chic had finally come to Hayes.

Julia, who leaned against the railing and was looking around, had also changed. Her lacquered flip had been replaced by a confusion of soft curls which fell gently to her shoulders. She wore a loose-fitting, embroidered peasant top. The only jarring note was her jeans, which looked like they'd been purchased yesterday. A few patches and some Clorox in the "wash" cycle would fix those. Most important of all, Julia's sorority pin was missing.

"Hey, Valerie," Julia called, catching sight of her. "Do you believe this turnout? Everybody came to the same realization at once."

Not likely, but they do want to be where the action is, Valerie reflected as she and Julia followed the stragglers inside and down to the basement. How was the SMC going to handle all of these people, anyway? But she said, "It's outtasight. How was your vacation?" Each summer, Julia worked as a counselor at a camp for the underprivileged in Wisconsin.

"A little depressing," Julia admitted. "The kids were great, but this year I was really struck by the differences in their backgrounds. If we don't end this war soon, some are doomed to Vietnam." The room was so full they couldn't move forward and had to perch on long tables shoved against the wall.

"What about the sorority?" Valerie thought she knew the answer to that question but asked anyway.

"I sent my letter of resignation in July," a look of sadness crossed Julia's almost-beautiful face. "But I intend on keeping up some of my friendships. It's just that stopping the war's more important than painting murals for rush."

"I really felt shitty about the trouble I caused you last spring. I was afraid you'd give me the brush-off when I called this morning."

"You know me better than that! Besides, you were right. I couldn't be a part of both worlds." Julia scanned the crowd, apparently looking for Adrian, too.

"I've been here a week, and I haven't been able to find him either. I hope he's OK."

"What?" Julia had the startled look of a child caught with her hand in a cookie jar.

"I'm talking about Adrian." Was something going on between Julia and Adrian? Since when was he into virgins? No way, Valerie thought.

"Oh, yes, Adrian," Julia replied hastily. "I don't see him anywhere, either."

Valerie wondered who Julia *was* searching for, but before she had a chance to ask, Louie Wexler called the meeting to order. Since there were so many newcomers, Louie spoke briefly about the history and function of the Student Mobilization Committee to End the War in Vietnam. Founded in 1966, it was part of a Washington-based organization that encompassed a wide spectrum of people: doctors, ministers, homemakers, returning vets, high school and college students. The SMC worked on a grass-roots level to unify these elements through local "actions" — marches, demonstrations and moratoriums. Recently, the SMC had also begun to call for nationwide activities, even publishing the *G.I. Press Service*, a magazine for soldiers who'd served in Vietnam.

"We stand for immediate and unconditional withdrawal of all U.S. troops in Vietnam and an end to the draft, along with free speech in the Armed Forces and for high school and college students," Louie paced back and forth, while the audience listened raptly. Valerie realized her concerns about the SMC's growth were unfounded. Louie could lecture about trash collection and people would sympathize. "We also support black America in its struggle for equality.

"In the past few years, membership has increased by the thousands," Louie continued. "Our fall offensive is focused on uniting even larger portions of the academic community. So on October 15, there's going to be a nationwide moratorium, a day of stopping 'business as usual' on every campus." Louie proceeded to outline the day's schedule of events.

"With this spirit of opening up lines of communication, I'd like to introduce tonight's speaker," Louie concluded, smiling graciously. "Dr. Richard Shaffley, vice-chairman of the Department of Economics."

Richard *Shaffley?* Valerie almost fell off the table as a tall man strode towards the podium. Could he be related to Adrian, whose last name was also Shaffley? She shrugged an "I don't know" in response to Julia's curious glance.

Even from a distance, Valerie noticed a resemblance to Adrian in way he carried himself and his craggy, almost sharp features. But why would Adrian want to hide any connection to this man, a professor and a liberal one at that? Because of Adrian's refusal to discuss his family, Valerie assumed he'd come from an ignorant, intolerant background similar to her own.

Richard Shaffley began to talk, radiating a maturity and assurance Adrian hadn't yet begun to possess. Valerie found herself drawn to the sensuality in his facial expressions and his ebullient movements, which were smoother versions of Adrian's jerky, almost melodramatic ones. No doubt this dude meant what he said, although his ideas were irrelevant — dialogue about "walking hand-in-hand with the Administration towards the long-range goals of ending the war and implementing a black studies department on campus." There was no eventuality about it, Valerie reflected, for even as they sat there rapping, babies were getting napalmed and blacks were rioting for equal representation. He was in over his head.

"Shut up, you honky fool!" Someone in the middle of the room shouted. "We don't want to listen to any more of your wishy-washy rhetoric." There was no need to be rude, Valerie thought. Shaffley was trying to help in his inept way.

"You may see things differently, but I, too, have a right to my beliefs," Shaffley kept his cool, further garnering Valerie's admiration. She would have immediately told the heckler to fuck off.

"We don't want anybody over 30!" Why did this voice, obviously muffled, sound familiar? "So get the hell outta here."

"If you're going to be abusive, you could at least show yourself," Shaffley replied calmly.

Two people stood up: a black fellow Valerie had never seen before and a caped figure in a top hat with a mask over his eyes. It took Valerie a few seconds to recognize Adrian in the costume. What was he up to? "When are you white idiots gonna realize we need results now!" the black shouted, thrusting out his fist in the standard "strike" gesture. "None of this sit on our hands and wait shit."

"That's not exactly what I said," Richard Shaffley countered.

Essentially Valerie agreed with the black fellow, but the people around her were beginning to snicker and mutter among themselves. They think this is a joke, Valerie realized. The SMC will lose its new-found credibility if Adrian and his friend don't stop their harassment.

"I strongly suggest you let Dr. Shaffley finish his speech," Louie stepped up to the podium with that don't-mess-around-with-me expression Valerie had come to respect. "Otherwise, leave. My apologies, Dr. Shaffley. Please continue."

"You asshole!" This time Adrian forgot to disguise his voice. Richard Shaffley took a step backward, and Valerie instinctively knew the father had identified the son.

"That's really all I have to say," The elder Shaffley's voice trembled. "Thank you so much for listening." Without waiting for the polite applause that followed, he hurried into the kitchen directly adjacent to the basement meeting-room.

That Adrian! Valerie fumed. *He* was being an asshole! This nice but misguided dude was at least trying to reach out and understand where the kids were coming from.

Adrian ought to spend some time with her family. Any attempt to communicate with her mother or married/engaged sisters was met with stonewall contempt and refusal to listen. They ignored her ideas and talked around her, centering their conversation on husbands and weddings and child care, making it clear that Valerie wouldn't count until she snagged a man. Valerie had taught herself to keep quiet and avoid family gatherings as much as possible, for she'd disrupted more than one with her infamous temper.

At least they hadn't publicly humiliated her, although her stepfather did a pretty good job whenever they were alone. Valerie turned to Julia and said, "You may not have noticed, but that was Adrian in the cape." Julia gasped and Valerie put a shushing finger over her own lips. "But don't say anything. Shaffley must be Adrian's father. The poor man's really bummed."

"Why is Adrian acting this way?" Julia asked, wide-eyed.

"Oh, he's probably tripping, and you know how he gets."

Julia stared at her blankly, and Valerie thought, of course she doesn't know. Sometimes her friend added new dimensions to the word "naive."

"Try to get Adrian out of here before he does any more damage to the SMC," Valerie told her. "I'm going to find his dad and try to make him feel better." Valerie headed towards the kitchen.

She didn't have far to search, for Richard Shaffley was sitting on the counter drinking coffee with Win and Shawn. When Valerie entered, Shawn told him, "Here's the person you should talk to."

Valerie looked into Richard Shaffley's confused, unhappy eyes. Something inside her came alive and she realized they might have more in common than just Adrian.

Julia stood around aimlessly after the meeting. Valerie had disappeared, Louie was busy signing up volunteers for the October 15 moratorium, and she hadn't yet glimpsed Win. And how could she, of all people, tell Adrian he'd made the SMC look bad and would be doing them all a favor if he departed?

And she was in no particular hurry to escort him out and return to her single room, a privilege she was entitled to as a senior. Miami Hall, her non-Greek dorm, was only next door, anyway.

Julia hadn't seen a familiar face since moving in that morning and eating a solo lunch and dinner in Dodge Hall, the co-ed cafeteria across the street. She'd met two out of three of her suite mates — girls who shared the cluster of five rooms and a bathroom, but they were seniors too and busy with their own lives. She hadn't felt this lonely since Rush Week her freshman year. Even then, the other girls had also been new and eager to make friends.

She was to begin student teaching tomorrow at Etna Elementary in Hamilton, another dreaded experience. Before she quit BGP, she'd arranged to carpool with four other sorority girls who were also student teaching in Hamilton. Julia's remark to Valerie about maintaining her Greek contacts had been bravado, for when she'd phoned the carpool's organizer to verify arrangements, it was made coolly clear that Julia's inclusion was solely due to her one-day-a-week driving commitment and contribution towards gas.

Adrian found her. "Oh wow, Julia. How are you?" he cried, opening his arms wide for a hug. He'd removed his mask and people stared at him. In addition to the black cape and top hat, he also wore eye shadow and rouge. What was he trying to prove?

"I'm fine," She was embarrassed to be seen with him, but awkwardly returned his embrace.

Adrian gestured towards a black fellow standing next to him. "I'd like you to meet Felix Watts. That's his nom de guerre for this year, anyway. He's late of Berkeley and Columbia." He giggled. "Or is it Columbia and Berkeley? I can never get it straight, especially now."

So this was the man who called Adrian's father a honky fool. Somehow he seemed more menacing than all the histrionics and bizarre outfits Adrian could muster.

Felix's narrowed eyes assessed her, found her insignificant, and his lips twisted into a scowl. "If this is as radical as it gets, I'm gonna change this institution's name to Whitebread U." He shook his long Afro in disapproval. "I haven't seen a brother or sister since I set foot on this campus. What do you do, keep them working as maids and janitors?"

What an awful person, Julia thought. True, there weren't many blacks at Hayes, but the ones she'd encountered at the Student Center seemed content to stay among themselves.

"Now, Felix, don't be a downer. I know we have a lot of work to do but by the end of the year, everyone will be burning buildings and bayoneting professors. In fact, I can think of one right now...." Standing on his tiptoes, Adrian surveyed the room.

She had to get Adrian out of here before he made another scene. "Look Adrian, I'm thirsty. Why don't we walk upstairs and get a Tab from the machine?" She was referring to her diet beverege of choice.

This produced shrieks of laughter. What had she said that was so funny? "Oh, wow, you're unbelievable, Julia," Adrian cried, his voice careening like a roller coaster. "I don't even need LSD when I'm around you. A tab from the machine, indeed! Wait 'til I tell the others."

Pushing himself in front of Julia with Felix in his wake, he rushed over to Win, Louie, and Shawn, who stood by the exit. They smiled expectantly. Win was as beautiful as she'd remembered with his warm red-brown hair and matching eyes and gentle expression. Julia had a fleeting image of his curtain of hair falling over her as he buried his head between her breasts.

She watched in hurt bewilderment as Adrian relayed her remark. Win and Shawn, too, seemed to find it hilarious and even Louie chuckled. The hell with them, she thought angrily. I was only trying to help. I didn't say anything stupid or rude. They can make their in-group jokes at someone else's expense.

She brushed past them without bothering to wait for an explanation or even say "hello." She glimpsed Louie's mouth opening to speak and saw the amusement drain from Win's face.

But she was too overwhelmed by all the changes in her life to want to do anything but go back to her lonely room and brood.

CHAPTER SIX

"**W**here the hell have you been?" Two weeks later, Valerie stood scowling in the middle of Julia's tiny room.

"I'm student teaching this quarter," Julia sat at her antiquated, scarred wooden desk. Hoping to avoid Valerie's piercing gaze, she stared at the lesson plan in front of her. "Don't you remember?"

"Don't pull that shit on me, Julia. You're back by four and the SMC meets after dinner. I've been busy too, but a whole lot of important stuff's been going down." Valerie flopped on the bed, unfazed by the fact that it was after eleven on a school night.

Valerie had been waiting for her on the steps of Miami Hall when Julia returned from her nightly sojourn at the library. The SMC gathering must have also just dispersed, for Julia noticed several longhairs leaving the Campus Ministry building next door. "Dean Moreland's issued a restriction against campus demonstrations," Valerie complained. "Do you know what that means? We have to follow some tightass, complicated application procedure so we can maybe hold the Moratorium. And it's less than ten days away!"

She jumped up again and began to pace. "It's like those bastards are one step ahead of us...they're trying to stop the Movement before it gains momentum. I think someone on the inside's ratting to the Administration."

Julia listened without comment. She had to get up at 6:15; her car pool left at seven sharp, whether she was ready or not. Fortunately the attitude of the girls she rode with thawed after they discovered Julia wasn't planning on smoking grass or passing out pamphlets. They'd even had a few meaningful discussions about Vietnam and the upcoming Moratorium.

The drive in was the most pleasant part of her day. From the moment Julia stepped inside that classroom, her world darkened. She'd been assigned as a student art teacher for sixth through eighth grades, an age grouping with which she had little empathy. She might have been able to handle it if the children had been younger, or if her supervising teacher, Miss Johnston, hadn't been such a picky horror. But her constant, critical scrutiny made Julia nervous. So she made foolish errors, pouring an unnecessary pound of wax into a batik vat or turning up a kiln too high.

This afternoon had been the worst. Julia had knocked over a small can of paint and watched, immobilized with dismay, as it spread all over the new indoor/outdoor carpeting. The kids snickered at Miss Brandon's newest mistake. Barely able to conceal her annoyance, Miss Johnston ordered Julia to wipe up the mess. The older teacher became almost apoplectic when Julia grabbed a small sponge, the nearest cleaning implement instead of a more absorbent rag. Finally three or four boys took pity on her and rushed forward with paper towels.

It had been different when she'd run the art program at Camp Wakanochee this summer. She'd only had eight or nine children at a time and they'd all been under age ten. Each camper picked whatever project he or she wanted to work on; Julia provided one-to-one guidance and advice. No one was looking over her shoulder waiting for her to slip up and the inner-city kids were usually appreciative of every kindness. Although she'd found the camp experience less than stimulating, it was heaven compared to student teaching.

"You haven't heard a word I said!" Valerie accused. "Don't you care any more?"

"You were telling me about Dean Moreland's restriction."
The problem was she cared too much. She simply didn't fit in —
couldn't Valerie see that?

"That was five minutes ago. What's eating you, Julia?"

My entire pathetic, pointless existence, Julia wanted to cry
out. I love to draw, but I don't know what to do with my life. And
I have insane fantasies about a man who barely knows I'm alive.
And your whole scene, as you would say, has no rules, no guidelines, so I don't know how to behave. She drew a deep breath, and
said, "I'm thinking about changing majors." Actually, she hadn't
given the possibility much consideration, but she suddenly realized she couldn't stand another day, another minute, in Miss
Johnston's stifling classroom.

"I figured student teaching might be a bummer." Valerie,
the theatre major, cherished the unstructured freedom of her department, even if nights and weekends were often given up to rehearsals.

"It's worse than that, Valerie. It's a living death. How can I
make a career out of something I despise?"

"You know, I saw some sketches you did for the sorority last
spring. You're really good. Why don't you change to art?"

"I started out as an art major my freshman year. But like my
Dad says, the only real security artists have is in being unem-
ployed. And I don't want to depend on my parents after I graduate." Julia's father had grown up during the Depression and put
himself through undergraduate and medical school. His example
had impressed her with the importance of making one's own way
in the world.

"I can relate to that," Valerie rubbed her chin. "What about
political science? Louie's a poli sci major and could tell you all
about it. Or psychology? You could ask my friend Vicki Viorst
what the requirements are. Or sociology...."

"That's it!" Julia cried. It was so simple, so obvious. Why
hadn't she seen it earlier? "Social work!" Not only would she be
helping the less fortunate on an individual basis which she enjoyed, but she could get a real job! She'd just recently read about
a shortage of caseworkers in *Campus Life* magazine.

"I think Win's a social work major," Valerie observed. "Although he probably wouldn't be much help. From what I hear, he cuts more classes than he attends." Julia was so excited about her new career that Valerie's remark about Win barely registered. "I'll go to the Registrar's tomorrow. It's only the end of the second week so I'm sure they'll let me sign up for a new course schedule." She was full of plans. "I'll probably have to stay here another year, but to be honest, I'm in no hurry to graduate and face the real world."

She reached over and hugged Valerie. "Thanks so much for giving me the idea!" For the first time in months, she felt weightless, carefree. So what if she didn't belong in a classroom? Women had other options, like nursing or social work. Pity it hadn't occurred to her sooner. She was struck by a sobering thought. "I hope Mom and Dad understand."

"Knowing your parents, I'm sure they'll want you to be happy," Valerie replied in an oddly hurt voice. Julia looked at her questioningly, but Valerie continued in her normal tone. "*Now* will you tell me why you're avoiding the SMC?"

As Julia related the conversation with Felix and Adrian, she waited for a condescending grin to appear. But Valerie explained patiently, "Oh, tab. Don't you get it? As in a tab of acid, not Tab the soft drink. Adrian is such a total jerk, especially when he's tripping. And Louie was so pissed at Adrian that night."

"Why?" Julia asked, still involved in spite of herself.

Valerie tossed her golden hair. "Adrian almost fucked up the SMC's strategy of appealing to as broad a base of people as possible. After you split, Louie told Adrian if he didn't get his shit together he'd better stop coming to meetings. I'm convinced Adrian needs counseling."

Now it was Julia's turn to be puzzled. Valerie had always taken Adrian's antics so lightly. "I thought you guys were good friends." On occasion she'd even wondered if they were lovers, but figured they'd tell her if they wanted her to know.

"Yeah and we balled a couple of times," Valerie replied, sensing Julia's curiosity. "But now I'm into more mature men." Her giggle had a nervous edge. "Or should I say they're into me."

Before Julia could ask any more questions, Valerie seized her arm. "C'mon, let's celebrate your new major."

"But it's 11:30 and I was about to put on my p.j.s...." She was tired, her physical alarm clock still set for 6:15.

"So? You're not student teaching anymore and they finally lifted curfew restrictions this year. A tiny concession, but progress nonetheless." She flashed her impish grin. "Hopefully the others haven't already split."

"What others?" Julia demanded, still stinging from the memory of the meeting. She wasn't about to subject herself to more ridicule, unintentional or otherwise.

"Oh, Adrian won't be there — he's already occupied," Valerie replied. "Probably Shawn, Win, Kirsten...maybe Louie."

In spite — or perhaps because of — her strong feelings, Julia was a little afraid of Win. What if she said or did something stupid around him? Every glance, every word seemed so weighted with significance, hidden meaning. Seeing Julia's continued hesitation, Valerie added, a trifle impatiently, "I'm sure people forgot about the whole incident two minutes after it happened. Now get your ass in gear!"

Perhaps she was being too sensitive. They hadn't really been laughing at her, only at what she'd said. And to see Win again.... Wordlessly she followed Valerie out the door of her suite, through the lobby, and into the crisp October night.

Instead of steering her towards uptown and Lenny's where Julia knew everyone usually gathered, Valerie headed towards the center of campus. She finally paused in front of three huge scrub pines that faced Vorhees Hall, the physics and chemistry laboratories.

"What are you doing?" Julia demanded as Valerie peered intently at first one tree, then another. "You could have used the bathroom in my dorm, Valerie...Oh my God!" she shrieked as a hairy hand shot out from beneath the middle pine and seized her leg. She stumbled forward and found herself face-to-face with a heavy-set bearded countenance almost as panicked as her own.

"Hey, man, I'm sorry I freaked you out," the beard apologized. "We heard someone snooping around and weren't sure you were cool 'til you said the name Valerie. Then we had to get you in here quick before the campus Cap Guns saw you."

"Here" was a hollowed-out underbrush; a hideaway perfect for a half-dozen people. As Julia stooped to enter, she saw Shawn and two other girls she'd never met before seated in a semicircle. The cloying smell of marijuana overrode the tree's piney scent.

The beard introduced himself to Julia as Bill Gordon, and his girlfriend as Vicki Viorst. Shawn commented that of course she knew Julia and had she met Kirsten Jasensky, Shawn's other housemate? Julia and Kirsten exchanged polite "hellos."

"Did you see Win and Jake?," Shawn asked. "They left a minute ago. They went uptown with Buffy."

"Who the fuck is Buffy?" Valerie demanded. Julia stared at the ground, trying to hide her disappointment. It had taken all of her courage to come here and she'd just missed Win.

Shawn chuckled and relit the wooden hash pipe. "I'm surprised you don't know her, Valerie. We, ah, liberated her from the Performing Arts Center. She's our nominee for Homecoming Queen."

"Oh, *that* Buffy." Nodding, Valerie took the hash pipe from Shawn and inhaled deeply. Everyone grinned at each other. Another private joke, Julia thought resentfully. Well, she'd be damned if she'd let them know their exclusion hurt. "I think it's great that the SMC has a candidate," she observed. "Someone who is politically aware can be a positive influence on those who aren't."

Everyone, including Valerie, burst into laughter. The tree shook with their movements as they rolled around, slapping each others arms. She'd done it again, made a fool of herself when she was being perfectly serious. Well, she'd had it. She was going back to her room and never coming out, except for classes. Julia began to crawl out of the underbrush.

Shawn pulled her back. Her grip was surprisingly strong for someone so ethereal-looking. "Buffy is a mannequin. Win and the others dressed her up like Marilyn Monroe and took her uptown to get the kids to vote for her. We want to show the Administration how meaningless their Homecoming ritual is."

"We wanted to elect a real dummy, not the kind that usually wins the title," Kirsten spoke for the first time. Despite her annoyance, Julia smiled. It was pretty funny, now that she knew Buffy's real identity. "Too bad I'm not in the sorority any more. I'd lend Buffy my pin."

Shawn said nothing but handed Julia the pipe, which had gone back to her instead of Julia. "Your turn." Her words held a hint of a challenge. The others looked at Julia in anticipation.

Julia could take the pipe and start chattering about Maudine Orsmby, a Holstein cow that won the title of Homecoming Queen at Ohio State in the twenties when her Uncle Saul was a student. She could pretend to puff, hoping no one would notice how inept she was. She could politely decline and probably further alienate herself. Or she could take a chance and tell them what she was thinking.

She opted for the last. "Like everything else this year, this is pretty new to me. Valerie showed me once with a joint. How do you smoke with a pipe?" Those seemed to be the magic words. They couldn't help her enough. Thanks to their experienced coaching, the smoke went down more smoothly each time the pipe was passed to her. And long before the grass affected her, she felt totally at ease, suffused by the same warmth and well-being she'd experienced last spring with Win. It was an intangible feeling of freedom and exhilaration, defying clear definition, an opening up of one's life to all possibilities.

And she learned about them. A fine arts major, Shawn planned to be a professional harpsichordist. She aspired to play with the New York Philharmonic or Boston Symphony. Yet for someone who wanted to devote her life to music, she spent most of the time talking about various stray animals she'd adopted and nursed back to health.

Kirsten appeared as talented as she was eccentric. Not only did she design and research all the outfits for student productions but the few she sewed herself were so exquisite that, according to Shawn, they found their way into professors' private collections or the university archives. Kirsten was headed for New York after graduation and Julia had a feeling she'd be successful.

Vicki and Bill, both psychology majors, were the touchy-feely loving couple. Unlike most romantically involved protesters who disdained mixing politics with personal commitment, they constantly kissed and held hands. They said they resolved their few differences with primal scream therapy and sensitivity training.

Everyone began to feel cramped in the small space and started to move around. In the middle of stretching, Valerie extracted a pine cone from her blue-jeaned rear end. "Prickly little sucker!" She tossed the cone through the branches of the tree. "How come you guys didn't want to get high at the house, anyway?"

What house? Julia wondered. She started to ask, but the words got tangled in her mouth.

"Oh, we're doing this for old time's sake," Kirsten said in her affected, theatrical tone. "A sort of sentimental journey as it were." Pale, bespectacled Kirsten reminded Julia of the White Rabbit in Disney's version of *Alice in Wonderland*. Why would beautiful, poised Shawn want to room with someone so cartoonish? Perhaps because platinum-haired Shawn really was Alice. Julia giggled at the analogy.

Shawn looked at Julia and smiled wistfully. Her eyes clouded, as though remembering something sad. "Kirsten, Laura, and myself shared a room in Edwards Hall last year," she explained. "Win, Stu, Jake, and Bill lived uptown in Hayes Village apartments. Sometimes whenever we wanted to toke, we'd meet halfway, which happened to be these trees here."

"Or these here trees, as we'd say back home in Kentucky," Vicki added, snuggling next to Bill. "I'd come in on weekends and visit Bill."

"Of course, this is no longer necessary since we all reside in the same dwelling," Kirsten commented. "However, it is occasionally beneficial to remind oneself of the hardships engendered in inhaling marijuana, not to mention the vicarious thrill of almost getting busted." She pronounced it "marihuana."

"Heavy emphasis on the almost," Valerie amended.

Julia was confused by Kirsten's onrush of words. "You all live together?"

"Are you sure you're not from the South?" Vicki teased. Bill leaned down and kissed his girlfriend.

Shawn glanced affectionately at them. "Considering most of us paired off last year, it seemed the best arrangement."

"Alas, not poor, lonely me, or Jake, who's enamored of all creatures female," Kirsten added. "Even Louie has the protest movement."

Julia began to match up couples. Vicki and Bill. Stu and Laura. Win and... She glanced at Shawn, remembering the day last spring when Valerie was arrested. Shawn leaning over Win's lap in the car, inviting Valerie to the wedding. Walking with Win towards the portico in their matching costumes. Win and Shawn. They were always together. It was so obvious.... How could she, Julia, have been so monumentally unaware?

Considering most of us paired off last year.... Her feelings for Win defied all logic. She barely knew him, yet she'd reacted so much to him at the wedding and even for an instant at the meeting. Her emotions even impaired her usually sharp perceptions of peoples' relationships.

If Win's already involved with Shawn, he certainly won't be interested in me, Julia decided. And girls never go after someone else's guy if they want to keep their friends. It had always been that way in high school and in the sorority.

Julia picked up a pine needle. It was fragile, slender, like the beginnings of a friendship or love. She snapped it in half. She would have to forget about Win. But that didn't mean she had to continue avoiding the others or the SMC.

Shawn stood up, brushing off her jeans. "We'd better split. I feel another monster headache coming on." So the pain in Shawn's eyes had been physical and not mental. There was nothing worse than a migraine. In spite of the fact that Shawn had Win, Julia felt sorry for her.

Kirsten pulled a pocket watch from her vest. "Oh dear me!" she cried. "It's nearly one o'clock. And I, with the early costume design class."

Julia grinned unsteadily. Kirsten really did remind her of the White Rabbit. Any moment she might burst into, "I'm late, I'm late. For a very important date." The big question was, would she, Julia, be able to handle it?

"Are you all right, Julia?" Valerie asked as they ducked out from beneath the tree. "You're so quiet."

The stars stood starkly beautiful against the moonlit night. Julia was tempted to tell Valerie to walk ahead with the others, for she wanted to stand alone and see if she could somehow become absorbed in the brightness of a faraway universe. Tiny Julia, lost in infinity, removed from life's petty shackles and useless passions....

"As I suspected, she's wasted," Valerie linked her hand through one of Julia's arms while Shawn took the other. "We'll see that you get safely into bed and to the Registrar's office tomorrow morning."

"Next time you'll watch her," Kirsten reprimanded. "Can't have too much of a good thing."

Julia wanted to hug them. They barely knew her, yet once she'd been upfront, they adopted her as one of their own. Neither money nor social standing could buy that kind of caring. But she didn't know how to put her feelings into words without sounding overly sentimental.

So she swore, "What the hell! I'm going to be the best goddamn social worker you ever saw!"

"Julia!" Valerie exclaimed. "I can't believe you're cussing. Far fuckin' out!"

Instead they laughed together.

CHAPTER SEVEN

On this particular Wednesday night, the Campus Ministry basement fairly crackled with tension. With the Moratorium scheduled for the following week, and pamphlets written, speakers arranged, and information booths organized, the students still had no official go-ahead from the Dean of Students, Edward Moreland. No one could seem to agree on a course of action, and several factions argued vociferously, even shouting down Louie's demands for an orderly discussion.

One group, lead by Felix and Adrian, insisted on immediately storming the Administration building and demanding a confrontation. Another suggested Hayes students migrate en masse to the nearby University of Cincinnati's "Day of Awareness" Moratorium. The rationale behind this was that an empty-looking campus and half-vacant classrooms on the fifteenth would serve as an object lesson for apathetic, negligent administrators. The majority felt the Moratorium should be held, regardless of official sanction. How could thousands of students be arrested, with only a dozen campus Cap Guns and half that number of Hampton Police? The end result was that everyone began talking at once and the meeting fell into total disorganization.

The solution seemed simple to Julia. Before anyone decided anything, why not make an appointment with Dean Moreland

and hear what he had to say? Perhaps he had a reasonable explanation: he could have misplaced the SMC's application or simply forgotten about it. Her sorority sisters who'd served on Moreland's Program Board had said he was jovial and kind, if opinionated. But as Dean of Students, he was undoubtedly honest and fair.

She caught sight of Louie leaning over the podium talking with a tall young man in an Air Force uniform with a red plastic F-111 fighter plane anchored to his military cap. She hurried towards them, anxious to communicate her idea. "Excuse me, Louie?" she ventured, reluctant to interrupt what appeared to be an intense conversation.

Louie waved her over, and said to his companion, "See, I told you we're not all immature savages. Some of us still have manners...Julia Brandon, I'd like you to meet General Waste-More-Men. He and his aide, General Hershey Bar, are two vets from California. They're here to tell us how to boil our draft cards so no one can read them instead of burning them and getting busted."

Among the rhinestone pins and memorabilia pinned to Waste-More-Men's chest was a huge button of Mad Magazine's Alfred E. Newman in a GI uniform under the caption, "Now *I'm* Worried!" Julia smiled. "It's an honor to meet you. I've always found humor one of the more palatable forms of protest. I don't mean to intrude, Louie, but we need to talk."

"Listen, I think Hershey Bar's still in the john puking up the dorm food," Waste-More-Men said. "I'll catch you later...Let us know when these assholes stop screaming at each other so we can make our speech and get out of this armpit."

"Nice attitude," Louie commented to the visitor's retreating back. "But I guess if I spent my life touring college campuses, I'd get tired of it too." He turned to Julia, his brown eyes glowing pleasantly. "You and I haven't rapped much this year. How have you been?"

"OK, I guess," She'd never felt the need for superficial chatter with Louie so she said, "Why don't you ask Dean Moreland why he hasn't responded to our application? Call Mrs. McCabe, his secretary, and see if you can get an appointment." Mrs.

McCabe coordinated Greek Homecoming floats each year. Julia had worked with her on BGP's and found her quite amiable.

"That's a good idea, Julia, but I've phoned several times and stressed the urgency of the matter. He has yet to return my calls. And the earliest his secretary says he can see me is the end of October."

"Oh." So much for her brilliant strategy.

"I think he's trying to avoid the issue." Louie explained gently. "Ignore the problem and it will go away. Unfortunately he's wrong, because we're not going to let him slough us off."

"Louie, what if *I* call Dean Moreland's office? I know Mrs. McCabe from BGP, so she won't associate me with the protest movement. I can pretend I want to talk to the Dean about joining the Program Board. And once I sit down and explain the Moratorium will be peaceful and orderly, he'll listen."

"I don't know, Julia. It's an awful risk for you to take. You might get on the Administration's troublemaker list. And that would be bad news for you. Especially on this campus."

Why was Louie being so overprotective? She was no longer a simpering sorority girl. "Hayes has changed a lot this year, and so have I. In case you haven't noticed, more and more students and professors are becoming involved in stopping the war. Besides, what I'm suggesting is insignificant compared to the daily slaughter in Vietnam."

Louie seemed to retreat into himself, to withdraw into an inner world. Too late, Julia remembered he'd been there and here she was spouting hot air on the subject. But the moment passed and Louie said, "You have a point. Their list is probably as long as a roll of toilet paper by now, anyway, and about as useful. But Moreland can be tough."

Julia shrugged. "According to my ex-sorority sisters, he likes co-eds. Who knows? Maybe I can turn that to my advantage."

"OK, go ahead, but be careful. Look what happened with Deputy Adams and you didn't even encourage him. Let me get everybody to shut up so we can reach a consensus."

After the crowd had quieted down, Louie motioned Julia to stand next to him. "Julia will attempt to speak with Dean Moreland tomorrow," he told the group. "If she doesn't get anywhere, then I'll visit President Carrell the day after. Although Carrell has an open-door policy, I've put off seeing him because I wanted to try to work within the constraints set by the Administration. We don't want to appear whiny or childish by running to the President complaining the Dean won't cooperate. But if Julia's plan doesn't work, we have no other choice. All in favor of this proposal, raise your right hand."

A sea of arms lifted in response, and Louie said to Julia, "I'm calling a special meeting tomorrow night. You'll give us a report then."

"Right," Adrian, Felix, and several others had walked out during Louie's speech. And despite Valerie's initial nurturing of Julia's liberalization, her former roommate had failed to attend the last several meetings. In fact, Julia realized, Valerie hadn't been around at all lately. Valerie could be involved in a play, although it hardly seemed logical that she'd immerse herself in the "Theatuh," as she jokingly called it when the protest movement was finally becoming a force on campus.

Julia took a deep breath. She'd have to do this on her own without the help of Valerie or anyone else.

"Hello, Mrs. McCabe?" It was 8:30 the next morning.

"Who's calling?" Dean Moreland's secretary sounded as if she hadn't yet had her first cup of coffee.

"Julia Brandon. Do you remember me from Beta Gamma Phi?"

"Of course I do, dear." The tired voice became infused with warmth. "You helped design that wonderful Homecoming float last year."

"I know it's kind of late, with Homecoming being only two weeks away and all, but is the Dean still interviewing applicants for the Program Board?" Her words came out in a gush. "I'd like to get in on at least the tail end of the planning." Julia hated fibbing even more than arguing with people, but she saw it as the only immediate route to Dean Moreland. Once she got in to see him and explained what the SMC was all about, she was confident he'd approve the Moratorium. If people like herself were joining the protest movement every day, then administrative support couldn't be far behind. Dean Moreland just needed to understand they weren't a bunch of wild-eyed radicals.

"Well, the Program Board meets on Fridays," Julia knew that already, and prayed the woman wouldn't suggest a Friday morning appointment when she had to have results by tonight. "And we certainly could use another body or two, with student volunteerism being down these days. How about 3:30 this afternoon? Dean Moreland meets with the Trustees after lunch, but I'm pretty sure he'll be through by then."

"Wonderful!" Julia hoped her relief wasn't too obvious. "I'll see you later." The SMC, and Win, too, from a safe distance), would recognize her as a heroine when she announced Dean Moreland had approved the Moratorium.

At first Julia thought she imagined Mrs. McCabe's frostiness as she waited in the anteroom shared by the Dean of Students and the Vice-President of Academic Affairs. But as the clock moved slowly towards 4:30 and Mrs. McCabe silently cleared off her desk and gathered up her purse and jacket, Julia realized she wasn't going to get to see the Dean.

Julia stood up also, the back of her legs sticking against the green naugahyde love seat, her sweater and skirt set left over from her BGP days damp from sweat. She asked uneasily, "Mrs. McCabe, do you know when Dean Moreland will return?"

"He's tied up in that meeting," The older woman fixed her with an icy stare. "Besides, you didn't really want to talk about the Program Board, did you?"

"No." Ashamed and embarrassed by what had unexpectedly turned into a painfully obvious deception, Julia looked away. Mrs. McCabe continued, "You protesters think you're so smart. But I have ways of finding things out. I'm disappointed in you, Julia."

"Look, I'm sorry I lied. But it's important that Dean Moreland approve the Student Mobilization Committee's application. Otherwise, we'll have to hold the Moratorium illegally, and there might be hell to pay...Sorry." She wasn't sure whether she was apologizing for the four-letter word or the SMC.

The Dean's secretary softened a little. "I know you're heart's in the right place, Julia. But you'd best stay out of this antiwar mess. Dean Moreland has a line on many of those people, and it will follow them the rest of their lives."

"What do you mean? Do you have spies or something?" She remembered Valerie's comment about an informant in the SMC.

"Sometimes I talk too much," the older woman replied. "I'm running late already and my family expects dinner on the table at 5:15. Wait for the Dean as long as you like, although I imagine he'll go straight home from the President's office." She buttoned up her coat and left.

Someone who'd been at last night's meeting must have tipped off Mrs. McCabe after I called, Julia thought. Or maybe my phone is tapped...Julia dismissed the last idea as irrational; after all, she was not a known radical. And Louie had warned her Moreland was skirting the SMC.

Louie had been right. Moreland had simply not returned to his office once he learned the true intent of Julia's visit.

The SMC came to the same conclusion that night after Julia told them what happened. She had never seen so many people get so riled so quickly. A group of students immediately started chanting, "Get Moreland out! Get Moreland out!"

"Will you all calm down!" Louie exclaimed, "We've got to use our heads, not our emotions."

Julia was angry, too. "And someone from this group informed the Dean's office I was representing the SMC, because I never told his secretary the real purpose of my visit," she said to the group. Win leaned against a paneled wall, studying her quizzically. He was with Shawn as usual and she avoided his gaze. "Mrs. McCabe practically admitted she had inside information."

This was greeted by a fresh roar of rage, and Louie pounded his fist against the podium with a fury Julia had never seen before. "SHUT UP, YOU MOTHERFUCKERS!" he shouted.

He turned to Julia, his eyes blazing, and said in a low voice, "You could have told me about the informer when we were alone. How the fuck are we going to find out who he is if he knows we're onto him?"

"I'm sorry," Julia mumbled, abashed for the second time that day. When was she ever going to learn how to handle things? Since there were so few rules, she had to be guided by her instincts which she'd rarely had to rely on until now.

The room had gotten quieter. "We have a right to be upset," Louie said so softly that the few people who were still talking had to stop to hear him. "And this bullshit has gone on long enough. So why don't we all meet at the Administration building tomorrow morning at ten when I go talk to President Carrell? A peaceful demonstration of solidarity will get us a lot farther than demanding Moreland's resignation."

Louie had come up with the solution as usual. Yet Julia had a feeling the SMC's troubles were just beginning.

CHAPTER EIGHT

By 9:30 Friday morning nearly 1500 students had gathered in front of the steps of the Administration building. Julia was surprised that neither Hampton police nor state Highway Patrol were there to greet them. Apparently the informer either hadn't gone to the meeting last night or had been silenced by Julia's comments about his presence.

The group was fairly well mannered. A few students waved spray-painted placards "Stop Campus Repression" under a circled, clenched fist. Another sign which read "Fuck Moreland" showing a hand with the third finger raised was quickly confiscated, but not after news of its contents had passed through the crowd with a ripple of laughter.

Louie hurried over to Julia. "I'm sorry I lost my temper last night. Sometimes things get away from me and it makes me mad. " He ran his fingers through his curly tan hair. The modified Afro was an improvement over last year's pony tail. It made his face seem older, sturdier. Louie would get better-looking as he matured, Julia decided. "But you need to be careful what you say in front of a crowd."

Louie had every right to be annoyed and she was glad he decided to forgive her. "I won't do it again. It's just that things are so complicated and I'm a straightforward person."

"I understand that." He extended his hand. "Do you want to come with me?"

Julia hesitated. "Do you think I can handle it?" After the fiasco with Dean Moreland's secretary, she wasn't sure. And Carrell was the president of the university.

"Carrell is a pussycat, compared to Moreland, and you had the courage to face him. Now come on."

His fingers were medium-sized with square-cut nails, his grasp confident, strong. "All right," she agreed with more assurance than she felt.

"Just remember this," Louie told her as they mounted the steps. "Think first, listen, and be willing to compromise. Sometimes you get the bear and sometimes the bear gets you."

They didn't have far to go, for they were greeted at the door by President Carrell. "I was just coming out to speak to the students," he said matter-of-factly. "What's the problem, Louie?"

Up close the president of Hayes University did not seem imposing. Nor did he appear particularly upset. And he seemed comfortable with Louie.

"Perhaps we'd better discuss this in your office," Louie replied. "If that's all right with you, of course."

"Fine. You know my philosophy." They walked down the deserted hallway. Secretaries and other University employees peered at them from inside offices and around corners. Why, they're afraid of me and Louie, Julia realized with a thrill. We do have some impact after all.

After Louie introduced her to the President, Carrell said, "Let me give you some background on this situation, Julia. Louie came to me last spring and told me about the Music Fest incident. We both wanted to avoid further dissention, so I instituted my open door policy, along with putting an end to police monitoring of University functions. In return, I expect student organizations to inform the Administration of any planned activities, such as demonstrations."

Louie never seemed to overlook anything. Julia had never met anyone who had his shit together so well, to borrow Valerie's expression.

"Which is why we are here today..." Louie began.

"First, let's have some coffee." Carrell's office, three times the size of Julia's dorm room and much more elegantly appointed with excellent reproductions of Chagalls and Picassos, was dominated by a large, round oak table. Carrell motioned for them to sit at the table, then strode over to an automatic coffee maker discreetly hidden on an inlaid shelf. He poured the black, steaming liquid into two cups engraved with the University logo. "Sugar? Milk?" he offered.

Louie wanted his plain, and Julia refrained from asking for saccharine, taking a packet of sugar instead. As she pinched a few granules into her cup, she noticed Carrell poured his coffee into a silly-looking mug with a caricature of a man with a moustache and the name "George" printed under it. She almost giggled at the sight of it because, except for the moniker "Harry," she'd bought an identical one uptown and had given it to her dad for Father's Day. She relaxed — George Carrell was human after all.

Carrell sat down next to them. "So what's this all about? I gather you students are upset about something."

Louie launched into a concise explanation of the SMC's application, of Moreland's negligence in responding, and finally of his and Julia's attempts to talk to Moreland. Carrell listened, his expression thoughtful. "I know Dean Moreland wrote a procedure for students this summer. As administrators, we have a responsibility to have knowledge of student activity."

"No one's questioning that, President Carrell," Julia said. "But Dean Moreland ignored our application and dodged me when he found out why I made an appointment with him. It seems as if he's trying to put a stop to the Moratorium before it's begun." She looked at Louie and he nodded.

"The only way we're going to resolve this is to get Dean Moreland's side of the story," Carrell went over to his desk to buzz his secretary.

Louie rolled his eyes toward the ceiling. "Oh, shit," he mouthed.

"What?" Julia whispered while Carrell spoke on the phone.

"I was hoping once we got to Carrell we could just go ahead and get his sanction." Louie's reply was barely discernable. "Now we're going to have trouble."

Less than two minutes later, a short, stocky bullet-headed man with an iron-grey crew cut strode into the President's office. He said with barely controlled impatience, "I'm in the middle of something, George. Is there a reason you called me here?" He refused to look at Julia or Louie.

"Sit down, Ed, and have a cup of brew," Carrell seemed unperturbed. After Moreland settled in a chair on the far side of the table without any coffee, Carrell said, "The Student Mobilization Committee applied to you a month ago regarding a Moratorium on October 15. Now we agreed the students have a right to hold demonstrations...."

"I'm very well aware of their application," Moreland interrupted. "But really, George, I have better things to do than worry about some spoiled, effete minority's whining about a war they're too chicken to fight."

Julia stiffened with anger. This man was the Dean of Students, yet he refused to acknowledge their civil rights. And who was he to condemn the protesters? It wasn't his life on the line. Edward Moreland seemed at odds with everything Julia's sorority sisters had said about him.

Yet it couldn't be easy for the administrators, either. Until recently, generations of college students had come and gone with hardly a word of complaint. And her experiences with Deputy Adams and Moreland's own secretary taught her not to jump so quickly. So she kept quiet.

"Excuse me, sir," Louie said, his tone a caricature of politeness. "But several thousand people, students and faculty alike, plan on attending the Moratorium and subsequent Free University classes. We've invited Dr. Benjamin Spock to speak, and Phil Ochs has offered to sing..."

"You've assumed a hell of a lot, haven't you?" Moreland snarled, giving rein to his frustration. "I never had any disturbances among the students until you transferred onto this campus last year. You're a troublemaker and I want you out."

"Now, just a minute, Ed," Carrell finally sounded distressed. "Try to be more objective about this. You're confusing issues with personal feelings."

"I'm not confusing anything. I fought in Dub-W Dub-W Two and I'm damn proud of my country." Moreland turned to Louie, his steely eyes spitting fire. "Cowards like you make me puke. Mommy and Daddy handed you everything on a silver platter. When things don't go your way — when you have to do something you don't want to do — you sit in your sandbox and cry."

Julia could keep silent no longer. "You're talking to the wrong person, Dean Moreland. Louie served in Vietnam. He knows what's going on over there. That's why he wants to stop it."

"That's even worse," Moreland glared at Louie. "The veterans come back to this country pumped full of crazy ideas and drugs. I think the Commies get to them."

"Ed, you've gone too far," Carrell reprimanded. "You've lost sight of the fact you're supposed to help the students, not censure them."

Louie stood up, his expression remote, as if Moreland's accusations had taken him to a faraway place. "Tell me, Moreland, who *is* the enemy?" Louie sounded numb, not at all like himself. "I was a medic there, and I could never figure it out. I sorted through maggot-covered guts and put them back into the dead bodies of my buddies. It was my job to make sure the Cong didn't plant mines there. It was also my job to cremate arms, legs, torsos, and heads of women and children who'd been blown apart by our soldiers. They mistook the villagers for North Vietnamese sympathizers." He was sweating, ashen. "I'd really like to know, Moreland. So maybe the next time I can look at a hamburger and not get sick to my stomach."

"Stop it, Louie!" Julia covered her ears with her hands. It was one thing to see remote, flickering images of combat on a TV screen, quite another to hear the grisly details from someone who had lived through it.... No, she decided, Louie was not as together as he appeared to be, for most people would be tormented by those memories for years.

Even Moreland was subdued. "This is not a discussion for a woman," he said to no one in particular.

"The subject of this conversation should never have happened in the first place," Julia retorted.

Then Louie seemed to come out of his reverie and said in a normal voice, "Julia, perhaps you should go outside and inform the others we're negotiating." He wiped perspiration off his forehead. "They might be getting anxious."

"If that's what you want, Louie." Once in the hallway, away from the oppressive tension of Carrell's office, Julia took deep gulps of air. Louie's revelations had shaken her to her very essence. She had to steady herself so she could face the protesters and tell them she knew little more than they.

CHAPTER NINE

As Julia stood outside waiting for word on the Moratorium, she caught a glimpse of Valerie hurrying across the Slantwalk in the direction of Wendling Hall, the economics building. Pushing herself towards the edge of the crowd, she waved her hands and cried, "Valerie! Valerie!"

Her former roommate stopped, glanced around, then saw her. For a moment, Julia thought Valerie was going to bolt in the opposite direction, but she paused instead.

Julia caught up with her and demanded, "Valerie, where have you been?"

"Busy," Valerie looked around, as if afraid someone might have noticed her.

"What's going on with you? Why haven't you come to the SMC?" In spite of her concern, Julia had to chuckle. "Now I sound like you a few weeks ago."

"Look Julia, I have a meeting in a few minutes." Seeing Julia's bewildered, hurt expression, she relented, "Oh, hell, I'm not brushing *you* off." She glanced uneasily at the protesters. "Adrian's not around, is he?"

"Adrian?" Now Julia was even more confused. "How should I know? I don't hang around with him anymore, remember? So I don't pay much attention to his comings and goings." Actually she couldn't help but notice Felix and Adrian had become insepa-rable, rather like Valerie and Adrian last year.

"I need to talk to someone," Valerie admitted. "And I know I can trust you. It's not eleven, is it?"

Julia glanced at her Timex. "It's 10:26, to be exact. Why all the paranoia about Adrian? You told me not to take him seri-ously."

"It's more than that. Is the coffee shop at your dorm open this early? We can go there and rap."

Julia was reluctant to leave. "I want to hear the outcome of Louie's meeting. I was there, you know. It was really exciting, until Louie started talking about his horrible experiences in Viet-nam."

"Louie did *what*?" Julia's last statement jarred Valerie out of her preoccupation. "That's one topic he never discusses."

"Dean Moreland goaded him into it. He implied Louie was a coward."

"Moreland's a gold-plated bastard. He's going to cause more problems on this campus than anyone can handle."

Julia knew she would find out about the Moratorium even-tually, but she might not have another opportunity to talk to Valerie. "Let's go, then."

Valerie waited until after the waitress had served them cof-fee to drop her bombshell. She and Julia faced each other in the uncomfortable, high-backed wooden booths that were a trade-mark of Ruddy's. Located in the basement of Miami Hall, it had the distinction of being Hampton's oldest operating eating estab-lishment. Both students and alumni lusted after its homemade doughnuts, served hot and dusted with confectioner's sugar. But food was the farthest thing from Valerie's mind today. "I'm hav-ing an affair with Richard Shaffley," she announced, closely watching Julia's expression.

She wasn't disappointed. Julia's mouth dropped open and her wide eyes grew even bigger than the quarter Valerie clutched in the palm of her hand for quick payment for her coffee in case Julia tried to guilt trip her. "Adrian's father?" If she leaned over any farther, she'd knock over her coffee cup with her tits, no mean feat, considering their relatively small size. "He's married, isn't he?"

"That's a dumb question, Julia," Slapping a quarter on the table, not really comprehending why she felt so angry, Valerie stood to leave. "I didn't think you'd be able to relate to this."

"No, no Valerie. Please sit back down." Julia's seaforest eyes seemed to reflect Valerie's own inner turmoil. "Why don't you explain? From the beginning." Neil Young's "Tell Me Why" was playing on the jukebox. How appropriate, Valerie thought as she slid back into the seat.

There really was no place to start. From the moment she and Richard met, each had known what the other wanted. An urgent desire, an uncontrollable passion was born between them, and neither could deny themselves.

They'd gone to bed the night of that very first SMC meeting. They pretended they were heading back to Valerie's place to rap about Adrian's problems, but within fifteen minutes, she and Richard had peeled off each other's clothes. Richard quickly taught her what a real orgasm was, and how it could be achieved over and over again with various parts of both their anatomies. Valerie's feelings about sex had done a complete turnaround that night.

But how could she explain that to an innocent like Julia, who saw Richard as part of the Establishment — a professor, a married man, father of fucked-up Adrian and his fifteen-year-old sister, Carrie? Richard was only a few years younger than Valerie's machinist stepdad, although from a vastly different world.

Valerie had been confident she could handle the affair. Students made it with professors all the time, and not just for good grades. For kicks, or to see what sex was like with an older dude. And at first she and Richard said little to each other. They'd simply made love, occasionally using *Joy of Sex* as a guide, mostly utilizing their own imaginations and inventiveness. Her precious little house came to symbolize the fulfillment of her erotic fantasies.

Soon they began spending every spare moment together. They'd meet at his office for a stolen hour between lectures, and lock the door, thankful the department secretary was located at the far end of the hall. They'd unzip and unbutton, and he'd enter her quickly — she liked it that way — further stimulated by the imminent danger of discovery. But once Valerie's passions were unleashed, she forgot everything, save her own pleasure and their mutual ecstacy.

If only they'd been able to keep the relationship on that level. But Richard began to confide in her — about how empty he felt; how his family blocked all attempts at communication; how he never enjoyed making love until he'd met her, that it had been a mechanical act to release tension. Valerie realized she'd found her soul mate, and it scared her. After all, where could a love affair possibly lead, with Richard vying for the department chairmanship, the married father of a boy Valerie had occasionally slept with? And Valerie had never gotten around to telling Richard about the casual sex with Adrian.

So she simply said to Julia, "There's really not much to relate. We ball constantly and I think I'm falling in love with him."

"Oh," Julia blushed at the word "ball." "Adrian doesn't know about this, does he?"

"No, and you'd better not tell him, either."

"I wouldn't dream of it. What about, uh, Mrs. Shaffley?"

Valerie studied the hardwood floor. Myra Shaffley was the last person in the world she wanted to think about. "According to Richard, she's one of those overweight, lazy housewives who sits by the pool all day drinking wine and gossiping."

"But she must have feelings."

"They certainly don't seem to involve Richard." Valerie felt an overwhelming need to defend him. "She doesn't even care when he comes home at night. Half the time he sleeps with me. The words 'selfish' and 'manipulative' crop up whenever he talks about Myra."

Julia seemed to accept her rationalization. "She sounds like Adrian," she observed with uncharacteristic pique. "He and that neoradical Felix are always storming out of meetings and advocating violence. They only seem to be out for themselves. They're certainly not concerned with the SMC."

"Maybe they'll go off on their own and form a branch of the SDS or Weathermen. That might not be a bad idea. The

SMC's become too moderate, too bound up with satisfying the Administration, from what I've been hearing lately."

"How can you say that, Valerie? Dean Moreland would love to see us off campus and you know it. Besides, do you want buildings to burn and our friends to get hurt?"

"If that's what it takes to end the war." Valerie had long ago given up on Gandhi. Like Martin Luther King, he'd been so submissive and caught up in principles he failed to see the total picture. And he, too, had gotten an assassin's bullet for his troubles.

"Oh, come off it, Valerie. Besides, I wonder about some people's motives. My sociology prof says student sexual activity increases in direct proportion to the amount of protesting on campus. And that a lot of kids are involved with the antiwar movement so they can pick up members of the opposite sex." Julia looked perturbed.

"Now *you're* getting the big picture." One more brick out of Julia's ivory tower wouldn't hurt, she decided. "Hell, that's probably one reason why Adrian's so screwed up. He'd like to think he's bi, and avoids the truth by doing crazy shit."

"Bi?"

"You know, like, bisexual. Everyone is, even though most of us lean towards the opposite sex. Not Adrian though. He's among those who prefer their own kind."

"You mean he's a homosexual?" Realization touched each one of Julia's features, making her appear even younger than her twenty-one years. "It must be awful for him."

"Not really. Not if you can handle it. Haven't you ever looked at a girl and thought she was beautiful?"

"Well, of course, Valerie. But I wouldn't want to go to bed with her. There's a big difference."

"Actually, it's a fine line, like when you see a good-looking dude and imagine what he's like in the sack. You've just been conditioned to think a certain way and repress your desires." Valerie briefly wondered what she'd said that made Julia look as if she wanted to crawl under the table, then shrugged. She didn't want to be late for her assignation with Richard. Besides, all this talk about sex aroused her. She rose, grateful that her moist vagina was hidden between her thighs. Women had an advantage in that area, anyway. "It's nearly eleven and I've got to split."

"I'll go with you. Maybe Louie's out of the meeting by now."

As they headed back to the Slantwalk, Valerie confessed, "I'm mixed up about this whole scene. I wish I could stop caring about Richard and just enjoy the fucking. But I can't." The last thing she'd had in mind was a commitment, to end up like her sisters. Especially to someone so already settled in his life. But would marriage to a college professor be so bad? No way in hell, she told herself firmly.

"If only we could turn love off and on like a faucet," Julia sighed deeply and Valerie knew her virginal ex-roommate understood. For someone so untouched by life, Julia showed great sensitivity.

They both saw Kirsten hurrying from the opposite direction at the same time.

"Hey, Kirsten," Valerie said. "You going back to the house?"

"Did you come from the Administration building?" Julia wanted to know. "Did you hear what came down about the Moratorium?"

"Yes, yes, and yes," Kirsten flashed her bizarre grin. "Yes, I'm going back to the house. Indeed I'm fresh from the Administration building. Yes, we are permitted to have the Moratorium...."

"We are!" Julia cried, exhilarated. "All that worrying....Oh that's wonderful!" If Julia had been a cheerleader, she would have done cartwheels, Valerie reflected, forgetting that she'd been as enthusiastic a few short weeks ago. One passion had simply replaced another.

"There are stipulations, of course," Kirsten said.

"It figures," Valerie commented. "What sort of picky constraints did the assholes slap on us this time?"

"We must be present at classes, for professors will be taking attendance," Kirsten sounded like a rebellious child forced to memorize a hated lesson. "We must begin promptly at nine and end precisely at four. We must restrict the Moratorium — or shall I say Morelandatorium — to the Slantwalk area only. Anyone demonstrating uptown will be incarcerated. That's busted, for those of you whose vocabularies are limited to two-syllable words."

"Thanks a lot, Kirsten," Valerie always enjoyed Kirsten's offbeat yet strangely sane takes on life. "I imagine some people are royally pissed off about all this bullshit."

"Precisely. In fact, those SDS rumblings are getting stronger by the hour. This may be the beginning of the end of all communication with those who have the misfortune of being over 30."

The campus bell tower began to chime. "People have no right to be upset over a few rules," Julia argued. "We're allowed to have the Moratorium, to show the world we feel Vietnam's immoral, and that's the important thing."

Valerie would have liked to toss a little more reality onto Julia's idealistic brew, but every moment with Richard was precious. As she said a quick good-bye and hastened towards Wendling Hall, she heard Julia tell Kirsten, "Louie says sometimes you get the bear and sometimes the bear gets you. Well, this time we won. So let the bear rattle his chains."

It's not that easy, Valerie added silently. In order to get what they wanted, the bear had to be vanquished for good.

CHAPTER TEN

On the day of the Moratorium, Julia hurried towards the Administration Building through the cloudy, cold dawn. She'd spent most of the night stenciling white doves onto black strips of cloth, stuffing them into grocery bags. What if she'd wasted an all-nighter producing these arm bands for nothing? What if only a few loyal protesters showed?

By 10:00, however, not a single band remained, and students were wrapping black crepe paper streamers around their upper arms as a cheap substitute. How gratifying to see her efforts, however small, so prominently displayed.

Even better, the Moratorium had turned into an Event with a capital E. Despite, or perhaps in spite of, the class attendance rule, with the more conservative professors scheduling quizzes or threatening to take points off for skipping class, much of the campus mingled with University employees, students from Hampton High, and even a few townspeople.

Although Dr. Spock had another engagement, Columbus native Phil Ochs thrilled the crowd with his rousing antiwar songs. Speakers included a Cincinnati-based rabbi, two local ministers, and, thanks to a surprise coup by Louie, His Honor the Mayor of Hampton himself. President Carrell and the usual assortment of activists were also present. Volunteers took turns reading lists of the Ohio war dead from the Congressional Record.

Yet as the day ripened and warmed, turning the sky a sunny October blue, Julia felt increasingly depressed, as if the event itself were an anticlimax to all the hard work. Her period had also come, which was probably why she felt so down. Her head pounded, her breasts ached, her stomach felt as if it were fighting a war of its own. Compounded, of course, by the lack of sleep and pressure involved in juggling courses and SMC commitments. Although the introductory Social Work classes were far less demanding and more interesting than student teaching.

As the afternoon wore on, the Moratorium assumed an almost playful air. Spontaneous Frisbee games erupted; students hunkered in large circles to listen to local rock bands; the cloying smell of marijuana filled certain sections of the Slantwalk. Yet Julia declined to participate, feeling very much removed from everything.

Something more was bothering her, she knew. Something she'd been fighting all quarter and successfully fended off until today when she'd had a chance to think. Her feelings for Win. She was afraid she was falling for him, and didn't know how to stop herself.

It became more intense every time she saw him. He and Shawn always seemed nearby — talking with SMC organizers, offering to help Louie, even passing out Julia's arm bands. They seemed so well-suited, so much a part of each other. Yet she couldn't shake the sense Win watched her when she wasn't looking.

He stood not ten feet from her now, his arm flung around Shawn's slim shoulders, chatting with a middle-aged reporter from the *Cincinnati Enquirer* and a T.V. camera crew and newscaster from the local NBC affiliate. They were discussing the New Morality. "Shawn and I live together," Win said. "But when I invited her home with me over Thanksgiving, my parents insisted she stay in a hotel. Not only doesn't that make sense, but it's downright repressive."

Julia felt her as if her insides were burned with acid, but her fascination with Win compelled her to continue to listen.

"Are you going to submit to rules you feel are hypocritical?" The reporter queried, fishing for a dramatic quote.

"My parents wishes, no matter how old-fashioned, do deserve a certain amount of respect," Win hedged. "And it is their house."

At least he was perceptive enough to recognize a baited question. A yellow Frisbee from a nearby game landed at Win's feet and he stooped to pick it up. He looked around, and his deep-set eyes met Julia's. He grinned, and she felt herself sink into his russet gaze. Dammit, she thought, I want you. Being near you is like having a hot fudge sundae placed in front of me and being told not to taste any. What are you doing to my head?

"Does that mean you follow every guideline your parents set down for you?" the newscaster challenged him while the cameraman zeroed in for a close-up.

"What?" Win said and the newscaster repeated the question. Win looked thoughtful for a minute. His glance shifted back to Julia then to the TV camera. He seemed to come to a decision. "Hell, no," He shook his auburn tresses, a graceful yet defiant gesture. "I do what I want on my own time. Take the stupid regulations surrounding this Moratorium, for instance. No protesters allowed uptown, mandatory class attendance. Don't think for a minute I'm going to walk out of a Free University discussion on how to avoid the draft to go to an irrelevant Spanish class!" Suddenly he tossed the Frisbee in Julia's direction and the TV camera followed its path, coming to focus on her.

The bright plastic sphere hit Julia in the middle of her sensitive stomach and she forced herself not to double over in agony. She was too much of a lady to let Win, Shawn, and viewers watching the 6 o'clock news know about her cramps.

What a show-off! The Frisbee fell untouched to the ground, and she snapped, "Win, you undermine the SMC when you talk about not following the Administration's guidelines. Your attitude's going to get everyone in trouble and they'll crack down on us even more." She strode away, hoping he didn't notice the tears springing beneath her eyelids.

She hurried over to the Cassidy Hall arch on the pretense of hearing the Psychedelic Scuzzballs mutilate "Satisfaction." She half-hoped Win would pursue her and try to talk. But she knew he wouldn't; after all, she'd practically yelled at him, in addition to making an idiot out of herself in front of the media people. By showing them dissent from within, she'd been almost as counter-productive as Adrian.

But she'd had good reasons for acting the way she had. Or did she? Win had been perfectly natural until he'd spotted Julia. Had his little performance been for her benefit?

She gradually became aware of someone standing close to her, silently commanding her attention. Julia looked up and was so amazed to see *Valerie* crying she forgot her own troubles.

"My God, Valerie, what's wrong?" She'd never sensed any-thing even close to tears in tough Valerie. Something truly terrible must have happened.

Valerie covered her eyes with trembling hands. She wore a red peasant blouse with round embroidered mirrors that seemed to magnify her sorrow. "Can't rap about this here," she mumbled.

"Well, then we'll go back to my dorm. I need my heating pad. Unlike some boys I know, it'll keep me warm and won't talk back." A joke, however feeble, might make Valerie feel better.

It had the opposite effect. "*You* got your period," Valerie said in an accusing voice. "I won't get mine for another nine months."

"What??" Julia could hardly believe Valerie was pregnant. She was too knowledgeable about birth control, having had sex since she was eighteen. "Are you sure, Valerie? You might be late. Look at what happened with Nancy."

As it turned out, Julia's ex-roommate and Valerie's predeces-sor hadn't been expecting after all. But she still married her "hometown honey," the Mrs. degree taking precedence over the one she could get at Hayes. But Julia knew how important gradu-ating was to Valerie.

"There's no such thing as "late" on the Pill," Valerie re-minded Julia grimly.

"You can't be sure until you go for a pregnancy test." Julia's father was an internist and various physical aberrations were oc-casionally discussed at the dinner table. "Sometimes your cycle gets messed up, even on the Pill. Do you have 21-day packets or 28-day packets? Have you switched prescriptions recently?"

"Cut the diagnosis, Julia. How does nausea in the morning sound to you? A bloated stomach? A sudden revulsion to meat, eggs, and even toothpaste? Classic symptoms. Straight out of your dad's textbooks."

"But how did it happen? I mean I know how it happened," she added quickly, wanting to fend off yet another jibe about her own innocence.

"I get what you're saying." For once Valerie didn't have the heart to go for the obvious opening. "One time! I fucked up just once and forgot to take the little yellow bastard! That first night Richard and I were together...But I took two the next day, thinking I could make it up. Shit! What am I gonna do?" She rolled her eyes heavenward as if beseeching a God she no longer believed in. "Besides, I have what is known in our family as the Stazcyk Curse. One shot is all it takes...More than one good Catholic Stazcyk has gone to the altar in the family way."

No one knows your own body like you do, Julia's father often told her. So Valerie was probably right, although Julia didn't want to upset her further by agreeing. "Does Dr. Shaf, uh, does Richard know about this?"

"No! I broke it off with him. He'd probably ante up the bread for my abortion but I'd never take his blood money."

Julia shuddered. Abortion was illegal in Ohio, and all she knew about it was whispered tales of coat hangers, of second-year med students with dirty fingernails performing operations, of fetuses being removed via Coke bottles. "So what are you going to do?" Julia asked, secretly wishing Valerie could somehow keep the baby.

For the first time, Valerie sounded hopeful. "I think I've got it all figured out. Since we're riding on the bus to D.C. for that march next month, I'll hitch to New York from there. There's a clinic that'll suction out fetuses under six weeks...."

Julia had an unbidden vision of her two-year-old cousin Scotty tearing around on his tricycle. She was about to reprimand Valerie for her heartlessness, when Valerie broke down all over again. "I know I'm killing a helpless baby, but what can I do? How can I support it, or even give it up for adoption? Richard can't leave his family, even living with me would permanently fuck up his career. And my folks would disown me if they found out." Her voice shook with desperation. "I have to finish my education. I have to show my stepdad he was wrong about me...."

Valerie was too proud to go to Richard for help and her parents would cut off what little money they gave her, forcing her to quit college. Someone had to be there for her. So she said, "Valerie, I'll go with you to New York. I hadn't planned on attending the march because I'm kind of behind on my schoolwork. But you shouldn't be alone."

Actually, Julia's reasons for not traveling to D.C. sprang from a fear of directly confronting her parents with her newfound beliefs. Like much of the older generation, they couldn't understand the students' revulsion towards fighting for their country. And since they called her every weekend, they'd wonder where she went. Not wanting to lie, she'd have to tell them. Julia especially hated upsetting her mother.

"Would you? That would be far out, Julia," Valerie was beginning to sound like her old self. "The clinic's supposed to be, like, safe, but still...."

"Oh, wow, if it isn't this year's fuck," a sarcastic voice interrupted them. Julia and Valerie jerked up their heads.

Adrian leaned against a tree, his arms folded across his chest, his angular face set in a sneer. "How is the old goat these days? Mother wouldn't know. He usually returns to the fold by this time, to put it delicately." He tittered.

Valerie did not reply and Adrian continued his tirade, "Father and I ought to compare notes. What a thesis topic that would make! 'An analysis of the time it takes father and son to reach orgasm using the same woman...'"

"Shut up, Adrian!" Julia cried. Valerie remained silent. Why was Valerie taking Adrian's abuse? Julia couldn't believe the three of them had been practically best friends last year, that she'd laughed at Adrian's jokes.

But then he said, "I couldn't help but overhear your conversation, Valerie. I'm really sorry you have to have an abortion. " He appeared sincere.

"Well, you certainly weren't responsible," Valerie replied with her usual spirit. "How did you find out about me and Richard, anyway? I tried really hard to keep it a secret."

"Nothing is hidden on this campus when you've grown up here. And I saw the horny bastard leaving my old house — the one he owns and you pay no rent on — when I stopped by to visit you a couple of times."

"Adrian, you and I need to rap." Valerie said. "Tell me about his other affairs."

Julia was totally confused. Why did Valerie want to discuss Richard with Adrian, who would do anything to discredit him? The whole situation was too convoluted for her comprehension. "I think I see Louie waving me over," she fabricated an excuse to extract herself. But Valerie and Adrian were so engrossed in conversation that neither acknowledged her good-bye.

CHAPTER ELEVEN

As soon as Valerie's pregnancy test came back positive, Julia called her mother to tell her she'd be going out of town November 14th. She phoned during the middle of the day when her dad was at work; Hester was easier to get around than Harry.

She hoped her nervousness wasn't obvious as she asked her mother about her and Dad's golf game and the medical practice. They'd moved on to a discussion concerning the fates of Julia's high school classmates, anything but life at Hayes, when Hester said, "What's on your mind, Julia? And how much will it cost?"

Julia could never figure out how her mother always knew when something was up. Ironically, Julia had also been debating whether to ask for a loan. Valerie would need some extra cash to defray the cost of the abortion and New York wasn't exactly cheap. "You're right on target, Mom," she laughed uneasily. "About $100, more if you can spare it. I need it for a weekend away."

"Where are you going?"

"Please, Mom, don't ask. Just trust me when I say it's for a good cause."

"You know I can't just give you the money without knowing what your travel plans are. You're not in some kind of trouble are you, Julia?" Hester reverted back to the accent of her native Hungary.

It was probably better to tell the less threatening of the two truths than unnecessarily worry her mother. Besides, Hester had been through so much in her youth and usually accepted others' foibles. "No, it's not me. My friend Valerie is pregnant. She has to go to a clinic in New York and wants me to come with her," Julia hated dragging Valerie into the discussion, but she saw it as the only way to avoid telling a direct lie about the Washington march.

"Ah, so your unmarried girlfriend needs an abortion. I'm sorry to hear that. But how are you going to get to New York on only $100?"

"Well, we have a ride part way...And I have some extra money I earned from last summer." Julia hoped she didn't sound as cornered as she felt.

"I suspect there's more to this than you're letting on."

"Look, Mom, we'll pay you back, OK? Why are you giving me the third degree? Don't you trust me?"

"Not when you're hiding something. You never call me in the afternoon during the middle of the week."

There was no way around Hester when she was onto Julia. Besides, she'd gotten this far without too much trouble; she might as well reveal the entire situation. "The students are organizing a march on Washington on November 15. Valerie and I are going to ride the bus with them."

Silence. For a moment, Julia thought they had been disconnected. "Hello? You still there, Mom?"

"What kind of march did you say you were going to?" The last time Julia had heard that tone was when she accordioned the family car into a pole at the Bexley High School parking lot. "With those radicals who throw dog doo at policemen?"

Julia cringed. Sometimes Hester had an incredible talent for triviality. "Now, Mom, we talked about Vietnam this summer. You even agreed that Nixon was wrong in sending in more troops than necessary. The march will be peaceful and well-organized. Besides, I'm not going to be there most of the time, remember?"

"Peaceful and well organized -- ha! Just like those riots in Chicago. With billy clubs and broken heads and people behaving like animals," Julia heard the tears in Hester's voice, as she reverted back to immigrant English. "I don't want you should go, Julia."

"What's this all about?" Her father broke in on the line. "Why is your mother so upset?"

Oh, no. She'd forgotten Harry took Wednesday afternoons off, a doctor's prerogative. This was going to be much worse than anticipated. Her father was an ultraconservative brick wall when it came to politics. But she decided to try to talk to him anyway. Maybe he'd listen if she approached him in a logical manner. "Mom doesn't seem to understand, Dad," she said in her most adult voice. "Each month, the Student Mobilization Committee to End the War holds a moratorium to remind the government about the people's opposition to Vietnam. Last month, we had a demonstration on campus. On the 15th, they're organizing a nationwide march in Washington...."

"And you want to attend?" Her father interrupted. "How could you even suggest such a ridiculous idea?"

"Will you let me finish?"

"There's nothing more to say. The discussion is closed. You're not going."

As usual, he was treating her like a child. The man wouldn't even allow her to complete a sentence! "How can you ignore the continued slaughter of innocent people?" Julia retorted. "If I'd been a boy or not smart enough to go to college, I could be drafted."

"That's not the point! The men in power have perfectly good reasons for what they're doing."

Bullshit, Julia thought, but said, "Give me one."

He paused for a moment then prevaricated, "I thought you had more brains than this, Julia. Especially the way you've been raised, with the utmost loving kindness and respect. Is that why you quit the sorority? So you could run around with a bunch of dope-peddling freaks?" Her father had expressed great disappointment when she'd resigned from BGP.

In a crude sense, he was right, and it infuriated her. "You know, I could have just sneaked to the demonstration and not told you," Julia sputtered, forgetting her vow to act calm and mature. "We could have hitchhiked like Valerie wanted, instead of taking the train after we got to Washington."

If Harry had been listening, he might have caught and questioned the inconsistency in her plans. But he was furious. "My word is final. I absolutely forbid you to attend that march. Or any more demonstrations, for that matter."

Julia knew it was futile to continue. When Harry Brandon made up his mind, that was it. But she was 21 years old, no longer a malleable, acquiescent child. And dammit, she was right. "Look Daddy, I'm sorry you feel this way. But I am going to continue to protest the war in Vietnam, whether you like it or not."

She could hear Hester weeping on the other extension, along with Harry's sharp intake of breath. Then he began to shout, "Listen to how you've hurt your mother, young lady. If you so much as set foot near those radicals, I'll cut off your tuition. Then you'll see what it's like in the real world...." He was practically breaking her eardrum, and Julia held the phone away from her. "I'll talk to you when you've settled down. Good-by, Daddy." Her hands trembled as she replaced the receiver on the hook.

Closing her eyes, she leaned against the wall. How could her parents be so rigid? Anything out of their frame of reference was met with resistance. It was almost as if they were afraid of new ideas. I'll never be like that, she vowed. I'll always try to listen to what people tell me, even if it's something I disagree with.

She'd make her own way if Harry really meant what he said. She'd move out of the dorm and get a part-time job. And she'd have no trouble obtaining a government-subsidized student loan with her grades, as long as she didn't mention that her father was a doctor. The phone buzzed and, without waiting for the other party to speak, she picked it up and said, "I don't think you've taken quite enough time to think things over, Daddy...."

"I'm not your Daddy, unless someone gave me a sex change while I was crashing," Valerie sounded like her usual offhand self.

"Oh, hi Valerie..." Julia related the argument with her parents. "Can you believe they forbade me to go to demonstrations?" she concluded, angry all over again.

"I'll believe anything from the older generation. They're a bunch of hypocrites, going around and pretending the kids are wrong. They make us fight, but they won't allow us the vote. Hey, I bet you need a little help from our friend -- I'll be over before you can say 'marijuana'."

"Sounds good," Julia said and they hung up. Not that grass was the answer, but it occasionally made life more palatable. And right now she needed some soothing. Julia had smoked in her room a few times before, usually with the girls in her suite. Although she never felt completely at ease, her dorm had a liberal reputation. As long as the girls remained discreet and didn't start pushing drugs, no one was hassled. Even the resident adviser, a graduate student in psychology, was rumored to be a toker.

The phone rang again and she jumped. So why was she being so paranoid? No one could bust her for *thinking* about getting stoned. This time it was her mother, who was still crying. "Julia, I never told you what happened to your Aunt Juliana, did I?"

Julia sighed in exasperation. What did poor, dead Aunt Juliana, whom Julia had only seen in brownish, faded photographs, have to do with an argument over a Vietnam protest march? "No Mom, not really." She struggled to sound patient.

Julia did know her grandparents and most of her mother's relatives had perished in concentration camps. Mom's older and only sister Juliana was a teenager when Mom sailed at age 10 to America to stay with a distant cousin in Columbus. The family had planned on joining her, but Hitler put a permanent end to their dreams. It was a subject her mother rarely discussed. But Hester's periodic bouts of depression, her emphasis on family togetherness, and the generosity heaped upon Julia, her sister's namesake, was an explanation in itself.

"My papa -- your grandpapa, may he rest in peace -- begged Juliana to come with me to America in 1935," her mother said. "The Nazis were beginning to influence the surrounding countries and Budapest was becoming more anti-Semitic. He wanted to make sure his two youngest children got safe passage -- my older brothers had graduated from the university and were married by that time. He and Mama and the rest of the family would follow, of course. Well, Juliana refused to go. She was determined to help organize a resistance movement. The Nazis were wrong, yes, they were evil and Juliana and my brothers Stefan and Asher and their wives swore they'd do everything in their power to stop them.

"Mama and Papa stayed, too, thinking they could buy their way to freedom if things got bad. Papa owned a successful clothing business, and he assumed he could always sell it, never dreaming the Nazis could just seize it, with their trumped-up laws against Jews. My family had a sense of obligation, or commitment, as your generation would say. So they were butchered at Auschwitz. I was a child, so I had no choice...." She began to sob again.

"Oh, Mommy, please stop," Unchecked tears flowed down Julia's cheeks. She hadn't called Hester "Mommy" since grade school. "Don't feel guilty about something you had no control over."

"I know. I understand that now," Hester replied a little more calmly. "But it took me years to recover. Let me get to my point, Julia. What I'm trying to say is, there are a great many injustices in this world, such as Vietnam. You can't go around trying to stamp out each fire. It's fine as long as you don't expose yourself to danger, as you would if you went to this march. I realize you feel badly that you won't be there to support your girlfriend. And I recognize you see injustice in Vietnam. But look what happened to my family when they tried to help others and disregarded their own well-being."

Julia knew she had lost. How could she defy a generation of martyred relatives? She was an endangered species, the last of her mother's line. "All right, Mom, I won't go to Washington," she conceded. "But I want you and Daddy to be aware I'm not going to give up demonstrating against the war. It is a free country and I'm an adult. He has no right to order me around, even if he does pay my tuition."

"All right, Julia," Hester's voice brimmed over with relief. "I never wanted to hold you back from your beliefs. I only try to protect you from harm. Just stay out of trouble."

What about the guys in 'Nam? Julia wanted to ask. How did they stay free from harm? But she didn't want to start the argument all over again.

"Believe me, things will become clearer with time," her mother reassured her. "One day you'll truly understand." They made polite conversation for a few minutes, then said good-bye.

"I knocked but you didn't hear me," Valerie leaned against the closed door, an unlit joint dangling from her lips. She wasn't smiling, and Julia wondered how much she'd overheard. Enough to realize Julia wasn't going to New York with her, no doubt.

"I'm really sorry, Valerie. I want to explain why I can't be with you," Julia began, having never told Valerie about her mother's near-miss with Hitler's death camps.

"Not necessary," With a wave of her hand, Valerie lit the joint. "It all boils down to the same bullshit. I'm just glad my parents don't scrutinize my every move." She handed it to Julia.

Julia took a drag and gave it back to her. Valerie's defiance masked her hurt over giving up Richard, the abortion, and God knew what else her family had or had not done for her. She let the remark pass. After she'd exhaled, she said, "Listen, Valerie, you can't go through the abortion by yourself. Why don't you just tell Richard? I'm sure he'll help in any way he can."

"No fuckin' way! I'm doing this thing on my own." Valerie inhaled deeply. "No more entanglements for Valerie.... In fact, I plan on paying Richard the two months back rent on the house. Adrian, Felix, and I are working on a little partnership to help finance expenses."

Her father's remark about dope dealers flashed through Julia's mind. "For God's sake, don't do anything illegal," Julia admonished. "Smoking grass is one thing, but possession of over an ounce could mean years in jail."

"Don't get all freaked out about it, Julia," Valerie was beginning to sound like Adrian. "I'm the one who's going through all this shit. But what the hell, it'll all be over in less than two weeks. Say, didn't you tell me you just got 'Abbey Road?' Let's put it on the stereo."

"OK." She hadn't had much of a chance to listen to her new record. She took it out of the colorful dust jacket with John, Paul, George, and Ringo crossing the namesake street. The rumors about Paul being dead were nonsense, she decided, just because he had bare feet. She told herself not to be too upset with Valerie. Hopefully, her disillusionment would pass.

Yet Julia felt guilty, as if she'd let down both herself and her closest friend. But if what Hester said was true, if life became less confusing as one got older, why did she feel increasingly enmeshed in its complications?

CHAPTER TWELVE

It was the weekend of the march, and just another Saturday night in the Beta Gamma Phi suite. Julia wished she hadn't accepted Betsy's invitation to pay her ex-sisters a visit.

In spite of everything, she and Betsy remained friendly, chatting once or twice a week on the phone, occasionally meeting for lunch. Since everyone Julia now associated with had gone to Washington, and Betsy's fiancé "Fast Eddie" DiCarlo was at the library studying for graduate school entrance exams, the two girls decided to spend the evening together.

They started out at Mario's, cramming themselves full of pizza. Over the thick, buttery crust topped with mozzarella cheese and chunky tomatoes and mushrooms, Betsy confided that the sorority was "troubled." Apparently Lydia was trying to force her right-wing beliefs on the sisters and they resented it. "BGP's hardly a hotbed of dissent, but everyone's entitled to her own opinion, don't you think?" Betsy asked as Julia nodded agreement, her mouth still full. Betsy went on to say some of the girls missed Julia and wouldn't it be nice if she stopped by the suite?

Julia hesitated. How would the girls react to her presence in their territory? Granted, most were amiable when they saw her on campus despite those first few weeks of aloofness when feelings ran high about Julia's "defection." And the suite was a home base for former high school cheerleaders, homecoming queens, most likely to succeeds, and class valedictorians, a place to let down perfectly coiffed hair. Julia had been among the latter category, a brainy, albeit attractive addition.

But Betsy insisted and Julia didn't have the heart to refuse. Besides, she had nothing else to do except catch up on her reading. And she desperately needed something to take her mind off what Valerie was probably enduring this very moment at the abortion clinic.

So here she sat, on the familiar powder-blue velveteen sofa, her bellbottomed legs propped up on a coffee table, her moccasins stashed nearby. The suite, with its stiff-looking arrangement of Queen Anne furniture and gallery of annual group photos tacked in neat rows along the velvet-patterned wallpaper, was what her parents would call goyishe. Funny how she'd never noticed it until now.

The girls, some in hot rollers, robes and pajamas, others popping in for a quick good-bye before a date, were mostly glad to see her. And she was happy she still had friends in the sorority. But their lives seemed so narrow to Julia, like a pair of child's shoes long since outgrown. She felt like standing up and shouting, "Quit pretending nothing's changed! Don't you see what's happening around you?" But years of being taught to say and do the proper thing would never allow her.

Lydia swept into the suite shortly after Julia and Betsy's arrival. Even though the sisters were clustered around Julia ("Gosh stranger, where have you been?" "Is it true boys with long hair are more, you know, passionate?"), Lydia ignored her stating, "Well, Trevor's gone out drinking with the guys again. I just don't understand this fascination between boys and bars!"

Several of the girls exchanged glances. Even Julia had heard that Lydia's pinmate was trying to dump her, although Lydia hung on to those gold and diamond studded Greek letters like a drowning person to a life preserver.

Then Lydia began holding forth on the merits of the ultra-conservative Young Americans for Freedom. Since Louie was constantly passing out all kinds of literature to SMC members, Julia was familiar with the organization. Basically a reactionary group

to the New Left, it claimed a nationwide membership of 51,000.
The YAF advocated hard-line policies in Vietnam and considered
Communism America's number one threat. Its so-called New
Right groups were springing up in colleges all over the country.
Members vowed to take demonstrators and even administrators
to court should they prevent students from attending classes
during demonstrations or close campuses during disruptions.

Lydia pointed to a pile of papers on an end table. "I want
you girls to help me distribute these," she said.

"Are those invites to the Beta beer blast?" asked a lively
blonde whom Julia had never seen before. Obviously a new
pledge, she didn't look more than 18. Suddenly Julia wished she
could wear those child's shoes again, so she'd have nothing more
serious to worry about than her next fraternity mixer.

"Absolutely not," Lydia replied. "'Tell It to Hanoi' is more
important than that, dear. This little newspaper is a proposal for
winning in Vietnam. We intend to distribute a million copies all
over the country. The YAF is going to put a stop to Communist
infiltration on campuses." Leveling a venomous glance at Julia,
she continued, "And we have important people backing us, too
— author William F. Buckley,

Senator Barry Goldwater, and Governor Ronald Reagan."
She added emphasis to the title of each. "Not media flakes like
Abbie Hoffman and Jane Fonda who support the protesters."

"Wasn't Reagan an actor, too?" Julia couldn't resist putting
in. "I saw him in that monkey movie, *Bedtime for Bonzo*, when
I was a kid. The chimp was so cute!"

Several of the girls laughed as Lydia grew pale with anger.
But Julia had no desire to repeat last spring's confrontation, so she
said quietly to Betsy, "It's getting a little uncomfortable in here,
if you know what I mean. Thanks for having me over. It was good
to see everyone." Without waiting for Betsy's reply, she slipped on
her mocs, grabbed her maxi coat, and strode towards the exit, but
not before she overheard one of the sisters comment, "I don't
think passing out YAF pamphlets has anything to do with the
sorority, Lydia. Besides, some of us may not agree with the
organization's philosophy. We haven't even made up our minds
about the war."

Lydia's doing them a favor, Julia reflected as she hurried outside Henderson Hall into the chilly night air. By being so dogmatic, she's getting them to question things and think about Vietnam. Otherwise, they'd be arguing about who to nominate for the Miss Hayes contest.

The campus bells chimed nine times, another sad reminder that it was 9:00 on a Saturday night in Hampton, Ohio. And she didn't have a date or anyplace to go to except her lonely dorm room. Stop the self-pity, she reprimanded herself. Think about where you should be now, standing on the steps of the Capitol Building holding a placard with the name of a G.I. who'd perished in Vietnam. The National Mobilization Committee planned a 36-hour "March Against Death" starting from Arlington Cemetery past the White House to the Capitol. How tragic there would be over 8,000 Ohio gravestone names to choose from.

Given that she was alive and healthy, how could *she* contribute to humankind? A degree in social work was one goal, but Julia needed something more concrete. She wanted to help those less fortunate than herself, the truly underprivileged.

Then she remembered VISTA and the Peace Corps. Just last year, a VISTA volunteer had given a lecture and slide presentation in Julia's dorm. The young woman spoke movingly of the improvements she and her coworkers had made in a hamlet in Appalachia. Julia and the other sorority girls had been impressed not only because the woman had been a former Tri-Delt and runner-up for Miss Ohio, but because of her conviction and dedication.

Since she had this extra time, why not go to the library and learn more about the programs? Obviously the first step was to find out how to apply for them. Many other students had the same thoughts, for the bookshelves where the reference clerk directed her stood in half-empty disarray. Only pamphlets about taking various Federal Civil Service tests and joining the Air Force Reserve remained. At least someone had the sensibility to scrawl a peace symbol on the cover of the last.

Nothing works, she thought with a rush of frustration. No matter how hard I try, I get stymied at every turn. "Well, shit on it all," she blurted, her voice sounding loud to her ears. Self-consciously she glanced to her right and left to see if anyone had overheard. This was after all a library, albeit an incomplete one.

"My sentiments exactly," said someone behind her. She whirled around and saw Win peering at her through the empty shelves. He wore a fringed leather jacket that emphasized his broad shoulders but had on something underneath that looked like a sweat suit. His hair was pulled back in a ponytail. Holding up a copy of the 1965 edition of *Europe on $5 a Day*, he said, "I have the same problem, too. They didn't have anything more recent than four years old."

"What are you doing here?" Each word came out as a gasp. Julia was so flabbergasted by his presence she spoke the first thing that came to mind. Why wasn't Win at the march? Why wasn't he with Shawn?

"I could ask you the same thing, but I won't. You might yell at me again or run away. I'd rather take that chance on another question: Why are you avoiding me?"

Because I'm afraid of you, she almost replied. Being near you is like trying to put my hands on an electrical current. You make me feel things I don't even know about. But twenty-one years of passive, feminine conditioning took over. "Well, you know, it's been a crazy quarter," she floundered. "A lot of stuff's been going down, that thing with Dean Moreland, and Valerie's been having problems, and all the demonstrations. I switched majors, too." She ducked her head to protect herself from his penetrating stare. "And besides, you have..." she caught herself just before she said "a girlfriend," "uh, so many friends, and one more wouldn't seem to make much difference."

"Ouch." Putting the book back on the shelf, Win winced as he pulled the stick from the leather peace symbol that held his ponytail. Was he referring to her reply or the fact that he'd yanked a strand of his hair? As he shook out his russet mane, Julia sighed in admiration. He really was the most beautiful man she'd ever met.

Win smiled at her, a radiant sunbeam that lit up his entire being. "In response to your question about my presence here tonight," he said in Nixonian tones, "My Mom and Pop didn't want me to go to the march. They were afraid I'd get hurt so I honored their request. What's your excuse?" He pointed an accusing finger at her. He did a decent imitation of the Tricky Dick and Julia giggled, relieved that the uneasy moment between them had passed.

Most protesters would have fabricated another reason, just to avoid acknowledging parental influence. He deserved an honest answer in return. "I caught the same thing, from my folks, too. My mother was a refugee from World War II so it's hard for me to go against her wishes. But I feel guilty about not going."

"I can relate to that," He shifted awkwardly from foot to foot. "Say, I just finished a five mile run and I'm hungry. Want to get something to eat?"

Julia couldn't believe it. She'd been waiting for Win to ask her out since she'd first seen him last spring. It was so simple, yet had seemed impossible five minutes ago. Unlike the sorority with its follow-the-numbers dating game, there were no rules, so anything could happen.

He stood there, studying her uncertainly, and Julia realized he half-expected her to refuse. "Sure," she said. "Where to?"

"Ruddy's OK?"

"Fine." Anyplace would have been wonderful.

As they walked to Ruddy's in the suddenly magical night, Win told her about his bodybuilding and running regime, indirectly explaining the presence of his sweatsuit. He also went through phases where he refused to smoke grass or take other drugs, just to cleanse his system. "I was a sickly kid who had all kinds of viruses," he said. "I got into the habit of physical activity to build myself up. I know it sounds weird, but I really enjoy it."

I bet you do, Julia thought, blushing at a mental picture of Win working out, his naked chest glistening with sweat. She was grateful for the dark which blanketed her expression.

At Ruddy's Julia discovered they had more in common than she ever imagined. In addition to being Social Work majors, they shared a passion for drawing and design. Win had started out in architecture, but like Julia's student teaching experience, found it too rigid and confining. "It was also a lot harder than I imagined it would be," he admitted.

They both came from affluent suburbs, although among their friends, this was hardly something to brag about. Win won hands down as they tried to outdo each other with tales of excesses among parents and neighbors. Indian Hills in Cincinnati had a hunt club *and* mansions built in the early 1800s, two unheard-of refinements even in Bexley. The second in a family of four boys and a girl, Win grudgingly confessed to being elected senior class president, voted Most Likely to Succeed and chosen for the lead in the junior/senior class play.

"It sounds like you were in the 'A' clique in high school," Julia observed after he informed her he'd gone steady with the Prom Queen. At Bexley, Julia had been just one of the girls, never selected for anything important, usually involved behind the scenes, although she had been a straight-A student. Her dates were rare and almost literally blind, bespectacled cousins of well-meaning girlfriends. "You probably never would have talked to me back then," she teased.

He seemed to take offense. "I was an asshole. I only looked for superficial things in a woman. There's more to you than exterior beauty."

Julia didn't know what to say. Was he implying she was beautiful? No one had ever called her a woman before. Win wasn't the kind of boy who used a line to make headway with a girl. He was his own person, neither obsessed with being a rebel nor with getting into a profession. Like Julia, he seemed in-between.

"I guess that's a compliment," she replied uncertainly.

He glanced around and she noticed Ruddy's had emptied out and was mostly dark. "We'd better split," he said. "They're turning off the lights."

They stood to leave. "Where are you living this year?" he asked. "I'll walk you back."

"First floor," Julia pointed skyward. "Two flights of steps and I'm home. So it's not necessary." For once, she regretted Miami Hall's convenient location. "But I'd like some fresh air before I go back to my room," she added, hoping she didn't sound too eager. As much as she wanted him to kiss her, she refused to throw herself at him.

So she kept her distance as they strolled into the alley separating Julia's dorm from the Campus Ministry building. "My house is that way," he indicated the next street down from Miami Hall. "Then turn left a block. Lucky us, we live right across from President Carrell."

His house. She'd forgotten about Shawn. She reminded herself that she'd merely joined the ranks of Win's acquaintances.

Then why was he looking at her like that, his hands thrust deep into the pockets of his baggy sweatsuit, as if trying to hide something? And why did she feel warmth rushing from the pit of her stomach to the place between her legs? She was conscious of a wetness there, a hot surge.

For a moment — a millisecond, really — she thought she glimpsed what was going on behind Win's eyes. Entwined naked, she and Win exchanged kisses with exploring tongues while his hands caressed her breasts, his fingers rubbed her erect nipples. Her back arched as he entered her again and again, his penis stiff, engorged. They cried out, lost in ecstacy. An incredibly vivid image, on the verge of actual sensation, yet having nothing to do with any experience she'd ever had. It was as if he'd opened his mind and let her inside.

Everything around her seemed liquid, softening. "Julia..." Win began in a velvet voice. He took a step towards her. She seemed to float forward to meet him.

Then he stopped. "Good night," he said and walked away.

Julia's mind reeled. Her entire life had changed in the course of that second. She'd been drawn to a precipice she hadn't known existed. That Win pulled back did not concern her. She was only aware of a singular overpowering feeling. And the only word she knew for it was love.

CHAPTER THIRTEEN

Even though Julia didn't see much of Valerie in the weeks that followed, Valerie did stop by to tell her the abortion had gone smoothly. Julia meant to spend more time with her friend, but life became unexpectedly busy: with finals coming up, professors began to pile on work and she'd become deeply involved with draft counseling.

As the December 1 draft lottery grew closer, droves of nervous high school and college students flocked to the Campus Ministry Building to learn about their options. Often they left even more disheartened, knowing they were truly victims of chance should their birthday draw a low number. In a way the draft lottery represented a sick sort of justice, Julia reflected. If Vietnam was a war of class and privilege, shouldn't that inequity be corrected? Everyone should have an equal shot at annihilation, regardless of race, creed, color, or economic status.

By unspoken understanding, Julia and Win avoided each other. They waved and said hello on campus or in a crowded meeting-room, but it went no further. What was the point? Win had Shawn. Yet the need was still there, pulsing, alive. And Julia told herself unrequited love was better than no feeling at all.

Through the SMC, Julia gradually became acquainted with the people in Win's house. She found herself increasingly drawn to them, fascinated by the freedom they felt to simply be themselves. Each was an individual, yet they were bound together by an almost mystical connection.

They took care of one another with a camaraderie and gentle humor Julia wouldn't have imagined possible among strangers. They were like a family without the pressures and personality clashes of people thrown together by fate and genetics. And they never seemed lonely.

She discovered she wanted to be a part of that, to simply be accepted for what she was. But although they treated her with warmth and affection, she was still an outsider. There was no need to include her, they had each other. Yet despite knowing she'd be inviting pain by seeing Win and Shawn together, Julia longed to break through the invisible barrier separating her and them.

Then the afternoon before the lottery drawing, as Julia was carrying folding chairs into the Campus Ministry living room for that night's Anti-Draft Be-In, someone pinched her rear end. Blushing and nearly dropping the chairs, she twirled around to face a wickedly grinning Jake. A heavy-drinking flirt, Julia found him to be the least complicated of Win's roommates. Always surrounded by "chickies" as he called them, he delighted in teasing Julia, propositioning her just to see how she'd react. Jake pointed at Win. "He bet me 50 cents I wouldn't have the guts to grab your ass."

Win turned away, feigning fascination with a conversation with Louie and Shawn. But he was so obviously distracted that the latter two stopped to stare at Julia and Jake. "You owe me four bits, man," Jake called out to Win, who looked as if he wanted to disappear into the floor.

"Here, buy yourself a beer," Win flung two shining coins in the air and Jake caught them with ease. "Next time, don't make an announcement, OK?" Avoiding Julia's gaze, Win strolled downstairs. Unperturbed, Shawn winked at Julia and continued talking to Louie.

Why had Win made the bet and then dodged her? Something more complex than a romantic relationship with Shawn was at play here. And what about Shawn? She seemed neither upset or jealous. Come to think of it, Julia had never seen Win express physical affection towards Shawn.

She decided to ask Valerie. If anyone knew her way around the sexual revolution, her friend did. Everyone espoused openness, honesty, and free love, but over the months, Julia had come to realize there were certain rules. The trick was you had to be on the inside to understand them.

So, despite her backlog of term papers, realizing she should use the precious time before tonight's Be-In to study for a Social Work quiz, Julia went uptown to the small red house to talk to Valerie. Although this was too delicate a matter to discuss over the phone, Julia had no choice. Lacking the funds to pay the bill, Valerie had her phone service removed.

Her former roommate was in a foul mood. "Do you believe those military motherfuckers are actually going through with the lottery?" She raged around the cluttered room like an angry bull. "If I had the means, I'd go back to Washington and bomb the basement of the Selective Service building."

"That won't do any good," Julia observed. "They'd just set up an office someplace else."

Valerie turned to her, her eyes blazing in frustration. "Since when are you the all-time expert, Julia? You weren't with the Yippies when they got their heads bashed in at the Injustice Department during the Washington march. They were only protesting the kangaroo court that was trying the Chicago Seven. What a farce! No, you were the good daughter who stayed on this nice, safe campus."

Without waiting for Julia's reply, Valerie continued, "The only language those military bastards understand is their own." Picking up a half-empty pizza box, she shoved it into an overflowing trash can. "Garbage begets garbage. If I've learned one thing lately, it's that you've got to beat them at their own game. See this, Julia?" She held up her hand which was partially covered with tomato sauce. "It could just as easily be blood. Safety is just an illusion. We're all one step from the big void."

Julia was becoming annoyed with Valerie's theatrics. "And you think violence will solve our problems?"

Valerie went into the kitchen to wash off her fingers. "The repression keeps getting worse. But don't worry; I'm not going to take to the streets with rocks and guns. At least not yet."

"Well, that's good to know. I was just about to call the CIA." Julia said loudly over running water. Then it abruptly stopped. "Just kidding!"

When Valerie walked back into the room, she said in a more normal tone, "So why are you here tonight?" She wiped her hands on her plaid shirt. "I know I haven't been around lately. Let me guess. Louie sent you."

"No actually, I came on my own. Although I wish you'd reconsider some of your ideas. Didn't you once tell me that all problems, even war, can be solved through love and peaceful methods?"

"Don't throw my words back at me, Julia. You sound like Richard. Besides what do you know about love? You're the proverbial virgin."

"You seem to have the opposite problem, so I could ask you the same question." Julia was weary of Valerie's touchiness, whatever the cause. And just as tired of being reminded of her virginity.

"Touche, Julia. I'm sorry I'm acting like a bitch. It's just that since the abortion..." she paused. "No, it started way before then, and has nothing to do with you. My temper just gets away from me."

"Well, put it back where it belongs." A woman on a mission, Julia wanted to keep Valerie good-natured. "If I have my way, I won't be a virgin much longer. I'm here for some advice."

"Oh, really?" Valerie's stonewashed eyes gleamed with as much interest as they had anger. "I haven't heard anything juicy in ages. Who's the lucky dude?"

Now that she had her friend's full attention, she wasn't exactly sure what to say. "Well actually, I don't think he, uh, knows yet. It's only been a few months."

"What!" she shrieked. "You've been holding out on me, Julia Brandon. I've been pouring out my guts to you all quarter and you never uttered a word. Now, what's going down?"

Quickly, and feeling a glow as she talked, Julia told Valerie about Win. She gave her friend a PG-rated version of the incident outside her dorm, ending with Win's bet with Jake. "I think he kind of likes me," she concluded. "If only he weren't going with Shawn. But what do you think, Valerie? Do I have a chance?"

For an agonizingly long moment Valerie stared at a flake of plaster as it drifted from the ceiling. Taking a deep breath, she cupped her face in her hands. "Jesus Christ, Julia. I just don't know what to say. And Win of all people."

"What do you mean?" Julia cried in an agony of panic.

"Sit down," Plopping on the unmade sofa/bed, Valerie picked up and lit her bong. Julia perched on the end and began to pull at the loose threads of an armrest.

"Want a toke?" Valerie offered, inhaling. "It'll make what I'm going to say, like, more palatable."

Julia shook her head. Getting high would only make her feel worse right now. "Get on with it, Valerie. If it's something awful about Win, I want to know."

"It's nothing about Win, really. It's everything about you. Everyone knows what you are, Julia."

Tears of humiliation sprang behind Julia's eyelids. Who had she been fooling all these months? Certainly not Win and his friends. Of course they know what I am, she thought, remembering Jake's less than kind comments about certain female SMCers. Plastic hippies. Sorority chicks hot for guys in blue jeans. The last 20-year old virgin on earth who isn't brain-damaged.

"Don't look so bummed out, for God's sake," Valerie was quick to reassure her. "You're the kindest person I know, Julia. It just that you're such a—how can I say this tactfully—innocent. Not just sexually, either. I mean about people, and what they're really like, what their motives are. This thing with Win is a perfect example. You've built up this big fantasy about him. Julia, do you honestly think he has one inkling of how you feel?"

"I don't know! That's why I came here tonight. To ask you if I should tell him."

Valerie took a final puff on the bong and put a piece of cardboard over the top of it to extinguish the hashish. "Great stuff. A little goes a long way. You should try it, really. I have joints, if you prefer those." Seeing Julia's impatient expression, she said, "No, don't say anything. At least not until you know each other better. Telling him now would probably scare the shit out of him." She shook her head. "Jesus, I haven't talked this way about a guy since high school."

"But what about Shawn? I really like her, you know. I'd feel bad if I took Win away from her."

"That's what I mean, Julia. Win and Shawn are friends. Read my lips...friends. Their living together doesn't mean a damn thing. Just like loving and balling aren't necessarily related. That's a lesson I learned a long time ago." Valerie stared sadly at the bong, then placed it on the end table. "Win doesn't 'belong' to anyone. He does his own thing. If he wanted to get it on with you he'd say something."

"But I can sense he likes me," Julia objected. "The look in his eyes..."

"I'm sure he admires the same qualities in you that most men do, Julia. But he knows that underneath the pretty hair and gauzy tops and seductively snug bell bottoms you're a nice, clean, idealistic girl. Who is into marriage, despite any claims to the contrary."

"So what are you trying to say?" In spite of learning that Win wasn't seriously involved, Julia felt depressed.

"Stop tormenting yourself with mind games. Don't make your fledgling friendship with Win into something it's not....Do you know what I think you should do?"

"What?"

"Find some nice dude who sort of turns you on and make it with him. It'll help get rid of your hangups and you'll be able to see things more realistically. Who knows? Maybe you'll discover you don't dig Win at all." She shook her head. "Christ, Julia, why did you fall for him? I know he's gorgeous, but why not one of the other guys? Louie's a fine person. Even Jake has redeeming qualities. But Win — well, he's a free spirit."

Of course Valerie was right. Win would never be attracted to someone as ordinary as she. She'd been acting like a thirteen-year-old with a crush on a movie star.

"Hey, are you crying?" Valerie came over and put a sympathetic arm around her. "Don't. Never weep over someone who won't cry over you. To use a stupid cliche, there are plenty of fish in the sea." Reaching over into the back pocket in her jeans, she pulled out a reefer. "This is the stuff I was telling you about. Acapulco Gold. It'll give you a real rush."

After a moment's pause, Julia took the joint. The doorknob rattled and Valerie said, "That's Felix and Adrian, so I'm going to split. You're not still pissed at me are you? You wanted me to tell it like it is, so I did. Would you rather I didn't say anything?"

"No, but I was hoping for a little encouragement."

"With what? Your daydreams? You would have continued with that fantasy until you really got hurt."

Julia sighed. "I'm not upset with you, Valerie. Not really. I guess I'm mad at myself for getting so carried away over nothing."

"Well don't be. You're only human. Like the song says, love makes a fool of us all. Even me, who's supposed to know better." The knocking changed to a loud pounding and Valerie yelled, "Just a minute, you assholes! I'm coming!"

"Not in your pants, I hope," Adrian shouted through the door. "We just combined psilocybin with windowpane acid and the results are outtasight! But we gotta get back to my farmhouse before we totally lose it."

"Why are you hanging around with Felix and Adrian?" Julia asked. "Everyone knows how messed up they are. Why not come to the Campus Ministry with me instead?"

"You haven't been around the SMC long enough to learn what a cop-out it is."

Then Julia remembered Valerie's conversation with Adrian on the day of the Moratorium. "You're not trying to get to Richard through Adrian, are you? Why don't you just contact him directly?"

"Don't try to figure out someone else's head until you understand your own," Although Valerie's rebuke was kind, her voice had an edge. "Stay as long as you like, but be sure to lock the door when you split. I won't be back 'til tomorrow night."

After Valerie left, Julia lay on her friend's rumpled sofa/bed, puffing on the joint and staring at the cracked ceiling. Valerie's life was as chaotic as her apartment but at least it was real.

Meanwhile, she, Julia, had her own obligations. Which did not involve getting stoned and feeling sorry for herself. She had a Be-In to attend. As she stubbed out the half-smoked reefer, she remembered what Kirsten had said about designing costumes for student plays: that the outfits were different but the guidelines were identical. The same could be said for relationships. In spite of the long hair and liberated rhetoric, nothing had really changed.

CHAPTER FOURTEEN

Julia arrived at the Campus Ministry building just as the first lottery number was being drawn. There were no available chairs left, or even any place to stand, but Louie, leaning against the far wall that connected the living room to the foyer, made space for her anyway.

Win, Jake, Vicki, Bill, and dozens of others huddled in front of the TV set at the center of the darkened room. The black-and-white picture flickered over their anxious faces, making them seem even younger than their early twenties.

Representative Alexander Pirnie from the State of New York pulled the first capsule from the water cooler-sized glass bowl. "September 14," he announced, his tinny, televised voice barely reaching Julia. The group breathed a collective sigh of relief. At least none of them was Number 1.

Conversation resumed a low hum as other Selective Service representatives drew subsequent numbers, posting them on a bulletin board. Louie, whose birthday fell on March 17, would have been No. 33, but he'd already served. "Either then or now, I guess it was fated," he remarked to Julia with a shrug. Occasionally she'd hear a groan if someone's birthday was selected, but it was never anyone she knew.

Julia relaxed. It looked as though none of the charmed circle in Win's house was going to be tapped. January 28, her own birthday, drew 77, practically making her a shoo-in if she'd been a male. "Once they get past 100, we'll be fairly safe," Louie said as the TV voice announced April 18 as Number 90.

"No!" Win's reaction was instantaneous and violent, shocking the already subdued group into dead silence. "Goddamn it, no!" He jumped up with a motion so forceful it moved the heavy loveseat he'd been sharing with Vicki and Bill. For the first time, Julia noticed neither Shawn nor Kirsten was present. Kirsten was probably at the theatre sewing costumes, but where was Shawn?

"Win, calm down for God's sakes," Vicki placed a hand on his muscular arm but he shoved it aside and ran from the room, stumbling over people's legs and feet in haste. Unseeingly he pushed his way past Julia, his russet eyes gone dark with anger and other, undecipherable emotions.

Julia felt physically ill. Not Win, she thought, watching him run downstairs. Win would never survive as a soldier. Holding a gun, his face streaked with grease for camouflage, jumping out of a helicopter into the steaming jungle. Crying out in agony as he was shot or captured and tortured by the Viet Cong. He would die, if not physically, then emotionally. Yet the indifferent finger of war had beckoned him.

Someone sturdy like Bill or thick-skinned like Jake might manage. But Win was too sensitive, too much an artist to endure the rigors of military life. Too much like herself. Even Louie had trouble handling the memories, as Julia well knew. After the Moratorium confrontation with Dean Moreland, Julia had approached Louie gently, saying, "I think it would do you good to rap about some of the things you went through."

He agreed, making her promise that she'd stop him if his stories became too graphic. And they had, but she kept silent, watching him gradually become more relaxed, less frantic as he shared the traumas he'd hidden too well. Compared to what he'd been through, her listening was a small price for the healing of his mental wounds.

Now another friend -- and Win was a friend, even Valerie couldn't deny that -- was hurting. Julia's draft counseling experiences taught her there were other alternatives -- service in a veteran's hospital through the Presbyterian church, for example. And his number was high enough that it wasn't an absolute guarantee he'd be drafted. Perhaps just telling him he had options would help.

He couldn't have gone far. Julia hurried down the steps after him, assuming he went to get his jacket from the makeshift coat racks next to the meeting room. She heard Win's voice in the kitchen. He stood by the phone talking softly to Louie. She began to walk towards them.

"But it's not fair!" Win burst out suddenly. "Stu and Laura and I had everything planned...." He saw Julia and stopped mid-sentence, staring at her as if she were an intruder.

Julia backed away. "I just wanted to get my coat," she mumbled, her face burning with embarrassment. As she slipped on her maxi coat, she thought, how could I have believed I could comfort Win? He has the others to turn to. Like Valerie said, I'm an acquaintance. Our "relationship" is nothing but a pipe dream.

As Julia was beginning to learn, love provided its own blinders. Next quarter the Psychology department was offering a new course in something called body language. She would to sign up for it. Maybe she would learn something about behavior so she wouldn't be fooled the next time she was attracted to someone.

Besides heightening her depression, Valerie's grass made her sleepy. But she still had to go back to her room and study for that damned Social Work quiz. Grateful that Win and Louie were now gone, and not wanting to encounter anyone else, Julia headed towards the basement fire door. Since it was disconnected from the alarm system, it wouldn't buzz, providing a convenient and discreet exit. The door was also unlocked from the outside, so one could slip back in undetected.

Outside, a bitter wind had started to blow. Craving the warmth of her dorm, Julia dashed up the steps and into Shawn's arms, nearly knocking her down. "Oh, I'm sorry!" Julia cried, peering closely at Shawn's tight, tired expression. "Did I hurt you?"

"No, I'm OK. I just have another bitching headache. Have you seen Win? He called, and I'm supposed to meet him in the kitchen." In spite of knowing Win and Shawn weren't lovers, Julia felt a knife twinge of envy. They were intimate friends, making Shawn a lucky girl. And she was so weary of being the outsider. "He was there a minute ago," she replied tersely.

Julia's annoyance escaped Shawn. "I've never heard him so bummed out," Shawn confided. "But I've got something that'll make him feel a whole lot better." She pulled a wrapped handkerchief from the pocket of her green army jacket. Opening it carefully, she revealed several button shaped discs about one-half inch in diameter.

Obviously it was some sort of drug but Julia had never seen anything like it. "What are they?" she asked, momentarily forgetting her troubles and the inclement weather.

"Peyote buttons. American Indians have been taking them for centuries during religious ceremonies. A friend out West sent them to me. I'd planned on saving them for a special occasion, but now..." she shrugged.

Amazed that another culture had used psychedelics long before Timothy Leary had even been born, Julia asked, "May I touch?" Shawn nodded, and Julia leaned over and picked one up. It was hard and brittle, resembling the mushrooms her mother sometimes put in spaghetti sauce. "What does it do?"

"The buttons are sliced from the heads of cactus flowers, making them the most natural form of mescaline. And the rush is even better than LSD. You have control over your visions and don't get those shitty flashbacks. The simplest object can just blow your mind, and colors and music are fantastic. It's impossible to describe. Want to try some?"

Dare she? What would it be like to have vivid hallucinations, to see her world explode in a collage of vibrant rainbows and acid rock? Julia was both attracted and repelled by the thought of anything stronger than grass. She'd shied away from LSD, afraid of bad trips. And although she'd never admit it, her father's warnings about chromosomal breakage and defective children worried her. These last few weeks, Harry had been mailing her photocopied articles from medical journals. Although she didn't understand the terminology, the findings were clearly based on scientific research.

But as Shawn said, peyote was completely organic. And it had been used for hundreds of years. This also might mean the beginning of a real friendship with Shawn and the others.

Then she remembered her test. "I have a two o'clock quiz tomorrow," she said regretfully. "I haven't even started studying. Maybe another time?"

"That's no problem," Shawn assured her. "You could trip with us tonight and I'd give you some speed tomorrow so you could cram. You'd feel kind of lousy later on, but it'd be worth it."

In spite of Valerie's advice to forget him, Julia wondered if taking peyote would draw her closer to Win. She touched the button with the tip of her tongue. It tasted a little bitter, but not too bad. "It's hard to believe something so harmless-looking can do so much."

"What are you doing?" a voice thundered. Julia was so startled she dropped the peyote button on the ground.

Win stood under the street light by the front exit, glaring at them. With his shoulder-length hair and fringed leather jacket he looked a little like Wild Bill Hickok. An angry Wild Bill who'd shoot at their feet and chase them out of town, Julia thought, forgetting that just a few minutes earlier she couldn't have imagined Win carrying a gun. "Just what the fuck do you think you're doing?" he repeated.

"What does it look like, Win?" Shawn retorted. "You called me up, practically freaking out, and I told you I'd bring the stuff right over. What do you want from me?"

This had the augurings of a serious quarrel. Julia could scarcely believe it. But she'd brought it about: obviously Win resented sharing his friends' dope. So she said, "Look, I'm sorry I lost the peyote. If we look for it right now we might find it. Or why don't I just pay you for it, Shawn? How much do I owe?" She began to dig in her purse for her wallet.

"That's what I mean! That's just what I mean!" Win cried. "Put away your money, goddamn it! Do you know anything at all about peyote, Julia?"

"Well, Shawn and I rapped about it," Julia replied, feeling both defensive and ignorant. "It doesn't seem to be anything I couldn't handle. Shawn even suggested that I mix it with speed so I can take my test tomorrow."

Frustrated, Win hit his head with the palm of his hand. "Wrong, Julia. Shawn can get away with something like that 'cause she's a doper from way back. But you've never taken any hard drugs. Did you know you could get violently sick to your stomach? That the visions could last up to 12 hours? That mixing mesc and speed could blow you away for weeks?"

"Honestly, Win," Shawn objected. "You're talking about exceptions rather than the rules."

"Stay out of this, Shawn. I'm trying to explain the facts to Julia." He turned to Julia, his voice gentle. "We've had friends really lose it because they weren't prepared. Remember what happened to Laura our sophomore year?" he asked Shawn. "We almost had to take her to the hospital."

Shawn nodded. "You have a point, Win. I forgot what the stuff can do. These headaches have wreaked havoc with my memory."

"And since when were you interested in psychedelics, Julia?" Win asked. "You don't have to trip to be accepted. At least not by us."

Julia sucked in her breath. How had he guessed what she was thinking? And how did he know she'd never ingested anything stronger than marijuana? The subject had never come up in any conversation they'd had.

Shawn rubbed her forehead, her china doll features twisted with pain. "Oh shit, the migraine's coming back."

Always the internist's daughter, Julia asked, "Have you seen someone about these?"

"Yeah, every specialist imaginable, and then some. They all tell me the same thing. 'We don't know. We've got to run some tests.' Been to opthamologists, brain surgeons, the Cleveland Clinic. Now I get to spend Christmas break at Johns Hopkins. It'll be so much fun," she added sarcastically. Shoving the peyote-filled handkerchief into her pocket, she buried her face in her hands. "Oh God, here we go again."

"We'd better get you back to the house," Deftly Win slipped his arm around Shawn's waist. "Come talk to me next quarter if you're really interested in tripping, Julia. But believe me, it's not necessary." He guided Shawn down the alley leading to their house.

Watching them go, Julia realized she had no desire to experiment with heavy drugs. She'd been foolish to think that would garner Win and Shawn's friendship. In that one respect, Win understood her better than herself.

But he'd shown he cared. And that was more than she ever anticipated. Julia went back to her room intending to study, but instead fell into a deep, untroubled sleep.

CHAPTER FIFTEEN

The three weeks' vacation over Christmas gave Julia a needed respite from the frantic activity and confusion of Fall Quarter. At first she reveled in the quiet of her childhood home and the cloistered closeness of old friends from Bexley High. But the arrival of her grades the last week in December shattered her fragile peace.

She'd never received anything less than A's and B's, so at first Julia thought the B, two C's, and until now, unheard-of D were a computer error. But a phone call to the Registrar's office revealed no mistake had been made, at least not in the Administration's record keeping. And of course, not all her professors would have incorrectly scored her papers. She had gone into finals with her mind full of other things and it showed.

She had to give her father credit, though. He only lost his temper once -- "What's gotten into you, Julia?" -- then retired to his study, grumbling.

Her mother looked at her sadly, questioningly while Julia, full of guilt, rationalized, "Well, I did change my major. And I had mostly B's until finals. Just my luck, all the tests were essay and you know how terrible I am at composition." But there was more behind her slipping grades than Julia's inadequacy in putting thoughts on paper. No matter how awkward an answer might be, knowledge came through. Hester blamed her daughter's distraction on the protest movement, but Julia knew it was more complicated than that.

And how would those grades affect her plans for VISTA and the Peace Corps? Fortunately, they only pulled her accumulated average down a little, but social science skills weighed heavily in selecting applicants. And her "D" had been in Social Work.

Her parents didn't come right out and say so, but she could tell they thought she'd made a mistake in switching majors. In a sense, she agreed. Although she liked the courses, and found them insightful and useful in learning about behavior, they didn't enthrall her like sketching or even designing a brochure for the SMC. Yet she never wanted to go back to elementary education.

Gloom hung over the Brandon's stucco and brick two-story house. Her parents' restrained hurt and disappointment became increasingly oppressive. Julia began to look forward to going back to Hayes with equally proportional eagerness.

As Julia crunched through a new snowfall the first morning of Winter Quarter, she vowed to get straight A's and vindicate herself. She'd accomplished it once as a sophomore and could do it again. Her mind was now clear: over break, she decided to take Valerie's advice. To accept Win as a friend and date other boys if given the chance. And her antiwar work would come second to her studies, although Louie told Julia the SMC did practically nothing during January and February. Mass mobilizations and snowy weather didn't mix. So she had every reason to do well this term.

"Hey, Julia!" Shawn hurried over as Julia mounted the steps of Kluver Hall, the psychology building. "On your way to class?"

Since Win was a Social Work major also, Shawn might be walking with him to a psych course. Julia's heart began to pound as she glanced about expectantly for Win's russet mane. But he was nowhere around.

She said, "Yeah, I'm enrolled in some crazy course called 'Body Language and Interpersonal Relations.'" She shrugged, not wanting Shawn to suspect she'd taken it for her own self-knowledge. "I needed a Mickey Mouse to fulfill my psych requirement."

"Far out. Win's signed up for that, too. Did you hear what happened to him?"

"No, I haven't even seen him." Julia's heart began to hammer in earnest. Had Win been drafted over Christmas? Because of the lottery, his deferment had changed, so anything was possible.

"You won't. He broke his hip skiing. A multiple compound fracture. You know Win — he had to go down the steepest slope. It was his first time at Aspen and he overestimated his abilities." She thrust a piece of paper at Julia. On it were Win's name, home address, and a list of courses, including the one on body language. "Can you send him your notes? He'll be bedridden for quite a while. But for once the Administration's being rational — they're letting him take his classes by mail so he can graduate on time."

"Sure, just let me copy down the information." Julie struggled to hide her disappointment by fumbling in her bookbag for a pen. Finally locating a pencil, she scribbled Win's address on the outside of her loose leaf notebook. "Tell him I'll mail photocopies of my notes at the end of each week." The bell rang and she fled. She could sense Shawn staring after her in bewilderment. Only later did she realize how thoughtless she'd been in not asking about Shawn's stay at Johns Hopkins.

In class, Julia mentally replayed the scene with Shawn. She'd gotten emotional all over again. *Damn it, I won't get caught in the same trap this quarter,* she promised herself as the professor prattled on about the schedule of tests, required readings, and projects. *In a way, it's a blessing Win won't be around. Nothing will distract me. And how much feeling can you invest in someone you send lecture notes to once a week?*

She ran into Betsy after class and they went for a quick lunch at the Student Center. Betsy's fiance "Fast Eddie" DiCarlo joined them, and soon they were discussing the Greek system and how it had fallen behind the times. Because Julia was now an independent, they spoke more freely than if she were still affiliated.

"Hey, Eddie, what's happening?" The boy standing in front of their table was tall, blonde, and definitely fraternity. Easing into a chair, he asked, "May I join you?" with the rhetorical air of someone who has always been welcome.

"Sure, Trev," Fast Eddie replied. "Have you met Julia? She's our resident activist."

Of course Julia recognized Trevor Marshall. Good-looking in a classic preppy way, with even features and a perpetually genial expression. Rich. A senior. And Lydia's pinmate for better or worse. Julia sighed; the Greek world of couples remained ever thus.

Trevor stared at her approvingly. "You used to be in BGP, didn't you? You look different, somehow. Better."

"Thanks," Suddenly shy, Julia twisted her fingers through a strand of her hair. It had grown considerably since last spring and tumbled down her back, a curly cascade.

Trevor turned to Eddie and thrusting out his chest, said, "Notice anything different, F.E.?" His gold and diamond studded fraternity pin glittered in the florescent light.

"You got it back! All right!" Trevor and Eddie slapped each others' hands, palm to palm. "How did you shake it loose from that bitch? Oops, sorry about the wordy dird, girls." Eddie didn't sound regretful at all.

Trevor looked uncomfortable. "Oh, you know how it is. She finally got the hint. After months of my not taking her anywhere." He shrugged, almost apologetically. "She's pretty upset, but she'll recover. And I'm a free man." He smiled at Julia, and she noticed his eyes were the color of mocha flecked with caramel. "What are you doing Saturday night?" he asked her.

Ah, the beautiful simplicity of the Greek mating dance! If only things were as clear-cut with the protesters. Before she had a chance to reply, Fast Eddie said in a high-pitched voice, "Why, going to the party with you, my dear." He fluttered his eyelids at Julia. "Right?"

"Well..."Julia hesitated. She'd planned on attending a benefit coffeehouse at Lenny's. Proceeds were to go to the SMC Defense Fund which provided bail money and attorney's fees to members, should they get busted. But Valerie spent all her time with Adrian and Felix and Julia hated the thought of walking in alone. Besides, Trevor was what she used to call a hunk. And he was asking her out on a date. This was a first step towards that longed-for real relationship.

"I'd love to," she told Trevor, her eyes sparkling. Trevor reached over and took her hand. Julia knew where she stood with him and liked the feeling very much.

In the weeks that followed, however, Julia struggled against depression. She told herself it was the time of year: she hated winter with a passion most people reserved for a rival football team. This year it was especially bad, with snowstorms every week and temperatures rarely above the twenties. Everyone ducked down their heads, listening to the echoes of icy footsteps instead of each other.

Except for encountering Shawn the first day on campus, she hadn't seen anyone from Win's house. Even Valerie had disappeared. Her phone was still disconnected — Julia made periodic attempts to call. Twice she'd braved the slippery trudge uptown to visit her friend with no success.

Her two dates a week with Trevor and her attempt to bring up her grades left her with little time. Besides, she didn't really want to think — not about the protest movement and its contradictions about sex, drugs, and changing the world. And not about how everyone but Julia seemed sure of their place in the universe.

But she kept her promise to Shawn. She mailed Win's installment of photocopied lecture notes each week. They were a life preserver of sorts, a link to what might have been. Julia inserted sardonic comments about the material, drawing caricatures of the professor and their classmates in the margins because she knew Win would see them. Even though the asides were almost as dumb as she when it came to Win.

Oh stop it, she reprimanded herself as she prepared for her regular Saturday night date with Trevor. You have someone else now. Someone who truly reciprocates your affection.

Last week's notes lay on her bureau. She'd meant to drop them in the lobby mailbox that afternoon, but had gotten involved in drawing a cartoon of the prof physically tied up in knots over body language. She'd mail them when she left tonight.

The phone buzzed. "Hello?" Julia said, expecting Trevor.

"Where the fuck you been hiding?" Except for "fuck," the words were distorted, making them almost impossible to understand.

An obscene caller, Julia thought, and began to hang up, but the voice persisted, "An' I thought we were friends. Ha! Why don't you be up front with me an' tell me why you're pissed?"

"Valerie?" Julia gasped. Valerie's perfect diction was practically unrecognizable. "Valerie, are you all right?"

"Wha's it sound like? I'm havin' a great time? Not that you give a shit."

Valerie was slurring her words, so it was likely a downer instead of a psychedelic. Over Christmas, Julia read arguments for and against all kinds of drugs. She still hadn't reached any conclusions, except what she decided after the incident with the peyote, that psychedelics and barbiturates weren't for her. But she understood what they could do to people. "Valerie, I tried to see you. Your phone's still out and you're never home. What's wrong?"

Valerie may have been strung out but she was aware enough to be on the offensive. "Wha's your problem, Julia? Why've you been avoiding us?"

Julia's conscience bristled. Although she could tune out Vietnam, these who fought and lived there could not. She had stayed away from all things political, easing back into her old way of life with ease. But she still had good reasons. "My grades were terrible last fall and I have to bring them up. And Louie's studying for his Law Boards this quarter, so between that and the weather, the SMC's virtually nonexistent and I...." Julia was about to confide she'd taken Valerie's advice about sex.

"Fuck the SMC!" Valerie interrupted. "Nothin' stops the SDS, not snow or rain or any fuckin' career plans. Why don' you come to our meetings?"

It was hopeless to argue with Valerie right now, but she had to try to explain. "Valerie, the SDS indirectly supports the Communists. They want to shut down businesses and allow unconditional college admissions for minorities. That's reverse discrimination, which in a way is as bad as segregation...."

"Face it, Julia. You're copping out."

"Now just a minute, Valerie...."

Julia's suitemate Janine poked her head into the room. "Your guy's in the lobby, Julia. He says your line's busy."

Always punctual, Trevor hated to be kept waiting. "Look Valerie, I have to split. I am not deserting anyone, not you and not the protest movement. We'll talk next week when you're in a better frame of mind."

"Yeah, sure. Go an' have a good time with your groovy Greek boyfriend." Julia winced as Valerie slammed down the receiver.

How did Valerie know about Trevor? Had she made a point of finding out or had it become common knowledge? Whenever she was with Trevor, Julia worried about running into the protesters almost as much as she dreaded encountering Lydia. Both would be awkward.

Could Valerie still be resentful over Julia's secretiveness about Win? No, that had been months ago and seemed inconsequential now. Something deeper was bothering her friend; Valerie had alluded to it the night of the draft lottery. Somehow she'd locate Valerie and get to the real problem.

"Oh, damn!" Just as she reached the lobby, she remembered Win's notes. Trevor frowned as she hurried back to her room to retrieve the package. He stared at the address when she returned. "Who's Randall Winfield?"

"Just an acquaintance with a broken hip." In a way, Trevor owed Win. Win was responsible for Julia's sexual awakening, for after a few drinks, she actually enjoyed making out with Trevor. She merely imagined he was Win. Of course she'd never tell Trevor that. Learning that she wasn't frigid, that she might be normal, was such a relief she failed to consider the implications of her fantasies. "What are you sending him?" Trevor demanded.

"These are lecture notes. We're in the same class." She clutched the package to her bosom. "You're awfully nosy tonight." Trevor never pushed her, sexually or otherwise, although they explored each others' bodies a little more each weekend. It was unlike him to be curious about anything outside his normal frame of reference.

"And you're awfully feisty. I just wanted to know 'cause it's addressed to a guy and you're my girl. I didn't want to find out you have a hometown honey waiting in the wings."

His words weighed heavily. She might have wanted to a serious relationship in the past but the movement had changed that. She needed to find herself before getting involved with someone else.

Julia flushed. His brown-gold gaze seemed to ferret out her guilt. "You don't have to worry about that!" she chirped. Could he sense her thoughts when they were making out?

"Well, see if you can find someone else to do it," Trevor placed his arm around her shoulders, a gesture of possession. "Why put yourself out?"

Julia sighed and thought of her phone conversation with Valerie. She was being pulled in so many directions. Everyone had an opinion, a stand. She wished she could confide her ambiguities to Trevor: how she could see all sides of a situation, how she felt incapable of adhering to one ideology while condemning the other. But he would never understand: an accounting major, he saw life as a series of checks and balances. Everything had its place -- guys were buddies you drank and played sports with and girls were for dating.

Suddenly she missed her rap sessions with Louie. If only he hadn't sequestered himself in the Law Library this quarter! She could use a friend with whom she felt totally at ease.

"I thought we'd catch the flick uptown, then go back to my room for a few beers or whatever," Trevor murmured in her ear, his annoyance forgotten.

Julia nodded. Although it was her least favorite time of year, someone cared about her. She had no reason to complain.

CHAPTER SIXTEEN

Most of Valerie's classes were in the Performing Arts Center, so Julia stopped by there after her own courses were done on Monday. Eventually she'd turn up and Julia was determined to talk to her.

She didn't wait long, for as she wandered the halls of the old building, she glimpsed Valerie and Adrian strolling down the steps towards the theatre-in-the-round. Valerie's usually shiny blonde hair hung in greasy strands and her clothes looked as if they hadn't been laundered in weeks. Dirty hippie, flashed through Julia's mind and she reprimanded herself for thinking that way about her friend. Between the botched affair with Richard and the abortion, Valerie had some terrible times. She was merely coping the best she knew how.

Julia stepped in front of them. "Hello, Valerie. Hello, Adrian."

"Oh, wow, if it isn't the sweetheart of Sigma Chi. Have you reached home base yet or are you still stuck on third?" Adrian tittered, and Julia thought in annoyance, one thing about Adrian, he's consistent. Consistently an asshole.

Valerie looked uncomfortable. "Cool it, Adrian," she said. "Look, I meant to call you back yesterday and apologize, Julia. But I never got around to it. We've been tied up in rehearsals."

"Really tied up," Adrian giggled. "It's totally kinky. We're still looking to cast a virgin, though. Or don't you qualify anymore?"

Julia scissored her arms across her chest. "Why are you so curious about everyone's sex life, Adrian?" she demanded. "Is it because you're not getting any?" Valerie stared at Julia in amazement.

Her observation hit a nerve. "She's not the little kitten we met last spring, is she, Valerie?" he snarled. "The pussy has claws now." Glaring at Julia, Adrian drew his fur coat around him, clambering down the stairs in a great show of offended dignity.

Julia knew she'd overstepped the bounds of any fragile friendship she and Adrian might have had, that she'd likely made an enemy. But she no longer cared. Adrian had been lost to her a long time. Only Valerie mattered.

Valerie hung her head. "Look Julia, I'm, like, really sorry I hassled you over the phone. I was really ripped on reds and THC...."

"Let's just sit down and talk, OK? No apologies, no explanations. Like we used to when we were roommates."

"I can't. I have rehearsal." Valerie started to walk in the direction of Adrian's retreat and Julia fell into step beside her. "It's an experimental play," Valerie explained. "Adrian's directing and I have the lead. They're waiting for me."

"Then how about dinner? You won't be rehearsing all night. Since I never paid you for the grass we smoked last quarter, it'll be my treat."

"You don't need to do that, Julia." They paused before the glass doors leading to the small theatre. Although Valerie kept her face blank, Julia recognized the tone of voice she usually used when dealing with "straights" or people she didn't trust.

Julia wasn't about to abandon their friendship without an explanation. "But I *want* to. I'll meet you at Ruddy's at six."

Worn down by Julia's perseverance, Valerie conceded, "We might not be through by six, or we might get done sooner. Wait for me, and I'll meet you."

"Great. I'll be studying in the piano practice room down the hall. Come get me when rehearsal's over."

"You know, Julia, Adrian's right in a way." Valerie shoved her hands inside the pockets of her grubby pea jacket. "You *have* changed." Without bothering to explain, she pulled open the door and went inside.

Well, maybe I have, Julia replied silently. And maybe it's not all for the best. But you've changed so much I hardly recognize you any more. And I want to know why.

In her search for an unoccupied practice room, Julia heard the horrendous cacophony of someone mutilating Bach by slamming down on the keyboard. Another lost soul undoubtedly suffering through winter doldrums, she thought. Curious about the offender, she peered through the tiny windows of the cubicle-filled hallway until she located Shawn. Before Julia could make a tactful, discreet retreat, Shawn glanced up with a tear-filled face. Recognizing Julia, she motioned for her to come in.

What had happened to this cool beauty who seemed to have everything? Pregnancy? Bad grades? A broken romance? Or those headaches.... "Hi." Tentatively Julia sat down on the piano bench next to Shawn. "What's going down?"

"My whole life is ruined!" Shawn sobbed. "My whole fucking life! All my dreams!"

"It can't be that bad, Shawn," Julia said, knowing that if Shawn's problem was medical, it could be worse.

"Remember those tests at Johns Hopkins over Christmas? Well, they had to do growth cultures which took several weeks. I finally found out the results today." Her voice trembled. "They've narrowed my so-called problem down to two rare fungal infections. Zygomycosis or Histoplasmosis. Zygomycosis can be fatal, causing permanent blindness. With my luck, I have it."

"Oh, God, Shawn," Julia put a consoling hand on Shawn's shoulder. Shawn had on a pink angora sweater almost as delicate-looking as she. "I'm so sorry." She felt like crying, too. But her father always said that overt pity for sick people rarely helped them.

"You didn't know me last winter when I was preparing for the Ohio State music competition," Shawn rubbed her tear-streaked face with the heel of her palm. Fortunately she wore no makeup or it would have smeared everywhere. "I had an outtasight chance at winning. I mean, I was the Fine Arts department's answer to Wanda Landowska, a famous harpsichordist who practically revolutionized the field.

"Then all of a sudden, everything started going blurry and I began to have these pounding headaches. It was as if my vision kept shutting itself on and off. I told myself it was eyestrain, and would disappear once I quit practicing so much. Of course it got worse and I had to drop out of the competition. The whole department was pissed at me because they thought I copped out." She sighed.

"I know the feeling," Julia empathized. Valerie had reacted similarly when Julia told her she couldn't go to Washington. Perhaps that was when things between her and Valerie started to go awry.

"Finally Win made me promise to tell my parents and see a doctor over the summer. Although I don't have much faith in organized medicine. They're only in it for the bread." She looked at Julia with her challenging expression.

"My Dad's an internist, and for all his gruff talk, he really cares about his patients," Having grown up within the medical establishment, Julia felt obligated to defend it. "Besides, we're not rich."

"Win told me where you came from, Julia," As usual, Shawn knew more than she let on. "And wealth is a matter of perspective. I know there are decent doctors. It's just they jerked me and my parents around for so long and it cost so much," She began to weep again. "Now I'll never get to study at the Royal Academy in London."

London. Julia's hand fell from Shawn's shoulder. On the night of the draft lottery, she'd overhead Win mention arrangements with Stu and Laura, who lived in London. Adrian had also talked about moving there last spring. The road map of their lives seemed pointed in that direction. Yet their plans appeared shrouded in secrecy, alluded to and then dropped.

But now was not the time to ask questions. Shawn, steeped in misery, needed someone to listen. "Of course, everyone tries to be cool and not say anything about my being sick," Shawn continued. "We have a dream and no one wants to bring it down.

But I really thought I'd get back to normal and start playing again. But the fucking quacks, I'm sorry, I mean the doctors, tell me I'm lucky I've stayed the same." She began to sob uncontrollably.

Not knowing what to say, Julia pulled her close and stroked her silky platinum hair. Shawn smelled of patchouli and a little bit like the animals she cared for. Julia wished she had the courage to tell Shawn she was beautiful and kind-hearted and things would work out for her, no matter what happened. But she didn't know Shawn well enough and getting in her confidence had been a matter of being in the right place at the wrong time. So she kept silent.

Finally Shawn grew quiet, and Julia asked softly, "Will you be able to finish school?"

"I think so. The damage has already been done, but my doctor is putting me on antibiotics in case the infection starts spreading again."

"So why do you think the disease could be fatal? It sounds like they have it under control."

"I don't know. I'm just so upset..." She drew a long, shuddering breath. "Actually, the Johns Hopkins guys are leaning towards a diagnosis of Histoplasmosis, the less serious infection. Mostly because my condition's been pretty stable since summer. And the fungus is found around the Ohio Valley, near where I grew up. So maybe I'm making it worse than it really is."

"You probably are," Julia found herself echoing her father. "Sometimes when you get bad news, you paint it blacker. Then you feel better when it's not the absolute pits."

"How come you know so much about this stuff? Oh, yes. Doctor's daughter."

"The psych courses help, too. I enjoy them, although they're not what I really want."

"Do we ever get what we want? When I was younger, I used to dream of becoming another Emily Dickinson. 'Dreams are but fragile bubbles, broken in an instant by thoughtless reality,'" Shawn's tone held an edge of self-mockery, so she obviously felt better.

"That's not bad. Ever thought of changing your major to English?" Why didn't Shawn realize she could do nearly anything she wanted, once she made up her mind? It was just that she hadn't yet tapped into the centrifugal force governing her life.

"There aren't any blind poets in the twentieth century." Shawn's composure settled back over her like a comfortable blanket. Julia hoped she'd said and done the right thing; with Shawn, it was difficult to tell. "Thanks for listening to my tale of woe, Julia. I guess I'll have to find other dreams, although Janis Joplin says, 'Don't compromise yourself.'"

"Only rock stars can afford to make such rash statements."

"Perhaps, but compromise often means selling out." Shawn looked her over thoughtfully. "Want to come back to the house and have dinner?"

How wonderful to talk to Louie and listen to Jake's off-color jokes and Kirsten's outrageous observations. She'd ask about Win and how he was mending. But she couldn't. "I made plans with Valerie. We haven't seen each other all quarter. Otherwise, I'd invite you to join us."

"No thanks," Shawn seemed to withdraw at the mention of Valerie's name. "Some other day, perhaps."

Translation: maybe never, Julia thought. Shawn was being polite, showing appreciation for sympathy rendered. The tiny opening in their magic circle closed back up. Julia wanted to weep with frustration. She'd never get in, no matter how hard she tried.

"There you are!" Valerie burst into the small room, making it almost claustrophic with her extreme irritation. "I've been searching all over for you, Julia! Those goddamn motherfuckers shut down rehearsal! Oh hi, Shawn," she added.

"Hi yourself, Valerie. I could've told you that this afternoon. Dr. Portman said he got a call from Dean Moreland ordering you guys to put your clothes back on or forget the play and take an F."

"What's this all about?" Julia asked.

Shawn opened her mouth to explain, but Valerie exploded with anger. "That sucks! They can stick it up their asses! I'm going to the ACLU...."

"I doubt the American Civil Liberties Union's going to be interested in a bunch of bare-assed theatre majors," Shawn remarked drily. "What point were you trying to make anyway? It's just an experimental skit that hardly anyone's going to see."

"There doesn't have to be a point! We can do what we want, when we want. They make us fight their war, and they don't even give us the right to vote 'til we're 21...."

"What *I* can't figure out is how Moreland heard about the nudity in Adrian's skit in the first place." Shawn speculated. "Except for me and Kirsten, no one outside the cast knew about it."

"Well, *someone* told him," Looking to vent her fury, Valerie turned to Shawn. "In fact, some motherfucker's been ratting on us all year." She whirled back around to face Julia. "Wasn't Shawn at the SMC meeting when you decided to make that appointment with Moreland? And she lives in the same house as Louie...."

"You're not implying that I..." For a moment, Julia thought Shawn was going to break down again, but she drew herself up ramrod-straight. "If you are, I demand an apology, Valerie."

"If the shoe fits, chickie," Valerie shrugged.

"Now just a minute, Valerie, "Julia objected. "Shawn would never betray a confidence." Julia couldn't believe Valerie would consider such a thing. What was wrong with her, anyway?

"Know what, Valerie?" Shawn's voice was soft and sweet with an undercurrent of acid. "You're full of shit." She rose and walked out the door, closing it like a whisper behind her.

"Are you out of your mind?" Julia demanded, now almost as angry as Valerie. "Anybody with sense knows Shawn wouldn't fink on anyone."

"I think I'm going to split, Julia," Valerie yawned, not bothering to cover her mouth. "I don't feel like eating right now."

Julia lost her temper. "Jesus Christ, Valerie! You call me up when you're bummed out on drugs and accuse me of avoiding you. When I try to get together to see what the problem is, you shove me aside. Then you make unfounded accusations and alienate people I care about. Are you or are you not my friend? Even better, do I want you for my friend anymore?"

Valerie's stonewashed blue eyes grew wide with alarm; at last, a genuine reaction. "Hey, wait a minute, Julia..."

"No, you wait a minute! You say I'm different, but look in the mirror and see if you can recognize yourself. What happened to the girl who believed in nonviolence, who had a love of life and a sense of humor along with wanting to make the world better, more peaceful? All I see is hostility and hate. You vacuumed away your humanity along with your baby...." Horrified by her own words, Julia clapped her hand over her mouth. "I'm sorry. I didn't mean that."

Valerie stood pensively in front of the piano. Julia couldn't read her closed-in expression or interpret the silence surrounding her, a whirlwind of charged thoughts. Valerie was capable of anything and seconds ticked by, seemingly forever. Finally she looked up, her face inscrutable. "You know, Julia, you're right. I'm going to call Shawn tonight and apologize. But first I want to ask forgiveness from you, my dearest friend. I've only thought of myself these past few months...."

Now that she'd finally reached Valerie, Julia was anxious to get at what was really bothering her. "I understand your hurt over Richard and the abortion," she interrupted. "I'm no psychiatrist, but I think your pain is caused by something deeper. You even alluded to it last fall when we discussed Win."

Valerie's smile did not touch her eyes. "Once again you're right, Julia, you're not a shrink. But you *can* help. Come to the SDS meeting tomorrow night."

"What does this have to do with our friendship?" Julia was thoroughly confused.

"Everything. We'll be able to relate better if you understand where I'm coming from."

"But Valerie...." She wanted personal communication, not political collaboration.

"Look, I admit it, I'm one fucked-up chick. You're the one who has her shit together these days. And you can help us." She was animated for the first time in months. "Promise?"

"Well..." Would it restore her camaraderie with Valerie? Besides, Valerie had a point: Louie's Law Boards and a few inches of snow were no excuse to shut down the protest movement. They hadn't stopped sending boys into Vietnam and shipping body bags out. And her studies and Trevor weren't enough: not with the war still going on. It was simply a question of balancing her priorities. "I can split anytime?"

"Whatever. And don't worry about Adrian. He'll behave. Right now he's down on women 'cause Felix's balling a white chick. To say Adrian's jealous is an understatement." She glanced down at herself. "Ugh. I look like a slob! I'm going home to clean myself up. I'd invite you over, but I didn't tell my tenants the cockroaches you were coming. No matter, because after tonight, the gig is up." She mimicked a cockroach being machine gunned by a can of Raid.

This was the Valerie she remembered and loved. "That's OK, because Shawn and I were rapping and I didn't study like I was supposed to. So far, I've got all A's this quarter and want to keep it that way. So I'd better hit the books if I'm going to your meeting tomorrow night." She'd learned from her mistakes.

As Valerie gave her the time and address, Julia realized once again Valerie had drawn her into something she was unsure of. But it had always worked out for the best. And Valerie was nothing if not sincere. Besides, what harm could one meeting do?

CHAPTER SEVENTEEN

Julia had never experienced anything like the SDS meeting. Held in a run-down apartment at the edge of town — Julia never got the tenants' name — it consisted of about twenty-five radicals shouting at each other at the same time. Topics revolved around the unfair treatment of the few blacks on campus, separation of the sexes in dorms, worry over CIA infiltration, and proposed retaliation against the Administration's shutdown of Adrian's skit.

No one seemed to agree on anything and by the end of two hours, Julia had a headache from the noise and was convinced she'd caught a cold. She alternately sweated and froze in the shabby room with its boarded-up windows and sporadic space heater. She desperately wanted to go back to her warm, quiet room and lie down.

Although Julia didn't know anyone except for Valerie, Adrian, and Felix, people seemed to recognize *her*. Julia was treated with a consideration and respect not apparent in their relations with each other. Even Felix engaged her in a discussion about draft alternatives, listening to her opinions with grave thoughtfulness. But his eyes were as flat and cold as the icicles outside and he still made her uncomfortable.

How odd that, instead of trying to sell her on their ideology, the SDSers seemed so intent upon putting her at ease. She assumed it was because she was a newcomer — a "novitiate," as Valerie jokingly introduced her.

"You're not splitting, are you?" Valerie grasped her arm just as Julia, in her coat, tried to exit unnoticed. "Let's get high at Adrian's."

"No thanks, Valerie. I don't feel well. Really."

"Oh, wow, you're not still pissed at me are you?" Adrian joined them. "I've been civilized tonight, *n'est`ce pas?*" His tone was friendly but he brutalized the French expression and Julia repressed an urge to correct him.

To refuse would be tantamount to rejection, she realized. Exactly the opposite of what she wanted with Valerie. Besides, she might feel better once she was high. So Julia, Valerie, Felix, and Felix's girlfriend, an anemic-looking redhead called Moonstone, piled into Adrian's creaky black Volvo. Everyone cheered when Adrian finally managed to start the car after several coughing and sputtering attempts. They discussed innocuous topics: the exceptionally frigid weather, getting Moonstone a pair of boots from the Salvation Army store in Hamilton. Perhaps I've been too harsh in judging the SDS people, Julia thought as they drove through the gently rolling winterscape. Except for Adrian and Valerie, I never gave them a chance.

Adrian's farmhouse was only a mile or so out of town, and it was spacious and clean, with Early American decor and wall tapestries and throw rugs. While Felix and Moonstone disappeared upstairs, Adrian played the gracious host, plumping up pillows, fussing over a few discarded items that happened to be lying around. "Can I get you anything to drink?" he asked Julia.

She couldn't resist jibing him. "A Tab, please. You know, the stuff that comes in a pink can?"

Valerie hooted with laughter while Adrian scowled. "Very funny, Julia. Keep it down, Valerie." He glanced at the ceiling. "We don't want to disturb the lovebirds." Julia waited for his usual innuendo, but none was forthcoming. Instead he looked sad.

Despite her anger at him over the past months, she felt a surge of pity. She knew about unrequited love. "Why don't you just kick them out? It's your place, Adrian."

Valerie cast her a warning glance. "It's not all that simple. Nothing's ever clear-cut, as tonight's meeting showed."

"Clear-cut? It was the most chaotic gathering I've ever seen!"

"Actually, we accomplished a lot," Adrian bent down to fumble with the plastic tubing on a bong. "Have you seen the THC, Valerie?"

"I think it's in the bathroom on the shelf by the sink."

"I'll be back in a flash." He disappeared around the corner.

"So are you ready to join us?" Valerie asked. The way she jiggled her knee revealed it was not a casual question.

"How can I make a decision based on a single meeting?" Once again, Julia was put in the uncomfortable position of wanting to spare Valerie's feelings. Only this time it was not over an outfit worn to a wedding. But Valerie had been on target then, too. "I'd like to know what I'm getting into."

"Trevor's pants, I hope," Adrian returned, holding a plastic bag with a small, bricklike substance inside. "That's his name isn't it? He's not bad-looking in an Aryan neofacist sort of way."

Warmth crept up her neck as she remembered Trevor's fingers brushing against her nipples. What exquisite agony it was to have a man's tongue licking her breasts! It was a prelude to a final uncoiling, an ultimate release she and Trevor hadn't yet achieved. But Adrian had chosen the worst possible description. "I'd rather you not use the word 'Aryan,'" she said uncomfortably. "My mother's family was killed by Nazis."

Oh, wow, what a bummer. Well, I was only making a joke." He shrugged. Why had she never before noticed that Adrian was oblivious to everything but his own problems?

They began to smoke. Julia took minute puffs. A concentrated form of marijuana, THC was several times stronger than grass. But the drug still alleviated her headache, and she found herself fantasizing about Trevor. Or rather, sex with Trevor. This Saturday, they planned to touch each other underneath their pants. Actually he'd been going too slowly, holding back because of the required ten day waiting period for the birth control pills she'd started taking. But she'd already been on the Pill two weeks and they could really lose their inhibitions. She wondered if her recent headaches were a side effect.

"This is great stuff," Adrian's eyelids were heavy from the dope as he laid the empty bong on the floor.

"How do you feel?" Valerie asked Julia. Neither girl had smoked as much as Adrian.

Horny as hell, Julia wanted to reply, but the last thing she needed was another discussion about her much-maligned virginity. "Out of it. You know. I don't mean *you're* out of it, Valerie." She giggled. "I think I better stop toking before I become totally incoherent."

"Hey, you seem to have things under control," Valerie gazed at Julia through steepled fingers. "You know, Julia, you have an in with everyone. The SMC. The Greekoids. And now us."

"Me? I hardly know anybody! You introduced me tonight, remember?"

"Think about it. You and Trevor-baby go to all the right parties. You lunch at the Student Center with your ex-sisters. Do you realize the YAF has recruited over 500 new members this quarter?"

And what had the protesters been doing? Julia wondered. "I believe you. Lydia practically runs it, you know. She's Trevor's ex-pinmate, so his brothers keep him informed, whether he wants to hear about it or not." The SMC better get organized, she thought.

"Look Julia, you've come a long way since September," Valerie rubbed her lower lip with her thumb. "So I'm gonna be upfront with you. Fascist pigs have been spying on us all year, reporting SDS and SMC activities to the Administration. We don't know who the leak is, but we'll find out. And two can play the game."

"What are you getting at?" Despite the dulling effects of the grass, a warning signal fluttered from her stomach to her brain.

"You're a smart girl, Julia," Adrian interjected. "*You* figure it out." His words rang with confidence.

Suddenly she no longer felt high. Tonight had been a setup. The SDSers had been nice to her for one reason only: to manipulate her for their own ends. "You want me to spy on the Greeks?" She was incredulous. "Some of them are my friends!"

"Hey, we don't give a shit about their personal lives," Valerie said. "We just want to know their plan of action. Even you admit the YAF has gained a big foothold. Do you want it to smother the protest movement?"

"You mean the Revolution," Adrian amended. "Ho Ho Ho Chi Minh. N.L.F. is going to win."

"Now wait a minute, you two!" Julia cried. "I certainly don't support the Communist Liberation Front."

"It's the National Liberation Front," Adrian corrected, glaring at her with bleary, slitted eyes. "And they are among the most politically astute...."

"Shut up, Adrian!" Valerie snapped. "That has nothing to do with this discussion. You're really ripped, anyway. Go crash."

"Oh, wow, Valerie, it's only my house." But he ambled upstairs, singing "Power to the People."

For a few minutes, the two young women sat in silence. Valerie kept playing with her lower lip, her shoulders hunched. Every instinct told Julia to turn Valerie down, to say she could never do anything so deceitful. But once again, Julia could see Valerie's point. The campus was engaged in a war of its own and the protesters were losing, at least right now. They needed an advantage.

Finally Valerie spoke. "Look, Julia I'm not gonna try to persuade you. I know ideologically I'm farther to the left than you. But we're both after the same goals. To end Vietnam. To prevent more needless killing. And the SMC isn't doing a fucking thing."

But that didn't mean it couldn't. "Let's contact Louie," she urged, hoping for an easier solution. "Even you admit he's brilliant. He'll think of something once he knows there's a problem."

"He's smart, all right. All he cares about is getting perfect scores on his Law Boards."

"I don't believe that. Louie would do anything to stop the war."

"Oh, would he? Well, listen to this. Moreland put Adrian, myself, and five other people on social probation because of our nude rehearsals. We went to Louie to ask for bread from the SMC

Defense Fund. We wanted to hire a lawyer to fight the Administration. He turned us down, with some bullshit dialogue about our case not standing up in court."

"He could be right, Valerie. After all, he's studying to be a lawyer...."

"That's crap! We're talking about repression here, a denial of basic freedoms! We hadn't even put on the play yet, yet somehow the Administration knew. And we have no recourse, no line of defense."

Julia buried her face in her hands. "Oh God, Valerie," she groaned. "Why me?"

"God is dead, but *you* are in a position to help us. If things continue this way, the movement will be pushed back further than even before the May Music Fest last spring."

Shawn's statement about compromise came back to Julia. Like Janis Joplin, Valerie was unwilling to back off — right or wrong, she stood up for what she believed. On the other hand, Julia had remained in the sidelines, shying away from direct confrontations, using her parents or her studies as a shield.

Even after all these months of commitment to the protest movement, in a sense she was still hiding. Now she had a chance to make a contribution, albeit a risky one. She thought of the unspeakable horrors endured by Louie and other veterans and soldiers. And what about radicals who'd been brutally beaten in demonstrations? How could she in good conscience say no, when her services were so desperately needed?

Her seaforest eyes locked onto Valerie's. "All right, Valerie. I'll try it. But I can't promise anything."

"Far fuckin' out!" Valerie leaned over and hugged her. "Don't tell anyone — not even Trevor-baby!"

"Are you crazy? If anyone finds out, I'll be pilloried, tarred and feathered!" She moaned again. "That means I'll have to attend YAF meetings and face Lydia. Maybe I should wear a disguise."

"Hell, no, Julia." Valerie advised. "Flaunt it. Imply you're turning right wing. That way they'll draw you in even more because they'll think you can tell them about *us*. It's an old Maoist tactic."

In spite of her doubts, Julia grinned, finding the role of heroine/spy intriguing, almost romantic. She and Valerie talked far into the night, planning their strategy. Their closeness had been reestablished, but on Valerie's terms.

CHAPTER EIGHTEEN

Actually, spying was boring. The only cloak-and-dagger aspect occurred when Julia made her "drops" of YAF minutes at a corner desk on the second floor of the library. She'd phone Valerie, who'd finally got her line in working order, or Adrian the day before with the time. She assumed they got the information, although she never saw anyone retrieve it.

Even YAF meetings seemed uneventful. Mostly everyone accepted Julia's explanation that the protesters had become too reactionary and she wanted to prevent future campus violence. Only Lydia cast her baleful looks and made sly comments. But because of Julia's relationship with Trevor, people interpreted Lydia's reaction as jealousy.

As February dragged into March, Julia became convinced the conservatives knew no more about the protesters than the radicals did about the YAF. Both groups regarded each other with equal enmity -- what the conservatives called "bullies and hoodlums" and "effete, intellectual slobs," the radicals had profanity for. And issues were highly charged, based on whatever facts a side chose. The right was as muddied as the left.

She tried to explain this to Valerie when Valerie called an emergency meeting behind the Campus Ministry building one subzero evening.

Valerie shook her head vehemently. "They don't trust you yet, Julia. They haven't let you into their inner circle."

"I don't think there *is* one, Valerie! The only real fanatic is Lydia, and she's been practically kicked out of the sorority because she's become so political...."

"Look, I didn't come out here to freeze my ass off and gossip about BGP. I wanted to tell you that my phone is tapped, so use a code when you call."

This was the stuff of James Bond movies, and seemed out of place at humdrum Hayes. Julia chuckled. "Valerie, you're getting as paranoid as Nixon. Who on earth would want to listen to your conversations?"

"The CIA, of course! Do you think I'm joking? I hear fucking clicks on my line every time I pick up the receiver."

"My phone clicks too, especially in this cold weather. I don't want to hurt your feelings, Valerie, but I think you're overreacting. It's not like you're building bombs or anything. And the campus has been quiet all quarter."

"Don't argue. Just do as I ask."

Julia shivered, and not totally because she was chilly. She'd come to realize there was a side to Valerie she knew nothing about. It was as if the abortion and rejection of Richard had released a subterranean rage. She still hoped Valerie would open up to her, although she dreaded her friend's reaction to her next words, "I needed to rap with you anyway. Finals are coming up and I won't have time to attend any more YAF meetings. And in the spring, I'm planning on becoming active again in the SMC. Besides, I don't feel right about sneaking around."

"OK, OK," Valerie replied impatiently. She wasn't even upset! "Just do me one last favor before you drop out of the YAF. Attend their big rally Thursday night. As you know, Moreland's the featured speaker. The topic's making Hayes safe for democracy or some imperialist shit like that. We need a head count, along with knowing what he said."

"Thursday night's my weekday date with Trevor," Julia objected. "You know how bored he is with politics. He doesn't even understand why I'm involved."

"Drag him along anyway. Once he sees you next to candy-assed Lydia, for sure he'll give you his fraternity pin."

"Oh, Valerie, that's not what I want." Once the initial excitement of discovering she was passionate had passed, sex with Trevor had become somewhat routine. And they still hadn't yet fully made love, much to Julia's frustration and bewilderment. For some reason, Trevor was in no hurry, preferring to satisfy their urges through mutual masturbation. "If I'd been dating him this time last year, I would have been ecstatic." Julia admitted. "But I'm not ready to settle down." And what does it mean when you have to fantasize about one boy to feel something with another? She didn't dare put that question to Valerie.

"Look, it's not important whether he goes or not. Just don't back out on me again."

Would Valerie ever stop guilt-tripping her about her failure to accompany her to New York? "All right, I'll be there. But this is the last time."

"Thanks Julia. You may not realize it, but you've been an incredible help." Two students strolled by and glanced in their direction. Valerie pulled up the lapels of her pea jacket in an attempt to disguise her face. "I have to split before someone sees me. Call me and say, 'The parrot lands at 9' or whatever time you want to leave your notes."

Julia had to giggle at Valerie's intensity. "Whatever you say, 007."

"Look Trev, it's just one meeting," Julia and Trevor stood in the lobby of Miami Hall on Thursday night. He looked especially handsome in a brown crew neck sweater and tan slacks which brought out the caramel color in his eyes. Expecting an argument, she put her arms around him, smoothing the short hairs at the nape of his neck. "I know you like the Boar's Head." Julia despised the place, with its blaring music and fraternity guys bombed on 3.2 beer. Even the Greeks called it the Whore's Bed, a more appropriate name. "The rally will be short, so we can go there afterwards," she placated.

Trevor gazed up at the multi-tiered stairway leading to the girls' suites. "Look at that pattern on the ceiling. Do you think it's part of the original building or was it added on later?"

What was the matter with him tonight, anyway? She'd volunteered to accompany him to his favorite bar and he ignored her. "Quit changing the subject, Trevor. I'm going to the rally, no matter what you say. I can meet you later at the Boar's Head if you'd like."

"I'm yours, baby. Whatever you want, I'll do." Absently Trevor patted her rear end. He seemed uncharacteristically preoccupied. "I need to discuss something important with you, but it'll just have to keep 'til afterwards." He smiled at Julia, as if hoping to pique her curiosity.

Before she could even think to ask, a familiar voice exclaimed, "Hey, Julia! How's it hanging?" and Julia turned to see Jake leering at her good-naturedly. His freak flag of a hairstyle, which he'd let grow even longer, flew in all directions, a whirligig of black curlicues spiraling down his back. His too-tight bellbottom jeans revealed a slender but well-proportioned physique. Julia sighed wistfully: like Win, Jake had a great body.

"Got a hot date, huh? Me, too." Jake picked up the lobby phone and began to dial.

Time and separation had not diminished her feelings for Win, although Julia had struggled to bury them. "Let's split, Trev." Suddenly uncomfortable, Julia hurried towards the exit.

"Who's *that* hippie?" Trevor demanded, his full attention restored.

"Someone I met at the SMC last fall," Without waiting for Trevor, Julia pushed open the door, praying Jake and his girl wouldn't be leaving at the same time. The last thing she wanted was a conversation about Win, although she constantly wondered when he was coming back to Hayes.

"You seem to be friendly with a lot of those weirdos. And they like you, too." Although he usually spoke about superficial things, Trevor occasionally exhibited moments of perceptiveness. Just last week, they'd encountered Louie eating pizza at Mario's. Louie had merely smiled and waved, but Trevor wanted to know about him also.

"I told you, I'm not active this quarter. I joined the YAF to hear their side of the story." In the broadest sense, it was true. Sort of.

The rally was held at Harding Auditorium. A volunteer passed out pencils and blank sheets of paper at the entrance, saying they would be needed later on in the program.

Julia and Trevor slid into a back row. Why sit in front, where Lydia could see them? Besides, if previous meetings were any indication, she and Trevor could slip out early and not miss a thing. Thank goodness her stint with the YAF was nearly over.

Nearly every chair in the huge auditorium was filled. Although much of the campus had adopted the scruffy look this year, only clean-cut types were present tonight. A good portion of the group consisted of townspeople -- middle-aged men in slacks and work shirts; construction workers wearing hard hats as a statement to their political beliefs. Others closer to Julia and Trevor's age were dressed for the office; the women wore subdued makeup, low heels, and inexpensive jewelry; the men had on neatly pressed bellbottoms and button down shirts.

Julia felt sick. It might as well be 1964, when Johnson sat smugly in the White House and the war machine was just beginning to vomit out its bloody putrescence of American boys. What was she doing here?

Her mood worsened during Dean Moreland's speech. According to him, the campus had gone to "hell in a handbasket," which drew appreciative murmurs from the crowd. The overall grade average of students was slipping; alumni donations had fallen; major projects had ground to a standstill because of fear of disruptions. Not only would this hurt the college, but businesses in town as well, as many who were here tonight were undoubtedly aware. Drastic, immediate action had to be taken.

"Give me your input on the sheets handed to you at the beginning of this program," Moreland told the group. "I'll call an emergency meeting of the Board of Trustees and push through the best suggestions, in the interests of town-gown relations. My surprise approach will overcome those who bow to the shrieking minority." Despite his play on Nixon's "silent majority" and the subsequent laughter, Julia knew he was referring to President Carrell. "We'll have a plan of action in place before Spring Quarter, when protests begin in earnest," Moreland concluded to enthusiastic applause.

The papers been left blank, so sly Moreland couldn't incriminate himself should his plan be discovered. As the audience scribbled, Julia realized Moreland was using his position as Dean of Students to achieve his own ends. He regarded the protesters as a personal affront to "his" university and seemed willing to do anything to stop them, even undermine Carrell who was trying to be fair. Yet she was beginning to understand this sort of duplicity was common in both the YAF and SDS.

Julia shifted anxiously in her seat. Forget Valerie, she thought. I'll call Louie as soon the meeting's over. He'll contact the president and tell him about this. Moreland has to be stopped before things go any further.

Volunteers began to collect the papers from the back of the room. Trevor took Julia's hand. "I'm bored as hell," he said. "You are, too, from the way you've been squirming. Can we leave now?" He tickled her palm, a supposedly erotic gesture which left her unmoved.

Julia sighed. Trevor had no concept of what was transpiring, nor did he seem to care. "What if this group and others like it are successful?" she demanded, attempting to stir up his conscience. "What if they squelch the protests, and the government continues to escalate the war? You'll be drafted, no matter what your lottery number." Trevor had refused to tell her, unwilling to enter into any discussion about Vietnam.

"I HEARD THAT, YOU TRAITOR!" Someone screamed in Julia's ear and she and Trevor leapt apart. "We have a spy in our midst!" Lydia stood in the aisle behind Julia and Trevor, pointing at Julia.

The entire auditorium turned to stare. With a groan, Trevor buried his head in his arms. Julia sat immobilized, thinking, this can't be happening. They can't be talking about *me*.

"You remember this girl, don't you Dean Moreland?" The gleam in Lydia's eyes said she'd been waiting for this moment for a long, long time.

"Yes, I believe I do," Moreland squinted at Julia in exaggerated recognition. "Her name is Julia Brandon," he informed the group. "She belongs to the SMC and the SDS. She made an appointment with me last fall under false pretenses. And now she's involved with the YAF under those same pretenses so she can inform the troublemakers of our activities."

They'd been watching her all along.... Valerie had been right about a small group being on the inside, trying to control events. But like Julia's understanding of Dean Moreland's motives, the knowledge came too late.

Pale and trembling, Julia rose in her seat. She'd walk out of here with her dignity intact and return to the SMC. No more spying for her, no matter what the reasons. She knew where she belonged.

Refusing to glance at Trevor — she didn't want to drag him into this — she edged towards the aisle. At least he could escape unscathed. "Not so fast, Julia," Now it's my turn, Lydia's pasty expression said. She was going to get even for all those slights, real and imagined, and especially for losing Trevor. "You've got to face the consequences of your actions."

"What consequences?" Julia retorted, repelled by Lydia's malice. She hadn't broken any rules or hurt anyone. The worst they could say of her was she'd passed information from one group to another, conversations that were a matter of public knowledge and not personal. "What can you do to me?" Despite her attempt to sound brave, the question came out sounding defiant.

She'd handed them their opening. "Kick her ass out of school!" a man shouted.

"We don't want any of you Communist troublemakers on campus!" A girl cried.

Julia stared at the sea of hostile faces. How would Louie handle this? Certainly not turn and flee from the room, which was what she'd initially planned. She'd be playing right along with Lydia and Moreland. There had to be a way to use this predicament to her advantage.

"Leave her alone, Lydia!" Trevor stood up and pulled at Julia's arm. "It's just like you to pull a stunt like this! Let's go, Julia."

"No. I'm not going to run away," Julia announced, her feet planted apart. "Even though I've been dishonest, you have too, Dean Moreland, by trying to stop the protest movement behind the President's and Board of Trustees' back...."

"We don't want you here, pinko!" Someone exclaimed, and the crowd began to chant "Go! Go! Go!" as pencils and papers flew in their direction.

"You don't understand! If we'd all quit acting like children and calling each other names, we could unite and end this lousy war...." This created a fresh roar of rage. A pencil hit Julia in the face, narrowly missing her eye.

Seizing Julia by the waist, Trevor started to drag her from the auditorium. Lydia leaned towards her and spat in her face.

"Oh, God...." God is dead, Valerie's voice whispered in Julia's mind. Horrified, she wiped the spittle off her cheek. It was wet and slimy, like an earthworm she'd once handled as a child.

"You stupid, jealous bitch," Trevor snarled at Lydia. "She's my girl and you just can't stand it so you have to make up lies!"

"They're not lies!" Lydia screamed. Julia and Trevor ran towards the exit. "She's playing you for a fool!"

Once outside, Trevor seized Julia by the shoulders and shook her. "Are you crazy?" he demanded. "What were you doing, arguing with a mob?"

Julia pulled away. Huddling against the stone archway that led to the sidewalk, she caressed her cheek. The spittle was nearly dry, but she could still feel the burn of the crowd's collective hatred. "Go home, Trev," she said dully. She'd been a fool to think she could persuade that group towards a balanced way of thinking. She'd been even more of an ass in letting Valerie and Adrian take advantage of her. It was time to trust her own feelings, at least when it came to politics.

Trevor towered in front of her. "What do you mean, go home? I'm not some casual acquaintance you can just send away. I'm in love with you, Julia." He leaned over to kiss her.

The word "love" didn't quite register. She knew Trevor liked her, wanted to go to bed with her, but love never entered her mind. She needed time to think.

Gently she pushed him aside. "You don't understand. I didn't myself until tonight. There's a core of people who want to destroy the protest movement. They're trying to set us against each other so we won't unite. But I think I halted them, at least for now. Moreland won't try anything, now that he's been exposed."

"Then Lydia wasn't fibbing. You *did* spy on the YAF. How could you be so stupid?" Instead of being angry, Trevor stared at her, frightened. "You didn't fake your affection for me, did you?"

If only Trevor were Win.... Yet Trevor had been good to her and she so much wanted to reciprocate his feelings. "Of course not, Trev," she said, glad for the darkness that hid her guilt. "It's just so difficult...." She began to weep in confusion and as a delayed reaction to the group's hostility.

Trevor embraced her, back on the familiar masculine territory of comforting a helpless female. "Now, now, baby. You know I hate to see my girl cry. It'll all work out." He sounded almost cheerful. "Besides, I bet everyone will think Lydia's pissed off because I was planning on asking you to marry me."

"What?" Julia froze, immobilized with shock. Had she heard right? Trevor was *proposing*?

"Why do you think I held back making love to you all these weeks? Do you think I enjoy celibacy? I respect you and wanted to wait until we were engaged." Placing his hands underneath her bulky sweater, he began to kiss her, his tongue roaming in her mouth.

She tolerated it for a few seconds — she never really enjoyed French kissing — and disentangled herself, replying, "But Trev, you never said a word to me. I had no idea...."

"It's a given, baby. You should know me well enough by now to understand I play for keeps." He looked at her almost slyly. "Don't tell me you want to face the big, bad world all by yourself, Julia. I'll even hang around campus for a couple of extra quarters 'til you get your degree."

"Trevor, this is totally unexpected." Couldn't he see the outrageousness of what he was suggesting? A lifetime together when they barely knew each other?

"Well, it's supposed to be a surprise," Trevor replied in what Julia mentally termed as his "aw shucks" demeanor. "These weren't exactly the conditions I'd hoped for, though." Gently he guided her towards the Sigma Chi house. "I thought we'd have a nice, romantic evening. Go back to the room for a little kissy-face, then I'd pop the question. Oh, well...." He reached for the inside pocket of his jacket. Was he going to give her a ring? Julia recoiled in dismay.

"Trev, let's think about this," she said, trying not to panic. "Some really nasty things went down tonight and your brothers might feel differently about me. You don't want to be involved with a outcast."

"Once we're engaged, you won't have time for that stuff," Again he wasn't listening. "You'll come home with me over Easter break, then we'll pick out a ring." Trevor came from nearby Hamilton so he made frequent trips back and forth. He pulled out several small metal circles. "Let me size your finger so I can tell Uncle Dan — he's a jeweler — what to look for."

At least he hadn't purchased a ring! Julia shoved her hands inside the pocket of her maxicoat. "But Trev, it's too sudden."

"I guess you need time to get used to the idea," Trevor conceded. "If it makes you feel better, you can give me your final OK at the Winter Ball next weekend. We'll keep it under wraps 'til then. Want to come back to the room?"

They paused in front of Fraternity Row. The Sigma Chi house loomed ahead, the tallest, most impressive building on the block. It seemed almost Teutonic with its dual-leveled porches and concrete Doric columns. Who was she, a simple Jewish girl from Columbus, to defy this bastion of Hayes tradition?

"No thanks, Trev. I want to be by myself. You don't mind, do you?"

"You sure? You still seem pretty shaken up."

"No, honest. I'm fine now." They kissed good-night, and Trevor disappeared inside the house, whistling and jiggling the jewelry sizers in his jacket.

Although she'd gotten into trouble, at least she'd put a temporary wrench in Moreland's machinations. And despite everything that had happened, Trevor wanted to marry her. Dare she refuse one of life's winners?

CHAPTER NINETEEN

Yet Julia took no action. She knew what she needed to do — tell Trevor her true feelings, confront Valerie with her refusal to no longer be manipulated, warn Louie about Dean Moreland's subterfuges. Yet the consequences might be dreadful, so she held back. The inertia was more insidious than fear, making her feel like a robot with only strung-up wires and microchips instead of a soul.

On the evening of the Sigma Chi Winter Ball, Julia stared at herself in the full-length mirror on her bathroom door. Her floor-length turquoise formal looked fine, heightening the coloring in her fair skin and dark hair. It hugged her figure, which now bordered on the voluptuous, thanks to water gain from those damn birth control pills.

But she was only thinking about her face. What would it look like after twenty years of marriage to Trevor? Already her eyes had lost their sparkle and her mouth seemed permanently turned down. At twenty-two, she felt like her life was over.

Yet a part of her wanted to be loved and cherished, the idealized, virtuous woman symbolized by TV characters like Donna Reed and June Cleaver. Trevor reminded her of their husbands: well-meaning, steady, offering security and stability yet no emotional closeness. Once they got over the fact that he wasn't Jewish, her parents would surely like Trevor. Didn't he stand for the kind of existence they believed in?

She wondered if she lacked something and expected too much from a relationship. Was Trevor's love the best future she could have? Would she regret turning away from it?

"Julia? Are you in the bathroom?" Her suitemate Janine pounded on the door. "Your phone's ringing."

Dashing towards her room, Julia grabbed the receiver, only to hear the clear hum of a dial tone. It had to be Trevor, even though he was a few minutes early. Not wanting to risk his annoyance at having to wait, she gathered her wrap, an elaborately embroidered shawl borrowed from another suitemate, and hurried into the lobby. At least it was balmier tonight and she wouldn't have to struggle with her maxicoat.

Trevor came walking in just as Julia caught a quick glimpse of a tall, russet-haired figure striding through the outside door. It can't be, she thought, her heart thudding uncontrollably. Win was still laid up; she'd mailed the last batch of lecture notes today.

"Nothing I like better than a woman who's on time," Trevor remarked as he awkwardly helped Julia with her shawl. He seemed to be hiding something behind his coat.

Diane, the resident adviser, approached them. "Someone just left this for you," she told Julia, handing her an oblong cardboard box.

"For me?" Julia said, flustered. Even seeing someone who resembled Win had unnerved her; how could she seriously consider spending her life with Trevor?

"You must be mistaken," Trevor said, pulling out a clear box with an orchid inside." Julia's corsage is right here."

For a girl who'd never been asked to her senior prom, she should have been swept away. But somehow the gesture — all the girls would be wearing flowers tonight — only made her feel more guilty. As Trevor put the orchid on her wrist, she turned to Diane. "That must be for someone else. Look inside; there's probably a card."

Diane started to say something, then thought the better of it. She glanced from Julia to Trevor and back. "Whatever. But if there's no card, I get to keep the flowers."

Julia drank four Harvey Wallbangers at the party. Finally Trevor, no modest tippler himself, warned, "Go easy on those, honey. You have to be at least a little sober for our announcement tonight."

No I don't, because there won't be one, Julia thought rebelliously. "Let's go to your room, Trevor-baby." She knew she was being louder than necessary, but was too drunk to care. All these people were two-faced anyway, pretending as though the confrontation at the YAF rally never happened. But she noticed them staring at her when they thought she was otherwise occupied.

She had to get him alone, to tell him she couldn't marry him. And he wasn't moving. She cupped her hand over his ear. "There's something we need to do by ourselves," she breathed. She owed it to him to have the discussion in private.

Trevor turned bright red. "I've been thinking about getting you alone all night!"

Clinching her firmly by the waist, he guided her through the ballroom. Elaborately dressed couples danced frantically to "Eli's Coming" by Three Dog Night. How prophetic, she reflected. Uncle Sam is just waiting for them to graduate or flunk out so he can show up with the induction notice.

"I knew this would be a special night," Trevor's caramel eyes glowed like a cat's when they arrived upstairs. "So Fast Eddie lent me his pad." But what did Betsy's fiancé's room have that Trevor's did not? Being a senior, he lived alone, so no one would interrupt them.

Trevor opened the door proudly, revealing the tackiest potpourri of cheap furniture Julia had ever seen. In the left corner stood an aluminum-plated naugahyde bar over which hung a mirrored, framed picture of two huge breasts. Magenta carpeting splashed across the floor and a black and white zebra fur stretched over the bed. Posters of naked women in various erotic poses adorned the walls.

"I can't think of a sexier place to be initiated into the garden of earthly delights," Trevor said, slamming and locking the door. "You've wanted me all these months. Now you're going to get me." He began to peel off his clothes.

Julia stood aghast. How could she tell Trevor she couldn't marry him, when she'd done nothing but encourage him sexually? It seemed too cruel to say something now. Besides, she'd wanted to be rid of that albatross, her virginity, for a long time.

And who was she saving herself for, Win? In her intoxicated state, she could almost hear Valerie mocking her. At least Trevor cared about her. And maybe, just maybe, making love with him would change things.

Slowly Julia began to unzip her dress. And even if it didn't, he wouldn't be so hurt, knowing he'd been the first.

"Let me do that, baby," Down to his boxer shorts, Trevor reached for the back of her gown. "Herman and the twins can't wait much longer."

Originally Julia had been amused by Trevor's nickname for his private parts, but now it merely seemed stupid. "I can do it myself," she retorted. Yanking off her formal and slip, she began unhooking her strapless bra.

"Please, Julia, oh please," Trevor leapt on her like a dog ravishing a steak, nearly tearing off the rest of her underwear. "You're so sexy." He buried his face in her breasts which were made full and tender by the Pill. "Even though you've put on a little weight this quarter. But that's good," he added hastily. "I like my women plumper." While sucking her on nipple, he slapped her rear end.

What happened to the hours of foreplay, the stroking of breasts and thighs that had brought her to the brink of tantalizing sensation? Why had she never before noticed his beanpole legs, his narrow, hairless chest? Had she been too caught up in her own fantasies to pay attention to what *he* was like?

But it was too late. He had thrown off the black and white travesty of a cover and pulled her on the bed. He began to poke, prod, and lick, and with horror, Julia realized she'd made the worst mistake of her life. She should have waited until she found someone she truly loved....

She was to about to cry out for him to cease when he suddenly inserted himself inside her. She shrieked in surprise — it hurt like hell — and Trevor exclaimed, "I knew you'd love it baby!" and began to move rapidly back and forth.

Stop, stop, she screamed inwardly as he filled her shocked and battered vagina. Leave me alone! Fortunately, after a half-dozen such thrusts, he bellowed like a bull, collapsing in a spasm of wetness.

Julia was disgusted. *This* was what Valerie and the others raved about? It was painful, it was gross, not to mention messy. Not doing *this* was what set her apart from everybody else?

"That was good, baby, real good." Trevor pulled away and began to wipe off his limp penis with a towel, presumably left under the bed for such purposes. He glanced at the rumpled sheet, grunting in satisfaction at the red stain there. "So I was right. No one believed me when I told them you were a virgin."

His callousness enraged her. She'd given him something she'd never be able to give anyone again. He violated her physically and now mentally. "So what are you going to do?" she demanded. "Parade the sheet around the Sigma Chi house for all to see?"

"Don't be ridiculous, Julia. It's just that nice girls don't usually associate with undesirable elements or cause near-riots. It gives them a bad reputation."

How dare he put her down for wanting to stop the senseless killing in Vietnam? He was spoiled and pampered and could undoubtedly maneuver his way out of the war anytime he wanted. Who was he to condemn her beliefs?

She grabbed for her dress and bra, hastily putting them on, nearly breaking the zipper halfway up. "Well, Trevor-baby, I'm gonna beat you to it." Seizing the stained sheet, she started for the door. "Gather 'round brothers, I've got a real flash," she shouted. "The last cherry at Hayes has finally been popped!"

"Jesus Christ, Julia!" Still naked, Trevor tried to tackle her, crying out in agony as he nicked his ankle on the metal corner of the bed. "Ouch! Shit! Please, baby, don't be upset. Look, if it makes you feel any better, I'm practically a virgin, too. I've only done it twice with prostitutes."

"What about Lydia?" Julia mocked him, one hand on the knob, the other on the bloody sheet. She would never go through with it — she was ashamed enough already — but Trevor didn't know that.

"What about her? She's as cold as the weather outside." Julia glanced out the window. The temperature had taken a nosedive and it had begun to snow on top of the four inches already on the ground.

"Besides, she never really liked *me*," Trevor continued sadly. "She only wanted to be pinned to a Sigma Chi." Standing there unclothed and rubbing his bruised ankle, he looked morose and vulnerable.

He had feelings like everyone. And in a sense, she'd been as bad as Lydia, using him for her own selfish ends, to hide from the unexplored regions of her heart. She felt a chill, and realized she'd forgotten to put on her stockings and underpants.

"Looking for these?" Bending down, Trevor held up the missing items. "I knew you were too much of a lady to leave the premises without them. That's one of the things I love about you, Julia. You have so much class."

Dropping the sheet on the floor, Julia walked over to the bed, her anger gone. "Look Trev, there's something I have to tell you. I don't think we're right for each other."

"Why not?" Hurt and bewilderment chased themselves across his perfectly even features. "I don't understand. You just had sex with me, for the first time in your life. Don't you *want* to get married?"

"I don't know what I want and I don't think you do, either." Julia said. "What do you expect to gain by marrying me?" She hated to use the words "I don't love you," knowing that, like their opposite, they could have an equally devastating effect.

Trevor became very still, then reached over and drew the zebra cover around both of them. "It's just that life is supposed to follow a pattern," he explained. "You go to school, join a fraternity, get hitched, find a job. All the guys I pledged with are engaged or about to be. And you seemed like the perfect partner — beautiful, intelligent, caring. You just have to get those crazy ideas out of your head."

Would he *ever* understand? "But my beliefs are based on what is really happening. The entire structure of our society is changing. You and your friends are clinging to the world we grew up in," she sighed. "I'm sometimes guilty of that too. But think about it, Trev. We barely know each other. And to embark upon a life together seems doomed from the beginning."

"I never really thought of it that way." He pulled her close. "Look, Julia, I really do care about what happens to you."

"And I care about you, too," Julia told him gently. "I've learned a lot from our relationship. But like spying for the SDS, it's something I should never have gotten into in the first place...." Seeing the distressed look on his face, she reached over and hugged him. "I'm sorry. I really thought it might work...."

Julia let him make love to her again, more from a sense of obligation than anything else. It was less painful the second time, but Julia still felt nothing. Trevor fell asleep immediately afterwards. She realized she would probably never see him again.

Wide awake and unexpectedly thirsty, Julia slipped back into her clothes and went over to the bar in search of something cold. The compact refrigerator held only beer and wine so Julia twisted open a bottle of Boone's Farm. She neglected to consider what she'd be doing to herself if she mixed wine with Harvey Wallbangers.

She took several gulps, thinking that if it weren't for Valerie and Adrian, she wouldn't be in this mess. Entangled with a man she never loved, convincing herself she had to have sex to be "normal," like everybody else. Goddamn Valerie and her manipulations! Goddamn Adrian and his sleazy jokes! They'd have to pay for leading her down the wrong path, she decided after another swig. And pay they would.

Still grasping the bottle of wine, she crept quietly from the room and hurried downstairs in search of her wrap. Snow or no snow, she'd find those two and give them a piece of her mind. They'd never get to her again.

The party had wound down. Only a few couples revolved to "Good Night, Ladies."

"Hey, Julia," Fast Eddie came up to her. "Where's Trev?"

"He crashed in your room." Preoccupied, Julia glanced around. "Have you seem my shawl?"

"Not leaving so soon, I hope." Fast Eddie caressed her bare shoulders with his fingers. "I just took Betsy back to her dorm."

His eyes were alight with the same lust she'd seen earlier in Trevor's.

Julia stared at him in shock and disgust. What a double crosser.... He was hitting on what he believed was his best friend's girl and his girl's best friend. She was about to make a cutting remark about him almost being married, when she remembered he had a car. "That's some decorating job you did in your room, by the way. You certainly have unusual taste."

"Thanks. Too bad you couldn't see it with me," Reaching for Julia's Boone's Farm, he drank deeply. "Got a little bored, huh? Trev's not the most exciting guy in the sack."

How would you know? she was tempted to ask. The next time she saw Betsy, she would warn her about this bastard. But right now, he might be able to help her. Even though she was gritting her teeth, Julia tried to make her smile pleasant. "Not a real man like you, right F.E.?"

"Actually, Fast Eddie's kinda inaccurate. Slow Eddie's more like it." A knowing smirk snaked across his All-American face.

Her plan might work, as long as she kept Fast Eddie under control. That shouldn't be too difficult, considering his brains were in his pants. "Why don't we go for a ride? There's a farmhouse in the country. The kids who rent it are out of town for the weekend." Once they arrived and found Valerie and Adrian, she could apologize for being mistaken and send Eddie on his way.

Snow was falling rapidly as they got into Fast Eddie's red Corvette. Julia was thankful for the bucket seats and stick shift separating them. She'd taken the half-full bottle of wine with her, promising him they'd finish it once they got there so he wouldn't drink it beforehand. She wasn't about to end up snowbound in a ditch with this creep.

"I could tell you were hot for me the first time I saw you," Eddie informed her as they pulled into Adrian's driveway. "Trevor kept insisting what a nice girl you were, but I know women."

"I just bet you do," Julia reached for the door handle. She started to thank him for the ride when he seized her arm and touched her fingers to his zipper. "Looks like you're wrong, Julia. The lights are on and I see people inside. How about a hand job here? Or we can join your friends for some group sex. Although right now I'm in the mood for manual intervention." His fingers seemed to turn into a vise as he let loose with a dirty laugh.

Julia thought quickly. The now-forgotten wine bottle was wedged next to her seat. She could threaten to hit him with it, but being stronger, he could easily wrest it from her. Or she could actually clobber him. But as much as she disliked him, she didn't want to cause him harm. At least not physical.

Deftly she unscrewed the bottle with her free hand. "I'll give you one you'll never forget," she promised, thinking, this is for Betsy. And Fast Eddie will never put the make on any friend's girl again.

Unzipping his pants, Eddie pulled out his penis. It was bigger than Trevor's and uncircumcised with that weird little flap on top. He groaned with anticipation as Julia bent down and calmly poured the remainder of the Boone's Farm over his erection. With detached amusement, she watched it wither as the cold wine made impact. "Fast Eddie's not such a bad name after all," she observed.

"You bitch!" He lunged at her. Quickly she tumbled out of the car and dashed towards the brightly lit farmhouse. He would never pursue her, not with his pants soaked and his cock hanging out.

She arrived at the door just as the Corvette's engine roared to life. He wouldn't try to run her over, would he? "Help! Help!" Julia banged frantically on the wood. Why didn't they answer?

"I'm a comin.' I'm a comin.'" Felix yanked open the door and as his eyes traveled over Julia, his usually sullen features opened up into a grin. "Well, Ah'll be God-damned! Cinderella done paid us a visit!" He spoke in a Southern dialect completely unlike his usual clipped Eastern tones. "You missin' your glass slippers, but, hey, that's OK. C'mon in."

Her flight from Eddie had sobered her. As she stepped into the living room, she saw Adrian, Moonstone, and two boys she briefly recognized from her single SDS meeting. Valerie was no-where around. Several wooden crates had been shoved into a corner and were partially covered by a throw rug.

Adrian broke into his high-pitched giggle. "Oh, wow. It's not Cinderella. It's the good witch Glinda. Cinderella was a blonde."

So was Glinda, she thought. They were obviously on some sort of high so nothing she would say would have any effect. Coming here had been a foolish act of drunken bravado: Valerie and Adrian didn't force her to lose her virginity. It had been her own doing, borne of her own insecurities and a desire to conform.

Moonstone whined, "I don't wanna go back to Kansas. I wanna go to Oz." She looked pleadingly at Julia. "Take me there, Glinda. Please."

The room seemed abnormally warm. The combination of cheap wine and Harvey Wallbangers suddenly began to churn in her stomach, and Julia knew she was going to be sick. It had happened once freshman year and had been miserable.

"What's going down now?" Valerie appeared in the doorway. "I can't even take a piss...." She saw Julia and her expression went from shock to fear to closed and almost hostile.

"Look, I'm sorry to bother you," Julia stammered, taken aback by Valerie's reaction. "I just needed a place to crash." She cupped her hand over her mouth praying, Please God, don't let me vomit. I will never, ever, do this again.

"Ain't no never mind, honey chile," Felix assured her. "'Cause after the Revolution come to Hayes, ain't gonna be nothin' left to bother."

Bile rose bitter and punishing in Julia's throat, and her stomach heaved as the first wave of nausea hit. "Bathroom," she gasped, and the horrible stuff sprayed all over her hands. As Valerie dragged her towards the toilet, Julia promised herself that from now on she would only do what she, Julia, wanted. No more push me-pull you from Trevor, Valerie, or anyone else. She would follow her own instincts.

If only everything would stop spinning, she could get her bearings and it would be all right.

CHAPTER TWENTY

When Julia woke up the next morning, bright sunlight streamed into an unfamiliar room. Where was she? What had happened?

Then the whole evening came back to her; a nightmarish rerun of astonishing clarity. Losing her virginity. The breakup with Trevor. Fast Eddie's huge, ugly penis. Throwing up in Adrian's living room. Struggling to pull herself upright, she felt as if every bone in her body had been pummelled, so she lay back down.

She became conscious of someone watching her. Valerie was perched on a narrow walnut chair, regarding her with a mixture of concern and annoyance. "You OK?"

"No." Even her mouth tasted putrid. Through one half-closed eye, Julia peered at her now ruined dress. The turquoise tulle was torn from careless pullings-off and reeked of vomit. She couldn't remember where she'd left her suitemate's expensive shawl. "I feel like shit."

Valerie handed her a glassful of a red, suspicious-smelling concoction. "Take this, then. It'll help."

"What's in it?" Julia demanded, wrinkling her nose. In her present state, it looked repugnant and smelled even worse.

"Don't worry, Julia," Valerie retorted. "I'm not slipping you LSD or anything like that. It's just the Stazyck cure for a hangover — tomato juice and a raw egg with a dash of tabasco sauce. But you better drink it or you'll feel like one of the dead."

Well, anything was an improvement.... Taking a deep breath, Julia forced down as much as she could in one gulp. Actually, it wasn't bad, considering the contents and the state of her stomach.

A few minutes later, Valerie helped Julia sit up. "Why did you come here?" she asked.

Valerie would never understand her confusion and ambivalence about sex, so she said, "I broke up with Trevor and wanted to rap with you."

"You certainly picked a hell of a time. It's a good thing I didn't take the acid last night or you'd still be lying in a puddle of puke."

Julia shuddered at the memory. "Could I borrow some clothes? I have to get out of this dress."

"Yeah, I have some extra things downstairs." She glanced critically at Julia. "If you can fit into the pants. Have you put on weight or something?"

"Unfortunately, thanks to the Pill. But I won't have to worry about that anymore."

"Trevor and you...?" Valerie asked, raising her eyebrows.

Julia nodded and, in spite of herself, flushed. Even though she was no longer a virgin, she was still modest. And, besides, she didn't feel any different, only slightly sore. "I would appreciate your not telling anyone. Besides it wasn't all that great."

Much to her surprise, Valerie neither expressed joy nor congratulated her. Instead, she said, "That's what I used to think before Richard. Unless it's someone you care about, it's no big deal." She shrugged. "Actually, I thought Trevor-baby was all right. Rich, too. You should have hung with him."

Julia was dumbfounded. "You of all people should understand, Valerie. He represents everything you despise!"

Valerie turned to Julia, her expression so forbidding it was almost frightening. "Go back to your Greekoid friends, Julia. You'll be a lot safer."

"What the hell are you talking about?" Julia demanded. "*You* were the one who encouraged me to get into the protest movement! So maybe I don't fit into your beloved SDS. But I certainly feel at home with the SMC."

"In an organization run by a baby killer?" Valerie mocked. "That is, like, the ultimate in hypocrisy!"

"I can't believe you'd say that about Louie. He's the most dedicated person I know. He does more than any of us!" Louie had told her no one would truly understand what happened in Vietnam except for other vets. Maybe he was right.

"He's motivated by guilt over the acts of savagery to the Vietnamese people," Valerie countered. "If he was really against the war, he would never have gone over there in the first place." She tilted her chin defiantly, as if daring Julia. "I'd spit on any veteran who crossed my path."

This had been coming for a long time. Their friendship was over. "Get out, Valerie. We have nothing more to say to each other." Ignoring the pains in her muscles and head, Julia began to yank on her dress. "I don't even want to borrow your clothes." Valerie turned and left without comment.

Julia was trying not to cry when she came downstairs a few minutes later. She could hear Valerie moving around in the kitchen so she went into the living room where Felix and Adrian were sprawled on the floor smoking a joint. "Have you seen a shawl lying around?" She vaguely remembered burrowing into it before the heat kicked on in Eddie's car. "It's not even mine; I borrowed it."

Adrian and Felix looked at her blankly, as if she'd asked about the moon. The room was excruciatingly neat, almost as if they'd cleaned up for Julia's benefit. As an afterthought, to get some sort of response from them, she said, "Where are the boxes?"

"Boxes?" Adrian stammered, his wiry body growing tense. "I don't know what you're talking about!" Felix regarded her silently through a thick haze of smoke.

"You know, those wooden crates on the floor," Julia babbled, knowing she'd blundered onto a forbidden topic. "There were three or four over in that corner." She pointed towards the wall.

"Sure you weren't tripping last night, too?" Felix's loud snort of disgust cut through Julia's aching head. "'Cause you sure were hallucinating. There were no boxes."

"Look, I may have been bombed, but I know what I saw. It was the worst evening of my life, and I'm not likely to forget it. Adrian and the others thought I was the good witch Glinda and you were talking with a Southern accent...."

"I don't rap like no Oreo," Felix strode over to her, and faced her, dark, fierce, frowning. "I grew up in Harlem, far away from Uncle Tom country. You were out of it and puked." He pointed to a wet spot on the rug. "Valerie spent the whole morning cleaning up your shit."

"I'm sorry." In addition to being confused, Julia felt humiliated and intimidated. She'd really made an ass out of herself last night and regretted it, especially losing her virginity. Yet she was positive she'd seen those crates.

Still, Felix was no one to argue with. "Oh, wow, you can't even remember where you put your shawl," Adrian interjected, his voice unexpectedly compassionate. "I'll take you home so you can get some sleep. We'll call you if we find it."

Julia almost didn't notice the cardboard box lying on her dresser when she got back to her room. It had already been opened, with a small envelope peeping out from beneath the tissue. Inside was a baby orange tree, according to the printed card taped on bottom. Actually, it was no more than a twig with minute leaves and tiny, fragrant white blossoms.

What an exquisite plant! She saw her name on the envelope and for a disorienting second, thought she recognized her own handwriting. She didn't dare hope, but hoped nonetheless as she tore it open. The note inside said:

> Julia—
> Sorry I missed you. Just wanted to let you know
> I'm back. Thanks for all the help with my course.
> —Your friend, Win

As fragile as it was, the beautiful tree was real. Just like her feelings for Win. And that had been him in the lobby. If only she had gotten to the phone in time! The evening — and possibly even her life — would have turned out so differently.

She postulated later that Valerie, Adrian, and Felix were dealing drugs, large quantities of marijuana and God knew what else. They must have just gotten in a shipment; hence, their paranoia about the boxes. Valerie had made good on her statement that she was going to earn money.

The finale of her friendship with Valerie filled Julia with sadness. She missed Valerie, but the person she'd been so close with no longer existed. So much of Valerie's anger was displaced, directed at others instead of internally. Julia wondered what was at the core; but until Valerie faced herself, no one would ever know.

Julia tried not to dwell on the events of that terrible night, sequestering herself in the library. She'd blown her finals last quarter, and was afraid of making the same mistake again. So she waited on the steps for the library to open at 7 a.m. and was inside when the lights blinked their last warning before closing.

Each night, she looked forward to returning to her room. The orange tree Win had given her flourished on the window sill where it would get the best sun. She tended the stripling with care, identifying with its growth, even talking to it. She planned on thanking Win at their Body Language final on Thursday. Phoning him seemed too aggressive.

Relieved of the burden of her relationship with Trevor, Julia found the solitude healing. She actually enjoyed being alone. Life would take care of itself as long as she followed her heart.

On the Wednesday night before her last final, the one with Win, Julia decided to take a few hours off. Except for a last-minute review, she had finished studying. The SMC was holding its weekly coffeehouse at Lenny's, having moved it forward two days, since most students would be leaving soon for Easter break.

Named after Lenny Bruce and modeled after the Cafe Wha? in New York City, Lenny's had been purchased a year and a half earlier by two aging, trendwise beatniks. Formerly a townie bar called The Silent Woman, it had undergone a renovation of sorts, which included the removal of an offensive sign of a headless female and various stuffed, antlered animals that had adorned the paneled walls. But the cigarette-scarred wooden tables, temperamental pinball machines, and unventilated rest rooms remained unchanged.

On her way into the bar, Julia dropped her contribution of two quarters into a coffee can labeled "SMC Defense Fund."

Typically, she didn't know anyone well, although she recognized many of the protesters by sight. She started to look for an empty table when someone called her name. Louie waved frantically at her, his Afro'd head bobbing above the crowd. "Over here!" he cried.

She elbowed her way through the smoky, dingy room and even though Louie smiled at her with undiluted joy, Jake, Shawn, and Kirsten glared at her. It felt wonderful, no, magnificent, to see them, but why were they so angry?

"Where the hell have you been, Julia?" Shawn spoke first. She looked well, considering her ordeal with her eyesight. "Don't you care about us? You could have at least stopped by the house!"

"You're the only one who truly appreciates my jokes," Kirsten lamented. "I wanted to show you my new poster of the Cleaver brothers — Wally, Beaver, and Eldridge."

"You're not still dating Howdy Doody, are you?" Jake demanded, casting a glance at Louie. "We don't approve at all, do we, Louie?"

Louie surveyed her up and down, gauging her. "I tried calling, but you're never in," he said. "We're organizing a demonstration against President Carrell's ROTC review and need your posters. We also have to figure out how to efficiently make hundreds of cardboard crosses to drop on the cadets when they march." Reaching over, he traced the outline of her chin. "And I missed our rap sessions, Julia. I know I was busy, but I'm sorry we lost touch."

"Oh," was all Julia could manage. She felt overwhelmed, as though a great burst of sunshine had exploded inside her. These were her people. She belonged with them. Why had she denied herself for so long?

Gentle fingers brushed her arm. "I thought I'd never see you again." Win stood close to her, holding a pitcher of beer with his free hand. Julia tried not to gasp. He was deeply tanned, and the sun had illuminated the highlights in his hair, turning it into a red-gold blaze. "Are you avoiding me?" He said anxiously. "Are you pissed at me?"

Mad at you? I love you! Julia wanted to fling her arms around them. She seated herself in the chair Louie had pulled out for her and said, "From now on, you'll be seeing a lot of me. I've learned who my true friends are."

"I'll drink to that," Win began to pour the beer. "By the way, I loved your little drawings. And our handwriting is so similar, I thought it was my own." His eyes caressed her, and unexpectedly shy, Julia ducked her head. It had been months since they'd seen each other.

"Yeah, Win had a great time studying on the beach," Jake remarked enviously. "He *says* he had a broken leg."

"Hey, man, I only went to Florida for a couple of weeks, during the last stages of recovery." As he sat down next to Julia, several women cast admiring looks in their direction. No wonder they want him, Julia thought. Not only is he beautiful but he's a gentleman. How could she have been so foolish in trying to stop loving him? At worst, he could reject her, but at best, fantasy could become reality. Besides, what could hurt more than turning away from her true feelings?

"Louie's good fortune is ours now, too." Win told her. "He got an almost perfect score on his Law Boards so tonight we're celebrating. And look who we ran into!"

Louie glanced from Win to Julia and back again and frowned. Draining his glass quickly, he poured himself another beer. Odd, since unlike the others, Julia had never seen Louie drink or even talk about getting high.

"Louie can get into just about any graduate school he wants," Shawn added. "He can practically write his own ticket."

Then why did Louie suddenly seem so bummed out, Julia wondered. What his GI benefits wouldn't cover, a scholarship or loan surely would.

But Julia was too caught up in her own happiness to worry about anyone else. Spring had come at last and she was going to savor every moment.

CHAPTER TWENTY-ONE

As if to verify their vows of friendship, Win and Shawn dropped by the first night of Spring Quarter and invited Julia for dinner. Win's house sat directly across from the President's residence, which was a gracious estate on an acre and a half. How ironic, considering the President's ROTC Review was to be held in a few days. In a perfect world they could pop over and ask "George" about the details.

Like most of the homes on the other side of Maple Street, Win's had been built during the '20s. Made of brown brick and wood, it stood two and a half stories high, with a fire escape on the left side and a mini-ladder centered below a window in the attic, making it a perfect spot to throw water balloons at passing cars when things got boring or during Finals Week. It boasted a front porch with a creaking swing and upstairs and downstairs suites, each with a kitchen, living room, and three bedrooms. In residence-starved Hampton, the house was considered a find, despite its lack of renovation and leaky basement.

Except for Louie, the others were present for the meal of spaghetti and red Zonin. But Julia's mind was so filled with Win she scarcely noticed anyone else. This was *his* kitchen, *his* living room, *his* wooden coat rack in the center hallway. No matter thatit was shabby, the rooms small and ill-kept, smelling of

Shawn's dogs and rabbits. It symbolized an intimacy she longed for, and much to her delight, was now privy to.

Throughout dinner and afterwards, she and Win stared at each other. Julia reveled in the fact they were finally together, and when Johnny Carson signed off at 12:30, Win walked her back to Miami Hall. "I don't have to worry about studying so much this quarter," she told him as they stood on the steps in front of her dorm. "My grades helped balance out the mess I made during Fall Quarter." Her four A's and one B more than satisfied Julia and her parents, raising her accumulated average back to its normal B plus.

Win took her hand in his. "Then we'll have more time to play," he replied, brushing her fingers with his lips, a caress as light as the touch of a bird's wing. Julia finally understood why women "swooned" in Victorian novels.

But Win was wrong, for Julia and the others were inundated with the minutiae of organizing the protest against the ROTC Review. Donations of materials had to be obtained from the few sympathetic local merchants; pamphlets had to be written and disseminated; the cadets' exact route needed to be pinpointed so protesters could strew cardboard crosses and flowers along their path.

Much to everyone's amazement, the SDS offered to assist. Louie agreed, although Julia, when she was finally able to corner him in the Campus Ministry building, told him about what had transpired last quarter with the YAF. She tried to warn him about the informer.

Louie shrugged her off and turned to answer someone else's question about a list of proposed reforms he planned to read during the ceremonies. With an exasperated sigh, Julia returned to the kitchen to cut out more crosses. The crosses still weren't complete the day of the ceremony, so Julia and Shawn spent a frantic morning trying to finish the tedious task.

"My eyes don't allow me to do much close work, so these are going to look like daggers," Shawn complained as she threw a half-dozen into a container. She looked elegant, even though she wore a T-shirt with a big peace symbol and bellbottoms with bric-a-brac around the hem. "Weren't you supposed to figure out how to do this with a minimum of hassle?"

"There is no simple way," Julia picked up the pattern that served as the master and began to trace over a poster-sized sheet of cardboard. "If we'd been dealing with tissue paper, we could have divided the crosses in half or done two or three layers at a time. But these sheets are just too thick."

"Mmmm," Shawn concurred, then said, "Win's very fond of you. How do you feel about him?"

Shawn's directness caught Julia off guard; she pressed so hard on the pencil it snapped and broke in two. "Oh damn...." Her cheeks blossomed red.

"I thought so," Shawn's smile was knowing but gentle. "You're afraid to show your feelings but they show through nonetheless. You shouldn't be. We all love each other. That's what life's all about."

Julia let the broken shards fall from her fingers. There were so many different kinds of love, and she didn't know how to separate them. "I wasn't sure if Win liked me that way." Her words sounded awkward to her own ears. "You just can't walk up to someone and tell them you're crazy about them. Especially someone as beautiful as Win."

Was Shawn's glance critical or merely cloudy because of her eye condition? "There's more to Win than his looks." Then in a kind voice, "You have nothing to worry about."

Before Julia could ask her what she meant, Shawn said brusquely, "We'd better get our asses over to High Street. The review's about to begin and they'll need what we've made."

Julia had the sense Shawn was trying to tell her something. She started to ask, but Shawn made a big deal about only two people carrying dozens of small containers filled with crosses and daisies and why couldn't anyone else help? So the moment slid by.

The trees were just beginning to bud and the air, although chilly, held a promise of softness. Demonstrators lined both sides of the road. Julia and Shawn quickly passed out containers while Louie read from his list of demands: abolish ROTC on campus; establish a Black Studies department; sever university ties with the military-industrial complex; and remove all negative sanctions from campus demonstrations. The crowd clapped and cheered after each item.

"I'm going to stop the parade and confront President Carrell with this list," he told them and they roared their approval. "Let's end the war now!"

"Here they come!" someone cried and feeling one with the group, Julia leaned forward, tense with expectancy. Louie started to sing, "Give Peace a Chance," and everyone joined in.

"Hey, I was looking for you," Win appeared, seemingly from nowhere. He handed her a daisy. "Don't forget to throw this at your favorite soldier." He moved close to her and she could feel the length of his body alongside hers. Julia leaned against him, dizzy with desire. For a moment they stood pressed together. Then Win pulled away. "I'd better go see what the others are up to." He vanished, his russet mane swallowed by the group.

Julia's body was a firestorm of sensation. Win's nearness excited her more than any foreplay she'd ever had with Trevor. Did Win have any inkling of his effect on her? If he liked her as Shawn said, perhaps he was taking things slowly. After all, they'd just begun spending time together.

"Holy shit, those aren't the cadets!" Someone further along the parade route shouted. "It's the fuckin' pigs!" A horrified murmur ran through the crowd and they filled the street, infected with the virus of fear. Julia strained to see, but was too short. She heard yelling and cursing, then suddenly people turned and fled. She found herself swimming in a tide of humanity, going the wrong direction.

Bill Gordon, for once without Vicki, saw her and grabbed her arm. "The YAF and townies have banded together! The cops are arresting everyone! Get the hell out of here!" He tried to pull her along with him, but she pushed him aside, thinking, I can't leave Win and the others in the middle of this.

"No," she replied and gasped as a boy no older than she seized Shawn. Glaring at the peace symbol on her shirt, he started beating Shawn on the head.

"Goddamn hippie!" he screamed, his expression murderous. "I risked my ass in Vietnam and now I come home to this!" Shawn cowered in terror. Covering her face with her hands, she struggled to protect her eyes. Julia was about to intervene when a campus security guard yanked Shawn and the veteran apart. Picking them up by their collars, he dragged them both away.

A few feet from where Julia stood, a Hampton policeman approached Felix. The cop carried a pair of handcuffs behind his back. Unmoved and unmoving, Felix stared at his potential jailer, his arms akimbo, his dark face defiant. Felix's really got guts, Julia thought with new respect. He's about to be busted and he's not even afraid.

Felix said something Julia couldn't hear and the cop skittered off. Admiration turned to horror as Julia realized that Felix must be the informant. How else could he possibly avoid arrest? As a leader in the SDS, Felix had been privy to the same information as Louie. And Felix had also known about Julia's activities in the YAF.

Before she could reflect further, the policeman turned to her. "I was just leaving..." Julia stammered. Terrified by his impassive demeanor, she fled, any second expecting to feel his hand on her shoulder, pulling her back. Julia didn't stop running until she reached the safety of her dorm. And then, out of breath and full of self-disgust, she thought, what a coward I am. I want to stop the war, but I'm afraid to do more than cut out crosses. Why didn't I let that cop arrest me?

The least she could do was try to help her friends who had been busted. And she wanted to tell Louie about Felix.

She trudged back uptown only to find even more chaos at the Hampton police station. All ages and types mobbed the tiny lobby. People sat on radiators and window sills. Gesticulating and shouting, they lined the floor leading to the holding area. Julia spotted Win and Louie near the entrance to the jail cells and headed towards them.

Win saw her first and, flashing his electrifying smile, exclaimed, "Thank God you weren't busted! They've got poor Shawn back there. I hope she's all right."

For once, Julia ignored Win. "Louie, I've got to rap with you. It's about the informer."

"Not now, Julia," Louie gazed in the direction of the cells. "They're releasing the others." The area flooded with even more people, among them Valerie and Shawn, who sobbed hysterically.

Gripping Shawn's arm, Valerie guided her towards them, rolling her eyes in annoyance. "Here's your roommate," she snapped at Win. "I had to babysit her the whole time. She can't handle anything."

"Don't do me any favors, Valerie," Shawn jerked away, her previously impeccable clothes mussed, her face streaked with dirt and tears. "Just leave me alone. I'm sick of this whole scene."

"Good, because there's no room for gutless wonders," Valerie retorted. Why did Valerie persist in condemning even those who were on her side? Anyone who got in her way was the enemy, not just the Establishment.

"What's wrong with you, Valerie?" Louie demanded, echoing Julia's thoughts. "You know Shawn can't afford to jeopardize her eyesight."

"Haven't you heard, Louie?" Valerie mocked him, her once impish features drawn into hard, brittle lines. "There's a revolution going on. Folks are bound to get hurt."

"Why don't you just cool it, Valerie," Win said, his eyes sparking with anger. "We don't need any of this bullshit."

"It takes one to know one," Valerie retorted. "And you're the bullshit king, Win." She started to leave.

But Julia said, "Valerie, I think you should hear this before you split. I know the identity of the informer."

The crowded room had one of those sudden, inexplicable moments of stillness, and Julia's statement echoed loudly. Seeing this, Valerie glanced around and, placing her hands on her hips, announced in her most dramatic voice, "Pray tell, Julia. Who *has* been spying on us all these months?"

Everyone was staring at her. "Well, perhaps I shouldn't name names," she hedged, not wanting to draw attention to herself, remembering the disaster at the YAF meeting. "At least not here in front of all these people."

"Go ahead, Julia," Louie encouraged. "Let's get this thing out in the open."

The near-silence passed and once again the station filled with chatter, albeit more subdued. "Well, I saw Felix talking to a policeman..." Julia began.

Valerie burst into derisive laughter. "*Felix*? You think *Felix* is the fink?"

"Valerie, the cop was about to bust him. Then Felix said something and he backed off."

"Yeah, Felix probably threatened to blow him away. Felix's one heavy dude. No one fucks with him," Valerie chuckled again. "That's a real gem, Julia. I can't wait to tell him."

"Actually, Julia makes sense," Win defended her. "The cops and the conservatives knew what was going down and had the parade route changed. The cadets are marching uptown even as we speak and our demonstration's a failure."

"And we shared all our plans with you SDSers," Shawn glared at Valerie. "Like you said to me once, 'If the shoe fits...'"

Valerie shook her head. "What a bunch of candy-assed idealists. You don't even know what's happening on this campus." As Valerie strode away, Julia resisted the impulse to run after her and shake some sense into her.

"Then why don't you tell us?" Louie called, a troubled expression stealing over his face.

"Quiet, everybody, I have an announcement," A man in a Hampton police uniform scrambled on top of a desk, and Julia recognized the deputy who'd threatened to rape her a nearly year ago. She shrank behind Win and Louie.

"My name's Cal Adams, and I've temporarily replaced Sheriff Evans, who had to retire on account of a mild heart attack," the cop said. He still looks like a weasel, Julia thought. Or a mean fox about to tear into a rabbit. "I just spoke with President Carrell on the phone," he continued. "I'm setting all of you free today, with a warning. We will tolerate no more disruptions or fighting."

"Fuck you, pig!" A heckler shouted. "You're only letting us go 'cause some of your redneck friends got busted, too."

Sheriff Adams smirked in the direction of the voice, his small eyes glittering. "Oh, you can protest all you want on campus," he replied mildly. "In fact, YAF leaders informed me they won't stoop to your level again and won't be suckered into helping perpetrate any more acts against this great country of ours. But if you bring your demonstrations into town, you're my responsibility. So you do so at your own risk. That's all I have to say." He jumped down.

"I can't stand this any more!" Shawn cried. "I'm getting out of here. No more marches. No more arrests. Things will only get worse, so I'm going back to the house and only coming out for classes." She started to leave.

"Don't be like that, Shawn." Win stepped in front of her, blocking her path. "You're just bummed out and scared."

"I mean it, Win. I've had it. You, Louie and the others can save the world. I've got to look after myself."

"The lady has the right idea," Cal Adams drawled. How long had he been eavesdropping? Once again, Julia tried to make herself inconspicuous. She looked different this year; perhaps he wouldn't remember her.

"I think the rest of you could take a lesson from her." Adams' probing gaze darted around and locked onto Julia's. Involuntarily she shivered, remembering his clammy touch on her arm and the hungry way he'd stared at her legs last spring. "I've kept track of what's been going on in the campus, and I know who the troublemakers are. So I'd walk softly if I were you."

"Don't threaten us," Louie warned. "Because if I see one shred of harassment, I'll have the ACLU on your doorstep so fast you won't have time to kiss your badge good-bye."

Adams smirked. "I know the law, mister, a lot better'n I did a year ago. I know your kind, too. Didn't they execute your relations for selling the H-bomb to the Russians?"

What he meant by "relations" was unclear. For an instant, Julia though Adams was casting aspersions on Louie's Judaism. She and Louie had found out they were the same religion when they bumped into each other at Hillel House during Yom Kippur services last fall. Then she realized Adams had no way of knowing and was probably referring to a Communist party affiliation. But Louie obviously shared Julia's initial line of reasoning for he promptly lunged forward, his fists bunched, "Why, you racist son-of-a-bitch," he snarled. "Let's step outside and hear you say that again."

Julia was incredulous. Louie was always in control, always rational, doing whatever was needed for the common good. Until this moment he'd made his feelings work for him instead of being dominated by them. Maybe she didn't know Louie as well as she thought.

Win laid a restraining hand on Louie's broad shoulder. "Let it go, man. Please. It's not worth it."

"You're right, Win," As quickly as it had come, Louie's fury evaporated. He dropped his aggressive stance. Adams swaggered off, emanating smugness. Having accidentally located Louie's weak spot, he'd made his point.

"C'mon everybody, let's split," Shawn begged.

At least we can demonstrate peacefully on campus without worrying about the cops and the YAF, Julia reflected as they left the station. One of the SMC's demands had been accomplished. Yet she found little comfort in the concession.

CHAPTER TWENTY-TWO

By early April, Hayes had erupted in its own riot of fragrant spring greenery. The blend of ancient trees, Georgian architecture, sweet air and sunshine produced a perfume of calm enjoyed by conservative and protester alike.

Having some unexpected free time, Louie strolled uptown to buy incense at Nirvana, Ohio, the local head shop. He didn't want to return to the Campus Ministry building where the sensitivity training people had taken over for a few days, or to his house, which seemed dark and confining on this brilliant afternoon.

Although the SMC continued to gather and demonstrate, things had quieted down. Louie had met with President Carrell twice since the ROTC fiasco and George, as he insisted upon being called, assured him that as long as the protesters stayed on campus, there would be no more resistance from either police or YAF. When Louie mentioned that the SMC wanted to have a peaceful candlelight march uptown, George promised he'd discuss the matter with Hampton officials and get back to Louie right away.

Yet two weeks had passed and Louie hadn't heard a word. It wasn't like George and the march was scheduled for tonight.

I suppose it's OK or they would have told us otherwise, Louie reflected uneasily as he ambled down the Slantwalk. After all, the mayor himself had spoken at last fall's Moratorium and certain storekeepers donated money and goods to the antiwar movement. Everybody knew that stand-in sheriff Adams threatened more than he acted. Yet Adams possessed an instinctive, cruel cunning. But did one fool merit canceling an entire march? And Adams still had to answer to town officials.

The song "Suite: Judy Blue Eyes" drifted from a cluster of dorms and a group of students sitting in a circle in an outdoor class burst into unexpected laughter. A barefoot couple tossed a Frisbee back and forth — both wore identical headbands, tie-dyed shirts, and bellbottom jeans. The girl's unrestrained breasts bounced beneath the thin fabric of her top. She reminded him faintly of Julia, and he sighed.

He waved at a pretty acquaintance — a freshman in a makeshift Indian print dress weaving a necklace of clover. She motioned for him to come over and join her, but he shook his head "no" and smiled. Some women, especially younger ones, found his so-called powerful position in the movement attractive, but he was in no mood for a casual relationship. Better to stay solo for the duration, finish his education and get established as a lawyer. It was just that on afternoons like this he *ached*.

He knew that what had happened with Hu'o'ng in Vietnam had everything to do with his reticence. He'd promised himself he'd never love so intensely again, but his resolve had begun to weaken as he'd gotten to know Julia.

Like the horse he could never tame at summer camp when he was a kid, Julia seemed to elude him. He'd been fourteen when his parents had sent him to a camp for "special children" which Louie now realized meant troublemakers. Actually it had been the best thing that could have happened, but at the time he'd resented the hell out of it.

Like the rest of the children there, he'd been given an unbroken thoroughbred colt to take care of, to teach him responsibility. But as soon as Louie thought he'd established rapport with the animal, that she believed he meant her no harm, she ran away. Each time she let him closer though, bolting just as Louie was about to put the lasso around her neck. It was one of the few things he'd tried for and couldn't achieve, and it had made him furious.

Yet when he returned to school the following fall, he stopped picking fights with other kids and skipping classes. He channeled his obsession with fairness and intense curiosity about the "why" of things towards studies and activities.

Like that skittish horse, Julia was independent and beautiful and so unknowing of her effect on others. Didn't she realize her promise? And why the hell did she waste herself on Win? And why had Win picked the one girl that he, Louie, wanted? With his rock star good looks and animal magnetism, Win could have just about any chick to warm his bed.

If Julia knew what he did about Win, she'd probably never speak to Win again. But Louie's code of ethics prevented him from telling her.

He entered Nirvana, Ohio and was immediately deluged with a cornucopia of aromatic smells, intricate jewelry, beads, mobiles, roach clips, hash pipes, so-called cigarette papers, and posters that cluttered shelves and walls in an organized madness. These head shops had sprung up everywhere virtually overnight and Louie wondered if such places existed in Saigon. Most of the items here were unheard of when his tour of duty ended in '66. But by then, Americans had begun to realize what Louie had learned through experience — Vietnam was a back street abortion bleeding the life from both countries.

After high school graduation, Louie enrolled at Cleveland State, intending to become a social worker like his mother. But the courses held no interest for him, so he enlisted in the Army, much to his parents' dismay. Louie, the eldest, was their only son and even his gentle-natured accountant father begged him to reconsider. But their pleas came too late, and Louis Eli Wexler, a nineteen-year-old nice Jewish boy from Cleveland Heights, was headed for what he thought was a great adventure.

And it had seemed that way at first, from behind his desk at a civilian hospital in Saigon. Louie was assigned to help out with admissions; that was where he'd met Hu'o'ng. Her father, a high-ranking South Vietnamese official, was to undergo a gall bladder operation.

Unlike American girls, who at that time struck Louie as brash and aggressive, Hu'o'ng was soft-spoken, gentle, highly cultured. They fell in love almost immediately and since both were virgins, explored the exciting terrain of sex together.

They'd only made love a few times when Hu'o'ng discovered she was pregnant. Since her family was Catholic, abortion was out of the question. As was typical of many Vietnamese, they sent her away in disgrace, to a village in the Mekong Delta. In a sense, Louie's punishment was even more brutal; his superior officer transferred him to work as a medic on the front lines. It could have been worse, Louie thought with a shudder. I could have been a grunt, forced to kill or be killed.

He'd been scared shitless the entire time. Saving lives had been the only impetus for sanity. That, and the too-brief, secret visits to Hu'o'ng and their infant son Hein, or Henry, as they liked to call him.

Upon completion of his tour, Louie tried to marry Hu'o'ng, but of course was turned down by the American military. As if a 20-year-old Vietnamese girl and a toddler would undermine national security! He'd argued so vehemently with his superiors he'd almost received a dishonorable discharge. Although Louie was shipped home practically by force, he promised Hu'o'ng he'd send for her. A vow he'd never keep, since he'd learned from another medic still in Vietnam that both she and the baby died in the '68 Tet Offensive.

He never told Julia or anyone else about his Vietnamese family. How could they possibly understand his agonizing loss? They were college kids, living in a fantasy world. Death was not real to them. Only Julia seemed to grasp the implications of what the protest movement was trying to achieve. To many of the others, demonstrations seemed an excuse to indulge in drugs, get laid, skip classes. Sometimes he wondered if his efforts were worth the results.

Depressed, Louie left the head shop empty-handed. He didn't want incense after all, just needed an excuse to avoid his lonely room. He puzzled over whether they should hold tonight's march.

As it turned out, the decision was out of Louie's control. By the time he arrived at the designated meeting point across the street from Campus Ministry, several hundred students had already shown up, candles in hand. As darkness descended upon

Hayes, they walked slowly, silently down the streets of campus. Others joined them along the path, an ever-extending line stretching nearly a half-mile long.

Unlike previous demonstrations, the mood of the crowd was somber and respectful and Louie thought, well, maybe they do understand a little. If enough of us come together in the right spirit, we will end this war.

Candles flickered, feet shuffled, the stars glittered brightly. The march turned towards uptown, and Louie made no effort to redirect it. After all, they weren't creating any disturbance. Perhaps some townspeople might join them.

The first marchers had almost reached Hampton Square in the middle of the village when Louie heard shouts. He hurried forward and found a small cluster of YAFers, blocking the tiny park that dominated the square. Except for the lack of townies, this was an instant replay of the President's ROTC review, Louie thought in annoyance. Only this time, we outnumber them 30 to 1. When will they learn to leave us alone?

Louie stepped on the sidewalk that separated the marchers and the cross-armed conservatives. "We have a right to be here, just like you..." he began, when blinding lights and the scream of suddenly ignited engines filled the air.

The street, which had been dark save for the candles, became brilliantly illuminated from above and to the side of them. Louie instantly recognized the thwup-thwup of chopper blades and blue and red sirens revolving atop what looked like twenty police cars.

A line of helmeted policemen approached them with billy clubs. Filled with terror, Louie shouted, "Run!" to both protesters and YAFers. "Get the hell out of here!"

"Oh, they won't hurt us," a short-haired young man replied. "We're on their side."

"You asshole!" Louie cried as the first tear gas canisters exploded. He saw the young man erupt into choking coughs as the park became permeated with fumes.

Louie fled through the square. Stumbling over a tree trunk, he fell into a bramble bush. He struggled to extricate himself, scratching himself in the process. The chopper had just airlifted him into the jungle; he had to save as many guys as he could. But where was his stretcher? He could hear them screaming but he couldn't do a fucking thing without his med kit.

The horrible sense of helplessness returned, along with the smell of sulphur, decay, and blood. Louie vomited into the bush.

Wiping his mouth with the back of his hand, he tried to pull himself together. Calm down, calm down, he chanted to himself. You're not in Vietnam. You're in the middle of a student riot.

Cold and trembling, Louie crept behind the stores that lined the back side of Hampton Square. He heard the pop of tear gas, and kept reassuring himself it was not gunfire; kids his age weren't being killed, only repressed because they wanted to stop more senseless murders. But what was the point? It couldn't bring Hu'o'ng or his son back. He knew he had to return to the Campus Ministry building where the others would reconnoiter. Although what he really wanted to do was huddle in his bed, pulling his misery behind him.

Louie started down fraternity row, assuming it safe, when he nearly ran into half-a-dozen Shawnee County police with a German shepherd. He ducked behind a parked car in the driveway of the Beta House, but not before he saw the dog leap onto the front porch. A male voice exclaimed: "Get this goddamn animal off me!" then a growl and a rending of clothes.

"Oh, shit, I'm bleeding!" The voice continued. "I was just sitting here minding my own business! Oh, shit!" The horribly familiar cry of the young discovering its vulnerability.

Rather than waiting to see the cops' reaction, Louie crept towards the house. Fortunately a back door was open, so he slipped inside. He knew first aid and could help. There were no more lines of demarcation among the campus groups now: the student was enemy.

CHAPTER TWENTY-THREE

As a result of the "Candlelight Massacre" so named by the protesters, several students were taken to the hospital, among them the Beta whose leg had been bitten through to the bone by the German shepherd. Other injuries were caused by the crowd itself and included bruises and scratches of varying severity. The police never touched the demonstrators, letting the tear gas and the implied threat of their billy clubs do the intimidation.

President Carrell issued a statement in the student newspaper, *Clarion*:

> •No one may forcibly or physically disrupt, either by action or noise, the regular business or function of the University or the adjoining Village of Hampton.
>
> •Picketing as a nonviolent means of advocating different points of view may be utilized outside University buildings only. However, no one may block stairs, doorways, or walkways to buildings. Any form of demonstration or gathering is prohibited in the Village of Hampton.
>
> •Persons may not coerce or intimidate students, faculty, or administrators in entering or leaving the

campus, its buildings, or classrooms.

*Any violations of these regulations or of any municipal, state, or federal laws, or any disruption or interference with the University's attainment of educational objectives or the Village of Hampton and its citizens, shall be considered misconduct.

Students responded by causing as much trouble on campus as possible: setting fires in classroom wastebaskets; picketing and tying up food service deliveries; threatening to blow up the electrical generator; simultaneously flushing all toilets at a prearranged time. The Hayes "Flush In" drained the Hampton water supply and nearly destroyed the sewage system, along with making national headlines.

Everywhere Julia went — in classes, at the student center, in the cafeteria — she heard the word "repression." The diverse campus elements had united, even igniting what Valerie once called the "filler people," those undistinguished, unaffiliated students whose seemingly irrelevant purpose at Hayes was to get a degree.

Like the flowers in mid-April, "strike" symbols blossomed everywhere. Nixon added fuel by increasing bombings in Vietnam and threatening to move troops into Cambodia. This spurred a fresh outburst of enthusiasm for the next Moratorium, held on the 15th of every month during the school year 1969-70.

Yet the clenched fist graffiti, impromptu speeches on overturned trash cans, and small flare-ups had become but background noise. For Julia had lost part of herself to Win: she only wanted to be where he was, feel his nearness, listen to his voice. She knew he cared for her, but how much was still a mystery. He rarely touched her, and often drifted in a world of his own.

They spent most of their free time together; or more accurately, Julia spent it at his house. They went to meetings, movies, and parties with whoever was around. Julia adored the people in Win's house but she was beginning to realize something deeper percolated beneath Win's passivity.

It spilled into their relationship a few days before the April Moratorium. Julia and Win were walking from Davison Hall, where they'd completed their respective two o'clock sociology classes. Win was in an expansive mood, having just turned in a major paper. For him, midterms were almost over, while Julia's had just begun.

He motioned towards a card table being set up at the center of Slantwalk by two Girl Scouts. "Let's buy some cookies then get stoned. Thin mints are far out when you're high."

"I can't, Win. I've been goofing off all quarter and I'm only halfway through with my reading for Principles of Sociology."

"Oh, come on, Julia. The test isn't until tomorrow and you can catch up this evening. I had Barrows, too, and he's a cinch."

It was unlike Win to try to persuade her and Julia glanced at him curiously. He looked particularly handsome today in a multicolored dashiki top that brought out the vivid hues in his hair and eyes. Slit open at the neck, it revealed russet curlicues on his chest and a pewter tear drop peace symbol she'd never before noticed.

Almost against her will, she reached inside the shirt and pulled out the necklace, trembling slightly as her fingers brushed against his collar bone. "That's beautiful," she said, avoiding his gaze, afraid he might think her too aggressive. "Where did you get it?" As she turned the peace symbol over, it glinted in the sunlight.

"At Yellow Springs over Easter Break. There's an artist's community, with all kinds of shops. They have far out things, like this necklace."

"Oh? I've never been." Julia had heard of Antioch College at Yellow Springs, but only in the context of her father's opinions: a hotbed of left-wing ideas, interracial marriage, and hard drugs.

"We'll go there sometime," Win promised. With a gentle yank, he drew the necklace from Julia, pulling her closer. His fingers burned in comparison to the burnished coolness of the pewter. "Please come back to the house with me."

Julia lifted her eyes to meet his. She saw the need, the same passion she'd recognized in the alley the night they'd talked at Ruddy's. So it hadn't been her overheated imagination, as Valerie had implied. Her stomach tightened. "All right."

Forgetting to purchase the cookies, they walked the short distance to his house in silence. Pausing before the psychedelic-swirl mailbox which rested precariously on the porch railing, Julia said, "I wonder if anyone got the mail," knowing that if the box was empty, someone was undoubtedly home. She prayed it wasn't.

Win reached inside and retrieved a pile of letters. Riffling through them, he pulled out an official looking envelope. "Hey, what's this?" His eyes widened as he scanned the return address. "Oh, fuck...." He ripped open the letter.

"What is it?" Julia demanded, her longing turning to fear as Win's normally placid features grew coarse with fury. "What's wrong?"

"Those bastards!" Win dashed into the house, dropping letters as he ran.

"Win!" Julia called after him. She picked up the torn envelope. It was from the United States Selective Service Administration in Cincinnati. Julia stared at it blankly, then realized Win had just been served with his draft notice. They couldn't wait a few weeks until he graduated? What kind of fuck-up was this?

Closing her eyes, Julia leaned against the porch, wondering why theirs was the only generation to resist its legacy of war. Was it because, prior to the nuclear bomb, fighting was considered a rite of passage? That the "ultimate solution" made people finally realize they could annihilate the entire race? She felt like weeping for everyone, including the Selective Service. Then she thought, what am I doing, standing here? Win needs comforting, not me.

Picking up the path of fallen cards and letters, she noticed one from Stu and Laura Porter in London. Funny, she'd almost forgotten about them. She could barely remember what they looked like.

Leaving all but Stu and Laura's letter on a ledge near the hallway steps, she hurried towards Win's room at the back of the house. "Win," Julia rapped softly on his door. "It's me, Julia. Can I come in?" She reached for the knob.

"Go away," His words were muffled, choked. Was he *crying*?

"Win, please let me in. I know you got your draft notice. You need to find out why it came so early. There are ways to get around it."

"Go back to your dorm, Julia," She could hear him moving around on the other side of the door, sliding the lock into place. "You said you have to study."

How could he be so insensitive? He was hurt, but he didn't have to shut her out. "All right then, be like that," she retorted, still more out of anguish for him than anger.

"Julia, I'll call you. OK?"

Defeated, Julia turned to leave. "By the way, you got a letter from London," she added. "I'll drop it off in the hall with the others."

"From Stu and Laura?" Win demanded in a frightened voice. "You didn't open it, did you? Slide it under the door."

Why would he think she'd snoop through his mail? With a sigh, Julia complied. The longer she knew Win, the less she understood him.

During the next two days, she waited for Win's call. The phone remained mercilessly silent, an unfriendly black presence. Julia tried to study, but couldn't concentrate. She didn't care any more, not really. The only thing she wanted was Win. Even if it meant dropping out of school and moving to London like he and the others had talked about last spring so he could avoid the draft.

She fantasized about a life in London. She visualized herself and Win strolling hand-in-hand down Picadilly Circus, going to the ballet and symphony, lying in front of a fireplace in their tiny flat. She stopped short, just before they made love. Was she frigid? Was Win receiving his draft notice at such a crucial moment in their relationship a divine favor? Did she want to risk what little they had for something, in reality, that seemed overrated?

She could have gone over to his house. But experience taught her that girls didn't pursue boys. "Let them come to you," her mother had advised when Julia was growing up. "Chase them 'till they catch you," girlfriends admonished. In both high school and college, among straights and hippies, Julia had seen the girls who openly went after boys rejected. This new idea, women's liberation, was the forte of frustrated old maids and lesbians.

Around dinnertime on the third day, Julia wandered into the lobby to get a can of Tab from the machine. Louie stood by the phone, lifting up the receiver. He looked as unhappy as she felt, not even bothering to smile when he saw her. "You saved me a call," he said abruptly. "I was coming over here to get a newspaper and Win wanted me to ask you over for dinner."

"Tell him thanks for the advance notice," Julia's reply was equally sour. She wanted to say no, to play it cool like she'd always been told, but she couldn't. Besides, Win was about to be drafted. "I'll be by in half an hour," she said in a kinder voice. Later she thought perhaps Louie could have waited for her so they could talk on the way to the house. But he seemed in a hurry to get back.

She rode her bike over anyway, taking care to wind the lock around a wooden pillar on the porch. "I'm here!" she called, standing in the tiny foyer. All the lights were off. Where was everybody?

Shawn poked her head over the stairwell. "We're eating upstairs! The boys' kitchen has been condemned by the Department of Health!" With crusted dishes piled high in the sink and half-empty wooden cabinets and filled with partially opened packages of junk food, the sink and refrigerator were undoubtedly filled with unspeakable life forms. Julia wondered if the landlord had called the city on them.

"Really?" she bounded up the stairs. "You'd better get rid of your dope then, if you want to avoid getting busted. When are they coming back?"

"God, Julia, you're *so* gullible!" Kirsten rolled her eyes and even Louie managed a grin. They were helping Shawn in the girls' kitchen.

Win sat in the living room with Vicki and Bill. Slumped on the battered couch, he stared morosely into a glass of wine which in a previous incarnation had been a Jif peanut butter jar. In spite of his indifferent treatment of her, Julia felt a surge of sympathy. He had good reason to be depressed.

"Hi, Win," Julia said softly, hoping for his radiant smile and the sparks that always seemed to fly back and forth between them.

"Hi, yourself," Win said indifferently as he stood up. "When do we eat?"

"Right now," Shawn replied, spooning macaroni and tuna fish casserole onto plates.

Everyone was lively, save Win, who barely touched his food. Julia could feel him staring at her, but he looked away whenever she started to say something to him.

After Julia and the other girls cleared the table, Win announced, "I'm going to Lenny's to find Jake. I need a little action tonight. Want to come, Louie?"

What did Win mean by action? Julia wondered. Was he going to pick up some chick and bring her back to the house? "Maybe I'd better leave," she said, edging towards the stairs.

"Don't be ridiculous," Louie told her, glaring at Win. "Shawn and I are going to stick around here and we want you to stay. But we do need some more wine. Can I borrow your car, Win?"

"Sure," Win shrugged and he and Louie clambered noisily down the steps in an obvious effort to cover their conversation. Julia figured they were talking about her.

Kirsten had a rehearsal at the theatre and Vicki and Bill went into their shared room to study, leaving Julia and Shawn to clean up the dishes and pots. Rather than giving Julia a chance to discuss her troubles with Win, Shawn spilled her own grievances. People hassled her because she wasn't into the protest movement; her parents bugged her because she was graduating this quarter and hadn't yet begun to look for a job. And she found keeping up with her courses difficult because of her eyesight. So Julia remained quiet.

A few minutes later, she heard the outside door bang open. Assuming it was Louie, she called, "Bring on the Zonin! We've been empty for too long!" Perhaps the wine would lift Shawn's mood.

Win capered into the kitchen, his deep eyes alight with joy. "I have something better!" He held aloft a plastic baggie full of pills. Red bullet-shaped capsules, huge round pink tablets, and tiny black-and-white caplets danced crazily together. "And I'm going to take them all! Anyone care to join me?"

"I'm going to be a drag as usual," Shawn shook her head. "You know I had to give up that shit when I started on antibiotics." Fortunately, her diagnosis has been for the less pernicious Histoplasmosis, although her eyesight would be permanently impaired.

Julia stood stiff with shock. Had Win lost his mind? Was this the same person who had ordered her not to touch mescaline until she was absolutely, positively confident she could handle the drug?

"OK, if you guys wanna be party poopers," Win went over to the sink. Picking up a still-dirty glass, he said, "Louie hasn't come back with the wine yet, so I'll have to wash these down with water." He turned on the tap.

Julia's eyes burned with unshed tears. "I'm not going to stand here while you kill yourself, Win. I'm splitting."

"Whatever turns you on," He filled the glass. "I'm going to die anyway, so I might as well enjoy it."

His apparent apathy spurred her anger. "You idiot!" Julia leapt forward, knocking the glass from Win's hand. It fell on the floor, turning into a shattered puddle of shards. Pills scattered everywhere, rolling under the table, into the heat register, into cracks in the yellow linoleum. "You don't have to take what's doled out to you. You have a choice."

For a moment they glared at each other, like two cats about to spar. Then Julia grabbed her Indian weave bag and fled.

"Hey, Julia!" she could hear him calling after her as she stumbled down the steps. How could he be so careless with his life? And how could she have been so foolish to fall in love with him when he didn't give a damn about himself or her?

"Julia!" She was outside in the darkness when Win caught up with her and seized her arm. "Stop! Please!"

"I have to get my bicycle," she attempted to squirm from his grasp.

"Not until we rap."

"Oh, *now* you want to talk," she retorted, the tears spilling onto her face. "Before you locked your door on me and ignored me and wanted to go uptown and find some *action* with Jake." She knew she sounded sarcastic and jealous but was too wounded to care.

"I'm sorry," Although Win hung his head and looked contrite, he refused to release her. "I was only thinking of myself and being drafted and how I was going to tell my family I couldn't go. My grandfather was career military, for God's sake and I'm afraid it will kill him. As it is, my folks force me to wear a hat when he's around so he won't see my hair." His eyes locked into hers. "You're the last person I want to see suffer." He wiped away her tears with his free hand.

She went soft inside. "Well, then let me into your head, Win. Don't shut me out." She reached over and caressed his angular cheek. He'd lost weight because of the stress of the last few days. Somehow he'd escape the draft. He had to.

"Oh, God, Julia, you are so beautiful," he whispered. "I can't resist you any more." His mouth came down on hers and she put her arms around his neck.

Every cell in her body came alive. His tongue slipped into her mouth and she gasped with pleasure at the unexpectedly exquisite sensation. "Oh, Win," she moaned, her tongue reaching to entwine his. He rubbed his erection up and down against her groin, and she felt herself falling into that chasm she now knew for certain existed.

She was vaguely aware of headlights and the crunching of gravel. Abruptly Win dropped his embrace and Julia struggled to keep her balance. "I'm an all or nothing man," he told her, his voice ragged. "I can't bear to be teased, even though I know you don't mean to. So please think this through, Julia. I mean it when I say I don't want to hurt you."

Louie slammed the car door and pretended not to see them as he started to scurry by, a frustrated look on his face. Louie's jealous, Julia realized in amazement. He likes me and that's why he's been behaving so strangely. Win seemed to notice it too, for he halted Louie's progress by throwing an arm around his shoulder and saying too heartily, "Hey man, let's go upstairs and get high. Grass and wine only, of course." Placing his other arm around Julia, Win guided them both back inside.

CHAPTER TWENTY-FOUR

Rather than being elated by Win's expression of passion, Julia found herself worrying about Louie. What on earth possessed him to fall for her? Because she listened to his stories about Vietnam? Because they were comfortable around each other? She had done nothing to encourage him sexually, hadn't even thought about him that way. Julia didn't want to hurt Louie but she didn't know how to avoid it, either.

And she was concerned about birth control. She'd abandoned the Pill months ago, hating what it did to her body. Yet the thought of making love without any protection never occurred to her. Some of her friends had abortions, and although she felt every woman was entitled to a choice, she could never do that to herself and an unborn child. Like so many things in her life, Julia couldn't live by the standards she tolerated in others.

She decided to get fitted for a diaphragm. Perhaps she could coax Shawn into borrowing Win's car so she could go to Hamilton. Shawn could make up a pretext for the trip because Julia was too embarrassed to tell Win the truth — that she wanted to go to the Free Clinic there.

Compared to its predecessors, the April 15 moratorium was boring. After the People's Lunch, the afternoon program dragged on with speeches about "Morality and War," and racism as it related to Vietnam and the Hayes campus. Issues were raised on extending the Equal Educational Opportunity Program to increase black enrollment, developing a plan of tutorial and support services for blacks, having each academic department set aside at least one professorship and graduate assistant position for blacks, and so on. Distracted by her problems, Julia glanced about.

It was then she realized she hadn't seen Valerie since that day at the jailhouse during the President's ROTC Review. Had Valerie dropped out one quarter shy of graduation? Or had she lost herself in an excess of drugs and self-indulgence? Even worse, had Valerie become so paranoid she'd gone underground?

Before Julia could contemplate further, Felix stood up to speak. Leaning over the microphone with a hellfire-and-brimstone approach reminiscent of old-time preachers, he shouted, "Instead of sitting on our asses rapping about equality, I propose we DO something." The chattering crowd grew quiet. Whatever his dubious political connections, Felix knew how to seize the moment.

"What do you suggest, brother?" someone asked.

"I say we pay a visit to the ROTC building," Felix said. "We gotta show them we mean business." This idea was met with cries of "Right on! Strike! Strike!" And the group began to move in the general direction of the Student Center.

Julia still suspected Felix might be the informer. She wondered if he was setting up yet another ambush and if the police would be there waiting for them. Still, like most undergraduates, she had no idea where the ROTC building was and curiosity compelled her to follow along. This time, she might even be able to prove something.

As soon they reached an inconspicuous brick structure tucked between the power plant and the Hayes chapel, Felix deftly broke the lock. A great cheer rose among the ranks. There were no policemen to be seen; apparently her theory was wrong.

The students surged inside. "Wow! Look at this!" Jake had found Julia on the way over and now pointed to an elevated deck. "Far fuckin' out!" The navigation bridge held a pair of anti-aircraft guns and a single-barrel gun mount. It was a simulated Destroyer vessel with barometer, compass, and other naval gear. Jake pulled a joint out of the pocket of his fringed vest. "Let's get up there and start tokin'!"

Still worried about a trap, Julia hesitated. "I don't know, Jake. What if the cops come after us?"

"Shit, we've already locked 'em out. This is a pretty solid building — they'll have to climb through the windows to get in. Besides, no one knows we're here."

Since it seemed more like a lark than a demonstration, Julia followed him up the steps. From her vantage point on top of the gun mount, she could see everyone's comings and goings. Jake lit the joint and they passed it back and forth. It was fun calling out to people, having them look around, puzzled, then find her grinning above them on the deck. Even more so because she was stoned.

Win joined them, scrambling up the metal stairs leading to the bridge. "Whenever I decide to finally hit the books, I always miss something," he complained good-naturedly. Since that night at his house, he'd been more like his old self, acting as if nothing between him and Julia had happened. Julia supposed he was giving her time to think things over, which put her at ease.

As Julia made room for him, she nearly slipped off the gun mount. "You'd better not smoke any more of that stuff or you'll shoot yourself," Win teased, taking the joint from her.

A rock band arrived around the same time as a hassled-looking petty officer. "Would you please stand clear of the bridge, away from the command posts?" he pleaded. Hoots and jeers greeted his request and knowing he was outnumbered, he left.

About 6:30, someone took orders for pizza. Julia and Win had moved to the relative comfort of the floor of the deck, their legs dangling over the edge which was supported by an iron railing. When their pizza arrived, they shared it between them.

Julia glanced down at the students boogeying to the Psychedelic Scuzzballs. "This is like a party," she giggled, still high from Jake's grass and the excitement of the event. "No I take it back, this *is* a party."

"Yeah, I know," Win replied, then looked at her in his sensual, penetrating way. He reached for the last piece of pizza. "Listen, about what happened a few days ago..." he began awkwardly.

He lifted up the piece, then changed his mind about eating it. "Want this? Otherwise, I'll throw it away."

"No thanks." His loss of appetite gave her courage; he needed reassurance, too. She said, "I need to borrow your car, Win."

"For what?" He stuffed the uneaten pizza into the delivery bag.

"I have to go the Free Clinic for a diaphragm," she told him softly.

Before Win could respond, Jake strode over to them, a girl on his arm. With her hair in a page boy with spit curls on the ends and creased, new-looking bellbottom jeans, she looked like a recent convert to the movement. She held a box full of what appeared to be junk and gazed admiringly at Jake. "Has anyone seen Adrian?" Jake tossed his black curls. "Me an' Sherry were liberating some loot an' he got a phone call in the office."

"That's weird," Julia said. "Who'd call Adrian here?"

"Did you take a message?" asked Win. "Nah, that's a stupid question. You never take any at the house." He peered into the box. "What is all this stuff?"

"Souvenirs of a memorable event," Jake winked at the girl. "You know, American Legion medals, trophies, platoon drill plaques, the usual military shit." He pulled out a ROTC training manual. "And this pornography." Tossing it back into the box, he said, "I was gonna sell 'em, but they're free to my friends." Taking out a medal, he started to pin it on Julia work shirt.

Julia pulled away from him. "Really, Jake, that's ripping off someone else's property. As much as we don't like them, we're only here protest the war...."

"May I have your attention, please?" The voice magnified by a bullhorn was only too familiar. Looking down, Julia saw a grim-faced Dean Moreland accompanied by Ken Dietz, student body president. Abruptly the room grew quiet.

"I am going to read Disruptive Behavior Statement Number One..." Moreland began and everyone, including Julia and Win, burst into laughter. What a title for simply asking students to split! Titters and giggles accompanied Moreland's canned speech which basically said that they were trespassers subject to arrest, and should leave now or face suspension. After Moreland was done, the crowd applauded, whistled, and stamped their feet. Julia noticed, however, that the rock band had disappeared, along with dozens of previously enthusiastic participants.

By now, Julia was familiar with Moreland's purple-faced anger. "I'm serious about this! We mean business," he shouted. Julia believed him. "I'm going to proceed to Disruptive Behavior Statement Number Two," he said, making an obvious effort to calm himself. This was greeted with snores and hand-blown farts; the joke had gotten old.

"The students present are now advised that they are officially suspended under the provisions of *Disciplinary Procedures*, Section 384," Moreland had regained his composure, although he was still yelling through the bullhorn. "The proper officials have been notified. Anyone remaining in the building will be arrested and charged with Breaking and Entering, which is a felony punishable by fine and imprisonment, and Trespassing, under the Ohio State Code."

"Hell, no we won't go! Hell, no we won't go!" The students chanted, raising clenched right hands in unison. Felix leaned over the railing above Moreland and shouted, "We ain't moving 'til you get rid of ROTC and give blacks freedom on this campus. 'Til then, you know where you can stick your fuckin' Disruptive Behavior Statements."

Wordlessly, Moreland handed the bullhorn to a beleaguered Ken Dietz and elbowed his way outside. Students cheered at his retreating back.

Julia and Win exchanged worried glances. "The party is over," Julia said.

"I know. We'd better split before the cops arrive." Taking her hand, he began to lead her downstairs.

Julia thought about the times she'd avoided taking a stand on Vietnam. She shook her head. Tonight she was going to stay, even it meant jail. She wanted to end the war, and if this was what it took.... "I'm not leaving, Win. You can if you'd like."

"Julia, you're going to get hurt. Look what happened to Shawn."

"That's not the point, Win. Sometimes you have to make sacrifices for everyone's good. If enough people unite, they'll have to listen."

The building began to rumble and the remaining students rushed to the windows. "Tanks!" someone exclaimed, "They've brought out the fuckin' National Guard!" Overhead, the roof rattled; obviously a chopper hovered above them.

The front and back doors burst open. While Shawnee County and Hampton police blocked the entrances, Highway Patrolmen began to remove students who quickly assumed the standard protest position, crossing their legs and linking their arms. The cops picked them up by their elbows; only when demonstrators actively resisted arrest did they use force, pulling them by their hair. Students retaliated by thrashing, biting, and kicking, increasing their activity for the benefit of the audience they knew waited outside.

Julia started towards the exit. "If we go peacefully, they probably won't hassle us too much," she said. Win followed her silently. She struggled with her own fear. What if Sheriff Adams were to demand an interrogation, alone? She glanced around; he was nowhere to be seen.

The Shawnee County policeman guarding the exit stepped away from the door. Instead of paying attention to her and Win, he looked into the crowd, and Julia realized he was giving them an opportunity to escape unnoticed and avoid arrest.

Julia held out her hands to the cop. "I want to stop the war. It's immoral, and this is one small thing I can do for the people who died."

Win hung back and she turned to him. "Go back to the house, if you wish. I'll be fine." Secretly she hoped he would stay with her.

"I shouldn't leave you," he replied, his face an agony of confusion. Julia's heart ached for him.

"I'll be OK, Win. Really. Besides, if the Draft Board sees you were busted during a demonstration, they'll ship you to Vietnam for sure."

"I don't have all day, you two," the cop said.

Win started to turn away, his expression still anguished. "I'll go back to the house and get the car and some bread for bail," he said. "Where are you taking her?"

"Hamilton Police Station," The cop grasped Julia's arm.

"I'll see you there," Win promised her. Maybe when he picks me up, we can stop at the Free Clinic, she thought, then chided herself for being so selfish. "Be careful, Julia."

Outside, the mace-filled air reverberated with sirens, screams, and shouts of "Fuck you, pigs!" An ambulance tore through the fabric of the crowd, leaving students fleeing in its path.

Julia gasped at the size of the milling mob; it looked on the verge of a full-scale riot. "Actually, you're safer on the bus," the cop told her. "Hope your boyfriend doesn't get hurt."

"Why, so he can be killed in Vietnam?" Julia retorted, then, immediately contrite because the policeman had been so reasonable, explained, "This isn't a game, you know. We have a purpose in doing this."

She stepped onto the school bus that held the arrested demonstrators. Everyone was jabbering about a student who had been trying to break up a fight between a cop and another protester and had been struck unconscious by a billy club. He had just been taken away by the ambulance.

"Who?" Julia was suddenly apprehensive.

"The SMC leader, Louie what's-his-name," A girl informed her.

"Louie Wexler?" Julia cried, horrified.

"That's him. We don't know if he's going to make it. His head was covered with blood."

Julia buried her face in her hands. "Oh my God," she said, her voice bitter. "Why do I keep calling on God? From the looks of things, He must be dead." Just like Louie might be.

"Right on, sister," Someone agreed as the bus headed toward Hamilton and an uncertain fate.

CHAPTER TWENTY-FIVE

Julia and the fifty other arrested female demonstrators spent the night huddled in a cold, barren holding cell. With one toilet and the stink of urine barely covered by disinfectant, the group's spirit quickly dissipated. Julia worried about Louie and, despite her doubts about the existence of God, prayed. Of everyone she knew, Louie was the most courageous, the most committed. He'd seen death firsthand and she'd thought it made him different.

But did it? she wondered. Had she drawn an invisible line between herself and Louie because he'd killed or experienced the slaughter of others? Did it make her any better than those who shunned vets or spat on them, calling them mass murderers and baby killers? The truth is, most of us would have reacted similarly, she realized. In a kill or be killed situation you do what you must in order to survive.

Every time a guard passed their cell, she asked, "Any word on the student who was hurt?" while the others clamored for release. No one seemed to know anything, and Julia paced back and forth in the space left to her.

Finally she tumbled into a corner and slept uneasily. When she awakened it was morning and a heavy-set matron holding a clipboard was unlocking the cell. "Everybody out," the matron announced. "We're going to return your identification and jewelry, but you'll have to find your own way home. The University has arranged for your release, but you will be charged with trespassing. Although, personally, I would have let you sit for a few more days."

"Fuck you," the girl next to Julia muttered.

The matron, thinking Julia had spoken, pointed an accusing finger at her and exclaimed, "I heard that. Come over here!"

"It wasn't me," Julia stammered, backing away. Why did she feel so guilty?

"What's your name?"

"Julia Brandon," Julia glared at the real culprit who pretended to look innocent. "But I didn't say it. Honest." The girl edged away from Julia as quickly as she could.

"Oh, yeah?" The matron scanned the clipboard, then scowled. "You're on here all right. From the looks of Sheriff Adams' notes you're a real troublemaker. Maybe we ought to ship you back to Hampton in a patrol car so you can have a talk with him."

"No! Please!" Julia pleaded, clasping her hands together. "I have to get back to campus. One of my best friends is in University Hospital with a concussion. And my boyfriend's on the verge of being drafted. Sheriff Adams has had it in for me since last year when I tried to post bail for my roommate." Of course the woman would never believe that Adams hoped to do more than interrogate Julia.

"You kids have no respect for authority," the matron retorted. "You spit in the face of everything. Come along quietly or I'll have to put you in cuffs." She reached for Julia's arm.

"I didn't say it. You've got to believe me!" Julia cried hoarsely. Even though her eyes burned with exhaustion, fear made her wide awake. "I can't speak for the others but I'm not disrespectful. Most of my mother's family died in the Holocaust so I value the few relatives I have left. And besides, everyone's entitled to their own opinion. Since you come from a different generation, I can understand your frustration."

The woman stared at Julia for a long moment, then said, "I don't know why, but I think you're telling the truth. Go ahead with the rest."

"Nice work," someone murmured as they filed towards the booking area to pick up their possessions.

"I wasn't lying," Julia snapped, not caring whether her voice carried. "I can't stand people who dish things out then leave others to take the rap. If I ever see that chick again, I'll kick her in the face." She knew she was tired and irritable, but she sounded as tough as Valerie, an unsettling realization.

After Julia got her things, she hurried to the station lobby. Perhaps she and Win could visit Louie in the hospital. The stop at the Free Clinic was forgotten.

Shawn, not Win, stood waiting for her. Seeing Julia's surprised disappointment, Shawn explained, "Win was here last night. He meant to come back this morning, but was so wiped out from all the shit that went down that he's still asleep. So I borrowed his Chevy."

How well she understood his tiredness. "But you're not supposed to drive, are you?" she asked. "Your eyesight...."

"I know I'm legally blind, but I can still operate a car if need be," Shawn replied with a touch of impatience. "Besides, I'm sick of hiding in the house." She handed Julia the keys. "You can take us back."

"Then we'll visit Louie. Have you heard anything about him?"

"Only that he's in fair condition. We called the hospital several times."

"They're feeding you a line," Julia said. "According to the kids last night, he was struck unconscious. His head was covered with blood."

"I don't know. Sometimes these things get exaggerated. Why don't you go back to your room and crash?"

"No, I want to go to the hospital," Julia insisted. "I must see Louie." Somehow she felt responsible, as if her not caring for him had made him take unnecessary chances.

During the drive to Hayes, Julia fought against falling asleep at the wheel. Every time she sensed Shawn watching her, she retorted, "I'm fine," ignoring her weary body's need for a hot shower and bed.

They arrived at the edge of campus. Everywhere Julia looked she saw soldiers in uniform, cordoned-off areas, and military trucks and transports. "What's going on here?" Julia demanded. "This place has become a war zone!" She suddenly came alert, drawing on untapped energy.

"Governor Rhodes called in the militia," Shawn replied. "He did the same thing at OSU and Kent. Rumor is Nixon's going to send troops into Cambodia, so the Man wants to be prepared."

"Those bastards! Didn't take them long, did it?" Julia pulled into the hospital parking lot.

In spite of their grim mood, Shawn chuckled. "We've got quite a selection. National Guard, State Highway Patrol, campus Cap Guns, and of course, Hampton and Shawnee County's finest. Take your pick."

Julia grinned, feeling a sense of extreme confidence, the upside of exhaustion. "Not a little nervous, are they? I'll handle this Guardsman at the entrance." If she could convince the hardened matron at the jail, she'd have no problem with the fresh-faced boy who looked even younger than they. "He'll let us in without any trouble."

Julia and Shawn approached him. "Excuse me, but our friend is in the hospital," Julia said politely. "Would you please step aside so we can visit him?"

"No miss, I'm sorry," The soldier's Southern Ohio twang still held the reediness of adolescence. "Governor Rhodes has declared this campus under a state of emergency."

Julia was determined to keep cool, despite the tiredness creeping back into her bones. "This has nothing to do with the governor. And it's a public hospital — anyone's welcome here."

"Sorry miss, I can't let you in," he repeated. An older couple walked out the door and he watched them pass with a pleasant, "Good day, folks."

"You allowed *them* entrance," Julia retorted, forgetting her resolve.

"They have relatives here, miss. You said you wanted to visit a friend. The campus is under martial law, so only immediate family and hospital employees are permitted access. Now please move; you're blocking the door."

"Why, that's the most ridiculous thing I've ever heard!" Julia cried, the ragged ends of her nerves unraveling. "You're discriminating against me because I'm a student!"

Shawn laid a gentle hand on Julia's arm. "We can come back another time, Julia. The people at the hospital were probably being straight with me when I called. I'm sure Louie's going to be fine."

"Then why won't they let us see him? We're closer to Louie than some of the so-called families this baby soldier lets through. And I want to talk to Louie. Now." She scowled at the Guardsman, for once unfazed by his uniform and helmet. His gun probably wasn't even loaded.

"What's going on here, Dave?" someone behind them asked. Julia and Shawn turned to see another Guardsman nearer to their age. "I go take a leak, and you've got trouble...." He stopped in mid-sentence and gazed at Shawn. "Jesus H. Christ. I don't believe it."

"Joey Lester?" Shawn trilled. Julia had never seen her friend smile that way before.

The Guardsman's expression mirrored Shawn's. "Shawn Collier." He spoke her name with reverence and they embraced. Julia and the young Guardsman stared at them incredulously.

"This is my steady from junior high," Shawn explained after she and Joey had finished hugging. "Then like a fink, he moved to Cleveland when we were sophomores. I always wondered what happened to you, Joey."

"Uh, Joe, if you don't mind," the Guardsman glanced at his comrade.

"Well, now you can let us in," Julia observed. "Let's go, Shawn."

"Not so fast," With a swift movement, Dave blocked the doorway, gun across his chest and legs apart.

Who was this kid to tell her what to do? "You have no right to stop me," Julia fumed. "You're just one of Nixon's puppets. You won't come out and openly protest the war like the rest of us but you wanted to get out of 'Nam so you joined the Reserves. I don't have to obey you."

"I resent that," Joey snapped, turning from Shawn's admirer back into a soldier.

Ignoring him, Julia glowered at Dave, who stood unflinching. She said, "Hell, I just tell it like it is."

"Julia was arrested during yesterday's demonstration," Shawn explained. "A night in jail can be pretty unsettling. Is there any way we can find out about our friend?"

Joey gazed at Shawn and softened. "I can go inside and check. Who do you want to see?"

With a sigh of resignation, Julia gave him Louie's name. While they waited, Shawn assured her, "Joey won't bullshit you. I've known him since he was a little kid and we used to tease him because he was so blunt." She tossed her silken hair, an uncharacteristic, preening gesture. "Can you believe I ran into him after all these years?"

"I'd stay away from him if I were you," Julia warned. "After all, he is in the military."

"We say we're open-minded but sometimes I wonder," Shawn observed in a quiet voice.

Joey came out with a man in a white coat. "I'm Dr. Gordiano," he introduced himself. "Which one of you was asking about Louis Wexler?"

"Me," Julia replied, her heart pounding. So she'd been right. Louie must be seriously hurt for the doctor to want to speak to her personally.

"Follow me, please." When they reached the lobby, Dr. Gordiano said, "How well do you know Louis?"

"We were pretty friendly last fall. He talked to me about his experiences in Vietnam. What's going on?" She tried not to show her fear. If the doctor knew how upset she was, he might withhold information.

"Oh, he's all right physically," Gordiano replied. "It was a relatively mild concussion. But I'm worried about his mental state."

"Oh, God...what do you mean?"

"He's slipped into a deep depression. He hasn't spoken a word since last night; he simply lies in bed and looks at the ceiling. It could be a result of the blow to his head, but I doubt it."

"I just got out of jail myself because of the riot," Julia rubbed her eyes. "But I'll do whatever I can to help."

"Right now, go home and get some sleep," Gordiano advised. "Louis's parents are on the way in from Cleveland, so they might help him snap out of this. I've seen this type of delayed stress reaction before, especially with men who have been in combat. But if you'd like, I'll leave your name with the admissions desk so you can visit him."

After thanking the doctor, Julia trudged back to her dorm. Shawn was still flirting with that sell-out of a National Guardsman, but Julia was too drained to care. Let the asshole drive her home in Win's car. Yet once in bed, sleep eluded her, even after her longed-for shower. Her thoughts kept returning to Louie; how he'd reached out to her all these months and she'd never noticed. And when she had, she'd done nothing about it, even though she considered Louie one of her best friends.

Not only has Louie helped me, but he's selflessly devoted himself to the movement, Julia reflected. And look what he got in return.

CHAPTER TWENTY-SIX

Except for the presence of militia on campus, the next few days were uneventful. Students and soldiers developed the strange sort of camaraderie sometimes found in a hostage-captor situation. Coeds placed flowers in gun barrels, made daisy wreaths for military necks, slipped peace symbol flags close to where the Guardsmen stood. In return, the soldiers, who were mostly young, whistled and flirted when they thought their commanding officers weren't looking.

Julia spent much of her time in the hospital with Louie, who slowly lifted himself out of his depression. She met Louie's parents, who, although his father painted instead of golfed for recreation and his mother worked full-time, reminded her of her own parents in odd little ways. They left after a few days, when they felt Louie was all right.

But Julia knew differently. When others were around, Louie seemed like his usual effusive self. But when he and Julia were alone, he grew morose. He resisted Julia's attempts to get him to discuss what was bothering him. Finally he lost his temper, accusing her of patronizing him, saying, "I don't know why you're so worried about me. I can take care of myself." He then told her about Hu'o'ng and his baby son.

After that, Julia avoided the hospital. She had only made things worse by meddling. Besides, he couldn't have cared for her as much as she'd believed, not after having the intense involvement of an almost-wife and a child.

Julia finally got fitted for a diaphragm, catching a ride with a suite mate who'd wanted to go shopping in Hamilton for a few hours. Feeling proud of herself and adventuresome, she inserted it that afternoon and went over to Win's.

Win and Jake were sitting on the front porch getting high. They did this with particular relish when they thought President Carrell's wife might come outside to do some gardening. It was their way of courting danger: smoking dope in the same vicinity as Amanda Carrell, never mind that she was across the street and not even paying attention.

They offered Julia the joint and she shook her head. "Uh, Win can I talk to you?"

Win handed it back to Jake. "Sure, Julia. What's going down?"

Julia blushed. "I mean, alone?"

"Don't mind me," Jake said. "I was just getting ready to watch TV. It's time for Scooby-Doo." Stabbing out the joint, he strode into the house, whistling.

"Well, I didn't want it anyway..." Win frowned nonetheless. He reached over and picked up the end of the joint, the roach, and relit it. He'd been smoking more lately, and had stopped running and going to the gym. Win's abandonment of self-caring disturbed her although she understood the reasons why.

"I don't know how to say this," she stammered and Win stared at her. "I have a diaphragm." There. It was finally out.

He looked away. "Oh, yeah? Well, that's cool." He stood and stretched his legs, shifting from one foot to the other. "I better go inside and start dinner. It's my turn to cook. I'd invite you over but we don't have enough food."

Didn't he understand what she was trying to tell him? "You're making this impossible, Win. I mean I have it inside me." She was so humiliated; she couldn't believe this was happening.

"I know what you mean, Julia. Look, I really have to split. We'll discuss this later." He stroked her arm gently before he walked away.

She stared after him, astounded. There was no graceful way to tell him, but he could have been a little more enthusiastic. What was wrong with her? No, what was wrong with *him*?

Win gave her conflicting messages. Arduous one minute, seemingly indifferent the next. Some of it was because of the draft, his uncertainty over the future, but he still hid a part of himself from her. If she could get to that, then she could get to Win. And she wanted him more than anything she'd ever wanted in her life.

She had no chance to mull over strategy, for the next day, Nixon sent troops across the Cambodian border and the campus once again erupted in violence. Dissidents tossed Molotov cocktails through the windows of the Administration Building and a gang of drunken fraternity boys raged through uptown, causing a general uproar.

The military tightened its grip, imposing a nine o'clock curfew. National Guardsmen stepped in whenever students congregated in small groups. The ensuing fistfights destroyed any rapport that might have sprung up between the two camps.

That weekend, rallies were held and reports of violence at other colleges filtered back to Hayes. Demonstrators burned down the ROTC building at Kent; broke windows and defaced businesses on High Street at Ohio State; staged a sit-in in downtown Cincinnati, blocking traffic for miles.

Her arrest and Louie's injury had come to no avail. What difference had they made? Vietnam was a war of the older generation — the same generation that still held onto the reins of their lives and refused to let go. Nothing was going to change, no matter how much they marched or boycotted or even advocated revolution. It would only breed more oppression.

Julia remembered her mother's remark about futile causes. Perhaps Hester had been right. The world was full of great injustices; one only needed to protect oneself from harm.

But still, she despised the hopeless feeling those thoughts gave her. And what about the boys still dying overseas or coming home physically and mentally devastated? And what about others who still might go, like Win? She wondered what their relationship would have been like without the specter of Vietnam. Would they be engaged? Or would they never have met?

At seven a.m. Sunday morning someone rapped softly on her window. Still half-asleep and forgetting to put on her robe, Julia lifted up the sash and peered down at Win.

His russet hair gleamed in the sunlight and a T-shirt and cutoffs emphasized his muscular body. Self-consciously she pulled her nightgown over her breasts. "What are you doing here?" she demanded, confused from being awakened.

"I was hoping you slept in the nude," he teased, flashing his radiant smile. "But we haven't seen much of each other, so I thought we'd spend the day at Shawnee Park. We'll have a picnic lunch and swim in the lake."

"Well, that wasn't my idea...us not being together, I mean," she retorted, starting to close the window.

"Julia, wait," Win placed his hand on the screen. "Please don't be like that. My Army physical's tomorrow and I've been going through hell. I need you."

Between his low lottery number and the fact that he'd be graduating in less than a month, the draft board must have refused to put off his physical. "Oh God, Win," Julia put her hand on the other side of the screen so their fingers mirrored each other. It was like visiting someone in prison, except she could feel his warmth. "Why didn't you say something sooner?"

"What's to say? It won't change the facts. Either I'll go or I won't." He looked at her imploringly. "But let's enjoy today, Julia. It's going to be beautiful."

"I'll meet you in front in a few minutes."

"Far out. Make it quick, though. The others are in the car and we want to get a good spot."

Why did it always have to be with the others? Julia mused as she pulled on jeans and a gauzy top. They didn't always have to come along. It was almost as if Win was afraid to be alone with her.

Her mood lifted as they drove towards Shawnee Lake. A state park and natural game preserve a few miles away from Hayes, it was a favorite springtime retreat for college students. A beach surrounded the huge manmade lake, making it nearly as beautiful as the real thing.

According to Kirsten, Vicki, and Bill, Shawn was at the library, where she'd practically been living these days. What a reversal from someone who'd refused to leave the house.

At the park, they located a grill and after an enthusiastic game of Frisbee, barbecued hamburgers and hot dogs. Afterwards, Vicki, Bill, and Jake wandered off in the woods to get stoned while Julia, Kirsten, and Win cleared away the remains of lunch. When the group returned, Jake suggested they go skinny dipping at a hidden cove they'd discovered last year. All but Julia agreed.

"I can't," she stammered, panicked. Except for her parents when she was a young child; Trevor, who had been drunk at the time; and the girls in the dorm showers, no one had ever seen her completely nude.

"You guys go ahead," Win told the others. "Julia and I will be along soon."

"Why are you so inhibited?" Win asked as they lagged behind their chattering friends.

"I've never done anything like that before," she hung her head, embarrassed by her own naivete.

"Neither had I, until a couple of years ago," He cupped her chin with his hand. "I know you haven't done a lot of things." He looked at her intently.

He thinks I'm still a virgin, Julia realized in shock. Yet she did nothing to correct the fallacy.

They reached the cove. In the distance, Julia could hear the others laughing and splashing. The area was heavily wooded, giving the illusion of privacy.

Not taking his eyes off Julia, Win began to strip. Mesmerized, she watched him. He had a beautiful, tanned body — broad, muscular shoulders, flat stomach, narrow hips, lightly sinewed legs. He did not bother to hide his erection. "Your turn," he said softly, his eyes challenged her.

Time seemed to stand still. Birds sang in the trees. A squirrel dashed across their path, taking refuge in a nest of wild clover. Julia's fingers hesitated at the top button of her peasant blouse.

"I'll make it easy for you," Win told her. "I'll meet you in the water." He strode towards the cove, leaving Julia to admire his smooth buttocks.

Alone, she undressed quickly and raced towards the lake, jumping in without bothering to test the water. The others seemed to take her presence for granted. Why shouldn't they? They were naked also. She relaxed. They were all men and women, they had bodies, they were, in a sense, a family.

Win swam towards her. "See, it's not so bad, is it? I must confess, though, I couldn't help but peek. You're even lovelier than I imagined." With that, he ducked his head under water and dove a few feet beneath her legs. Julia giggled and she and Win chased and tried to dunk each other. The sun beat down on them and she'd never felt more alive or content.

Soon they were both out of breath, and he said, "I'm getting wiped out. I know a beach where we can catch some rays without being seen."

As Julia started to swim with him, he called to the others, "We'll be back in a while."

The isolated stretch of sand was surrounded by scrub pines. Accustomed by now to her own and Win's nudity — almost reveling in the freedom of walking around unclothed — Julia thought nothing of getting out of the water and following him up to the shore.

Reaching behind a tree, Win pulled out a black garbage bag. It held two towels and an unopened bottle of Jack Daniels whiskey.

"I was hoping this stuff was still here," he said as he laid the towels side-by-side. "I meant to come back last spring and get it but never had the chance. Do you suppose the whiskey's still any good?"

"Might as well try," Julia watched as he opened the bottle and took a swig.

"Not bad," He offered it to her. "In fact, it's real smooth."

"No thanks," Julia shuddered.

"Don't you like Jack Daniels? It's the best."

"I don't touch hard liquor any more. Not since last winter." She waited for him to ask why so she could tell him about Trevor.

Instead, he reached over and captured her breast, fondling her nipple with his firm, strong fingers. Julia moaned softly and Win moved closer. "I mean it when I say you're exquisite." He began to kiss her neck, his tongue making slight indentations.

Her arms encircled his waist. "Everything's in place, I presume," he murmured in her ear, and for an instant, she had no idea what he was talking about.

Oh, yes, the diaphragm. "It's back at the dorm," she whispered, no longer caring. Let them make love and damn the consequences.

"Jesus Christ!" Win dropped his embrace and Julia jumped back, startled. He drew up his legs, burying his head in his arms. She stared at him in disbelief as he exclaimed, "How in the hell could you forget it?"

"You don't have to yell at me," Julia replied, suddenly close to tears. "I didn't think to put it in. You said the others were coming, so it never occurred to me we'd be alone." Why was birth control always the woman's responsibility, anyway? "It's not like a rubber that you can keep with you at all times." She glared at him.

"Do I look like I'm carrying a wallet?" Win lifted up his palms. He shook his mane, his long hair hiding his expression. "Look, I'm not mad at you, OK? Just disappointed and really, really frustrated. But I'd better split right now before I lose control and do something we'll both regret. C'mon, let's go back." Without waiting for her, he dashed into the water.

Everyone was tired, so the ride home was quiet. Julia tried to get in back, but Win insisted she sit next to him, touching her and looking at her with regretful eyes.

Julia condemned her own lack of sophistication. Of course she should have thought about the diaphragm. But why couldn't they just go ahead and make love? Was he afraid of even the implied commitment of pregnancy? She was ready to forge a life together. Why wasn't he?

They pulled in front of Julia's dorm. Win turned to her and said, "I'll meet you at the rally tonight, then we'll go back to my house."

There was no mistaking his message. "I'll be there," she promised him. "This time I'll remember."

CHAPTER TWENTY-SEVEN

The rally began at 7:30 in front of the Administration Building, just as dusk settled over the campus. Early May was the height of spring, reminding Julia of last year's Music Fest, when the protest movement was a fault line over an abyss of discontent.

Look at us now, she reflected, glancing around at the thousands of milling students. I don't even know most of these people. And from the appearance of some, I wonder if they even go to school here.

Win came up behind her in his usual silent way and slipped his arm around her waist. Moving his hand so it rested a few inches below her breasts, he whispered, "We'll split early if that's OK with you."

Julia stirred and sighed. The wetness between her legs was more than contraceptive jelly. "We can go now if you'd like."

"Let's wait a couple of minutes," Win told her. "I want to hear what this dude has to say." He pointed to a wild-haired young man in an Army jacket who was about to take the microphone. "He's supposed to be an expert on draft evasion."

"Who is he?" Julia asked. "He's not from around here."

"He's not a draft counselor, either," a voice behind them said. Julia and Win turned to see Valerie. Her clothes were clean, her blonde hair freshly washed. She even wore pink lipstick. "He's a professional agitator, a Weatherman brought in by the SDS. I've been looking for you all day, Julia." Valerie went on. "I've got to rap with you."

Julia stared at her, dumbfounded. She'd expected Valerie to be disheveled and disgruntled and if she hadn't seemed so worried, Julia would have said Valerie looked happy. Too taken aback to express anger at Valerie's past treatment of her, she asked, "What's wrong?"

"I can't tell you, not here. We've got to talk." Valerie picked at her fingernails which Julia noticed were manicured with clear polish. She'd never known Valerie to paint her nails. Or fiddle with them, either.

"We were just leaving," Win said, tightening his arm around Julia. "Julia and I have plans."

"Please, Julia," Valerie pleaded. "I wouldn't ask for your help unless it was an emergency."

Even though they were no longer close, she felt the pull of old ties. "Can't this wait 'til tomorrow, Valerie? Win will be in Cincinnati and you and I'll have time."

"There is no time, don't you see? It's just about run out for all of us." She ducked down. "Oh shit, there's Adrian. He didn't see me, did he?" Adrian stood a few feet away with his back to them and Julia shook her head. "You're the only one I can trust, Julia."

Julia looked at Win for guidance. "We might as well humor her, Julia. But don't let her keep you more than a few minutes." He released his grip. "You're paranoid, Valerie, do you know that?"

"And you're hornier than hell, Win," Valerie retorted, with a touch of her usual asperity. "Don't worry, you'll get your rocks off before they ship you out. Believe it or not, some things are more important than sex."

Win muttered under his breath as Julia and Valerie hurried towards the edge of the crowd. "Why did you talk to him that way?" Julia demanded. "Does it bother you that he cares about me? That you were wrong about him wanting to find one special person?"

Valerie looked at Julia and shook her head. "Still the romantic, aren't you? That's irrelevant right now. We've got to get away as soon as possible. Ever been to the Cliffs?"

Julia stopped. "That's almost a mile from here!"

Grasping Julia's elbow, Valerie steered her behind the Administration building away from the military encampment. "I'll explain it to you on the way over. It's a matter of life and death."

"Then you can just tell me right now. There's no one around. I mean it, Valerie. I'm not budging until I know what this is all about." Crossing her arms, Julia stood, unmoving.

Valerie looked at her with respect. "Whatever happened to the passive sorority girl? Now I know how Dr. Frankenstein felt when he brought the dead back to life. But at least I helped create someone who thinks for herself. All right, Julia. You deserve an explanation."

At the beginning of the quarter, after her arrest at the ROTC march, Valerie had gone to see Richard Shaffley. "I told myself I wanted to talk to him one last time before I graduated," Valerie recalled. "Then he totally blew me away — he said he loved me, but was afraid to seek me out because he thought I hated him, just like his own son did. I almost had myself convinced I hated him, too, until I realized love and hate come from the same emotion." Before Julia could question that outrageous idea — she certainly didn't love Adolf Hitler, for instance — Valerie continued, "He and Myra separated last January. She went back to Philadelphia and took Carrie with her. That shit Adrian never said a word, even though I know he was in contact with his mother."

"Richard was alone all that time and didn't call you?"

"He said he needed to think things through, to reevaluate his life and figure out where he'd gone wrong," Valerie replied. "He didn't want to mess me up again."

"I can't believe someone that old would have those kinds of problems," Julia said. She thought of her parents and their friends, people she'd known from childhood who'd stayed at the same job, with the same spouse, address, and phone number. They had no trouble with their identities.

"Experience only makes you better at hiding your fears," Valerie told her. "Contrary to popular myth, you don't stop hurting inside when you turn thirty."

Although she'd moved in with Richard, Valerie went on, she maintained her commitment to ending the war. She continued with her SDS activities, planning to marry Richard in July and go with him to the University of Florida where he'd accepted a teaching position. "We want to make a new start. Luckily for me, Adrian and Felix got so involved with the subversive shit that's been going down they didn't notice my physical and mental change of venue."

"Subversive?" As far as Julia knew, Valerie hadn't been involved in anything more destructive than supplying the entire campus with marijuana and other drugs.

"Don't you wonder where the stuff for the Molotov cocktails comes from? You know the SMC didn't plan the trash can fires or the building break-ins. And although most of the campus thought the flush-in was a big joke, we counted it on it fucking up the entire sewage system. And we almost succeeded."

Julia began to comprehend what Valerie was telling her. So she hadn't imagined the boxes in Adrian's living room; she'd merely been naive enough to think their contents harmless.

"Do you think this shit is spontaneous? It's planned, Julia. By a core group of people truly dedicated to stopping the war. While you and Win have been making goo-goo eyes at each other, while Shawn's been fucking her National Guardsman, and Louie's been running around getting clobbered, we've been orchestrating the methodical overthrow of the system. But now it's gone too far. Even for me."

The remark about Shawn and the National Guardsman confused her even more. "My God, Valerie. What are you talking about?" Despite the warm evening, she felt a chill.

"Tomorrow they plan on blowing up the Administration building. No advance phone calls, nothing. I can relate to people getting hurt for the cause, but not random murder."

A feeling of unreality stole over Julia, the same sensation she'd had when Lydia had spit at her during the YAF rally last winter. She stroked her cheek. "Maybe they're making idle threats. They wouldn't actually kill anyone, would they?"

"I know you and Win think I'm paranoid, Julia, with all my talk about the CIA and phone taps and shit. But Felix is for real; like I told you before, he's one heavy dude. Felix, Adrian, and a couple of others are supposed to rendezvous at the Cliffs at four a.m. tomorrow and pick up a cache of ammo we hid there. Once Felix attaches the timing device to the plastique, they're going to break into the Administration building and plant a bomb in the basement."

So this was what Valerie had been doing all this time. They're out of their depth. "We've got to tell the police. Now."

"No pigs, Julia. No pigs!" Valerie whirled around, her face rigid with anger and fear. "Think of what they'll do to me — us, since you know about it, too — if we get busted. Ten years in jail for me, at least! And you, well, you might as well forget about ever having a career or marrying a decent guy."

"That's not what I want out of life," Julia countered. "I love Win, and whatever he wants will make me happy."

"But what about me?" Valerie began to cry, huge gulping sobs. "I finally got my shit together, after my life fell apart because the abortion...."

"What *did* happen, Valerie? Why don't you talk about it?"

"Because it makes me sound like a neurotic fool. I mean, it was, like, so unimportant.... Sex is no big deal, right, and what my asshole stepfather did was nothing compared to the vast experience *I've* had...."

Julia hoped her silence would pull out whatever had been tormenting her friend.

"It was just a lot of innuendos, attempted kisses, and fast feels when he thought no one was looking," Valerie continued. "I was the youngest, the so-called free spirit, and he kept telling me how hung up I was. I mean, I was this innocent teenager who went to an all-girls high school and he was the machinist who felt like he was missing out on all the free love that was supposed to be happening. But God, he was an adult and my mother's husband...." She trailed off.

"So when you found someone you cared about, you got scared and split at the first sign of trouble."

"Right on." Valerie seemed relieved to have her feelings in the open. "But you have to help me. We'll get the ammo and take it back to my old house. I told Richard I needed to spend the night there and clean 'cause we're putting it up for sale. Tomorrow morning Richard and I will dump the stuff in Shawnee Lake."

"So Richard knows about this, too?".

"No. I told him it's a bushel of bad grass laced with strychnine. I don't want to burden him with this; he's got enough on his head. If we get caught with the ammo, he can claim ignorance, even take a lie detector test. Somehow I'll escape and go underground." Valerie's words sounded convincing, but her expression was frightened.

Separation from Richard would ruin Valerie's chances for happiness forever, and she'd suffered enough. How unfair if Valerie had to become a fugitive, just as she'd gotten her life together! "All right, Valerie, I'll help you, but you've got to let me phone in an anonymous tip to the cops about the activities at Adrian's farmhouse. I don't like the police myself but this sabotage has to be stopped before someone really gets killed. And what will Felix and Adrian do when they discover the ammo is missing? Won't they start asking questions?"

"I hadn't really thought about that," Valerie conceded. "But promise me you'll call the pigs after Richard and I get rid of the evidence. I may have to go to court, but as long as they can't prove anything, I'll probably get off." She attempted a joke. "Know any decent lawyers?"

With a stab of guilt, Julia thought of Louie. He could help them out of this mess. But he was still in the hospital, and besides, he was upset with her.

It was nearly dark by the time the two girls reached the Cliffs. Elongated shadows loomed like ominous fingers ready to grab them and the woods seemed devoid of animal sounds. "Are you sure we're not being followed?" Julia demanded, unable to shake the sense that someone was watching. "You are being straight with me about this, aren't you?" Could she be indirectly aiding the radicals by moving the contraband to a more convenient location?

"I swear on my great-grandmother's grave," Valerie replied. "I know I used you in the past to gather information and I'm truly sorry about that. But we operate on a need-to-know basis. And when Adrian, Felix, and the rest of us first mobilized, we agreed on a course of action. You, on the other hand, wavered between being the model daughter and the self-involved hippie."

Julia resented Valerie's last remark, but was too worried to take offense. "But Valerie, your activities make you worse than the police! Don't you see you're breeding more violence?"

"That's where you and I differ. That's why I never told you much. But now the situation's too intense, and only we can put a stop to it." Valerie paused before two boulders. "This is the place." A flat stone rested between the tall rocks. Pointing to it, Valerie said, "Help me push this off. The stuff's in a hole underneath."

They each grasped an end and after much effort, finally moved the heavy stone. Two burlap bags lay in the hole.

"Fortunately, it's only a couple of M-16s and bullets, plastique, and a few sticks of dynamite," Valerie explained casually. "We won't have much trouble getting it back."

Julia stared at the bags. In them was material designed to kill human beings. The contents of her stomach started to work their way towards her throat. "I'm going to the police." She turned to leave.

Valerie grabbed her arm so hard Julia was sure her fingers had made marks. "Listen to me, Julia Brandon! I can relate to where you're coming from. But we have to do it my way or you'll permanently fuck up all our lives including innocent people like yourself and Richard. Tell me, how else can we escape unharmed?"

"I don't know, Valerie. This is wrong." Julia shook her curls away from her damp face; the sweat from fear and exertion had made her long hair feel heavy. As much as she hated to admit it, Valerie's argument made sense. There really was no other solution.

"Of course it's wrong! That's why I'm risking our asses to stop it." Sensing Julia's acquiescence, Valerie released her grip. "Now let's be quick; curfew's in less than an hour and I know you want to get back to the rally. And we have to take the longest route back to my place so we won't run into any pigs."

Valerie hoisted one bag over her shoulder and slowly Julia picked up the other. It was lighter than it looked. Their eyes met. "Julia, you're the best friend I've ever had," Valerie said softly. "You were always there for me, even when I treated you like shit.

I hope you get whatever it is you finally decide you want. You deserve it."

"Oh Valerie," Julia wanted to weep. Why was she being so sentimental *now*? She struggled to hide her emotions. "Are you sure we're doing the right thing? I can't help but feel we should go to the authorities."

They started to walk. "I'm positive," Valerie said. "Let's not discuss this any more, OK?"

They hurried through the growing darkness. They encountered no one, so Julia told herself they were safe.

CHAPTER TWENTY-EIGHT

They reached Valerie's house a few minutes later. Everyone was still at the rally so campus and uptown were deserted, even of the usual tanks and trucks. Julia sighed in relief as they finally closed the door inside the barren-looking living room and secured the bags in the kitchen pantry.

The few remaining pieces of furniture were coated with dust, and the air reeked of stale smoke. Julia was dying to open a window, but didn't fearing someone outside might overhear their conversation. Strangely enough, the usually overcautious Valerie seemed confident they'd arrived undetected.

"Look at all this dust!" Valerie exclaimed, blowing a white cloud off her secondhand sofa. "My mother and sisters would shit if they ever saw this. They consider themselves Guardians of the Spotless Surface. Looks like I've got my work cut out for me. You'd better go back to the rally before Win puts out a contract on me for taking you away from him." She dismissed Julia with a wave of a rag she'd picked up off the floor.

Yet Julia felt she should stay. "You're not safe here alone," she said. "When Felix and Adrian discover the weapons are missing, they'll come looking for them."

Valerie took a half-hearted swipe at a nicked coffee table. "Why would they suspect me?" She shrugged. "Adrian blabbed about the ammo to at least twenty people, so it could be anyone."

"But what if they do?" Julia insisted. "Stay at Richard's, or at least spend the night in my room."

"Look, I can't leave the stuff.... And besides, by the time those assholes even consider that a radical chick like me might defect, Richard and I'll be back from Shawnee Lake. No one will be able to prove anything."

"I don't know, Valerie. I have a bad feeling about this."

"What can go wrong? Remember, Richard's coming here at dawn." Her stonewashed eyes sparkled, making them an almost vivid blue. "But knowing him, he'll get lonely and decide to drop by tonight." She started to nudge Julia towards the door. "So everything's cool. I know you and Win have plans, so go to it." She did a leering imitation of W.C. Fields.

Grasping the knob, Julia turned to face Valerie. "When you move to Florida, promise me you and Richard will buy a split level house, get a dog, and consider having 2.5 kids. I think that's what you need. The Stazyck tradition."

"No way, sister," Valerie flashed her impish grin. "Haven't you heard of women's liberation? Now get the hell out of here."

Julia started down the asphalt path towards High Street, then turned. Valerie stood, watching. "Hey, Julia, take care," she called. "I love you."

Her friend had never looked more fragile or vulnerable. "I love you, too, Valerie. Please be careful."

"I promise. Stop by tomorrow; Richard and I will be here painting walls. See you then." As Valerie closed the door, Julia was comforted by the sound of the chain sliding into the lock.

But as she walked through uptown, she found herself getting agitated all over again. How could Valerie let things go this far without telling anyone? And why hadn't she at least confided in Richard? He might have convinced her to do something about the weapons before now.

No one had bothered to turn on the street lights even though darkness had fallen. Lost in musing, Julia headed into the black-looking campus without a thought to staying on the

Slantwalk, the central and most well-traveled path. Instead she shuffled through the grass, taking the most direct route to the Administration building.

"Just a minute, young lady," someone shouted. Deputy Adams strode towards her, shortening the distance between them with every word. "You've violated curfew and I'm going to take you in." For an instant, Julia felt extraordinary relief — here were the authorities, someone whom she could warn. Then she remembered that cops were the enemy, especially Adams. If it had been anyone but him, she might have broken down and told anyway. But as it was, she had to get away from him.

Feigning composure, she glanced at her Timex. The illuminated hands read 8:54. It's not nine yet," she said, her voice even, knowing his compulsion for rules. "The rally's still going on."

With an unexpected movement, Adams seized her wrist and looked at her watch. "The clock in my car says different, but I'll give you the benefit of the doubt. You still won't make it back to the rally in time." He stank of sweat and chewing tobacco; his fox eyes seemed to glow in the night. "But I'll let you try." He released her.

Determined not to let Adams know he unnerved her, she calmly turned in the direction of the Administration building. Were those footsteps echoing hers? She refused to look behind her.

Adams answered her unspoken question by saying, "This place isn't so different from Vietnam, least not according to my brother Danny's letters. We've got good guys — the law and the townies — and Cong — you hippies."

Julia decided not to answer but quickened her pace. She could hear Adams speeding up his.

"You wanna know how Danny bought it?" His voice mocked her. "He stepped on a mine in the jungle and got his legs blown off."

Julia felt with a rush of sympathy. Adams had been a victim, too, channeling his grief into hatred of the protesters. She stopped and faced him. "I'm sorry about your brother. But you have to understand we're trying to prevent the killing of more people like him."

"No, magnolia blossom." He shook his head. "You and your friends are a bunch of pinko cowards afraid to stand up for your country. You see the war as an excuse for sex, drugs, and rock and roll. Folks in uniform like me and the veterans — we're the real heroes." He seemed almost desolate standing there in the dim light, patting his billy club. His life revolved around his authority, Julia realized. "Look at your watch now, magnolia blossom, and I bet you'll see it's after nine. Look's like you're gonna miss your rendezvous with lover boy."

How could he possibly know about Win? Her surprise must have been visible, because he said, "I have spies, or to be more exact, a spy. He lets me know what you hippies are up to. Of course I can always guess." Lifting up his billy club, he stroked it up and down suggestively. "Now it's *my* turn."

There was no mistaking his intent; he meant to come after her. Without replying, Julia started to run. The campus was still deserted — she thought the students would be coming back — so she zigzagged around buildings, hoping to encounter anyone.

No luck. Drenched with perspiration, she ducked inside the Cassidy Hall arch to catch her breath. She had to stop, just for a few seconds. But she thought she heard footfalls and took flight again. How could Adams possibly know where she was? He must have a sixth sense.

This was how hunted animals must feel. "Oh, please go away." She barely realized she'd spoken out loud. Where was everybody? Normally the campus teemed with people. She would have given her soul for the sight of a National Guardsman.

She stumbled in the direction of the Administration building. *Someone* had to be there. If she could only hold out a little longer.

The front lawn was uninhabited; the podium and microphone stood empty. Students had returned to their residences with a full military escort.

She was sure Adams still stalked her. Her heart pounded as she backtracked towards a clump of trees in a last ditch attempt to hide.

Strong hands reached out from behind the tree and pulled her down. Julia screamed and began to scratch with her little remaining strength; her assailant clamped his fingers over her mouth. Hysteria had taken over; Julia started to bite him, then realized the person holding her was Win.

"Oh, thank God," she burst into tears, hugging him. "I thought you were Adams. I thought he was following me. It was a nightmare." Her words tumbled over each other and he stroked her hair.

"Shh, Julia. It's after curfew. I waited for you here because I knew something happened. Otherwise, you'd have come right back to the rally."

Julia clung to him. "What are we going to do if Adams finds us here?"

"You don't know if he was tailing you for sure...he'd probably split anyway, once he saw me. He's a coward who uses his goddamn badge to terrorize defenseless women."

Julia was about to comment that she wasn't entirely helpless when Win began to kiss her. All thoughts and words flew out of her head until the crunching of boots indicated the return of the militia. Breaking off their embrace, Win peered around the tree. "It's only a couple of Guardsman on sentry duty." he whispered. "They probably won't notice us if we sneak around the back."

When she thought about that night later, she could never clearly recall the trip back to Win's house. Not like what followed afterwards. Every motion, every nuance, replayed itself over and over in her mind, allowing her a chance to relive it even as she was living it. Time had become fluid yet motionless.

As soon as they reached Win's bedroom, they peeled off each other's clothes. She remembered Win telling her, "I'm going to be as gentle as possible — the first time." And her cries of pleasure as she willingly fell into the chasm she'd once feared so much. Losing oneself was ecstasy and she wanted more and more. Who knew so many different body parts could produce so much bliss?

She never shared the details of that night with anyone. Words would only make what they shared seem crude and somehow cheapen the beauty of their consummation, of the shucking of their inhibitions to complete the fusion of desire and soul.

Only near morning, when a breeze from an open window wafted across their entwined, sweat-slick bodies, did she wonder how and where he'd gotten his experience. The thought filled her with shame. What business was it of hers? Win loved her; tonight had been proof. "I love you," she murmured.

His eyelids fluttered — had he heard her? — but he only moaned softly and nestled his head further between her breasts.

She noticed his pewter peace symbol had twisted itself around his back. To wear it to the Army induction center would be like waving a Viet Cong flag in the face of the military, and Win was absent-minded enough to forget to remove it. Gently she unhooked the necklace, placing it on the nightstand next to the narrow bed. Please let him fail the physical, she prayed. Maybe his recently healed leg or his childhood sicknesses would rescue him.

Just before drifting off herself, she thought how wonderful it was that she and Valerie had found happiness at the same time. She believed all facets of the prism of love had been revealed to her.

CHAPTER TWENTY-NINE

The first thing Julia noticed when she awoke the next morning was that Win's peace symbol was not on the nightstand. Win had gone also, presumably to take his physical. Julia hoped he had the sense to remove the necklace before the actual examination.

She yawned and stretched, as content as a cat in the sun. Julia wondered if she looked any different. She certainly *felt* different, as if a giant spring inside her had been unwound.

She jumped out of bed, suddenly embarrassed by the fact that she was lying naked in Win's bed and feeling aroused.

She glanced outside. It looked well after ten; if so, she'd already missed two classes. Oh well, she thought, I'll get the notes later this week. Grades and even schooling were no longer a priority.

After dressing, she went into her purse to put on lipstick. As she dug through her Indian print bag, she saw a flash of silver and pulled out Win's peace symbol. How wonderful; he had given it to her as a gift, a promise of things to come.

Smiling, she wandered into the boys' kitchen. A National Guardsman stood on a stool, pulling cans off the wooden shelves. "Just what the hell do you think you're doing?" Julia demanded, assuming he was searching for marijuana. "Do you have a warrant?"

Shawn drifted through the doorway, looking as radiant as Julia had felt before seeing the National Guardsman. "You remember Joey Lester, don't you? He's helping with some spring cleaning. It needs it, don't you think?"

"I guess so," Julia remarked, then said grudgingly to Joey, "I didn't recognize you from the back. I though you were a narc."

"No problem," Joey wiped his forehead with the sleeve of his uniform. "This is a lot more work than I thought. Let's break for lunch, honey." He glanced at Julia. "I'm making omelets. Care to join us?"

Walking over to Joey, Shawn slipped her arm around the flak buckle that encircled his waist. Remembering last night's encounter with Adams, Julia shuddered. How could Shawn even touch anyone in a uniform? They'd probably been screwing under this very roof while Win agonized over being drafted.

"I'd rather not," Julia's reply was brusque. "I'm leaving now."

"Don't be like that, Julia," Shawn pleaded in her gentle voice. "Win will be back soon and we'll borrow his car and pick up Louie."

"He's being discharged today?" Julia had no intention of riding in the same car with Joey, but she was glad to hear Louie was well enough to go home.

Shawn nodded. "At one o'clock to be precise." She gazed adoringly at Joey. "Try to be happy for us, Julia. We're buying a ring next week."

First Valerie, now Shawn. Everyone was getting married, despite their rhetoric against the institution. In spite of her happiness with Win, Julia felt left out. "I'd think twice about that if I were you," she said, watching Shawn's cheerful expression drain away. "How you can you even associate yourself with one of Nixon's pawns?"

Joey opened his mouth to speak, but Shawn rushed to his defense. "I'm tired of sneaking around and worrying about what my so-called friends will think." Julia had never seen her so angry. "Each of us chooses our own way of dealing with this war. You have no more right to condemn Joey's solution than Win for wanting to avoid the draft. You guys are as hypocritical as the straights."

So the others had been giving her grief, too. Good for them. "There are more honorable ways to avoid Vietnam than becoming an enemy of the kids trying to stop it," Julia replied. "But I'm not going to debate moral issues — I know I'm right. Just remember the old saying, Shawn, if three people tell you you're drunk and you think you're sober, go sleep it off anyway."

Shawn remained silent, uncertainty crossing her delicate features.

"I'm just a soldier assigned to do a job." Although his tone was harsh, Joey looked more bewildered than angry. "And you've got an attitude problem, Julia. It would be better for all concerned if you removed herself."

"With pleasure," Julia retorted. "Have Win call me when he gets back, will you, Shawn?" Without waiting for a reply, Julia marched out. She would talk to Shawn alone later, before she permanently messed up her life.

Rather than going directly to Valerie's to check on her friend and Richard's mission to Shawnee Lake, Julia decided to return to her dorm for a quick shower. As she approached campus, however, she heard the scream of sirens. Students ran in every direction.

Julia touched the arm of a frantic passer-by. "What's going down?" she asked, her stomach clutching with fear.

"Kids were killed at Kent State. Someone's planted a bomb in the Administration building!" He dashed off.

"A bomb?" Julia cried. "A bomb?" Her first thought was that Valerie had again deceived her. All that bullshit about getting rid of the weapons and being friends forever!

Anger overcame hesitancy and logic. Julia raced towards the Administration building, elbowing her way through students, not caring whose toes she trod on or books she knocked down. She had been an unwitting party to this and she was going to put an end to it. But metal barricades and armed militia impeded her progress. "Let me through!" She jumped from sentry to sentry, begging anyone who would listen.

Finally one Guardsman pulled her aside. "Calm down, miss. There's no way we can let you pass. Although the building has been evacuated, we've got a hostage situation, too."

"Hostage?" Julia demanded, bewildered. Valerie hadn't said anything about taking prisoners.

She turned to the students behind her. "Does anyone know what's happening?"

"Sort of," A freshman girl Julia recognized from the SMC spoke. "A group of Weathermen are threatening to blow up the Administration building unless Carrell gets ROTC off campus. They have some other demands, but I'm not sure what they are. Anyway, one of their chicks defected and that Felix dude found out about it. He's gonna blow her away if she tells anyone where the bomb is. He's got Dr. Shaffley, too."

"It's in the basement!" Julia cried. "The basement!" How could Felix possibly know that she and Valerie had absconded with the ammo? And why didn't he confront them last night, instead of waiting until today?

"We realize that, miss," said the Guardsman who had been listening to their conversation with undisguised interest. "We don't know the exact location."

Valerie....The militia had cordoned off a 100 square yard area in front of the Administration building, making it difficult to see exactly what was going on. When Julia squinted, she could glimpse Valerie's blonde hair shining in the sunlight. Richard stood close to her. Felix was pointing an M-16 at their heads.

Julia felt as if her breath had been taken away. In order to steady herself, she tried to focus on something trivial, the green and yellow curlicues on the Indian print dress of the freshman next to her. The cloth had been one of Nirvana, Ohio's best-selling bedspreads.

Several feet in front of Felix, Valerie, and Richard, stood two radicals Julia knew by sight. The tall boy on the left held the other M-16.

"Did you hear about Kent State?" The Indian print girl was asking her a question.

"Kent State?" Julia repeated blankly.

The girl turned a hate-filled stare onto the eavesdropping Guardsman. "His brothers-in-arms decided to open fire during a demonstration. Musta felt good to use those guns and see those kids bleed to death, huh?" The Guardsman's expression deadened; his military mask slid into place.

"Cool it, willya?" Someone behind them said. "We've got enough hassles without causing any more. Here comes Carrell; I want to hear what he has to say."

Passing through the barricades with bullhorn in hand, President Carrell stopped several yards in front of the Administration building. For the first time, Julia noticed the bomb squad clustered next to him, identifiable by their dark clothing. Julia wondered what the initials SWAT on their backs stood for.

Different from the easygoing, informal administrator of last fall, Carrell seemed stooped, his face collapsed in lines of worry. Felix tightened his grip on the rifle. Julia stood unmoving, paralyzed with helplessness. She felt responsible. If only she'd gone to the police last night instead of waiting! Even Adams would have prevented this.

Carrell lifted the bullhorn to his lips. "Listen everyone." His voice was ragged. "I just got off the phone with President White of Kent State. Four students were killed there and nine others wounded. I am saddened beyond words."

A somber murmur rippled through the crowd, and Carrell's tone grew firm. "This will not happen at Hayes. I am sending away the militia." Now a cheer began to bubble up, and the Guardsmen looked skittish.

"I am also shutting down the school, effective immediately," Carrell continued. The bullhorn seemed to amplify the determination in his voice. "Students can finish their courses by correspondence or take a pass/fail option on work already completed."

"Marshmallow! Fuckin' marshmallow!" Felix shouted, spitting out the words. "You think you're gonna get off that easy?"

"I'll negotiate your demands on two conditions," Carrell said. "First that you release the hostages, and second, that you give us the location of the bomb."

For long moments, President Carrell and Felix faced each other. The silence was so deep Julia felt it would never touch bottom. It seemed to go on forever.

Then it occurred to her something was missing. Like those drawings with a tiny but vital detail askew — "What's wrong with this picture?" And then it came to her: Adrian. Where was he? Why wasn't he out there with Felix and the other Weathermen? Because he's the link behind all this, a voice whispered in her mind. He was the spy, the informer. His absence was an admission of guilt.

Last night, Adams had mentioned someone who'd told him everything. He knew exactly what the protesters were up to. Although Adrian claimed to detest Adams, she remembered him once remarking they'd gone to the same high school. In the small town of Hampton, they could have easily maintained contact over the years. The phone call for Adrian during the ROTC building takeover could likely have been from Adams.

Because of his involvement with the protest movement, Adrian could have given the Administration advance warning of student activities. Dean Moreland's knowledge of the real purpose of Julia's visit regarding the fall moratorium and the disastrous ROTC review demonstration of a few weeks ago were perfect examples. Unlike Felix, wimpy Adrian's adeptness at avoiding arrest could not be attributed to his fierce demeanor. Adrian had to be the common denominator between the protesters and the Establishment.

Somehow Adrian had found out about Valerie and Richard. He must have spotted Julia and Valerie at last night's rally, followed them, and after Julia had left Valerie's, tipped off Felix as to the location of the weapons. What better way to get even with his hated father and ex-lover?

That bastard, Julia fumed. When I see him again, I'll expose him for the traitor that he is.

With agonizing slowness, Felix lowered his rifle. She felt herself breathe again, felt the others next to her exhale. Time reconnected with motion.

With a gesture of his hand, Felix indicated for Valerie and Richard to leave. The SWAT unit started towards the porch but Felix waved them away with the butt of his rifle. "I got the control device, so don't you worry about the bomb," he shouted. "Gives me a little bargaining power."

Lowering his bullhorn, President Carrell opened his mouth to reply. The words never came out; instead everything was shattered by an incredible blast.

From where Julia stood, it seemed as if the Administration building caved in upon itself, collapsing in an organized, symmetrical pattern. First the front porch, then the top three floors fell upon the center like a souffle taken too quickly out of the oven. The commotion was unbearable; instinctively Julia covered her head and ears with her arms. Then a few — perhaps ten — seconds of astonishing stillness.

Julia looked up. All that remained of the porch and most of the Administration building was a pile of rubble. The SWAT team and the two radicals who had been closest to the building stumbled away from the perimeter. Some were covered with blood. Because it was an implosion rather than an explosion, President Carrell and the majority of the crowd had been spared injury from flying debris.

The militia immediately took charge. "Clear out! Clear the area!" Waving their rifles, they had no problem persuading the students to leave. Most had already fled.

Julia stood unmoving. She felt paralyzed, as if suddenly caught between sleep and waking. Where was Valerie? Valerie, Richard, and Felix should be digging themselves out from underneath the mess. If she waited long enough, surely they'd emerge.

"Julia." Someone behind her said. "Julia." The tone grew more assertive. Turning slightly, she became aware of Louie's presence. Where had he come from? He was holding on to her as if she were going to fall apart. Which was ridiculous. Everything was fine. What was taking Valerie so long, though? She should be out of there already.

"Julia, listen to me," Louie's voice seemed far away, as if he were talking to her through the reverse end of a megaphone. "You've had a terrible shock. You need to go back to the dorm and lie down."

"They're not dead, if that's what you're thinking," Somehow, somewhere she found the word. She stared incredulously at Louie. "Look at that bandage on your head! You're the one who should be in bed!"

"Julia, please listen to me," Louie repeated patiently. "I know what you're going through." He glanced at her arms. Following his gaze, she saw that she'd raked herself so deeply with her fingernails that she bled.

Strange how, even though blood dripped from her arms, she experienced no pain. Therefore, Valerie must be alive. "Valerie's all right," she said in a monotone. "People just don't get killed like that."

"They do, Julia. It happened all the time in 'Nam. You and I talked about it. I'll walk you back to your dorm." He grasped her elbow.

"No. Let's go to your house," Julia said. "I want to see Win." Win will make it better, she thought. He'll love me and everything will be the way it was.

"Not now, Julia."

"Why not? I need him." Although she was having trouble breathing, her brain was starting to function again. "He's done with his physical by now."

"Julia, Win cannot bring back Valerie," Gently Louie started to guide her in the direction of Miami Hall.

Once again, jealous Louie was trying to come between her and Win. "I know it's hard for you to accept that Win and I love each other, but that's no reason for you to keep us apart," she said.

Louie winced. "Can we talk about this later?" He ran his fingers through the unbandaged part of his head. "You really need to lie down."

Julia pulled away. "No, I'm going to see Win," she repeated in a childish whine.

"Jesus, Julia, why do you have to get stubborn now?" Louie's eyes grew bright, as if covered with cellophane. "He's not there."

"Are you saying they drafted him right away?" Although things around her began to tilt crazily, Julia managed to keep her voice steady.

"No, of course not. It's just that he, he...." Louie could not bring himself to complete the sentence. "Julia, please let me take you back to your dorm."

Julia crossed her arms and began to rub her palms back and forth, smearing the blood from her scratches, irritating them even more. "I am not budging until you tell me what you know." Maybe saying the same words she'd spoken to Valerie less than 24 hours ago would bring Valerie back, would return things to normal. Maybe the words had a special magic, like a witch's spell.

"Stop hurting yourself!" Louie seized her hands, practically crushing them with his own. "Win has left Hayes. Permanently."

This was, of course a nightmare. Julia knew she'd wake up and find herself in Win's bedroom. Valerie and Richard would be at Valerie's, painting walls. For a few seconds, she squeezed her eyes closed, willing herself to sleep. Although the darkness provided a release, it was suffocating. She opened her eyes.

Louie stood there, tears flowing down his cheeks. Why was *he* crying? Because she loved Win and not him? Because of Valerie? Because of the destruction they'd wreaked upon themselves? Instead of being overwhelmed with emotion like Louie, she felt like a statue, with an impassive exterior and a hollow core.

She was barely conscious of Louie holding her, of him speaking. "Julia, I'm sorry. Win heard about Carrell shutting down school at his parents'. He called to say he's staying at home for a few days while he packs for London. He's been planning to move in with Stu and Laura for months. I kept asking him to tell you...."

Everything swirled together like a psychedelic crazy quilt. Solid objects lost their boundaries, but Julia glimpsed a black hole where she could escape. Before she slipped into the comforting void, she thought, at least I'm better off than Valerie. My soul was sold for a night of passion, while hers went for a few ounces of plastique....

PART TWO

TRANSITION

May 1969 – June 1971
London, England

CHAPTER THIRTY

15 Bloomsbury Lane   12 June 1971
Finchwood, Elstree
England TW8 4JP

Dear Shawn:

I know it's been almost a year since we last wrote. Forgive me for not getting in touch with you sooner. I just got back from a nine-month trip on the Continent.

So you got married. I guess congratulations are in order. I mean, it's your life, Shawn, even though it's different from what we thought it would be. But, really, engraved wedding invitations! Your mother's idea, I hope.

I'm glad your eye condition has stayed the same. Your note didn't mention Hayes — haven't you talked with anyone? Stu got this gossipy epic from Adrian, who by the way didn't seem too broken up over his father's death. I know he despised the old man, but still. Even though the explosion was an accident, it was unbelievable that something like that could happen at Hayes.

Adrian's all the way out in California in the UCLA film school, in case you didn't know. Yet somehow he's managed to keep tabs on almost everyone. According to his grapevine, Louie made Law Review at Columbia and Kirsten's designing costumes for an off-off-off (Is three "off's" enough?) Broadway play in New York. Vicki and Bill are doing a *Harrad Experiment* scene in Colorado and Jake's working for his Dad, selling cars in Cleveland (lucky asshole drew a high lottery number, so why's he wasting his life pushing autos?)

Julia

Win paused, then scratched out the word "Julia." He couldn't bring himself to think, much less write about Julia. Adrian's letter had stated that after dropping out of Hayes, Julia had simply disappeared. Adrian had phoned Julia's house, only to be told by her mother never to call again.

It was as though Julia had died alongside Valerie. But how could she be so angry and bitter? Of course she must have been devastated by Valerie's death and hurt when he split suddenly. But why sever ties so completely? Like the rest of the world, he had no way of knowing what would transpire on the day of his draft physical.

That morning he had wakened around ten. He and Julia were still intertwined. After gently extricating himself — he wanted to rouse her and continue last night's lovemaking, but she looked so peaceful — he had dressed quickly, conscious of the fact that he had to be at the induction center before noon. Remembering how much she'd admired it, he had put his pewter peace symbol into Julia's handbag.

He had to stop at his parents' and pick up the letter his father's friend had written for him. Dr. Silverstein was an orthopedic surgeon who attested that Win's "recently shattered and poorly healing leg" made Win unfit for military service. Rather than taking the honorable route of draft evasion, Win had broken down and called his father the weekend before. Although Pop had served during World War II and Win's maternal grandfather was a career officer, he had no problem with wanting to make sure his sons stayed out of Vietnam. He did have strong objections to Win's London plans, asserting that his second oldest was ruining his life with so drastic a move. So Win tried to avoid the subject and, in doing so, his parents. But there was no way around them that day.

Forty-five minutes later Win had arrived at his family's Indian Hills estate. He was surprised to see Pop's Mercedes in the driveway and as soon as he walked into the house, he'd known something was drastically wrong.

"Oh, thank God you're here!" His mother sobbed, rushing over to him and giving him a hug.

"What's going on?" Win asked. Had someone died?

"Didn't you hear the news?" Elliot Winfield demanded. Like Win, he was tall, muscular, and russet-haired, only his athletic predispositions ran to conventional sports such as golf and tennis, whereas Win preferred the solitude of bodybuilding and hiking.

"You know that old car radio doesn't work." Win had bought and paid for the '59 Chevy his sophomore year, refusing the old man's offer to subsidize a higher-class vehicle. Subsequent summers had been spent at various construction jobs earning money for the move overseas.

"Someone's planted a bomb at the Administration building at Hayes," the elder Winfield said. "They're holding hostages."

Win never made it to the induction center. Rather than taking the medical deferment, Pop had arranged for Win's name to be dropped from Selective Service records due to a clerical oversight. An old war buddy in Washington owed Elliot Winfield a big favor.

When Win went back to Hayes to pick up his gear two days later, everyone had gone. It was then that he realized he didn't even have Julia's home address. Between the rush to get to London and the hassles with his family, he never got around to looking her up. By the time he'd thought of Julia again, he had already moved in with Stu and Laura.

And, to be honest, he didn't want to be responsible for another person. Too many things were happening in his life.

Someone was standing in the doorway. Win turned around on the too-small stool that went with his too-small desk and faced Stu. Heavyset with a receding, dun-colored frizz and a snub nose, Stu had the thick facial features of a Russian peasant. His gestures and manner of speaking were overblown and almost prissy. How long had Stu been staring at him?

"It's dinnertime," Stu smirked. "Come and get it." Much of what Stu said was tinged with innuendo. Win had found this hilarious at Hayes; now it was annoying. Especially in the light of recent developments in their relationship.

"I'll be there in a minute," Win replied flatly. "I just want to finish this letter to Shawn."

"Laura's putting the food on the table, so why don't you just wait?"

Win sighed and stood up, bumping his knees on the edge of the desk. He would never be comfortable in this scaled-down half of a double located just outside London.

Yet in many ways, the house was similar to their places back at Hayes. Furnished with castoffs — Indian print bedspreads on couches and tables, imitation Persian rugs and huge throw pillows on the floor, macrame wall hangings — a tactful real estate agent might call it cozy. And despite the lack of central heating, it had enough rooms — a living room, a bathroom, a kitchen and dinette, two bedrooms. The place might suit slim, petite Londoners, but not a 6'2" hulking Midwesterner. And although Stu and Laura were overweight, they were also a good half-foot shorter than Win.

When he'd first arrived in London, he'd been enchanted by the difference between the two cultures. All things American seemed brassy and overabundant. He'd fallen in love with the small town of Finchwood, pretending he was in a 1940s movie when he walked down the quaint main street to their home. The greengrocers, laundry, bookstore, sweets shop and antique dealers seemed new in their cleanliness and upkeep despite bullet holes in some buildings, a reminder of World War II's Blitz.

Overhanging hedgerows gave the area a bucolic flavor. There were few cars; most people got about on foot or bicycles.

But now Win preferred the hustle and noise of London. Their place was considerably less well-tended than their neighbors.' On a street with identical houses where the lawns were impeccably nurtured and trimmed, their garden overran to a riot of nasturtiums, primroses and weeds of unidentifiable origin.

And although the townspeople were fanatically courteous, Win sensed a lack of acceptance. Perhaps it was due to his, Stu, and Laura's unconventional living arrangements. Or perhaps because Mrs. Northrup, the landlady who lived upstairs, rented out her place during the day to a couple engaged in an adulterous affair. Whatever the reason, the polite scrutiny surrounding him whenever he had dealings in town made him increasingly uneasy.

Stu and Laura were already eating when Win sat down at the table. He almost said, "Fondue, again?" but stopped himself. Laura had enough on her mind and the last thing either of them wanted was to instigate another tirade from Stu. So Win merely slipped into the chair and picked up the long, tiny-pronged fork.

Stu, he noticed, had drunk nearly half of the bottle of wine which he'd placed near his plate for easy access. Laura had barely touched hers, although most of the apples and bread on her side of the fondue pot were gone. Too bad Laura seemed to be gaining more weight — with her ebony waterfall of hair; her fine, narrow nose; almond-shaped eyes; and delicate mouth, she could be exquisite. At a certain angle, in a certain mood, she reminded Win of Julia.

As Win speared an apple slice and dipped it into the bubbling cheese, Stu asked, "So what did you say in your letter to Shawn?"

Win flinched, fork in mid-air. Why did Stu always want to know his every move? It made him feel stifled, smothered. The cheese dripped on the table.

Laura stood up to get a towel from the kitchen but Win said, "Relax Laura, I'll clean it up." Damned if he'd give Stu the satisfaction of an immediate answer.

When he returned, Stu was pouring himself yet another glass of wine. "I knew Shawn was desperate because she realized she was damaged goods," Stu was telling Laura. "But I can't believe she married a fucking pig. Who's peddling toilet paper, no less!" He laughed, an abrasive sound not unlike leaves being raked up off the sidewalk.

Win thought Shawn was being foolhardy also, but loyalty compelled him to defend her. "The guy makes a good living selling bathroom supplies to companies. And maybe she loves him."

"Bullshit!" Stu took a huge gulp of his wine, then helped himself to a refill. "Love was what we felt for each other at Hayes, my man. We made a vow and like everyone else, Shawn broke it. Everyone's selling out, turning into fucking androids, model citizens."

Now it would start. The rap about the promise they'd made before Stu and Laura had left for London. Win avoided Laura's anguish-filled gaze. The past two years had been full of disappointments for Stu. He remained an assistant set tech at the BBC, while his classmates at the Royal Academy of Dramatic Arts won bit parts and commercial work. Laura's job as a manageress in a day care center was still their main source of income. Win kept telling Stu to keep on trying, yet Stu insisted on blaming his failures on the fact that their utopia hadn't materialized as planned.

The bond between Win, Stu, Laura, Shawn, Adrian, and Kirsten had been forged during the fall of their sophomore year at Hayes. The others — Jake, Louie, Vicki, Bill, Valerie — came into their lives later. Involved in the theatre in various capacities, the original six drifted together during the production of an anti-Vietnam play *Amerika, Hurrah*, directed by Adrian. The summer prior, the so-called "Summer of Love" of 1967, Adrian had hitchhiked to Haight-Ashbury, then the center of hippiedom. If Adrian were to be believed, he took the Electric Kool-Aid Acid Test, and participated in the world's first Be-In. He came back to college tuned in and turned on, sexually and politically liberated.

Adrian had been like the Pied Piper, drawing them in with his tales of ecstacy. It was theirs, too, for the taking and soon they were smoking joints and talking about free love.

Inhibitions could not be removed overnight, but as the leaves withered and snow drove them inside, they began to experiment with each other's bodies as well as with mind-expanding drugs — LSD, mescaline, psilocybin. Pulling closer together, they shared their innermost thoughts and vulnerabilities.

For the first time in his life, Win felt as if his mental shackles had been removed. Although he'd always been liked — he shuddered at the word "popular" — it wasn't for who he really was inside but for the role of All-American Kid set forth by his family. The Winfields of Indian Hills, Cincinnati were strictly "Leave It to Beaver" — no screaming, yelling arguments, merely rational family discussions. Mom in the kitchen or out shopping and Pop making hundreds of thousands for himself and others on the stock market, never mind the poor souls who took a beating every day or the fact that the profit was derived from the military-industrial complex. Nary a racist remark was heard in their home but they lived in an exclusive suburb and belonged to a country club that knew few Jews and no blacks.

That year, Win reveled in his newfound freedom. He could bare his soul, bang his head against the wall if he wished and Stu, Laura, and the others accepted him, without the trappings of wealth or prestige, without consideration of how he dressed or his looks. All they asked was that he love them in return.

By January, they had all but moved into Adrian's house. In order to stay in school, they played it fairly straight during the week, but weekends were different. It was an unwritten rule — anyone could have anyone else. No objections or strings attached. They existed for each other's pleasure and Win, whose previous sexual experience had been limited to a few furtive encounters with a high school girlfriend, quickly learned the intricacies of male and female intercourse.

Looking back on it in clinical terms, it seemed almost revolting. But it hadn't been like that at all. They had experienced a form of unconditional love, the way a parent accepts a newborn baby or someone cares for a cat or dog.

Spring came, and with it a new burst of passion and freedom. They met others like themselves — free-spirited acquaintances who passed in and out of each other's lives like extras in a movie.

For this minority of self-described "freaks," the campus became a loosely organized playground. They piled in cars to Shawnee Lake and "tripped out" on the spring flowers. They explored the different aspects of campus life — beauty pageants, frat parties, baseball games — then satirized the same in the experimental theatre. In the middle of the night, they snuck over to the elementary school playground for games of hide-and-seek.

But the original six remained closely knit. Stu invariably had a major part in campus plays, so on opening nights, they dressed in their most elegant finery, courtesy of Kirsten's sewing, and strolled en masse to the theatre, drawing admiring glances from the other freaks. They were better than a family because they'd chosen each other through friendship rather than blood. No one was ever lonely, at least it didn't seem to Win at the time.

By junior year, they began to scatter. Jake and Bill moved into a two-bedroom apartment with Win and Stu. Bill's girlfriend, Vicki, was somewhat of a prude, hogging one bedroom on weekends because she went to school in Toledo and that was the only time she and Bill could spend alone. And Jake was an avid heterosexual, much to Stu's extreme irritation. Win and Shawn's relationship evolved from casual sex into a platonic, constant companionship, while Stu and Laura paired off. Adrian remained in his little house, spending more time with Valerie.

The SMC became a viable force on campus due to Louie Wexler, who'd transferred from Cleveland State. Originally Win and the others resisted Louie — he'd served in Vietnam and that made him a baby killer by association. But once they talked to him and witnessed his extreme intelligence, they became ardent supporters. But Louie erected his own barriers, avoiding the sex-and-drugs scene that had become such an integral part of their lives.

At the end of their junior year, Stu won a scholarship to London's Royal Academy of Performing Arts. Laura volunteered to go with him — with only tuition and a small stipend, Stu's life would not only be lonely but impoverished. Separation was imminent.

The thought of anything breaking them apart was excruciating, at least to Win. So he suggested that the original six move to London when they graduated in 1970. The rest agreed, although Win noticed a certain drawing back; Shawn had begun to worry about her headaches and Kirsten talked of nothing but Broadway. And Adrian had already begun to get into his own weird scene. But Stu and Laura were absolutely thrilled, making them exchange a vow of sorts. So at that last orgiastic gathering — Stu and Laura's wedding — the original six made a promise to only make love with each other until they came together the following spring.

Only Stu and Laura had kept their word. Win's downfall had been Julia.

"So the others copped out," Stu said when Win first arrived in London, raw from the shame of his arranged escape from the draft and the horror of Valerie, Felix, and Richard's deaths.

As Stu had caressed his shoulder with a meaty hand, Win suppressed an unexpected shudder of revulsion. "But I knew I could count on you, Win. Laura and I have been lonely for a long time." Their physical deprivation was to be extended — Win had been unable to bring himself to touch neither Stu nor Laura for months.

By now quite drunk, Stu leaned over the table so his face nearly touched Win's. His breath reeked of partially digested wine and cheese. "Like a bunch of rats deserting a fucking ship." He slurred his words. "When is your turn gonna come, Win?"

He knows, Win thought, ducking his head so his curtain of hair covered his surprised expression. Win hadn't even had the heart to mention his plans to Laura yet.

"If you talk like that, you're going to drive him away," Laura said, casting a pleading glance in Win's direction. As if *he* could control Stu.

"You'd hate that, wouldn't you Laura?" Stu replied. "Six inches for you and not for me." Win's sex drive had returned on the Continent, but only for women. He felt compelled to give Laura comfort, deriving pleasure because he pretended she was Julia. If Laura sensed something was amiss, she never let on.

"Now you sound like a jealous husband," Laura's lips twitched. The last thing Stu wanted to be accused of was conventionality, a sure way to get him to ease off.

"*Moi?*" Clutching his chest and rolling his eyes, Stu pretended to fall over from shock. In spite of himself, Win smiled

"You'd never leave us, would you Win?" Laura asked hopefully.

"Never-never land is a fantasy place," Win lifted his head to face her. "Only Peter Pan got to stay there."

What happened at Hayes, what happened with Julia, hadn't been enough to change his mind about Stu and Laura. What happened on the Continent had.

CHAPTER THIRTY-ONE

When Win had first arrived in London, he was sure he'd done the right thing. He could no longer tolerate living in the barbaric land America had become. Even the ivory towers of academia had been transformed into a bloody battleground. And he had to prove he could make it on his own, without the influence of his family or their money.

The only real problem was Julia. Her presence in his life had been an unplanned-for occurrence, an unfortunate aberration. Drawn to her beauty and naivete, he'd fought against his impulses all year, struggling to hide his feelings. Despite her proclamations to the contrary, Julia Brandon was the kind of girl you married. And no way was he going to end up like his old man, saddled with four kids, a big mortgage, and a standing tee time by age 28.

Julia was also inexperienced. Dropping out of a sorority and putting on worn blue jeans did not a liberated chick make. Much to his disappointment, she even wore a bra, the straps of which would often show through her flimsy tops.

So Win and the others left Julia out of the sex-and-drugs scene which had mostly dissipated by their senior year anyway. Stu and Laura's departure had removed the backbone from communal life. Although the people in Win's house remained close, relations were platonic. As graduation drew nearer, everyone grew more preoccupied with their own fates.

Several times Win had debated over telling Julia about what had transpired between him and the others. But he'd followed the instinct that had warned him to keep her away from the Bacchanalian debauchery of Stu and Laura's wedding reception the spring he and Julia first met. She would have been permanently frightened off. And he couldn't bear the thought of no relationship at all, even though it probably would have been best for her.

Except for Louie, they'd all agreed that Julia was better off not knowing. And Louie went along with the majority, conceding that yes, sometimes you had to protect the innocent.

Win despised himself for selling out with Julia, too. Like the animal he was, he just couldn't stay away. But dammit, she wanted him so badly. If it hadn't been reciprocated.... Their night together haunted his dreams, coloring his fantasies whenever he was with Laura or other women.

Divine retribution for the way he'd screwed up his life characterized his first months in London. Although Win found a job immediately in a small architectural firm, the nine-to-five routine was oppressive, his coworkers cold because a foreigner had been hired instead of an Englishman. Although he adored the elegance and cosmopolitan atmosphere of the city and the refinement and wit of the people, everything was so much smaller, older, and closer together, making him feel like a brash, oversized outsider. And Stu and Laura tried too hard to accommodate him, deferring his rent, offering him grass or sex whenever he seemed the least bit down. They even kicked out a paying boarder so Win could move in. He'd felt physically and mentally hemmed in.

Many times he wanted to return to the States. But the thought of facing his family stopped him. He couldn't show them what a failure he was by running away from this, too. He was determined to make a life for himself on these inhospitable shores.

Win had always dreamed of traveling. And maybe once he learned his way around Europe he'd have a better idea of how and where he might fit in. Perhaps a few months of being completely on his own would put his life into focus.

So, after giving his employer a week's notice and bidding Stu and Laura goodbye — incredibly, they were upset to see him go, despite his constant bad humor — Win hopped a ferry across the English Channel. Upon arriving in France, he stuck out his thumb. With only about $100 in his pocket, he had to conserve every penny. He'd never been more terrified in his life.

A green Volkswagen van with rust in the same spots as his old Chevy puttered by, was about to pass, then abruptly pulled over. The driver, one Mike Swenson, was a tawny-haired ex-surfer from San Diego. He and Win liked each other immediately; both were into Nautilus, hated the war, and had fantasized about seeing the world since they were kids. Mike's artistic bent ran to guitar, whereas Win loved to build things, especially theatre sets. Although each had an appreciation for the other's talent, both were practical enough to know that any money that would be made would be through less than legal means; in other words, selling dope.

Mike's parents were divorced. Although his mother still lived in California, his dad was a diplomatic attache with the Austrian embassy. "If we get into hassles with the fuzz, Dad will bail us out," Mike assured Win.

The first three months of their journey were blissfully uneventful. From France, they meandered through Spain and Greece, living in hostels or staying with natives they'd met on the road, becoming friendly with expatriate hippies of all nationalities. Because expenses were minimal, they had little need to sell hash to supplement their income, only parlaying their wares whenever the mood struck.

Both attracted women, but Win invariably extricated himself from romantic encounters, saying he was too stoned or tired or wanted to be alone. Finally Mike sat him down and asked what was wrong. "I didn't think you were gay, Win, although that's cool. But I know you must be hurting, man, 'cause I hear you in your sleep."

Win looked away, embarrassed by his nocturnal dreams of Julia, the evidence of which he found on his sheets the morning after. He was even more disgusted because Mike noticed. But women frightened him, everything did. Although he was living out his fantasy and wandering the earth, he still felt like a coward.

"None of the chicks turn me on. They all seem used. Who knows what kind of diseases they might be carrying around?"

A thoughtful expression crossed Mike's perpetually tanned features. "Yeah, man, you might have a point there." After that, Mike slowed down his sexual activities.

They left the shining white beaches and relaxed poverty of Greece for Istanbul, a tangible descent into metaphysical darkness. Native women wore veils and the men smiled showing their teeth but their eyes were cruel. There was nothing romantic about being poor in Turkey. Ragged little boys pulled at their sleeves, begging; cripples made do without the benefit of prostheses; vicious cats roamed the garbage-laden streets in search of scraps. Everywhere they went, they were watched.

"I think we'd better get rid of our grass," Win told Mike.

"Are you fucking crazy? Man, I plan to *buy* more stuff! Turkish hash is the best in the world."

"And Turkish prisons are the worst, from what I've heard."

"Don't worry, Win. Like I said before, Dad's got diplomatic immunity. Everything's cool. Besides, we're running low on bread and this is a perfect opportunity to stock up."

Win paced their hotel room — Istanbul hostels were too filthy for even their less-than-pristine lifestyle — while Mike went on the dope buy. He almost wept with relief when his friend came back with a full knapsack, red eyes, and a silly grin on his face. "You gotta try this stuff. Toldya it would be no problem."

And so it seemed through Iran and Afghanistan. They maintained low visibility, avoiding sales in the big cities, staying away from the obvious drug dealers and hippie hangouts. They limited trade to other American college kids on the road. Yet Win couldn't shake the feeling that somehow, somewhere a trap awaited them.

Several times he considered parting from Mike. But he'd developed a genuine affection for the laid-back Californian's kindness and generosity. And, in most matters, Mike respected and listened to Win, expressing admiration for Win's intelligence and common sense. After months of loneliness, Win basked in a friendship without the strain of past history or sexual tension.

Win began to feel more acclimated by the time they traveled through the breathtaking Khyber Pass to Pakistan. The Rainbow Hotel in the city of Peshawar was a hippie mecca of sorts, with tripped-out freaks roaming the streets, painting brightly-colored murals of their psychedelic visions on the walls. Even the natives were more accessible, hawking dough balls and betel leaves rather than begging from so-called rich Americans.

Because Peshawar seemed more Western, Win and Mike eased their self-imposed restrictions. The dope business was booming but the stash had run low. This was to be their last relatively safe opportunity to make money until they reached Katmandu, an estimated eight weeks away. Win and Mike planned on experiencing India and Nepal first, two countries not known for their extensive student populations.

Their combined cash totaled a meager $150 in various currencies. A friendly Pakistani had approached Mike in the hotel lobby that afternoon, saying he had several bricks of high-quality Afghani hash for sale. Mike had agreed to a rendezvous after dark.

This time Win insisted on accompanying him. No way was Mike risking his ass alone. That evening, Win and Mike wandered down the end of the bustling main street. With elaborate casualness, they paused in front of a corner stall in the marketplace, the prearranged meeting place. The vendor selling vegetables nodded; a three-wheeled cab appeared from seemingly nowhere, wending its way through the crowds towards the two Americans. The driver, a short man in a red fez leaned over and whispered, "You want hashish?"

Win felt as if he was in the middle of a Humphrey Bogart movie, *Casablanca* or maybe *The Maltese Falcon*. All he needed was a narrow-brimmed fedora and Lauren Bacall.

Mike nodded and the man grinned, revealing a gleaming silver tooth. "Get in, then." They did, and the vehicle, which absurdly resembled a golf cart complete with fringe, tore off into the night, careening through the zig-zag streets.

Within seconds, Win was lost. "Are you sure these dudes are up front?" he murmured to Mike.

The driver apparently heard the concern in Win's voice because he turned around and nodded emphatically. "No police, friend. We no want trouble."

Minutes later they arrived in a residential district. Two men stood in front of a nondescript, run-down house. Although one was taller than the other, they looked oddly alike; bulky and dark-complected, with sweet faces. They could have been twins.

They introduced themselves as brothers and the driver, Ahmed, as a cousin. Hell, this is a family operation, Win thought in relief. These out-of-shape dudes aren't going to turn us over to the cops and put themselves into any danger.

Ducking through the narrow door, they went into the house while Ahmed stood guard outside. The smaller brother, Hosain, disappeared into the other room. Win could hear him jabbering loudly in Urdu over the phone. Ten huge slabs of brown hash stood stacked on a wooden table in the main room. Win's mouth watered. The slabs reminded him of giant Hershey bars back home. How he missed tasty, unwholesome junk food! He'd even settle for the abominable English hamburgers he'd once scorned in the imitation American restaurants in London.

Big Brother, who had an unpronounceable name like Zulfikar (it sounded like "fucker," to Win and he'd had to keep from laughing), turned to Mike. "Hundred dollars American for the whole thing," he said. "You try first."

"I don't need to smoke it." Leaning over with the bored air of a connoisseur, Mike took a pinch from the topmost brick, rolling it around on his tongue. His eyes lit up but he said, "Not bad. I'll give you eighty. Fifty American, thirty in rupees." At all times, Win and Mike kept about $80 worth of American currency on them; five dollar bills came in extremely handy during border crossings and other touchy situations.

Although the bricks would be worth thousands in the States, Win had no idea Mike planned on purchasing so much hash. Not only would it deplete most of their money, but the logistics of hiding and transporting what looked like ten pounds of the stuff would make what had previously been commonplace bribes to officials extremely risky. Win opened his mouth to object.

Big Brother grinned. "I am a nice guy. I take your fifty bucks." He chortled. "As your President Kennedy used to say, 'You drive a hard bargain.'"

The oversized Pakistani's abrupt switch to Americanisms amused Mike also. He laughed and, pulling two $20s and a $10 from his jeans pocket, handed them to Big Brother. Later Win would reflect that at this point Big Brother showed them he knew much more than he'd initially let on.

Then one of the hugest men Win had ever seen burst into the room. The Pakistani equivalent of a Sumo wrestler, he wielded a club the size of his right forearm. Pocketing the money, Big Brother looked at Mike and sighed. "You foreign hippies must learn not to interfere with our commerce. We are a poor country and we need to keep whatever money we make — how to say? — in the family."

Mike seemed not to grasp the realities of the situation. "Hey, you set me up!" he wailed. "My dad's a diplomat and I have immunity. And besides, I'm an American."

"Above the law, eh?" Big Brother laughed nastily. "Well, I must tell you, we are not the police. We make our own law, carry out our own justice." Descending upon Mike, the man raised the club. Big Brother closed in, presumably to help with the job. They seemed to have forgotten about Win, who had remained silent.

Instead of panic, Win felt a calm acceptance. There had to be a solution.... He was strong, physically fit, and had the advantage of surprise. With a quick movement, Win knocked the club from the one assailant's hand, loosening the grip of the Big Brother. Pulling Mike with him, he dragged his companion towards the door. "Let's get the fuck out of here!"

Win had momentarily stopped the two men, but brother Hosain still blocked the entrance. Shoving Hosain aside with all his force, not caring about the man's groan of pain as his head made contact with the wall, Win propelled Mike towards the street.

There stood cousin Ahmed, calmly guarding the three-wheeled vehicle, unaware that the scuffle inside had gone in favor of the Americans and not his relatives. Placing his finger over his lips, Win motioned Mike to sneak around the back. Not a second too soon, for the Pakistani sumo burst outside, shouting in Urdu and gesticulating wildly.

Win and Mike took off down the darkened alley, running as frantically, their direction random. Nothing was familiar; it was like being trapped in a maze with no exit. Although it didn't appear they were being followed, they kept up their pace until they finally reached a busy thoroughfare.

A cab pulled up alongside the sweating, panting Americans. The driver, a young man about their age, smiled at them. "You get hurt? Bad men here if not careful. I take you to police."

Win and Mike stared at each other, then shook their heads. "Just tell us how to get back to the Rainbow," Win said.

Later they laughed about the incident. But at that moment when they looked at each other and saw that both had wet their pants, they knew their dope-dealing days were through. They had been lucky, and privately Win thanked God.

Between wired loans from Mike's mother and father, they scraped through India and Nepal. A true child of divorce, Mike skillfully obtained the maximum donation by playing one parent's generosity against the other's. They stopped at the Burmese border, feeling the closeness of Vietnam. Refugees and draft deserters served as painful, immediate reminders.

They parted with regret, knowing they would probably never see each other again. Win took Mike's dad's address in Austria, promising to repay Mike as soon as he got a job in London.

Hitchhiking back to England, Win met a lovely Canadian girl whose green-blue eyes and satiny skin reminded him of Julia. Much to his delight, his sex drive returned.

Nearly a year had passed since Win had left Hayes. He'd lived a lifetime and had come close to death or at least serious injury. But he'd redeemed himself by saving Mike. And whatever mistakes he'd made were in the past. It was up to him to build his future.

CHAPTER THIRTY-TWO

Within a week of his return to London, Win knew he could no longer stay with Stu and Laura. Not only had he outgrown the relationship, but Stu's constant angst made life intolerable. When had Stu stopped trying to change things and begun to blame everyone but himself? Or had he always been like that?

Win's parents had never liked Stu. But Win had attributed their disaffection to Stu's freakish attitudes and loud mouth. Had they perceived something that he, Win, had not?

On the night of the fondue dinner, after finishing his letter to Shawn, Win joined Stu and Laura in the living room.

As usual, they were plopped in front of the television; Stu in the easy chair, Laura on pillows on the floor. In the corner sat a threadbare Queen Anne chair; that was Win's place. It stood empty, waiting.

Canned laughter erupted from the TV. Stu scowled. "Nigel can't emote his way out of a toilet stall. And off screen he's the biggest nelly you ever saw." Nigel Holmes had been hired as a dresser at the BBC a year before Stu. But he'd quickly graduated to small walk-on parts on various comedies. Tonight marked the debut of his first speaking role.

Glancing up, Laura saw Win. Happiness fleeted across her plump face. "Come join us," she offered.

Win perched on the edge of "his" seat. "Stu, would you mind tearing your eyes away from the telly for a second?" He was barely conscious of using the British term for 'television.'"

"Shit, I'll do you one better." Gracefully, for someone who had consumed so much wine earlier, Stu flipped off the TV. He stared at Win, his beige eyes cold. Win shifted uncomfortably, wondering if Stu knew what was coming. Maybe he even wanted Win to split. The thought gave Win courage; it would make what he had to say easier.

"OK, Win, you have my undivided attention," Antagonism etched itself in Stu's every word. "When Nigel asks me what I thought of his performance tomorrow, I'll have to lie. I was going to anyway, but I won't be nearly as convincing. Now quit twitching and spit it out."

Self-consciously, Win straightened his back. Stu had the disconcerting habit of pointing out others' quirks. Although Win understood this as a way of establishing superiority, it put him further on the defensive.

"I'm moving out," Win blurted. "As soon as I can find a flat and a job."

"Well, aren't we the proper Englishman?" Stu sneered "First you ask me to turn off the telly and now you're looking for a flat. Well, tally ho, old chap. I'm going back to Nigel." He stood up. "But first I need another drink. Care to join me, Laura?"

"Look Stu, I know you're hurt," Win said. "But you had to be aware that I haven't been happy with our, uh, situation for a long time."

Stu refused to look at him. "And what about me?" He demanded. "What about *us*? We've known each other for almost five years. We planned on spending out lives together. You're just looking out for your own ass, Win."

"No, Stu *you're* the one who's being selfish," Laura rarely took a stand on anything, and Stu whirled around and stared at her in surprise. "People change, it's a part of life. Nothing remains static."

"Well, then why don't you go with him, Laura?" Without waiting for a reply, he lumbered into the kitchen.

Win walked over to Laura. Despite her size, she looked small and vulnerable. He clasped her chubby hands into his own. Her nails were bare and short from the practical work of caring for children. "I'm sorry, Laura," he began.

"Don't be. Something happened to you at Hayes, Win, during that year all of us were separated. You'd pulled away from Stu and me, even before you went on the Continent. Do you want to talk about it?"

Without truly understanding why, Win wanted to very much. So he told her everything, beginning with his infatuation with Julia and finishing with his brief fling with the Canadian girl while hitching back to London. He sensed Stu standing in the doorway listening, but he didn't care. Confession gave too intense a relief to stop now.

"So you see, I'm not even bisexual," Win concluded, trying to hide his relief. "To be perfectly honest, I haven't figured out who I am. But I know one thing for certain: I have to be on my own for a while. I need space."

He heard Stu go into the bedroom, shutting the door behind him. The anticipated fireworks, the tears and rancor hadn't materialized, leaving Win with the vaguely uneasy feeling that he'd missed something. Didn't these situations have repercussions?

"You can stay with us for as long as you'd like," Laura said. "And you're welcome to visit me anytime." Her implication was clear. On the two occasions he and Laura had made love, she had obviously enjoyed it; he'd been simply relieving the demands of his libido. But Stu hadn't touched Laura in months and Win felt sorry for her. Both he and Laura knew that Stu was getting his sex elsewhere, possibly even with the much-maligned Nigel.

"Why do you stay married to him, Laura?" Win asked. "You'd find someone else in no time. You're very pretty, even more so if you'd lose weight. " This was not Win's first attempt to prod Laura to shed pounds. Usually he said something after they'd been intimate.

"I've been wondering myself since the week after our wedding," she admitted. "But Stu accepts me for what I am, cellulite and all. And he needs me. Can you imagine how lost he'd be if *I* split?"

That's a hell of a reason for marriage, Win thought. He'd never consider such foolishness for himself. He said, "You ought to think more of yourself, Laura."

Laura shrugged. "There are givers and takers. Stu takes what I give."

Which am I? Win wondered. Since he'd extricated himself from the relationship with Stu and Laura relatively unscathed, he didn't want to test his good fortune by opening up an analysis of his personality. After pecking Laura good-night on the cheek, he went to bed.

Moving out was more complicated than it sounded. There were the seemingly clear-cut matters of finding a job and locating a place to live.

Decent apartments in London were scarce. Win's visit to a real estate agent resulted in his being told that rentals comprised less than ten percent of the housing market; they were either outrageously expensive or located in less than desirable neighborhoods. Besides, she informed him with the refined tact of the English, shouldn't he first obtain employment so he'd know where to look?

The search for work was even more frustrating. Win's trip on the Continent helped him realize that he needed to spend his life doing something he loved. What he wanted was set design, not slaving away in an architect's office with T-squares, slanted desks, and artificial light. The nine-to-five treadmill seemed like a living death.

But he had no practical experience, save his summer construction jobs and his set designs at Hayes. And he was an American. So who would hire him?

Win decided to try anyway. Damned if he'd be like Stu, defeated before he began. He spent the next two weeks combing the West End, starting with the larger, state-subsidized Royal Shakespeare and National Theatres, working his way through the less lucrative, commercially managed enterprises, and finally to the struggling experimental companies. As he'd intuited, he came up empty. Most of the time he was shunted off to underlings; stage managers were always too busy to see him.

After one particularly humiliating incident at a seedy warehouse in which the producer-cum-director ordered Win out, screaming that he couldn't even pay his regular people, a stagehand hurried after Win. An avant-garde production was hiring at the Theatre Upstairs in the Royal Court. Mounting it required more people than they'd planned for. Perhaps they were still looking for someone.

Because the Theatre Upstairs was an exclusive nightclub with a prestigious string of hits, Win hadn't even considered employment there. He wanted to feel hope but didn't dare as he trudged towards the address given him by the stagehand.

The well-dressed crowds at Sloane Square seemed to mock him, and he wondered, what will make these English thespians any different? Although they claimed to be egalitarian, most looked down upon him as a scruffy American hippie.

The street addresses were so erratic he missed the building. After backtracking, he went up the stairs as instructed and into a darkened round room dominated by empty tables. "Hello?" Win called. No answer. "Great," he muttered. "No one's even here." He turned to leave.

Suddenly the room grew brilliant with light, revealing the most bizarre set Win had ever seen. In one corner of the Odeon-carpeted stage stood an oversized Coke machine. Across from it was a laboratory of sorts, with a wheeled hospital bed that had exaggerated switches and dials. A rainbow-crested box and a huge screen rested center stage. The Saturday matinee-type red curtains topped off the effect of an excruciatingly tacky "B" horror movie.

Even more peculiar were the actors. Some were entwined in the various positions of the *Kama Sutra* while a tall, curly-haired fellow in a sequined black corset with fishnet hose and platform shoes towered over an overweight greaser, ready to stab him with an ice pick. One girl in a wedding dress sported vermilion hair, while a muscular blonde beach boy wore only a loincloth.

Had he stumbled into some sort of cultish sexual snuff ritual? Win edged towards the exit. "Uh, excuse me. I'll be going now. Sorry to interrupt."

A short man with soft grey hair and brilliant blue eyes stepped out from behind the curtain. "American, are you?" he inquired.

"That's right," Win stammered, glancing at the door. Why did it suddenly seem so far away? "I'm from Ohio," he added, for lack of anything better to say. The entire cast burst into laughter, dissolving their frozen tableau.

"What's so funny?" Win demanded, annoyed. Damn the British and their peculiar sense of humor, anyway!

"Not Denton, I hope," The curly-haired fellow laid the ice pick on the box. They were only playacting after all.

"You mean Dayton?" Win asked. "I'm from Cincinnati, only about fifty miles away...."

This induced another round of hysteria and the grey-haired man smiled at Win. "Our play, 'The Rocky Horror Show' is set in Denton, Ohio. It's a spoof of sorts as you can see." He stuck out his hand. "I'm Sam Kepler, a backer."

"Randall Winfield. Pleased to met you." Win's grip was firm. If he wanted to get a job, he had to act confident. And here was someone who could help him. "I heard you were looking for more stage crew."

"You seem like a nice enough chap. And you're a good sport." Kepler turned towards the stage, apparently addressing one of the actors. "How about it, Richard?"

"We'll have to check with Jack, but it's all right by me," a voice replied from behind the screen. "He's going to fit in just fine if he's from Ohio." This resulted in another wave of amusement.

This time Win laughed along with them. He had a job, and if the cast's camaraderie was any indication, this play would be a success.

The door slammed open and a slender redhead in a tailored suit strode into the room. Glancing around disdainfully, she demanded, "Is this what you called me away from work for? I am not impressed!"

"You sound just like Queen Victoria." Placing his arm around her shoulders, Sam Kepler said, "People, I'd like you to meet my lovely daughter Dulcie."

"Planning to shock the shit out of me, were you?" Dulcie gave her father an affectionate squeeze. "I recognize your handiwork, Dad. Shame on you!"

She turned to Win. Although at first glance she appeared almost plain, her even features had a patrician elegance. She carried herself with style and grace, qualities Win had just begun to appreciate in a woman. Her expression was serene but her intense blue eyes, so like her father's, sparkled with humor. "I see you were the unfortunate recipient of this practical joke meant for me."

"Not so unlucky," Win replied. "I think I have a job here. Now all I need is a place to live."

"Oh, we can help you locate a flat," Dulcie replied breezily. "I manage several of Dad's buildings in the City and we'll make sure you don't get gazumped."

"Say what?" Who said Americans and Brits spoke the same language?

"Cut out of an apartment the day before you move in," Sam explained. "It happens all the time, especially to Yanks. But now that you're one of the crew, we'll simply have to take you in."

"Right." Win grinned at Dulcie and her father.

That evening, as he rode home on the subway, he realized that he'd been attracted to a woman who hadn't reminded him of Julia. And once he moved out of Stu and Laura's, the last tie with his life at Hayes would be broken. Only memories would remain.

PART THREE

REALITY

March 1985, Ocho Rios, Jamaica
June 1985, Hayes University
July 1990, London, England

CHAPTER
THIRTY-THREE

What Julia faced on that shimmering beach over a gulf of fifteen years was not Win. It was her own feelings.

With a shock, she realized that the man with the russet hair was much closer to twenty than thirty-five. And although he resembled Win in build and coloring, his facial features were completely different.

"I'm sorry," Julia stammered, taking several steps backwards, stumbling in the soft sand. "I thought you were somebody else."

"That's all right, love," the young man replied in a British accent. He glanced at her appraisingly, seeming to find her attractive despite their disparity in years. "Listen, if you want to talk any time, I'm available. Come along, Rusty." He whistled for the dog, then turned to leave.

"You OK, lady?" Julia became aware of the Jamaican guide still holding her arm. "We go back to the Dunn's River now. No need to be afraid. You can finish the climb."

More than anything, she wanted to think. About her past and why she'd spent so much time and energy repressing it. And why even seeing someone who reminded her of Win produced such a strong reaction. "I don't think so," Julia extricated herself from his grasp. "I need to be alone. Tell the others I'm not going on the rest of the tour."

"But why..." he began, then, noticing Julia's expression, backed away. "No problem. Just be back to the ship on time. The *Morning Glory*, right?"

"I will."

Julia barely reached the women's rest room next to the snack bar before tears overtook her. As she sobbed, she prayed no one from the ship would overhear. She didn't care whether the natives did; in this impoverished country, they knew about suffering and would probably understand.

She thought she'd resolved this years ago. Why was it coming back to haunt her now? Then she realized that, for the first time in almost a decade, she'd had a chance to be alone, to think. She wasn't enmeshed in the role of Congressman's wife, mother of two wild and crazy first-grade twin boys, or freelance artist accommodating clients. She was Julia, a stranger with whom she'd apparently lost touch.

After Valerie had been killed, Louie was the only person Julia could talk to. Because he'd been there, he understood her pain; everyone else seemed overly solicitous or morbidly curious. Although she was determined to cut all ties with Hayes, and made him promise not to tell anyone of her whereabouts, she couldn't bring herself to turn her back on his seemingly unconditional friendship.

The year after the explosion, Louie stopped by her parents' home where she lived at first. After she enrolled in a commercial art program at the Columbus College of Art and Design, he'd visit her campus apartment en route between Columbia and his hometown of Cleveland. Although she had developed her own group of friends at Jefferson Publishing where she also worked part-time as a pasteup artist, most of the men were either gay or married, so she began to look forward to Louie's unencumbered male companionship.

Louie was spending one such weekend with her during his Easter break a few days into OSU's spring quarter. Julia had run low on groceries and wanted to cook dinner, so he went to the corner store and came back full of news about a candlelight march close to Julia's apartment. Didn't she wonder what the antiwar movement was like? Wasn't she curious to see where it had gone? During the past year, neither of them had been active, Julia because of what had happened at Hayes and Louie because he had no time, between law school and his part-time job. Against her better judgment, he persuaded Julia to go with him that evening to check it out.

Julia saw it as a small way of repaying Louie, who had done so much for her. And what could possibly happen that she already hadn't experienced?

At first she and Louie stood on a side street, watching. The kids seemed younger, less committed. They were there in numbers, but their lifeless chanting and nonchalant air revealed how little they understood the purpose of the march. The gathering was a contrivance, a social amenity seasoned with a dash of fear of repercussions from the Establishment. Even the cops, a handful of Columbus police, looked uninterested, talking and joking among themselves.

Then a policeman seemed to reach for his holster and Julia was gripped with a sense of overwhelming panic. He was going to pull out his gun and shoot the students! Her legs locked in terror and, as had happened just after the explosion, she couldn't catch her breath. "That cop..." was all she could manage before she blacked out.

When she came to, she was lying on the floor of a small bar. Louie and a ponytailed waiter knelt over her with a paper bag. "Something really freaked her out. She hyperventilated and fainted," Louie was explaining.

She struggled to get up, but Louie insisted she breathe into the bag until her respiration returned to normal. After what seemed like hours later, they finally left.

"Julia, I'm sorry I dragged you to that demonstration," Louie said as they climbed the steps to her apartment. "I should have known it would be traumatic."

"It wasn't," she replied shortly. "It looked like the cop was going for his gun, and I overreacted."

Louie turned to her in exasperation. "When are you going to face this thing and get on with your life?"

"I don't know what you're talking about." Inexplicably furious, she turned the key in the lock, shoving open the door.

Seizing her, Louie said, "Goddamn it, Julia...." And began to kiss her.

Instead of pushing him away, she found herself responding. It had been so long, and the throbbing, burning ache for sex that Win had awakened, that had been buried under the pain of the past year, came voraciously alive. Louie led her over to the couch and started to make love to her. She moaned, rubbing herself against his erection.

She pulled off her T-shirt, unhooked her skimpy bra. Louie buried his curly head between her naked breasts. "Oh, God, I want you," she gasped, as he covered them with hot, wet kisses. She began the slide towards mindless, exquisite passion. "Oh, Win..."

An instant after the words escaped her lips, she recognized her slip. But it was too late. Louie jerked away.

"Louie, I didn't mean that!" She tried to embrace him, but he was already handing her clothes.

"Get dressed."

"Louie, I'm sorry," she said, tears of disappointment gathering at the corners of her eyes. Her body ached to complete the act they'd initiated.

Without replying, he started putting his gear into his backpack. She pleaded with him to stay, but he refused to even look at her. Finally he said, in that irritatingly concise way of his, "I don't care how much you've been through. I won't be a stand-in for anyone."

"But it wasn't that way at all, Louie. I was actually feeling something."

He stopped cold, his expression so enraged she thought he was going to strike her. "It isn't me you want, it's a good fuck. You can get that at the bar down the street."

She slunk into the bedroom, waiting there until he left. She knew he spoke the truth. Although she found Louie attractive, no one could ever replace Win.

After completing her courses, she moved to New York a few months later to try her luck as a commercial artist there. She debated about phoning Louie. She missed their long, comforting rap sessions. But she decided not to: she was going to make it on her own or not at all.

The men she dated there seemed shallow, ruthlessly ambitious, self-serving. Louie's comment about sex for its own sake seemed to haunt her; she found the act mindless, mechanical, empty. After two short and disastrous affairs, she opted for what she hoped was temporary celibacy. Besides, her career as a commercial artist had become all-encompassing, requiring most of her time and energy.

In the spring of Louie's last year in law school, Julia finally called him. She figured he'd be leaving the city soon; they could at least part friends. And he'd probably met someone else by now.

Louie seemed thrilled to hear from her, and quickly informed her he'd broken up with his girlfriend of several months, another law student. Apparently the experience had overshadowed his and Julia's last encounter, which he seemed to have forgotten, or at least forgiven. They began to see each other, never discussing Win and rarely Hayes, and drifted into a relationship that soon crossed from platonic to a full-blown affair. It was comfortable, it was right and by the end of the summer, they married, moving to Cleveland shortly afterwards.

Between caring for Adam and Abe and attending to her career, Julia had little time and no desire to look back. Then in 1981 Louie decided to leave his law practice, quitting local politics to run for Congress. After that, it had been one upheaval after another, with Louie's career taking precedence over everything. They'd had to move to Washington, away from their mutual friends and many of her professional contacts. She had to start all over again and despised the back-stabbing and butt-kissing so endemic in Washington.

Although they still expressed affection for each other, she and Louie seemed to be drifting. Each cancelled school play, dinner, and evening together drove them a little further apart. This cruise was a perfect example — Louie backed out because of last-minute problems with his subcommittee, promising he'd make it up to her later.

And there was another cause for dissent. Louie had told her a month earlier he'd been invited to address the graduating class at Hayes this June. Julia couldn't believe he'd accepted: after what they had gone through, how could he go back and act as if nothing had happened?

"Except for that last month or so, my memories are basically happy," he told her. "Why can't you see beyond that?"

"Fine. Go by yourself and have fun reminiscing. Give Dean Moreland and Sheriff Adams my regards, and stop by the rebuilt Administration building at Valerie and Richard's grave." The bodies had been so crushed, they were never recovered.

"Why are you still running away, Julia? And why are you so angry?"

"I am neither," she'd replied coldly. "I simply have no desire to return to that place. It holds nothing for me."

Crossing his arms, Louie had fixed her with a penetrating stare. "I'm hard-pressed to believe that, Julia."

Something crashed and Abe began to cry. Julia and Louie rushed to the family room to see what was wrong. Abe had overturned a lamp in pursuit of one of his toy men and was unharmed, although scared. The moment for discussion passed, and the subject not brought up again, although Louie mentioned to their friends how much he was looking forward to returning to Hayes. Julia had kept silent.

Maybe that was my mistake, she thought now, as she washed her face free of sunblock and tears. I tried to bury a part of myself with Valerie and Richard. Maybe I *need* to face this, to explore the past.

Julia got a Diet Coke at the snack bar and flagged a taxi to take her back to the ship. Louie would be pleased to know she'd changed her mind about going back to Hayes. What she might uncover there — about Win, Valerie, and her own true feelings — might not make him as happy, if he still loved her.

CHAPTER
THIRTY-FOUR

Julia's return to Hayes a few months later was less than triumphant. Claiming yet another emergency, Louie postponed his visit until Saturday, telling Julia to go ahead to their room, which they'd reserved for the entire weekend. Because it was graduation, hotels in Hampton had been booked up months earlier and the travel agent could only get them a suite because Julia absolutely refused to stay in the dorm. Going back there was bad enough — she didn't need to relive it, for God's sake.

Then their sons decided to fly in with Louie. Athletic little Abe had an important baseball playoff and Adam was invited to a birthday party Friday night. Well, Louie will have to take care of the logistics of *that* along with juggling his meetings, Julia thought in grim satisfaction.

A thunderstorm out of Washington National, delayed, then finally cancelled her flight and all passengers had to be shuttled to another plane. And now, the idiots at the car rental place in Cincinnati couldn't find her reservation. "All we have left are fifteen-passenger vans, ma'am," sniffed the rental agent, taking in Julia's disheveled hair and white linen jacket, which had become stained with sweat and the grime of travel. "Your name wasn't on the list and it *is* graduation weekend for several colleges."

That was the last straw. "But this isn't my mistake!" Julia shouted. "And I have to suffer for your incompetence!"

Then she saw a uniformed young man holding a placard with Louie's name on it. Without offering an explanation to the rental agency android, she walked over to him. "What is this?"

"Congressman Wexler's wife?" The driver, obviously a student, grinned widely and thrust out his right hand. "I'm Jerry, your chauffeur. The University sent me to escort you and your husband around campus. The limo's out in front."

"You've got to be kidding!" She ignored his hand. Leave it to Hayes to provide special treatment because of Louie's position and seeming influence. They knew where they could stick *that.*

Then she remembered she had no transportation. And there was the matter of her and the kids' luggage — Louie forgot such necessities as toothbrushes and favorite toys so she'd packed for them in advance.

"Oh, all right," she conceded. Jerry headed over to the car rental booth where her luggage stood unattended. He must think I'm a bitch, Julia reflected as she slid into the back seat of the luxurious vehicle. He undoubtedly overhead the fracas about the rental and I wouldn't even shake his hand.

To make amends, she asked politely, "Do you do this often?"

"Every chance I get. Me and three other guys from Hayes work for a limo service based in Cincinnati. Mostly we get rock stars." For the first time she noticed he wore an earring, and almost smiled.

"They can get pretty wild," he went on. "Ever hear of Van Halen?" Julia shook her head no. "I chauffeured them in '84." He proceeded to launch into a discourse about the group's backstage antics and recent replacement of their lead singer, including the destruction of hotel rooms if certain requirements weren't met, such as the removal of brown M&Ms from candy dishes. "But they always pay for the damage."

Julia wondered if the driver would have been as intense about Vietnam. Probably so, she decided. Youthful passions rarely change, although times were certainly different.

As they reached the outskirts of campus, Jerry asked, "Didn't you go to school here or something? I know Congressman Wexler did."

Although it was nearly nine, the campus was still bathed in a golden dusk. Things were recognizable but definitely askew. Additional buildings had sprung up; old ones razed; the university had even acquired a nearby women's college. The newer structures seemed big and imposing, almost alien.

And the students... strolling back and forth with earphones and portable radios, they resembled walking isolation booths. Nowhere could Julia see the passionate interchange of ideas and thoughts she remembered so vividly.

Although it was a weekend, no one kissed, and few held hands. The campus appeared to be devoid of sex, although Julia suspected students were more sophisticated and discreet about it. And everyone *dressed* — in chinos, in matching skirts and blouses or slacks and shirts, even an occasional suit. Hayes seemed like a different country now.

Still, seeing it again opened up a floodgate of emotion. The memories made her want to weep. "Yes, I went here," she managed, hoping her voice didn't sound as choked-up as she felt.

"Hey, you want me to drive you around? I mean it's been fifteen years, right? And the campus has a lot of cool new stuff. Don't get me wrong, the older buildings are great, too."

There was something infectious about his enthusiasm. "Well..." she began.

"I'll take you uptown," Jerry offered, turning onto Spring Street, where most of the important buildings were located. "The alumni always go on about how they hardly recognize it."

But I'm not an alumni, Julia wanted to reply but didn't, not wanting to initiate a slew of questions.

She glanced outside her window. There stood the Administration Building, impassive, seemingly untouched by time, intact. Completely restored, it had resumed its normal functions as the clockwork of the university, a dull harbinger of records.

As if it were that terrible day, the explosion replayed itself in Julia's head. She saw it as clearly as if it were actually happening: bits of concrete flying, the tremendous noise, followed by ten seconds of deadly silence. Then waiting for Valerie, Richard, and Felix to emerge....

An incredible sense of loss engulfed her. Julia felt as if the breath had been seized from her. Her heart pounded so loudly she barely heard herself say, "I've changed my mind. Forget about uptown."

"Are you sure, Mrs. Wexler? You'll really be amazed."

Any moment she was going to explode. She had to get out of this car and away from everyone until she pulled herself together. "Just please, take me to the University Hotel. Now."

Jerry looked at her in the rear view mirror, his blue eyes perplexed. "Look, Mrs. Wexler, I know I'm probably out of bounds here, but do you want to talk about it? I can tell you're upset. And I've kept a lot of secrets."

How could she explain the destruction of so many lives to this innocent youngster, whose biggest worry was the breakup of his favorite rock band? "No thank you, Jerry, but you're very kind. And I don't need to be chauffeured around in a limousine. I got around on foot fifteen years ago and so did my husband. So take the weekend off — you don't need to tell anyone." Let the University pay for it, she thought. And Louie could find his own damn way around campus.

"Whatever you want, Mrs. Wexler. But I'm on call for you and the Congressman while you're here. So if you can't reach me at the Alumni Office, I'll give you my number at the frat house just in case."

As soon as she got to their suite, Julia phoned Louie. Without even saying hello, she launched into a tirade about her terrible trip. After she'd finished, he apologized, "I tried to catch you this morning before you left and tell you to fly in with us, but must have just missed you. I should have realized how upsetting coming back here alone would be."

"And you think your presence would make it easier?"

"Well, I hope so, Julia. I was there, too."

"Sometimes I wonder, with the way you've been acting these days." She told Louie about the limousine, thinking he'd be annoyed at her dismissing the driver. But he didn't seem to care. "I'll have a car waiting when we arrive in Cincinnati. And we'll get an earlier flight out, if possible. Why don't you order room service, or get a bite in the restaurant? Get a glass of wine, it will help you relax."

After she hung up, she felt guilty. It was her own anger she was feeling, not anything Louie had done to her. After all, she'd come here of her own volition.

She thought about calling him back to apologize and didn't. She could make amends tomorrow. He'd had enough for one day, and he had to get the boys to bed. As she went down to the hotel lobby to get some dinner, she thought, I guess I do need Louie more than I care to admit.

The dream came to her after she'd fallen into an uneasy slumber. She and Win were walking towards the Performing Arts Center. Which was strange in itself, because all her dreams of Win involved them just missing each other — at a demonstration, a party, even his house. They never had face-to-face encounters or spoke.

Unlike the rest of campus, in which buildings of all ages reflected the harmonies of Georgian architecture, the old theatre had inexplicably become an iconoclastic clash of red brick, steel, and glass. Still, Julia located a stairwell where she and Valerie had an intense conversation about drugs and Richard and life so long ago, then looked up and discovered a huge skylight. She found the addition oddly reassuring.

Intending to make love, she and Win wandered behind the theatre, their arms around each others' waists. Julia could smell the fragrant greenery, practically touch the ripeness of spring in the cool air. She ached with desire; she couldn't wait to feel Win inside her.

They reached a clearing. She and Win lay down beside each other, their bodies barely touching, both of them anticipating the ecstacy to come. Then the sobbing began. Without a word, Win hurried off to investigate the source of the sound. Julia watched lazily as he disappeared into a tangle of trees.

But something about this place.... The woods, so friendly and full of sunshine, became spookily familiar. Suddenly apprehensive, Julia jumped up and went after Win.

As she approached another clearing, she saw the two boulders. Then the memory hit her — this was where Valerie had hidden the ammunition! She glanced around again to make sure. Yes, this was part of what they'd once called the Cliffs. She was terrified.

The keening started anew, this time much closer, more intense. Following the noise, Julia peered from behind the trunk of a tree. Win had his arms around a tall, sticklike figure, who was obviously in distress. "You can talk to me, man," Win was saying.

"I can't. You'd hate me if you knew the truth. And you'd never understand," a familiar voice replied. "It was all my fault! If only I could bring them back!"

Adrian! Guilt had driven him back to where he, Felix, and Valerie had hidden the ammunition — a criminal returning to the scene. Adrian seemed much older than she and Win and was nearly bald. His wrinkled face and bent carriage revealed a man drained of all vitality. Dorian Gray in reverse....

But no, it wasn't Adrian after all. The person in Win's arms was changing, transforming into someone, no *something* else. With horror, Julia recognized Valerie, not the Valerie of fifteen years earlier, but Valerie as she would be today if she'd been buried in a grave. A skeleton of dust and bones, a head with staring eye sockets and long, greyish blonde hair.

The death's head turned to Julia. "Nothing is what it seems.... You've got to face the hate to reach the love." Paralyzed with fear, Julia opened her mouth to scream. Nothing came out except a ringing sound.

CHAPTER THIRTY-FIVE

The phone, it had to be the phone. As Julia struggled towards consciousness, she became aware of sunshine streaming into the room. It was morning, thank God.

She grabbed the receiver. "Hello?" she cried in a frightened voice, putting her hand on her cheek. It was covered with tears.

"Julia? Are you all right?" Louie demanded. He sounded so concerned, so *normal*. She slumped down in relief. "We're in the lobby and they won't let us up until you give us your room number."

"You woke me up." What time was it, anyway? She glanced at her clock: 7:45. Louie had meant what he said about taking an early flight. "I'm in 101. The Lucy Webb Hayes Suite."

"We'll be right there." Julia could hear her sons chattering in the background. It sounded like music after the horror of her nightmare.

At breakfast, Louie said to Julia, "I have something to show you. Actually, two things. Do you think you can handle going to the Performing Arts Center?"

"I don't know...." Julia told Louie about the nightmare, leaving out the part about her and Win making love.

"There's something I need to do first," she said. "I need to take the car so I can talk to Cal Adams. Then I think I'll be able to meet you."

"Why?" Despite his rise in politics, Louie still had difficulty disguising his emotions. At least with her.

"Because I think he has some answers. It was as if Valerie — or at least her spirit — was trying to tell me something."

Louie looked bemused. "Don't tell me you believe in ghosts now, Julia?"

"Not exactly, but there is an awful lot of unexplained phenomena. Even the Performing Arts Center was supposed to be haunted."

"And still is, from what I've heard. All right, Julia. But let me go with you."

"No, I need to do this alone. Adams can't hurt me any more than I've already been hurt."

The Hampton Police Station was still small and dingy, with an air of casual inefficiency. Yet it wasn't nearly as intimidating as Julia remembered.

Still, the young man behind the desk could have been Cal Adams fifteen years ago, and Julia had to conceal her shock and fear. Could it be his son? It never occurred to her that Adams had been married at the time, although she pitied his wife if he was. "Officer Adams, right?"

This fox face was an open book; surprise was evident in every feature. "How did you know? I just started last week."

"Cal Adams was the acting sheriff when I was in school in 1970. You look a lot like him."

The young policeman relaxed. "Oh, that's my uncle. He's been sheriff for years now. I'm Virgil."

"And I'm Julia Brandon Wexler." They shook hands, and Julia said, "Your uncle and I weren't exactly friends, but I'd like to talk to him. Is he around?"

"Nah, he's rarely on duty during the weekends. Me and Gary — that's the other officer — usually take care of things. It's usually pretty quiet. But I can call him for you, if you like."

"Even better, can you take me out to his place? I wouldn't ask but..." she gave Virgil the short version of the explosion and her and Valerie's part in it. "It's important I learn the truth. I've felt responsible all this time, like I could have somehow prevented the tragedy. And your uncle knew the informer." If Adrian had a part in Valerie and his own father's deaths, then he would hear from Julia. Somehow she would find him and make him pay. Although she felt sorry for Felix's family, he and Adrian had brought the ammo to campus and were therefore both accountable.

Young Virgil seemed genuinely sympathetic. "Uncle Cal doesn't say much about that time. I think he was real unhappy, 'cause my dad died in the war and people were so nasty to vets. I was a kid, then, so I don't remember much. But after my mom moved back to Hamilton in '73, he was like a father to me. He never married.... In fact, he talked me into joining the force here."

Perhaps Adams had mellowed over the years. "Do you think he'd open up to me?"

"Why don't we stop by his house and I'll tell him you're waiting outside? The worst he can say is 'no.'"

Julia followed the cruiser into an older section of Hampton, where the homes were smaller and closer together. They pulled in front of a shabby but well-tended residence. "Julia Brandon...what was your last name?" asked Virgil as Julia rolled down her window.

"Just tell him Julia Brandon." Best to leave Louie out of this; he and Adams had despised each other.

She seemed to wait forever. Was she doing the right thing by facing Cal Adams? Would he even talk to her? Or would she have to spend the rest of her life wondering who betrayed her and Valerie?

Finally the screen door opened and a skinny, balding man emerged alone. As he came closer, Julia saw it was definitely Cal Adams. And he looked unhappy.

As Virgil drove away and waved, Julia wondered about the wisdom of what she was doing. Was she placing herself in physical danger? Yet out of his uniform, without his weapons, he seemed unimposing.

Julia rolled down the window as Adams approached the car.

"I'd invite you in, but the place is a mess," he said. "I wasn't expecting company." His voice had the gravelly sound of a lifetime of alcohol and cigarettes.

"Then we'll talk right here. It's a beautiful day."

Julia got out of her car and Adams glanced at her appraisingly. "So, Julia Brandon, as pretty as ever. I bet you're married with a packet of kids. What can I do for you?"

A *packet* of kids? He must mean passel. Julia resisted the urge to correct him.

"Your nephew must have explained why I wanted to see you," she said, hoping he would start talking first.

Adams did not reply. He wasn't going to make this easy, but at least he had shown up.

"The last time we spoke, it wasn't, uh, under the best of circumstances." She stumbled over her words, but forged ahead nonetheless. "You said there was an informer, someone who told the police about the protesters' activities."

"I remember." Why did Adams look so sad? He didn't seem to want to talk to her but apparently something inside him had compelled him to.

Then he said, "You know, I been a pretty good cop most of my career, except those first few years when all that protesting was going on. I'm thinking about running for Shawnee County sheriff this fall. It figures you'd show up about now and remind me of my one big mistake." There was an apology inside those words, and Julia wondered why.

"What are you talking about? *You* had nothing to do with the weapons."

Adams snorted. "If I was smart, I'd refuse to see you. But Virgil said you felt responsible and guilty. And that bothered me. You're the last person who should feel that way."

In spite of her instinct to go slowly, Julia pressed, "Then who was the informer?"

As always, the direct approach backfired with Adams. He gave her his old sneer, "I always was a sucker for you, even though I knew I never had a chance. It always made me mad how you hippies had everything handed on a silver platter — education, money, sex. While us poor slobs fought in the wars and the streets preserving law and order."

"Look Sheriff Ad, I mean, Cal," Julia said firmly. "I'm not here to be flattered or argue right or wrong. I just want to know the name of the person who told Felix that Valerie had taken the explosives."

"There ain't no such person." He seemed to deliberately mangle his grammar.

"What?" Julia couldn't believe it. Was he joking? But his expression was serious. "But how did Felix find out?"

"Who knows? He was a professional agitator, a mercenary type, hired by the underground. He'd been trained in guerrilla warfare, and traveled from campus to campus. The FBI had a file on him a mile long. Shit, he probably figured it out on his own. You kids were so damn easy to read, anyway," he said, forgetting he and Julia were approximately the same age.

She felt as if she'd wandered into an optical illusion. She'd perceived things one way, but they were totally different. "But there *had* to be a spy, someone who told you about our activities. So many of our plans went haywire! You seemed to anticipate our every move!"

Adams chuckled, but was clearly unamused. "What did you expect, with your leaflets and your mass meetings and your so-called secret plans? You kids were your own worst enemies. Any fool could figure out what you were up to. Take that messed-up ROTC demonstration in the spring of '70, for instance. Common sense said the protesters'd be there; it was a damn military review."

Something still nagged at her, a missing link. "But if the police knew about the Administration building takeover, why didn't they prevent it?"

The look on his face made her feel as if she'd kicked him in the stomach. He avoided her gaze. "We didn't have a handle on everything and besides, we only had a couple of FBI plants."

Seeing her grow tense with suspicion, Adams explained, "It was no one you knew or even spent time with. And we went after the heavy duty dope dealers, the hard core revolutionaries like Felix and your friend Valerie."

Julia sucked in her breath. "So you knew about the weapons."

"Yes, but not where they were kept. At least not 'til the very end."

"So you did find out. How?" Adrian must have had a hand in this somewhere.

He became strangely quiet, and Julia said, "Cal, please be honest. I've had my hunches but I've never said a word to anyone. And I promise I'll never repeat whatever you tell me."

He sighed. "Would have made no difference, anyway. By then I knew myself. I followed you and Valerie that night to the Cliffs." So her intuition had been right, she had sensed someone! Only it had been *Adams*, not Adrian. But why hadn't he done anything?

"I saw what was in those bags you took to Valerie's. I figured what the hell, maybe you'd blow each other up. It'd only be justice. Got my wish, too."

"And you got even for your brother who died in Vietnam," Julia finished his unspoken thought.

"Yeah, you could say that," Adams hunched over, pulled out a cigarette and lit up. "Wasn't worth it, I can tell you. I've had to live with those deaths all these years, and shirking my duty as an officer of the law. Didn't bring Danny back, neither. Virgil still grew up without a daddy."

"I suppose we were all at fault," Julia was thinking aloud. Adams relaxed, finally freed of a burden he'd carried alone for too long. "It was no one and everyone's doing." Her voice was thick with tears, this time of relief.

"I think we'd better stop blaming ourselves," Adams turned away, but not before Julia glimpsed a glimmer of wetness in his eyes.

"Some things are just fated, I guess." The truth gave her a sense of empowerment. "Thank you for telling me. I needed to know."

Adams' gruff manner returned. "All that ruckus you hippies made did no good. World's still a shithole."

Like most men, Adams was fiercely protective of his emotions. "Well, you could look at it that way. Or you could consider how attitudes changed after Hayes, Jackson, and Kent State and a few years later towards Vietnam vets. People pulled together in an effort to rectify the war's wrongs. And civil rights for minorities and women has come a long way, too." Of course, there was

South America, South Africa, and AIDs, but they didn't need to get into that.

"Little Julia Sunshine. You're still the same. You end up with that red-haired fellow, magnolia blossom? The cheesecake you were supposed to meet that night?"

"You mean beefcake," Julia said. All Adams needed was to arrest a body builder and call him "cheesecake." "No, I married Louie Wexler. You probably remember him. He headed up the Student Mobilization Committee. Now he's a Congressman."

"Oh, yeah. I heard about him. Local hothead makes good." Adams nodded. "Well, at least you showed some common sense in that department." He turned and practically jogged back to his house, as if he'd had enough for one day.

What did he mean by that? Adams hadn't told her everything and likely never would. Julia wondered what else she'd missed about her time with Win and the others.

I may never know, she thought as she started the car. But at least she'd uncovered some answers and that made her very happy.

CHAPTER THIRTY-SIX

Julia sped towards the Performing Arts Center. It was 1:30; she was supposed to meet Louie and the boys a half hour ago. Louie's speech wasn't until tomorrow, but the University was giving a cocktail party in his honor tonight. Knowing Louie, he'd neglected to pack his tie or matching socks so she had to get back to the hotel, go through his things, then rush uptown to purchase the forgotten item before the stores closed. Sometimes she wondered what he'd do without her, although he hardly paid as much attention to her as when they'd first married.

She parked the car and hurried inside. She was so intent on finding Louie and their sons she failed to notice the renovations to the august old building. She finally spotted her husband in the first floor hallway, his hand on the arm of a petite, pretty woman with flowing black hair. She appeared to be flirting with him. Where were the boys, anyhow?

The woman's eyes widened when she saw Julia, and Louie turned around. "Oh, there you are!" he said with a smile. "I was just about to call the police, but then I realized you were *with* the police."

"Speaking of missing persons, have your forgotten our sons?"

"Don't worry, they're with Laura's little boy and her nanny. They're much happier playing video games than wandering around campus with us."

Laura... Now Julia remembered where she'd seen the woman before: the wedding on the steps of the Performing Arts Center the first spring she met Win. Her mind's eye released a torrent of mental snapshots: Julia's own out-of-context pink minidress; Adrian and Valerie getting outrageously ripped on hashish brownies; her and Win's first, timid conversation; Louie's confident commitment; Shawn's golden, glowing beauty. Everyone intact, whole, untouched.

Laura was about seventy pounds thinner than Julia remembered and very sexy-looking. She had lured away Win, and it looked as if she was now trying to do the same with Louie. "That's nice of you, but the hotel concierge has arranged for a baby sitter," Julia said coolly. "We need to get back, Louie. The party's in a few hours and I want to make sure you have everything."

Louie ignored the hint. "Laura's a professor in the theatre department here, and she's kept track of everybody over the years. We were just catching up."

"It's nice to finally meet you, Julia," Laura's voice was warm and gracious. "I've heard so much about you — in the past and today."

Win...this woman must know what happened to Win.... But before Julia had a chance to ask, Louie took her hand. "I said there were two things I wanted to show you; one of them's right here. Have a look." They paused before the main auditorium and he pointed at a large plaque.

Julia read: "The Stazyck Theatre. Named in honor of Valerie Rose Stazyck. Born: August 7, 1949, Died: May 4, 1970. 'Ye shall know the truth and it shall set you free.'"

She stood quietly, choked with tears. She couldn't remember the last time she'd wept this much, perhaps shortly after she'd lost Valerie and Win. But then she'd felt frozen inside. Now the ice was thawing, breaking up to reveal the true feelings underneath. "My God, Louie," she said, as he put his arms around her. "Why didn't you tell me about this?"

"I wanted it to be a surprise. I knew it would mean a lot to you. There's something else. Although the University re-named the economics building after Dr. Shaffley, a bunch of us are getting together to start an endowment in both Valerie and Richard's names."

"Actually, it was Adrian's idea," said Laura.

"Adrian? He hated his father!" Julia was shocked.

"Adrian didn't realize how much he loved him until after Richard died," said Laura. "He and Adrian's mother despised each other, so Adrian and his sister felt like they had to choose sides, to assign blame. Of course, it took him a few years to figure it out...."

"The scholarship will be an annual stipend for students who want to pursue their dream careers but don't feel like they have the security to do so," explained Louie. "It will provide for extra schooling, if necessary."

"Sort of like myself back then...." Julia mused.

"That's the idea."

Somewhere, Valerie was smiling down at them, Julia suddenly realized. It wasn't so much a physical presence as a sense of spiritual reassurance. As if a light the color of Valerie's golden hair had slipped inside Julia's soul and given it a hug. I'm here, it said. I'm with you. No matter where you go.

Julia wiped her eyes, then turned to Laura. Now she could deal with the rest of it. "Louie said you knew what became of the others. Obviously except for Louie, I haven't a clue."

"Do you want the short version or the long one?"

Louie said, "Why don't you two confer over a cup of coffee while I go back to the room and sort through my stuff? If I need anything, I can get it myself."

"Maybe you should pick up Adam and Abe, too. We don't want to impose." Julia wondered if Stu and Laura still held crazy "sex, drug and rock 'n roll" parties.

"Your sons will be fine at my house," Laura reassured her. "Gretchen will give them dinner, and we have a futon so they can nap there."

"What about Stu?" Julia couldn't help but ask.

"Stu?" Laura burst into laughter. "Now there's someone I haven't worried about in eons! I dumped him long ago. I decided

I wanted a child, though, so I adopted Malcolm ten years ago. He's Vietnamese."

Did Louie ever think about his long-deceased lover and son? He seemed unperturbed and said, "He's a charming child. Very well-adjusted."

Laura was not the man-eater Julia had originally thought. What had really happened? And how had everyone turned out? "Let's go, Laura. We need to talk."

Back at the Student Center, Laura gave Julia a sanitized version of what had transpired between her, Stu, Adrian, Win, Kirsten, and Shawn so many years before. But Julia figured it out: in the context of what Laura told her, Win's behavior made sense. Julia supposed that, deep down inside, she'd known something had been going on, because she never questioned Win or the others closely about their relationship. It was almost as if she'd been afraid to find out.

One thing bothered her, though. "Did Louie know about this?"

"I think he and Win argued over not telling you, with Win being the one who wanted to keep it a secret."

"Then why didn't Louie say something afterwards?"

"I don't know, Julia. You'll have to ask him."

They both grew silent. Finally, Julia said, "So what became of everybody?"

"Do you mean everybody, or Win?"

Julia flushed. "C'mon Laura, give me a break. I cared about the others, too. More than I should have, because for them, it was probably just a casual thing. They might not even recognize me if they saw me on the street. But I would know them. It's haunted me for years." She hadn't even admitted that to herself.

Laura reached across the table and squeezed her hand. "I didn't mean to give you a hard time. I know you've been through hell. I loved them also."

According to Laura, Shawn had gone back to school to be trained as a veterinary technician and was still married. She, Joey, their two children, and accompanying menagerie lived in a sub-urb of Dayton. Jake also married, sold cars in Cleveland and had four children. Kirsten had finally made it to Broadway with her costume designs. Adrian lived in San Francisco and produced documentaries about AIDS and other social issues. Stu periodically stayed with his family in Akron between stabs at a career in acting. And Win still lived in London....

Julia could keep quiet no longer. "We all turned out pretty ordinary, didn't we? And we thought we were so special, so enlightened."

Laura leaned back in her chair. "We were going to create the perfect utopia....What a bunch of bunk!"

"The world needs people like that. As long as it's not me, anymore." Julia knew that as long as she held onto the truth, she would continue to heal. "So what about Win?"

"There's not much, really. He married an English girl and, like most everybody, has two kids. He renovates and redesigns old theatres. To be honest, I haven't heard from him in years, although he sent me a change of address a card a few months ago. Do you want his new address?"

Julia laughed uneasily. "When would I ever go to London?"

"You never know. I'll give it to you anyway."

The rest of the weekend passed as if in a dream. The cocktail party was wonderful; Louie's speech to the class of 1985 garnered a standing ovation from both graduates and audience. And Julia reveled in her newfound sense of peace and security. She and Louie made love with renewed ardor. She could hardly wait to get back to Washington to begin some watercolors she'd been thinking about for years but hadn't yet had the nerve to attempt.

But as she and Louie were on their way to their home in Georgetown and the boys were asleep in the back seat, Julia said, "Why didn't you tell me about Win and the others?"

Softly Louie pounded his fist on the steering wheel. "I knew that was coming. And I honestly don't know why. Perhaps because you might not believe me? Because I didn't want to lose you or make you angry? Because it was better to do nothing and leave it alone? I just don't know. But I do know one thing. I love you, Julia."

"That was never an issue, Louie. After we slept together the first time, there was no one else. I fell in love with you and that was it."

"I may possess your body, Julia, but never your mind. What would you do if you came face-to-face with Win?"

Thank God the darkness hid her expression. "Why nothing, probably. Just say 'hello' and catch up on old times. It's been years." Julia had no idea how she'd handle the situation. What if she fell in love with Win all over again?

Louie seemed satisfied with her answer. "We've put the past behind us. Now it's time to move forward."

CHAPTER THIRTY-SEVEN

In the summer of 1990, as part of his duties on a subcommittee that was investigating health-care reforms, Louie was asked to visit several medical facilities in England. This presented a sticky question, because Louie debated utilizing taxpayers' money to finance such an expensive trip. Not only were such jaunts the target of public criticism but Louie was that rarest of creatures, an honest politician.

Finally, he decided on a compromise: he would combine the trip with a second honeymoon and use his own funds for personal expenses. It had been years since he and Julia had gotten away by themselves.

Julia hesitated at first. She was just now beginning to make progress as a "serious" artist; a small but prominent New York gallery was mounting a show of her watercolors. Adam and Abe were going to be bar mitzvahed in a few months; all those millions of details needed to be attended to. And she and Louie had recently purchased a larger home in Chevy Chase, so money was tight, especially since she'd cut down on her commercial art work to paint.

But Louie had to go regardless, and except for the cruise, Julia had never been outside of the United States. And it would give them some time alone. How ironic that they were to stay in London, of all places.

In addition to their passports, luggage, and English currency, Julia had Win's address and the peace symbol he'd given her so long ago. She had no plans for either.

During the past five years, however, Julia and Louie had been in contact with many of the people they'd known at Hayes to obtain support for the Stazyck/Shaffley Scholarship for Alternative Studies. Most were enthusiastic about the project, because they'd ended up doing something totally different from what college had prepared them for. Like Julia, they'd buried their true ambitions under peer and parental expectations. The extra year or two of study would provide a student with the freedom to pursue a dream career, even if it meant dropping out of traditional college to go to a specialty school, such as an art institute.

Julia was happy to see Kirsten successful and Shawn content. Still, Jake had gone fat and bald and was hardly recognizable from the freak-flagged flirt of so long ago. Nowadays, whenever she looked through the Hayes *Alumni Bulletin*, she marvelled at how middle-aged the pictures from her class years looked. But she didn't perceive herself or Louie or the others that way at all.

Perhaps the most amazing was Adrian. Julia was apprehensive when he came to Washington to meet with Louie about setting up the scholarship, especially when Adrian insisted on seeing Julia. But he and Rick, his Chinese-American lover, were as kind as could be. Between the loss of his father, with whom he'd never reconciled, and the death of his previous lover from AIDS, Adrian had developed a compassion and sensitivity which helped make his documentaries successful. In fact, it was most of Adrian's money that was being channelled into the scholarship.

And Julia had her own sorrows. Her mother and Louie's father had passed away within months of each other, and her father was now in a rest home. Only Louie's mother lived independently and his sister resided nearby in Cleveland, available whenever she was needed. With Harry in such frail health and her being the only child, Julia debated the wisdom of leaving the country for three weeks. But she had to live her own life and she could fly back immediately if something happened.

After checking into their hotel in Russell Square, Louie began phoning the various medical facilities and verifying appointments made by his aide in Washington. "You'll be on your own some of the time," he told her. "It may be a problem when we're traveling around the countryside. But there's so much to do in London." Little did he perceive the irony behind his words, Julia thought. Had he completely forgotten that Win lived here? The 1994 Senate race had been on his mind and his name had come up several times to replace the Democratic incumbent who was retiring. But still...Louie couldn't be *that* complacent, could he?

The first few days were hectic, with media interviews, dinners and luncheons, and "official" tours of various landmarks. But as Louie began to settle in and their political obligations dropped off, Julia found she had more time to tour the various art galleries and the British Museum. On Saturday, she planned to go shopping in Picadilly and on Oxford Street.

But as morning turned to afternoon, she grew tired of lugging her packages from store to store. Everything looked the same after a while and she felt conspicuous among the fashion-forward, swaggering youth who swarmed to these places. They reminded her uncomfortably of the past. Why must we all make the same mistakes? she wondered.

So she went back to the hotel and took Win's address and the peace symbol out of her carry-on. The pewter was still as shiny as the day he'd slipped it in her purse. On impulse, she picked up the phone and dialed directory assistance. "I'm sorry, but that number's X-listed," the operator told her when she gave her Win's name.

"Excuse me?"

"It's an unlisted number. We can't give it out."

Deflated, Julia sank down on the bed. Why on earth would Win have an unlisted number? What had life thrown his way to make him want to hide? No one had heard from him in years. It was as if he'd died. What was he running from, anyway?

She pulled out her *Frommer's* guide and looked up Haslemere, the small town where Win lived. It was about a half hour's ride from Victoria Station. Each July, a festival was held there, featuring handmade instruments, a street fair, and concerts. What a perfect excuse....

Trains ran frequently, so there was no problem getting back in time for dinner. Louie had said he'd return around six. Julia scribbled him a note about the festival and headed for the subway station. What did she have to lose?

Apparently dozens of other people had the same idea, because the tube to Haslemere was packed. Julia listened to the lilt of British accents all around her. She wondered if Win talked like an Englishman, or if he said "fuck" or still smoked dope. She doubted it. He'd probably immersed himself in his new culture and forgotten who he was, where he came from. Well, she'd just have to remind him.

Then the old fear came back: What if she was still in love with him? What if he held the same power over her? Would she abandon her husband, children, and career to be with him? Would he do the same for her?

I've had so many questions for so many years, she thought. It's about time for some answers.

According to the rest room attendant at the train station, the address was within walking distance. On her way there, she passed a street vendor selling ice cream. She wanted to stop and get some, but decided not to, fearing she'd mess up her clothes. Self-consciously she pulled out her compact and checked her makeup. The bright daylight showed the faint age lines in her skin; at forty-two, she was grateful they weren't more pronounced.

Win lived on a peaceful side street, full of large, beautifully tended cottages. In fact, the whole town was lovely, with green, rolling hills and a river running alongside it. It reminded her of the Beatrix Potter books she used to read to the boys when they were little.

She finally reached No. 26. Her heart pounding, she raised her hand to knock, when the door opened. She faced a woman who looked a few years older than she, with plain, classic features and faded reddish hair. For a moment, they stared at each other.

Then the woman demanded, "Who are you?"

Intimidated, Julia backed away. "I'm Julia Brandon," she replied, unconsciously dropping her married name. "I think I'm a friend of your husband's. Randall Winfield?"

The woman smiled, and the harshness in her expression and tone disappeared. "Oh, I thought you were one of those door-to-door people. They come 'round here often, especially during festival time. Come on in, then."

"Well," Julia hesitated, clasping together her suddenly clammy hands. "Win wasn't expecting me...."

"Oh, you *are* an old friend. No one's called him that in years. Win's in London this afternoon. He'll be back shortly. Why don't you come in and we'll have tea and chat."

Maybe this wasn't such a good idea. After all, here she was, barging in on Win's life. Having a "chat" with what obviously was his wife, for God's sake. She could only imagine her reaction if she walked in the door of her own home and found *Win* sitting here.

"Look, maybe I can come back," Julia said. "I'm visiting here with my husband and had nothing to do this afternoon, so I just thought I'd stop by. But it's obviously inconvenient...." She realized she was rambling while Win's wife just smiled at her.

"Julia, is it? I'm Dulcie. Come on in. I insist."

Well, she could either run the other way or go inside. And Dulcie was certainly gracious. So she stepped into the foyer and followed her down the cool, dark hallway and into what apparently was a family/sitting room. Julia perched awkwardly on the edge of a chair, while Dulcie asked, "Would you like something to drink? Coffee? Tea? Soda?"

"Tea would be fine, if it's already made. Otherwise, I'll have a glass of ice water." Dulcie disappeared into the kitchen and Julia tried not to crane her neck at the family portraits. It looked like they had two children, a boy and a girl. And Win appeared as handsome as ever, at least in his pictures. She'd have no trouble recognizing him. A large painting of the daughter in horseback riding regalia — she was a beauty who strongly favored Win — hung over the mantelpiece. Julia wondered what her younger brother thought of that.

Dulcie came back in with two china teacups and a tray full of small sandwiches. "I always serve tea in the afternoon, even if it's no one but me. Sammi should be back any moment, though. She's thirteen. That's who I was waiting for when you came to the door." She sat down and for the first time, the two women really looked at each other.

Although Julia saw someone close to her in age and perhaps experience, the haunted expression in Dulcie's blue eyes revealed a woman who had suffered deeply. Something was very wrong here.

Dulcie averted her gaze. "So you knew Win before he came to England. College perhaps?"

"Yes, we were both in the same year in Hayes, although I didn't exactly graduate. I dropped out and became an artist, much to my parents' disappointment. Although they were happy with my choice of husbands." Why was she saying such things? And to Win's wife, of all people?

"Well, Win doesn't talk much about the past. Mostly he's involved in Dad's firm — we restore old buildings, theatres and such. That's where he is today, negotiating on acquiring a theatre. Another company wants to make it into one of those dreadful multiplexes...." She sighed. "Since Dad retired, Win's taken on more and more."

"I know the feeling. My husband's thinking of running for the Senate. He's there but he's not, you know?"

A glimmer of recognition lit up Dulcie's plain face. "Oh, you're the one who married the Congressman, the one who did so well? Laura, was it, wrote Win about it a few years back. He was happy to get the letter, and then after he opened it got really quiet." She glanced at Julia shrewdly. "I see why now."

Julia stood up. "Look, I have to go. Thanks so much for the tea...."

A door screeched open and Julia jumped. It had to be Win. What on earth had compelled her to do this? "That better be Sammi," said Dulcie, and the girl from the portrait rushed in, wearing jodhpurs and boots. Along with her physical attributes, she radiated the same untrammeled sexuality as her father.

Dulcie seemed to forget about Julia. "Samantha, you are late. Why didn't you call me?"

"Mo-ther, I had to groom Topper and we stopped for lunch," Sammi wailed. "Do I have to report to you *every* minute?"

"Yes you do, and you know why. Especially with all the pandemonium at the festival...."

Sammi noticed Julia. "Who's this?"

"A friend of your father's. She's from the United States."

Sammi rolled her eyes at Julia. "My mother is *such* a pain," she said in an American accent. "I'm bilingual — I can speak Brit and American. Impressive, huh?"

"You and my sons would get along fine. They're almost thirteen."

"Oh yeah?" Sammi put her hand on one hip and tossed her long, auburn tresses. "Are they cute?"

Before Julia could respond, Dulcie practically shouted, "Sammi, go in your room and change right now! That's enough!"

"Mother, you are a psychotic, paranoid nutcase! Ever since Jordan...." Without finishing the sentence, Sammi ran from the room. Somewhere in the house, a door slammed shut.

Dulcie sat down, defeated. "I'm terribly sorry about that display of temper. Sammi thinks of no one but herself these days."

"That's all right, my kids are like that, too." But her mind was a whirl of confusion. Who was Jordan? And why did Dulcie seem so overprotective?

As if reading her thoughts, Dulcie said, "Jordan is — was — our little boy. He was killed three years ago." She lowered her head, as if she didn't want to face Julia — or anyone — ever again.

How horrible to lose a child. That had to be the greatest of life's sorrows. Impulsively Julia went over to Dulcie on the couch, putting her arm around her thin shoulders. "You don't have to talk about it if you don't want to. But sometimes it helps."

Suddenly Dulcie burst into huge, racking sobs. "I should have been there for him, I should have been there for him," she kept repeating. Julia held her tightly, stroking her soft hair, wondering how on earth she could bring comfort to this poor woman.

After a while, Dulcie grew calmer. "It was one of those fluke accidents." She looked up at Julia, her eyes surprisingly dry. "His book satchel got caught in the door of a school bus and the driver didn't see. It happened so fast, no one had time to react. He was only seven...." She trailed off, as if she could hear her child's screams.

Julia was at a loss for words. Something like that had happened in Washington several years ago, and Julia had gone around the house for weeks afterwards, warning her sons about the dangers of buses and other vehicles. No wonder Win had an unlisted phone number; the press must have hounded his family mercilessly. One could only guess at the depths of their heartache.

The two women sat quietly for a minute or so, then Dulcie said, "We try to carry on as if nothing's happened, but it's bloody near impossible."

"If you don't mind, I'd like to give you some advice," Julia finally found her voice. "Face your pain. Because if you run away from it, it only gets worse." She knew; she'd lived in a self-imposed cocoon for nearly fifteen years.

"I suppose that's wise. But Win doesn't seem to want to discuss it."

He's still hiding, Julia realized with a twinge of sadness. How well she understood Dulcie's frustration. "He never opened up much back then, either. So it's up to you to take the initiative."

"I suppose," Dulcie sighed, then looked at Julia, some spirit finally glimmering in her blue eyes. Now that we're being honest, I suppose I can ask. Were you in love with him?"

Am I in love with him might be a better question, Julia thought but said, "Yes, I was. Very much. But I didn't really know him." Except in the Biblical sense, which undoubtedly greatly colored her perceptions. "So perhaps I was infatuated with the *idea* of Win, not the actual person. And we were just kids." Julia pulled the pewter peace symbol from her purse. "He gave this to me a long time ago. Now I want to return it. Just so he never forgets."

"Are you sure? It must have great sentimental value."

"I don't need it anymore. And now, I really am leaving." As Julia stood up so did Dulcie, who, much to Julia's amazement, smiled and hugged her.

"Thank you, Julia. I do feel a lot better. Maybe your coming here was fated by forces larger than the both of us. I've kept this inside for so long.... It's not every day that I bare my soul to a total stranger, and my husband's ex-lover at that."

CHAPTER THIRTY-EIGHT

His hour with the therapist finished, Win took the early train back to Haslemere. He hadn't told Dulcie about his Saturday sessions with the psychiatrist. She was already so emotionally fragile he didn't want to burden her further. And his morning appointment at the Regency Theatre had been postponed.

He still had the deposit check for twenty-five thousand pounds in his briefcase, so there was no need to return to his office to drop off the signed contracts. If those bastards delayed one more time in their attempt to ante up bidding between Win and his competitor, Win decided, he would tell them to stuff it. Unlike human beings, buildings could be replaced.

Until Jordan's death, they'd coasted along as a happy family. Now there was a void; two devastated parents and one powderkeg teenager simply getting by. Time wasn't healing this wound as everyone had said it would — it was festering and getting worse. Win's feelings of uselessness had become so overwhelming that in desperation he'd turned to his father-in-law for advice. Sam had recommended Dr. Wellsley, who'd treated Sam's second, younger wife for depression after her double mastectomy and subsequent successful chemotherapy.

Like himself, Dr. Wellsley was an American. She was also about Win's age and very attractive. She appeared to be happily married, with photos of her husband and children prominently displayed around her tastefully decorated office.

This is how low I've sunk, Win thought as he opened up his London *Times*. Wondering about the love life of someone who's supposed to heal me. He and Dulcie hadn't had sex in months — she'd lost interest, and Win had grown weary of trying. Would he ever make love again? Would he ever have the chance to?

The train was unusually crowded for a Saturday and Win remembered the festival. Jordan used to love July — every weekend, he'd beg to go to the concerts and booths with their colorful assortment of foods, games, and toy musical instruments. He taught himself to play the recorder and lute and was really quite good, for a seven-year-old.... But now the festival was just another inconvenience, another painful reminder.

Usually he was in a better mood after his sessions with the psychiatrist, but not today. It seemed as if they were making no progress at all — Win still felt helpless and angry, Dulcie was constantly depressed, Sammi was becoming more uncontrollable, and Jordan was still dead. Sometimes it made Win feel like he wanted to die too, but his work saved him.

The past few years had brought success like never before. Every building he renovated and redesigned sold at five to seven times the price that he and Sam's company had purchased it. Win's Midas touch made the old seem glamorous again, tripling the company's already impressive holdings. They were making the leap from well-to-do to rich, a miracle of sorts in the depressed British economy with its high taxes.

And he still loved the elegance, civility, and culture of his adopted city. If only Sammi would learn to appreciate theatre, fashion, and art.... But with her passion for horses and competition, she seemed more like Win's late grandfather than either him or Dulcie. It had been sweet, gentle Jordan who had been Win's soul mate.

Enough, Win told himself, fighting the black, smothering slide into sorrow. There's nothing you can do about it. It was fate. You and Dulcie weren't even around when it happened.

Unseeing, uncaring forces had decided that Jordan's time on earth was up, as they would and had with Win and everyone else before and after him.

He settled into his *Times*, which was filled with the usual — the struggle towards financial recovery; the marital rumblings of the royal family; local bits of interest; unrest in Israel and the former Soviet Union. But then his eye fell on a headline, "Ohio Congressman Investigates Health Alternatives" and there it was, a picture of Louie, and, of all people, *Julia*.

Glad to be out of that gloomy house, and guilty at feeling happy it hadn't been her baby so cruelly and mercilessly wrenched from her life, Julia stepped into the sunshine. Although England was much cooler than steamy Washington and even Ohio in the summertime, it was a glorious day.

Everyone seemed to be smiling as Julia walked back through town and the festival. All generations mingled easily: mimes plied their silent but effective trade; clowns in face paint capered, the bells on their curved hats pinging; men and women clad in Elizabethan costumes worked the crowd with flutey, Shakespearian tunes. How different from the May Music Fest at Hayes of so long ago! How frightened she'd been then and how free she felt now. She wanted to embrace the world.

Julia realized she was hungry. She'd become so preoccupied with her quest that she'd skipped lunch. Where was that ice cream vendor? She'd find him and treat herself to the largest cone he had.

She'd left Dulcie neither her address in Washington nor her phone number at the hotel. Why should she? After all these years, could she honestly believe Win would call her? He'd made no attempt to contact her before and, surely, if he'd wanted to, could have found her. And from the way Dulcie talked about him, he sounded like an aloof stranger, not the sensitive, passionate boy she'd once fallen in love with.

And from every indication, he was well-to-do. Who knows, he might be suspicious, thinking she wanted to blackmail him about his sexually active past to raise funds for Louie's campaign. Stranger things had happened....

She finally spotted the vendor, who was mobbed with a group of children. She'd grab another snack and wander around the festival for a while, then come back for it later. For once, she was in no hurry.

Win was astounded. He knew that Julia and Louie had married, but couldn't believe she was here in his city. He wondered where they were staying. Would Julia even talk to him? Laura's letter had stated she'd been very curious about his fate during her visit to Hayes, but still, the manner in which they'd parted.... And God, she was still beautiful, at least if the picture was halfway realistic. He felt the stirrings of desire. Another country heard from. Dulcie had better get herself together or he'd start looking elsewhere.

Could there be a future with Julia? So much had happened, so much water under the bridge, as the saying went. And what about Louie? Did he love her? He was a politician, and everyone knew what self-centered power-hungry bastards they could be, although Win had to admit that Louie had more integrity than anybody he'd known during his time at Hayes. But still, people changed. Look what happened to him. Except for his accent, he looked and acted every inch the prosperous Englishman.

At the stop before Haslemere, a group of young toughs got on the train and sat near Win. With their tight leather duds, oddly shaved heads mixed with long hanks of hair, and rings and rhinestone studs in various parts of their anatomy, they caused a stir among the passengers.

Win ignored them. They were out for kicks and possibly the occasional pocketbook or belt pack of the unaware tourist. But conscious of the twenty-five thousand pound check in his briefcase, he moved it from next to him to between his legs.

The article mostly centered around the differences between the American and British medical systems, with very little about Louie, save he was a prime contender for the 1994 Senate race. The caption under the headline identifying Louie and Julia stated that they resided in Washington and that she was a commercial artist and noted watercolorist.

At last, Julia had her ice cream and, although it wasn't Baskin-Robbins or Haagen Daz, it had been worth the wait. But now she was tired. It was after four and she needed to rest before tonight's dinner, one of the last evenings she and Louie would have alone before they began their trip around the countryside on Monday. And it had been an exhausting, draining afternoon.

She strode toward the train station, glad she'd spent some time at the festival and could describe it to Louie. She would have hated to lie about what she'd done with her day. But she'd never tell him about her visit to Win's. It would just hurt his feelings.

Truthfully, she didn't understand herself. She'd loved Win, had been willing to follow him anywhere and devote her life to him. Yet she might have ended up like Dulcie, a prisoner to her own fears, hiding from the world. Valerie's death and Win's desertion had forced her to cope with adversity. Yet she felt as if she'd had a narrow escape from an even greater tragedy.

She reveled in the moment, the sunshine, the smoothness and sweetness of the ice cream....

Win got off the train, his briefcase and his *Times* secured under his arm. The punks were still nearby and he knew they could be damn clever; his own Pop had his wallet lifted on Trafalgar Square when he and Mom were visiting from Cincinnati a few years ago. He'd be glad when this festival was over.

Dulcie, ever the devoted housebound wife, had made dinner, he was sure. It would be nice to go to a restaurant once in a while, to be among friends.

I'm going to start insisting that we do things, he vowed. That we get out more and become involved in life again. This can't go on.

Then he saw Julia. She — or someone who looked just like her — was smiling and eating an ice cream cone, about to board a train on a nearby platform. He was so shocked the briefcase and paper fell from his grasp.

The punks whisked by him, obscuring his vision. And his briefcase was gone.

"Stop, thief!" Win shouted, sprinting after the culprits. "Come back here, you bastards!" They were fast, but not enough.

A bobby standing guard by the entrance had already grabbed the one with the purple hair who wielded Win's briefcase.

Then Win remembered Julia and whirled around. She was gone, the train pulling out of the station.

After he retrieved his belongings and made sure they were still intact, he turned towards home. It couldn't have been Julia, he told himself as he shuffled up the walk of his house. What would she be doing all the way out here? The festival attracted mostly locals and international music lovers, and Julia was an artist. Julia had been on his mind, and he'd glimpsed a woman who reminded him of her.

Julia was thinking this as she hurried towards the platform: I will never see Win again. And I can live with that. All those years of subconsciously searching for him had finally come to an end.

No matter what happened — whether her marriage with Louie endured the trials of his political demands; whether her career would take her to the success she'd worked so hard for; whether her children would grow up strong, happy, and healthy, as she'd prayed — she had herself, and could take care of herself. Which was all, really, her parents who had loved her with all their hearts (she knew that now) had ever wanted. As she wanted for her own family.

Julia never saw or heard the commotion at the station. She boarded the train and headed back to the rest of her life.

Photo: Creative Image Photography

Sandra Gurvis is the author of nine books and hundreds of magazine articles. Her titles include *Careers for Nonconformists* (Marlowe, 2000), a selection of the Quality Paperback Book Club, and her articles have appeared in *People, YM, The World & I,* and many other publications. A college student herself during the protests, she has written extensively about the era and is currently working on a nonfiction book about the '60s, *Where Have All the Flower Children Gone?* to be published by the University Press of Mississippi.

She lives in Columbus, Ohio and can be reached via her Web sites: www.sgurvis.com and www.thepipedreamers.com.

Colophon

The Pipe Dreamers is set in Adobe
Garamond. Some of the most widely used
typefaces in history are those of the six-
teenth-century type designer Claude
Garamond. Robert Slimbach visited
Plantin-Moretus museum in Antwerp,
Belgium, to study the original Garamond
typefaces. These served as the basis for the
Adobe Garamond romans, the face used
for the body of this book. Parts and chap-
ters are opened with Alternate Garamond
with swash capitals.

Designed and set in the foothills of the
Adirondacks by Syllables using Adobe
software which provided electronic files
used to create plates for printing.